JUSTICE LEAGUE
ADVENTURES

DAN SLOTT, TY TEMPLETON, FABIEN NICIEZA,
JOSH SIEGAL, CHRISTOPHER SEQUEIRA
WRITERS

MIN S. KU, JOHN DELANEY, CHRIS JONES
PENCILLERS

DAN DAVIS, MARK PROPST,
RANDY ELLIOTT, CHRISTIAN ALAMY
INKERS

JOHN KALISZ
COLORIST

KURT HATHAWAY
LETTERER

JUSTICE LEAGUE ADVENTURES. Published by DC Comics. Cover and compilation copyright © 2003 DC Comics. All Rights Reserved. Originally published
in single magazine form in JUSTICE LEAGUE ADVENTURES #1, 3, 6, 10, 11, 12, and 13. Copyright © 2002 and 2003 DC Comics. All Rights Reserved.
All characters, their distinctive likenesses and related indicia featured in this publication are trademarks of DC Comics. The stories, characters, and
incidents featured in this publication are entirely fictional. DC Comics does not read or accept unsolicited submissions of ideas, stories or artwork.
DC Comics, 1700 Broadway, New York, NY 10019. A division of Warner Bros. — An AOL Time Warner Company. Printed in Canada. First Printing.
ISBN: 1-56389-954-X. Cover illustration by Bruce Timm and Alex Ross. Back cover illustration by John Delaney. Publication design by Peter Hamboussi.

The Justice League consists of the greatest super-heroes the world has ever known — coming from different parts of the world and even from other galaxies!

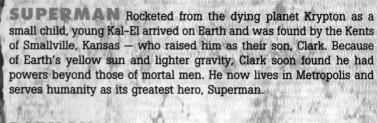

SUPERMAN Rocketed from the dying planet Krypton as a small child, young Kal-El arrived on Earth and was found by the Kents of Smallville, Kansas — who raised him as their son, Clark. Because of Earth's yellow sun and lighter gravity, Clark soon found he had powers beyond those of mortal men. He now lives in Metropolis and serves humanity as its greatest hero, Superman.

BATMAN After seeing his parents brutally murdered, young Bruce Wayne dedicated his life to fighting crime — perfecting his mind and body to transform himself into Gotham City's guardian, so that no one would ever have to face the same tragedy. He now dons the cape and cowl of the Batman to strike terror into superstitious and cowardly criminals.

WONDER WOMAN Diana was once Princess of the Amazons, the legendary race of female warriors of the island nation Themyscira. The Ancient Greek Gods gave her the gifts of great strength, superior speed and the power of flight, to use in her role of Amazon ambassador to "man's world." Diana is equipped with silver bracelets that she can use to deflect bullets, and a golden lasso that compels anyone bound by it to tell the truth.

FLASH Young Wally West was the victim of an electrochemical accident that granted him the power of super-speed, greater than even Superman's. As a side effect, his sped-up metabolism also demands food constantly, and on occasion his mouth is faster than his brain.

MARTIAN MANHUNTER The last survivor of an ancient race of Martians, J'onn J'onzz has found a new home on Earth and uses his powers of telepathy, intangibility and shape-shifting to protects its citizens. His one weakness is intense heat or flame, which can take away his powers.

GREEN LANTERN John Stewart serves the intergalactic peacekeeping force known as the Green Lantern Corps, assigned to Earth as a member of the Justice League. Like all GLs, Stewart is armed with a Power Ring — its unique alien energy shapes itself at his command to create tools or weapons, or provide power for any world-saving task at hand…as long as he recharges it every 24 hours.

HAWKGIRL Shayera Hol was a detective on her home planet of Thanagar. Here on Earth, she uses her police training to help her survive in unfamiliar surroundings, and has begun protecting the people of Earth with the Thanagarian technology and weapons she brought with her.

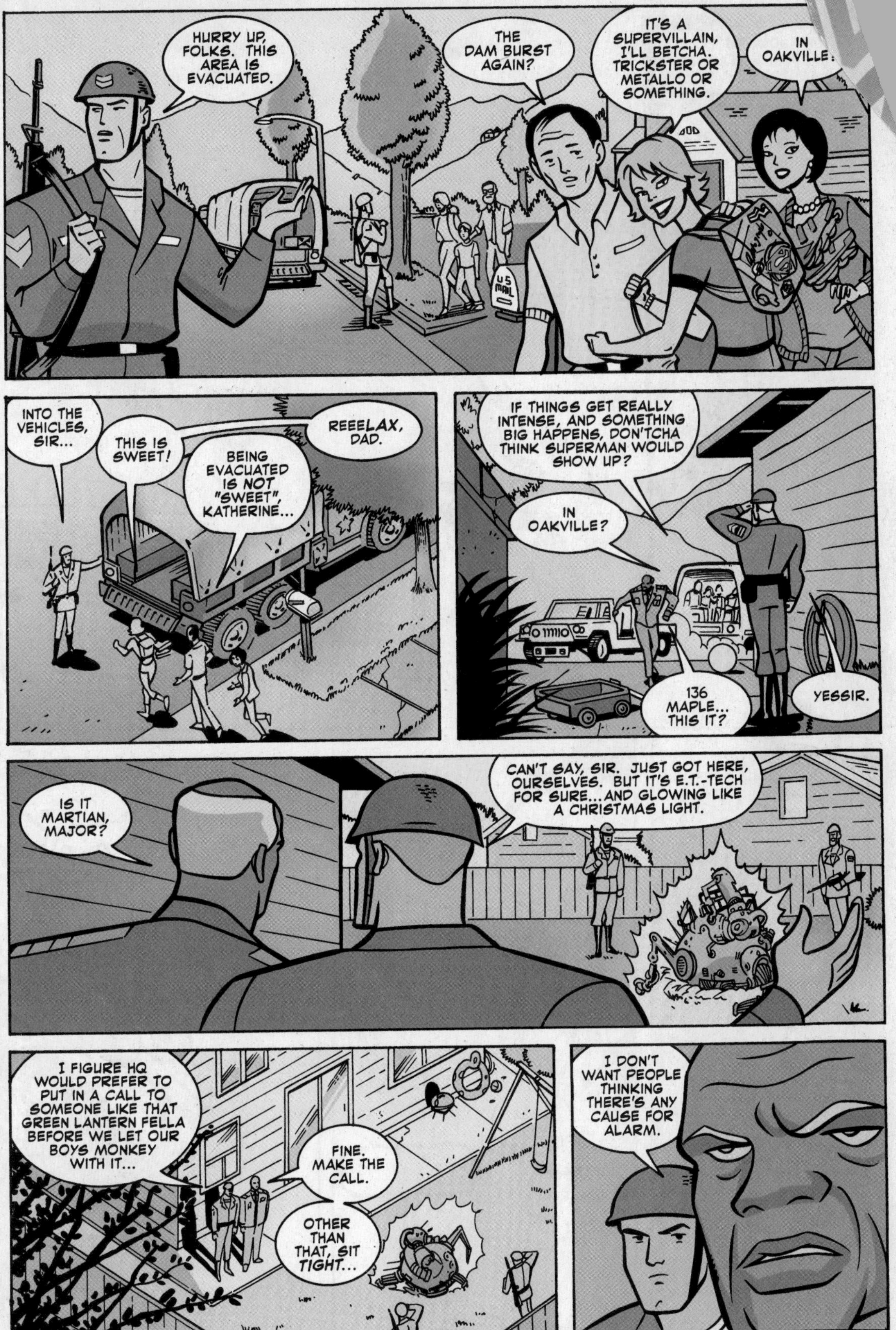
HURRY UP, FOLKS. THIS AREA IS EVACUATED.
THE DAM BURST AGAIN?
IT'S A SUPERVILLAIN, I'LL BETCHA. TRICKSTER OR METALLO OR SOMETHING.
IN OAKVILLE?
INTO THE VEHICLES, SIR...
THIS IS SWEET!
REEELAX, DAD.
BEING EVACUATED IS NOT "SWEET", KATHERINE...
IF THINGS GET REALLY INTENSE, AND SOMETHING BIG HAPPENS, DON'TCHA THINK SUPERMAN WOULD SHOW UP?
IN OAKVILLE?
136 MAPLE... THIS IT?
YESSIR.
IS IT MARTIAN, MAJOR?
CAN'T SAY, SIR. JUST GOT HERE, OURSELVES. BUT IT'S E.T.-TECH FOR SURE...AND GLOWING LIKE A CHRISTMAS LIGHT.
I FIGURE HQ WOULD PREFER TO PUT IN A CALL TO SOMEONE LIKE THAT GREEN LANTERN FELLA BEFORE WE LET OUR BOYS MONKEY WITH IT...
FINE. MAKE THE CALL.
OTHER THAN THAT, SIT TIGHT...
I DON'T WANT PEOPLE THINKING THERE'S ANY CAUSE FOR ALARM.

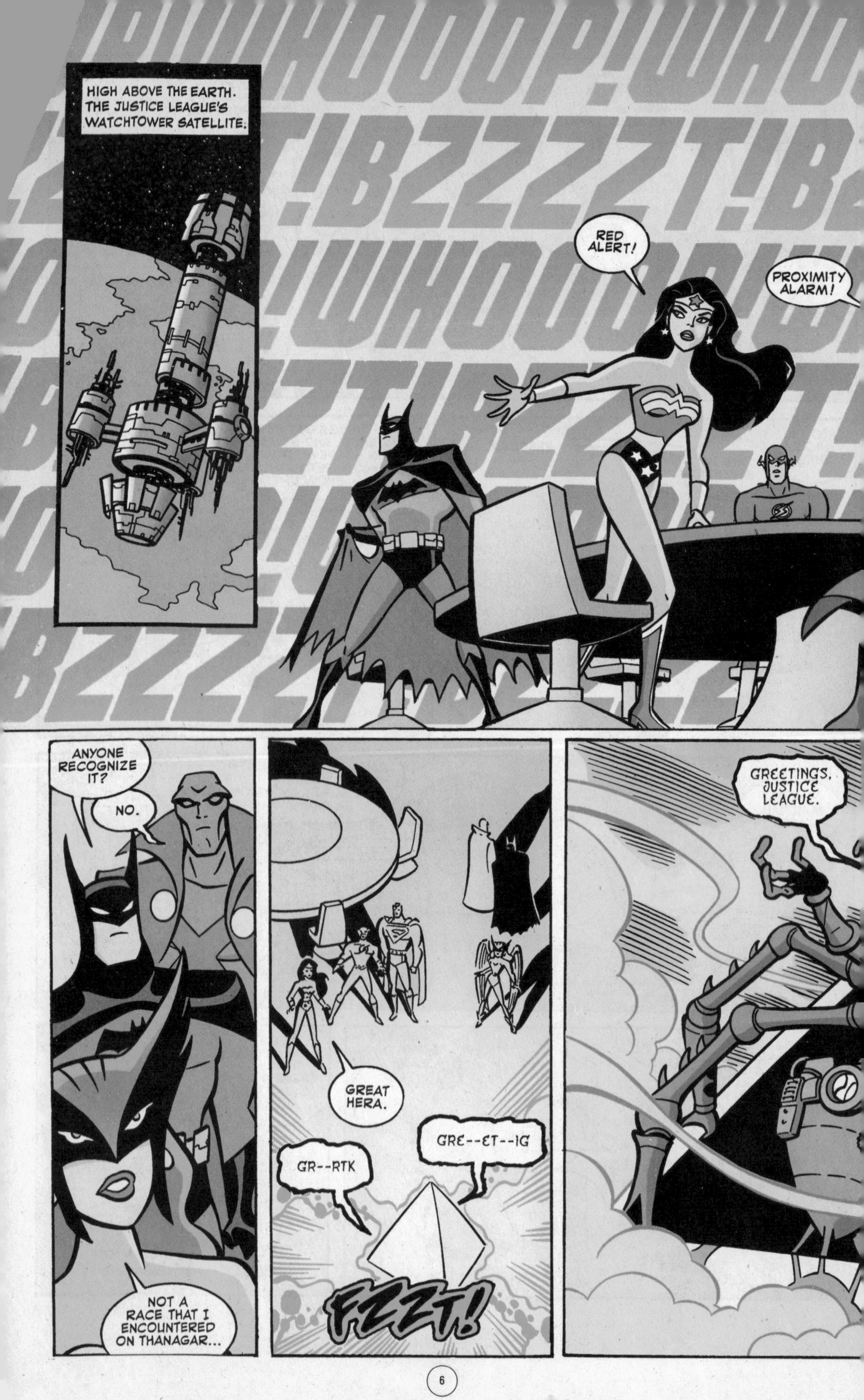

HIGH ABOVE THE EARTH. THE JUSTICE LEAGUE'S WATCHTOWER SATELLITE.
RED ALERT!
PROXIMITY ALARM!
ANYONE RECOGNIZE IT?
NO.
NOT A RACE THAT I ENCOUNTERED ON THANAGAR...
GREAT HERA.
GRE--ET--IG
GR--RTK
FZZT!
GREETINGS, JUSTICE LEAGUE.

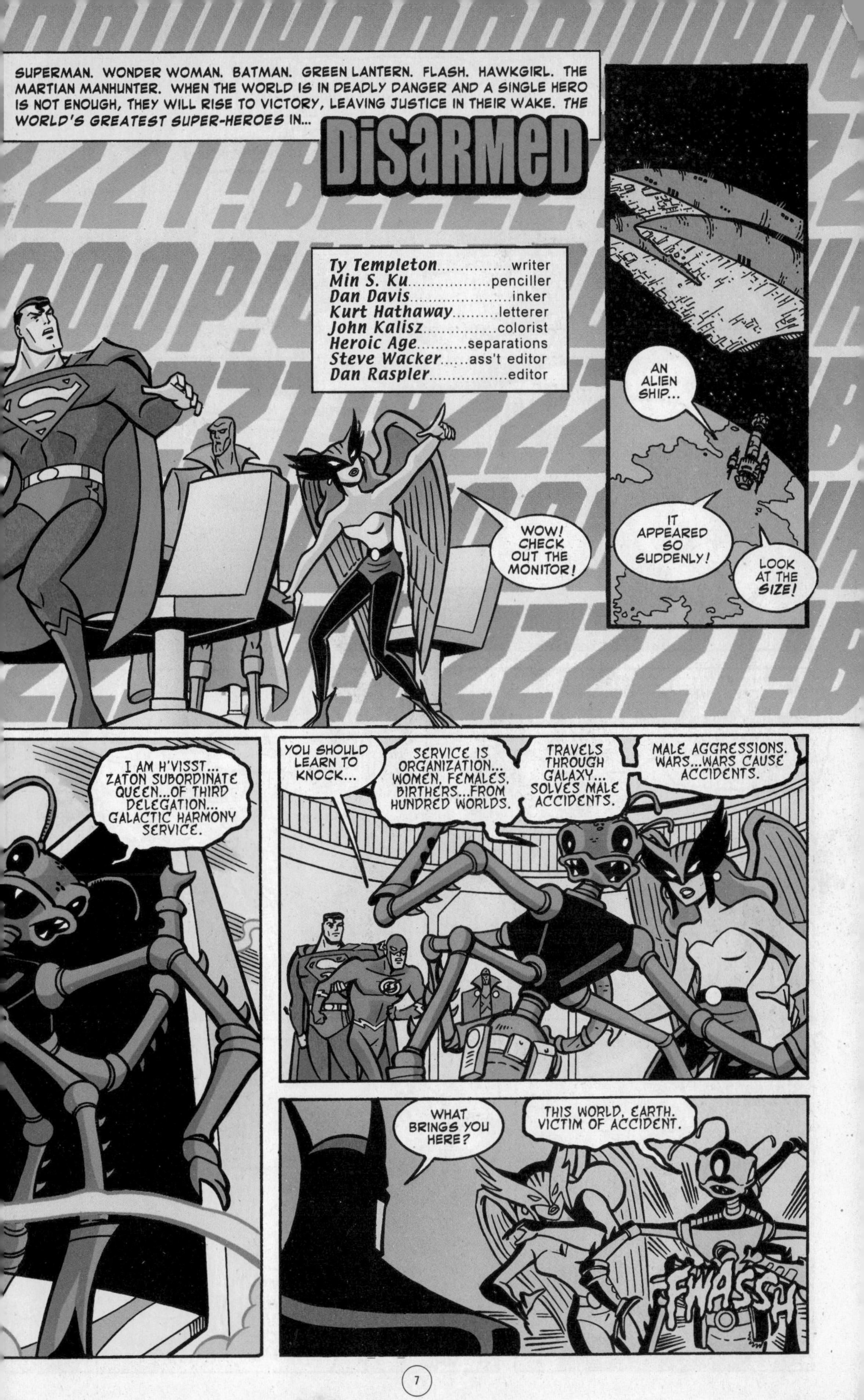
SUPERMAN. WONDER WOMAN. BATMAN. GREEN LANTERN. FLASH. HAWKGIRL. THE MARTIAN MANHUNTER. WHEN THE WORLD IS IN DEADLY DANGER AND A SINGLE HERO IS NOT ENOUGH, THEY WILL RISE TO VICTORY, LEAVING JUSTICE IN THEIR WAKE. THE WORLD'S GREATEST SUPER-HEROES IN...
DiSARMeD
Ty Templeton................writer
Min S. Ku..................penciller
Dan Davis......................inker
Kurt Hathaway..........letterer
John Kalisz...............colorist
Heroic Age...........separations
Steve Wacker......ass't editor
Dan Raspler.................editor
AN ALIEN SHIP...
IT APPEARED SO SUDDENLY!
LOOK AT THE SIZE!
WOW! CHECK OUT THE MONITOR!
I AM H'VISST... ZATON SUBORDINATE QUEEN...OF THIRD DELEGATION... GALACTIC HARMONY SERVICE.
YOU SHOULD LEARN TO KNOCK...
SERVICE IS ORGANIZATION... WOMEN, FEMALES, BIRTHERS...FROM HUNDRED WORLDS.
TRAVELS THROUGH GALAXY... SOLVES MALE ACCIDENTS.
MALE AGGRESSIONS. WARS...WARS CAUSE ACCIDENTS.
WHAT BRINGS YOU HERE?
THIS WORLD, EARTH. VICTIM OF ACCIDENT.
FWASSH

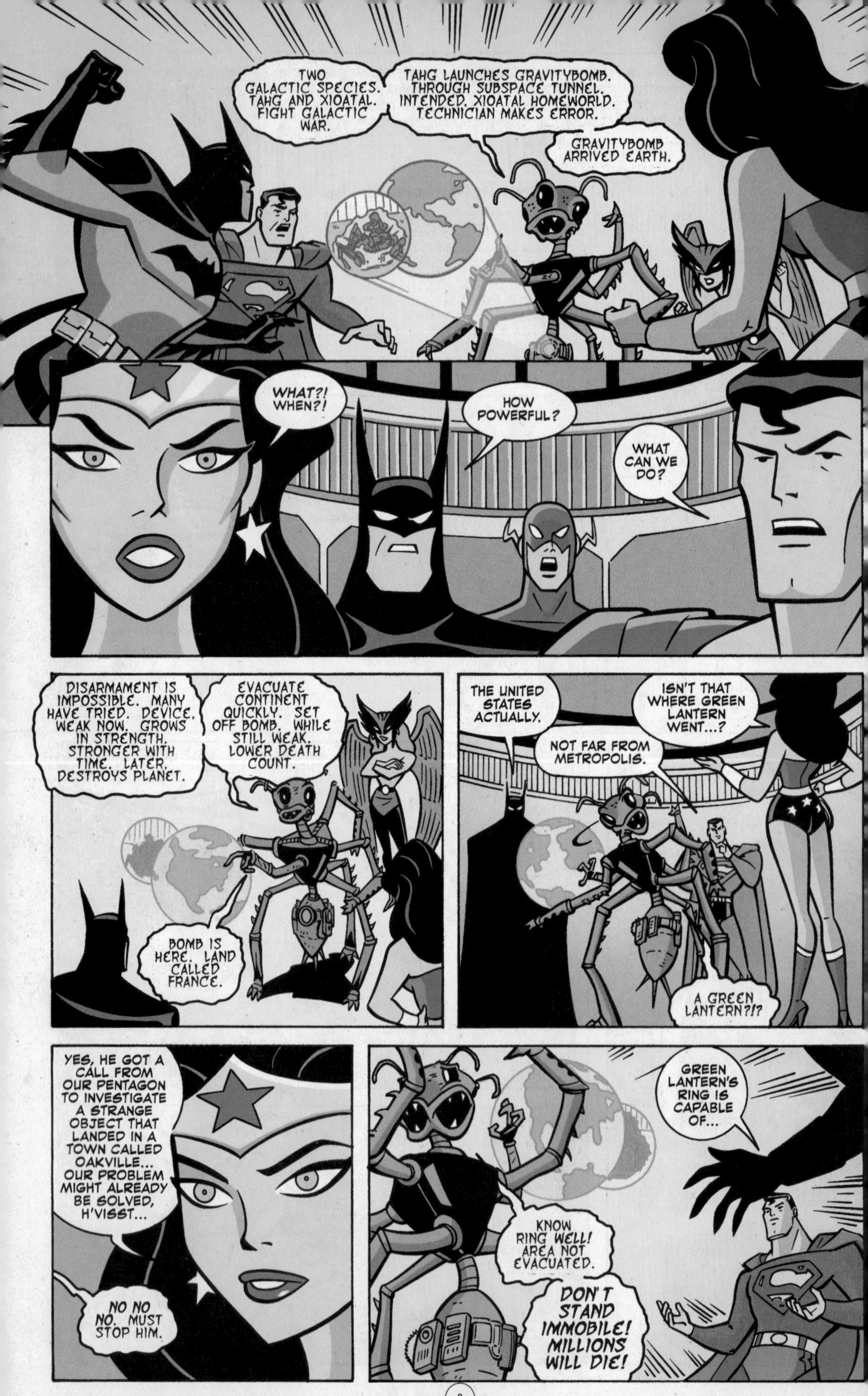

TWO GALACTIC SPECIES. TAHG AND XIOATAL. FIGHT GALACTIC WAR.
TAHG LAUNCHES GRAVITYBOMB. THROUGH SUBSPACE TUNNEL. INTENDED, XIOATAL HOMEWORLD. TECHNICIAN MAKES ERROR.
GRAVITYBOMB ARRIVED EARTH.
WHAT?! WHEN?!
HOW POWERFUL?
WHAT CAN WE DO?
DISARMAMENT IS IMPOSSIBLE. MANY HAVE TRIED. DEVICE, WEAK NOW. GROWS IN STRENGTH. STRONGER WITH TIME. LATER, DESTROYS PLANET.
EVACUATE CONTINENT QUICKLY. SET OFF BOMB. WHILE STILL WEAK. LOWER DEATH COUNT.
BOMB IS HERE. LAND CALLED FRANCE.
THE UNITED STATES ACTUALLY.
ISN'T THAT WHERE GREEN LANTERN WENT...?
NOT FAR FROM METROPOLIS.
A GREEN LANTERN?!?
YES, HE GOT A CALL FROM OUR PENTAGON TO INVESTIGATE A STRANGE OBJECT THAT LANDED IN A TOWN CALLED OAKVILLE... OUR PROBLEM MIGHT ALREADY BE SOLVED, H'VISST...
NO NO NO. MUST STOP HIM.
GREEN LANTERN'S RING IS CAPABLE OF...
KNOW RING WELL! AREA NOT EVACUATED.
DON'T STAND IMMOBILE! MILLIONS WILL DIE!

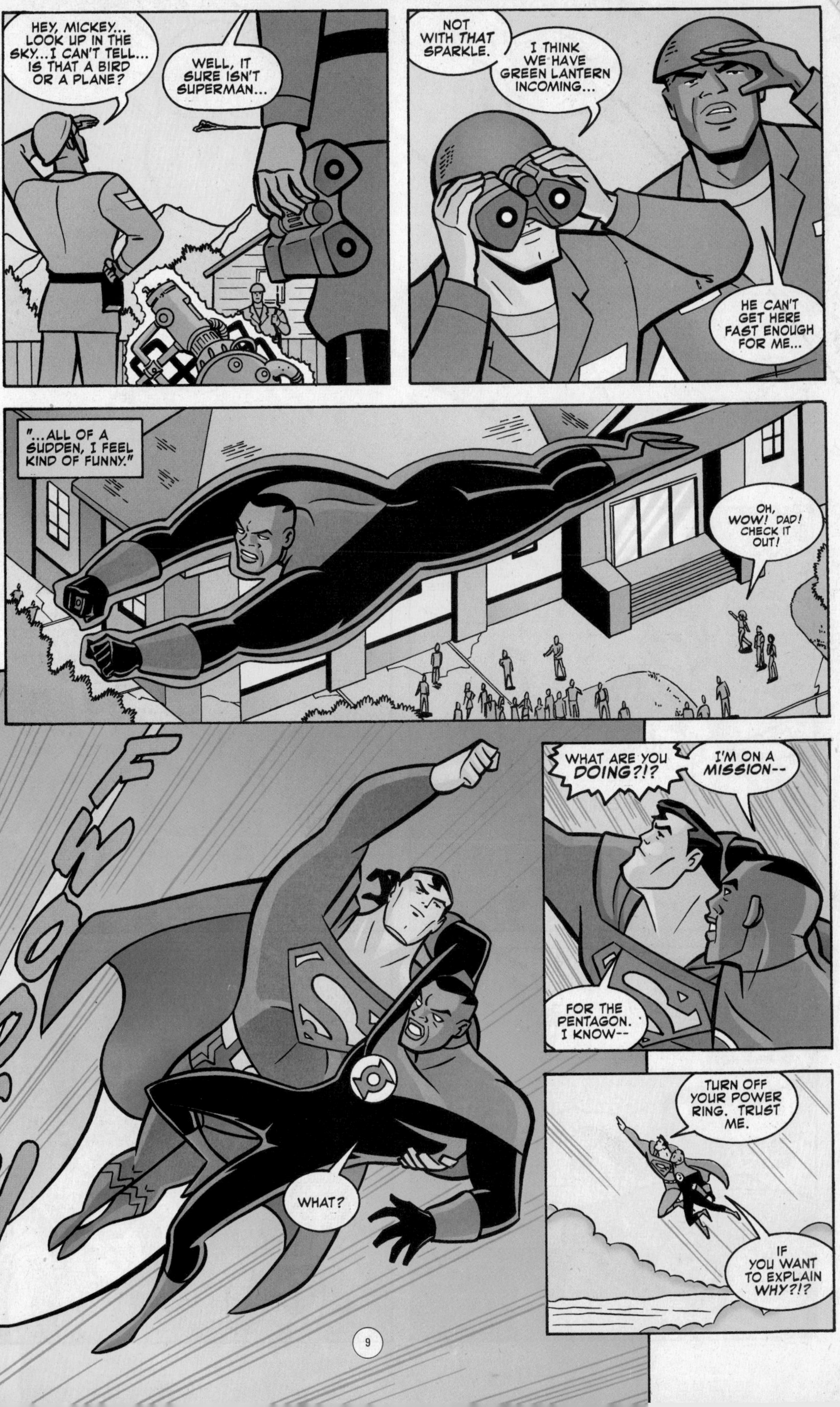
HEY, MICKEY... LOOK UP IN THE SKY...I CAN'T TELL... IS THAT A BIRD OR A PLANE?
WELL, IT SURE ISN'T SUPERMAN...
NOT WITH THAT SPARKLE.
I THINK WE HAVE GREEN LANTERN INCOMING...
HE CAN'T GET HERE FAST ENOUGH FOR ME...
"...ALL OF A SUDDEN, I FEEL KIND OF FUNNY."
OH, WOW! DAD! CHECK IT OUT!
WHOOSH
WHAT?
WHAT ARE YOU DOING?!?
I'M ON A MISSION--
FOR THE PENTAGON. I KNOW--
TURN OFF YOUR POWER RING. TRUST ME.
IF YOU WANT TO EXPLAIN WHY?!?

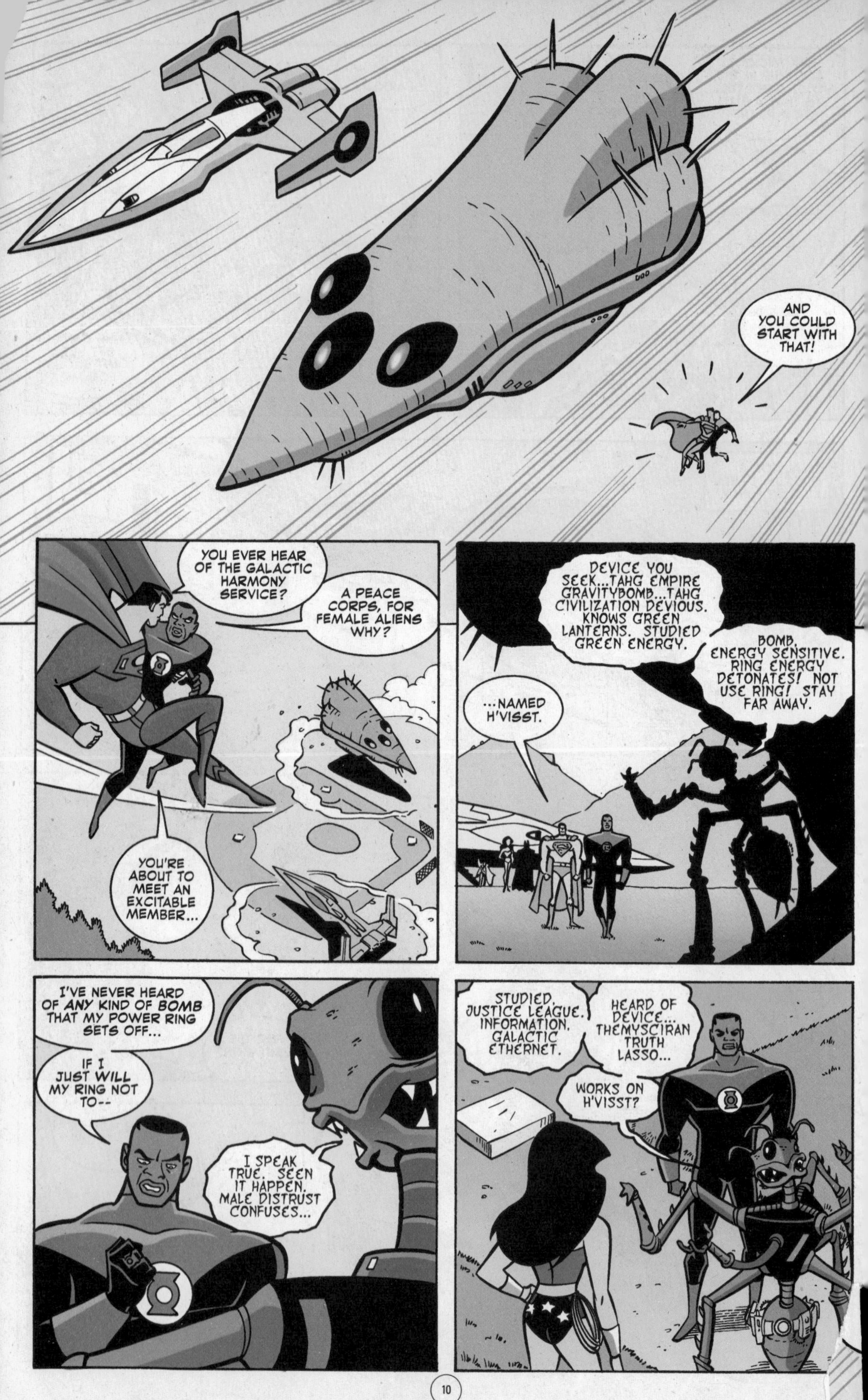
AND YOU COULD START WITH THAT!
YOU EVER HEAR OF THE GALACTIC HARMONY SERVICE?
A PEACE CORPS, FOR FEMALE ALIENS WHY?
YOU'RE ABOUT TO MEET AN EXCITABLE MEMBER...
DEVICE YOU SEEK...TAHG EMPIRE GRAVITYBOMB...TAHG CIVILIZATION DEVIOUS. KNOWS GREEN LANTERNS. STUDIED GREEN ENERGY.
...NAMED H'VISST.
BOMB. ENERGY SENSITIVE. RING ENERGY DETONATES! NOT USE RING! STAY FAR AWAY.
I'VE NEVER HEARD OF ANY KIND OF BOMB THAT MY POWER RING SETS OFF...
IF I JUST WILL MY RING NOT TO--
I SPEAK TRUE. SEEN IT HAPPEN. MALE DISTRUST CONFUSES...
STUDIED. JUSTICE LEAGUE. INFORMATION. GALACTIC ETHERNET.
HEARD OF DEVICE... THEMYSCIRAN TRUTH LASSO...
WORKS ON H'VISST?

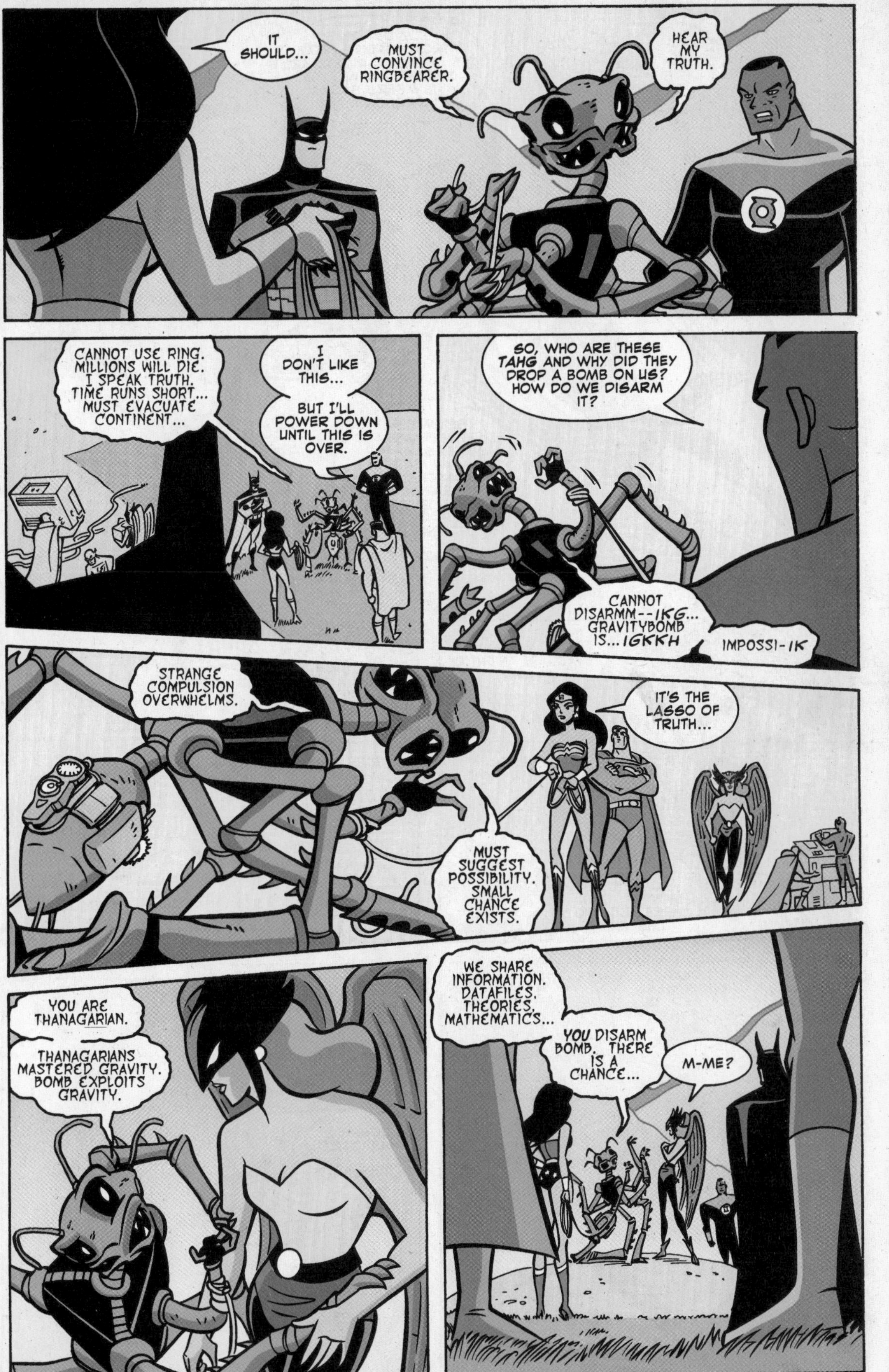
IT SHOULD...
MUST CONVINCE RINGBEARER.
HEAR MY TRUTH.
CANNOT USE RING. MILLIONS WILL DIE. I SPEAK TRUTH. TIME RUNS SHORT... MUST EVACUATE CONTINENT...
I DON'T LIKE THIS...
BUT I'LL POWER DOWN UNTIL THIS IS OVER.
SO, WHO ARE THESE TAHG AND WHY DID THEY DROP A BOMB ON US? HOW DO WE DISARM IT?
CANNOT DISARMM--IKG... GRAVITYBOMB IS...IGKKH
IMPOSSI-IK
STRANGE COMPULSION OVERWHELMS.
IT'S THE LASSO OF TRUTH...
MUST SUGGEST POSSIBILITY. SMALL CHANCE EXISTS.
YOU ARE THANAGARIAN.
THANAGARIANS MASTERED GRAVITY. BOMB EXPLOITS GRAVITY.
WE SHARE INFORMATION. DATAFILES. THEORIES. MATHEMATICS...
YOU DISARM BOMB. THERE IS A CHANCE...
M-ME?

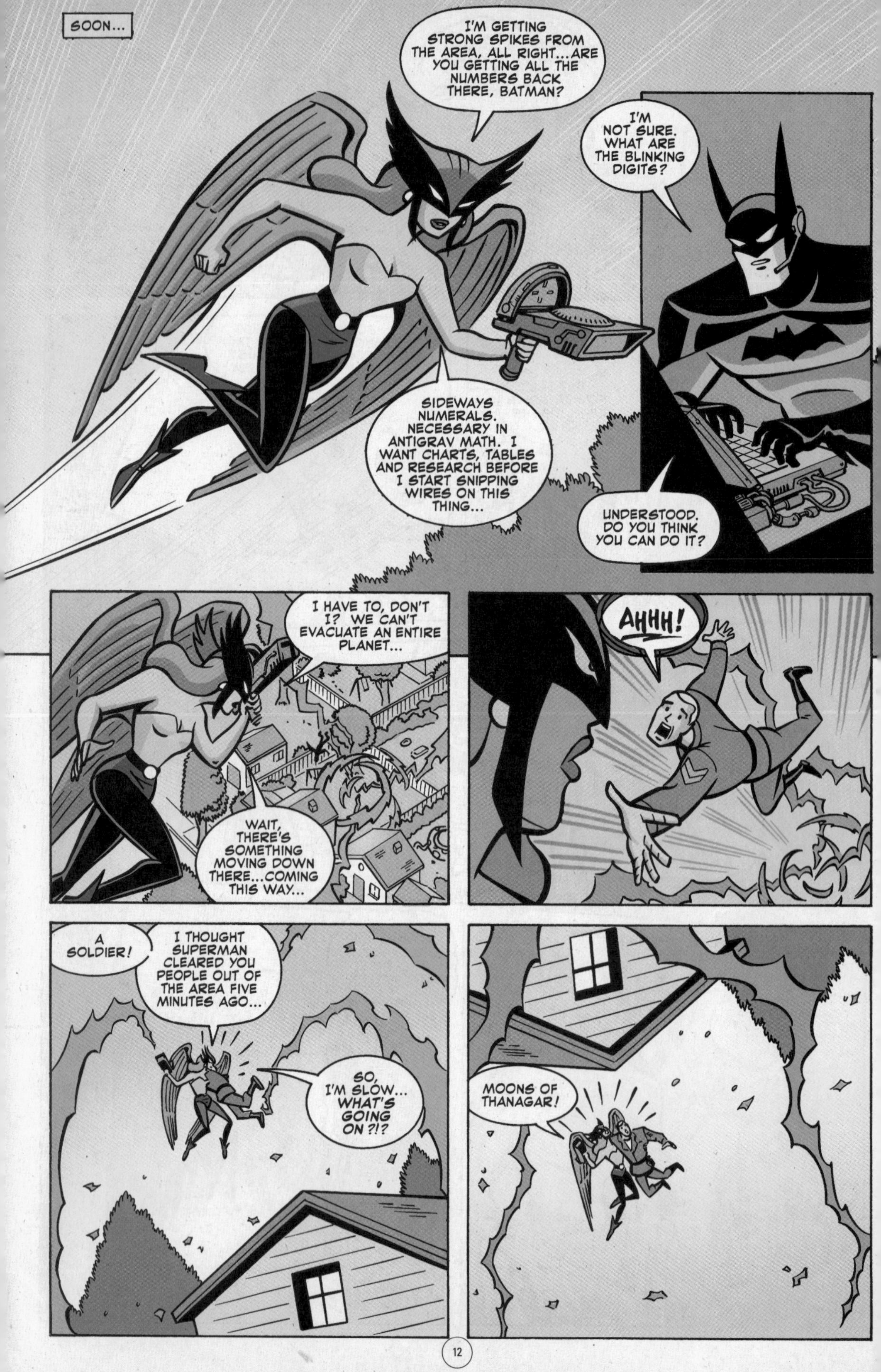
SOON...
I'M GETTING STRONG SPIKES FROM THE AREA, ALL RIGHT...ARE YOU GETTING ALL THE NUMBERS BACK THERE, BATMAN?
I'M NOT SURE. WHAT ARE THE BLINKING DIGITS?
SIDEWAYS NUMERALS. NECESSARY IN ANTIGRAV MATH. I WANT CHARTS, TABLES AND RESEARCH BEFORE I START SNIPPING WIRES ON THIS THING...
UNDERSTOOD. DO YOU THINK YOU CAN DO IT?
I HAVE TO, DON'T I? WE CAN'T EVACUATE AN ENTIRE PLANET...
WAIT, THERE'S SOMETHING MOVING DOWN THERE...COMING THIS WAY...
AHHH!
A SOLDIER!
I THOUGHT SUPERMAN CLEARED YOU PEOPLE OUT OF THE AREA FIVE MINUTES AGO...
SO, I'M SLOW... WHAT'S GOING ON?!?
MOONS OF THANAGAR!

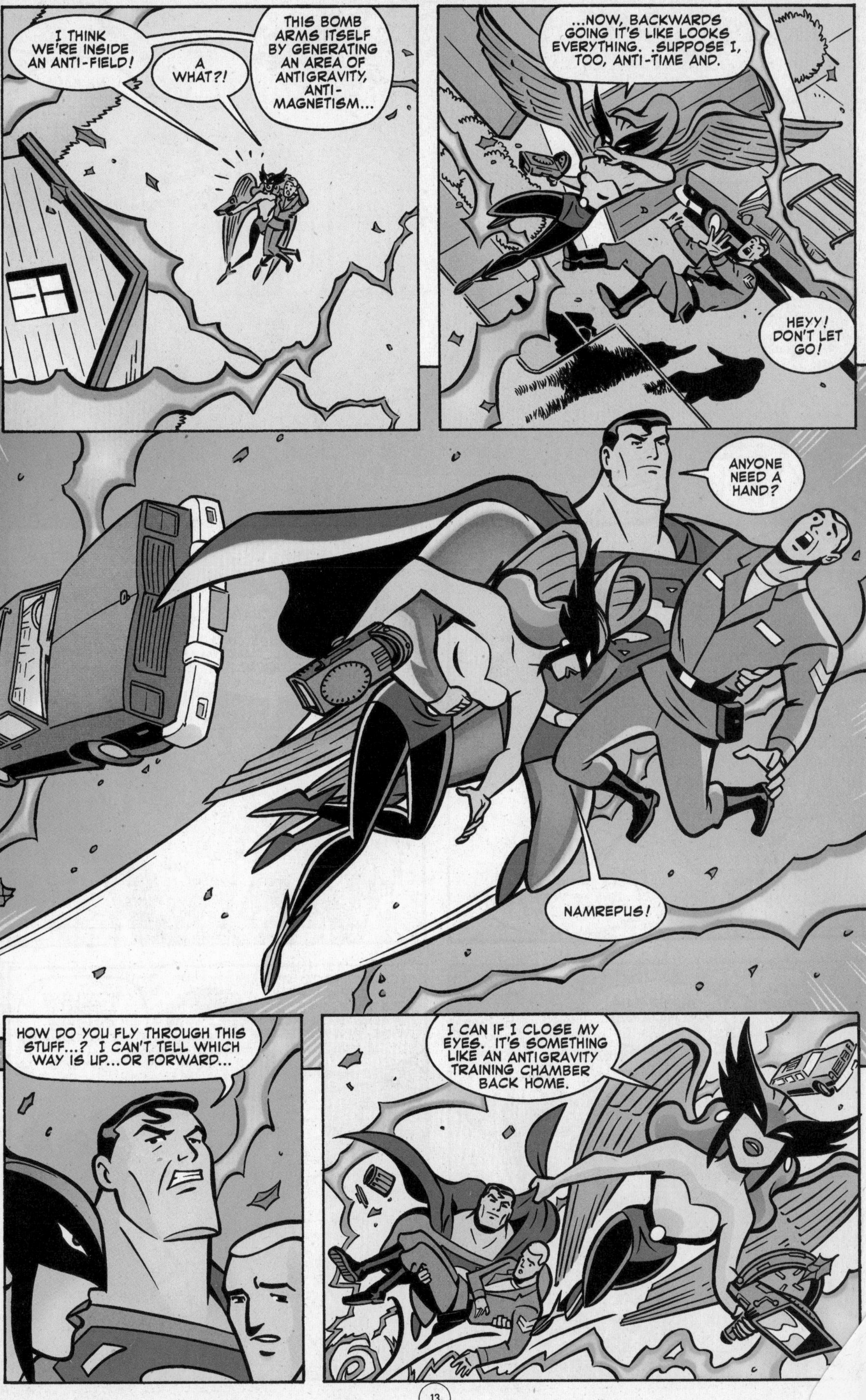
I THINK WE'RE INSIDE AN ANTI-FIELD!
A WHAT?!
THIS BOMB ARMS ITSELF BY GENERATING AN AREA OF ANTIGRAVITY, ANTI-MAGNETISM...
...NOW, BACKWARDS GOING IT'S LIKE LOOKS EVERYTHING. .SUPPOSE I, TOO, ANTI-TIME AND.
HEYY! DON'T LET GO!
ANYONE NEED A HAND?
NAMREPUS!
HOW DO YOU FLY THROUGH THIS STUFF...? I CAN'T TELL WHICH WAY IS UP...OR FORWARD...
I CAN IF I CLOSE MY EYES. IT'S SOMETHING LIKE AN ANTIGRAVITY TRAINING CHAMBER BACK HOME.

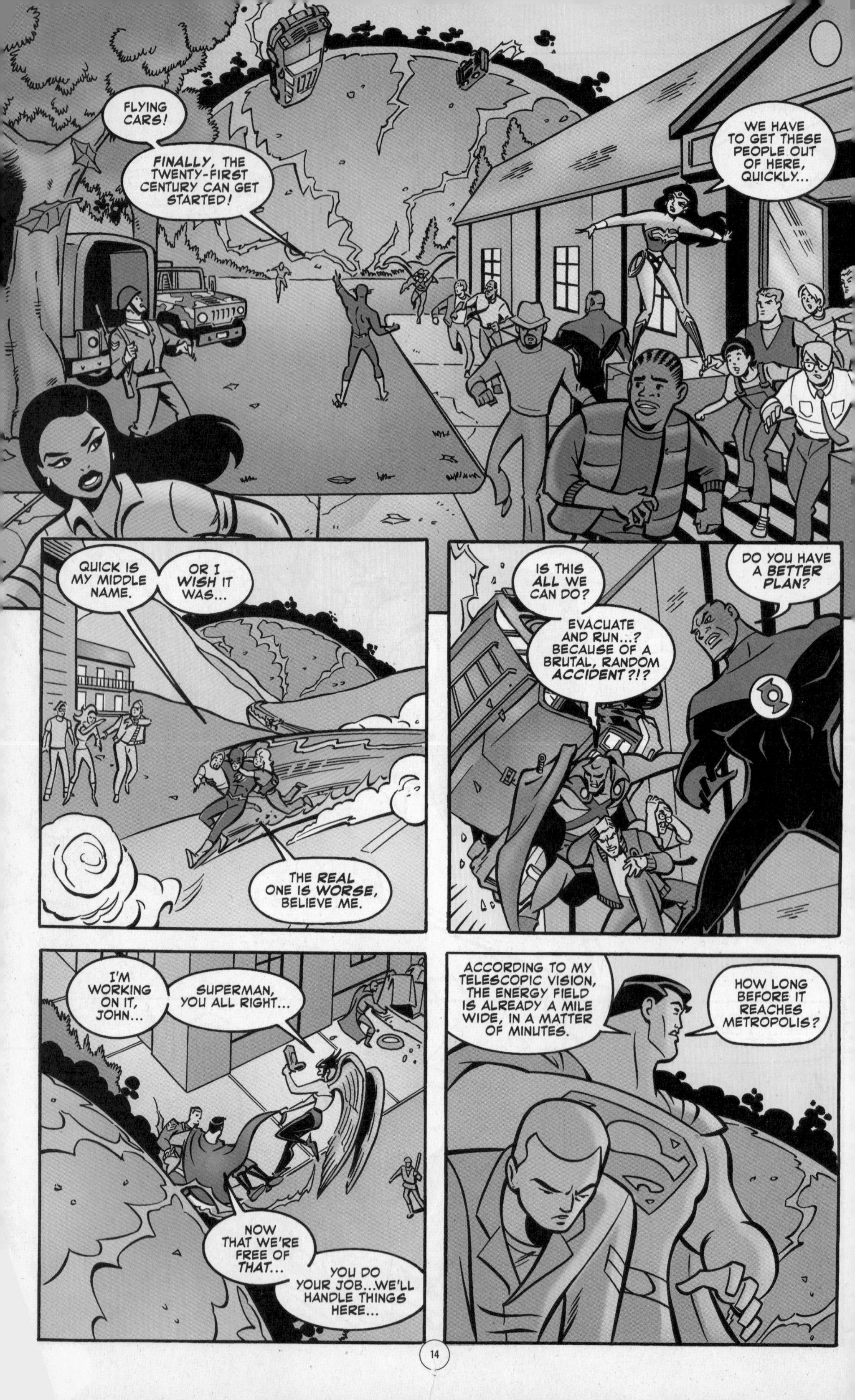

FLYING CARS!
FINALLY, THE TWENTY-FIRST CENTURY CAN GET STARTED!
WE HAVE TO GET THESE PEOPLE OUT OF HERE, QUICKLY...
QUICK IS MY MIDDLE NAME.
OR I WISH IT WAS...
THE REAL ONE IS WORSE, BELIEVE ME.
IS THIS ALL WE CAN DO?
EVACUATE AND RUN...? BECAUSE OF A BRUTAL, RANDOM ACCIDENT?!?
DO YOU HAVE A BETTER PLAN?
I'M WORKING ON IT, JOHN...
SUPERMAN, YOU ALL RIGHT...
NOW THAT WE'RE FREE OF THAT...
YOU DO YOUR JOB...WE'LL HANDLE THINGS HERE...
ACCORDING TO MY TELESCOPIC VISION, THE ENERGY FIELD IS ALREADY A MILE WIDE, IN A MATTER OF MINUTES.
HOW LONG BEFORE IT REACHES METROPOLIS?

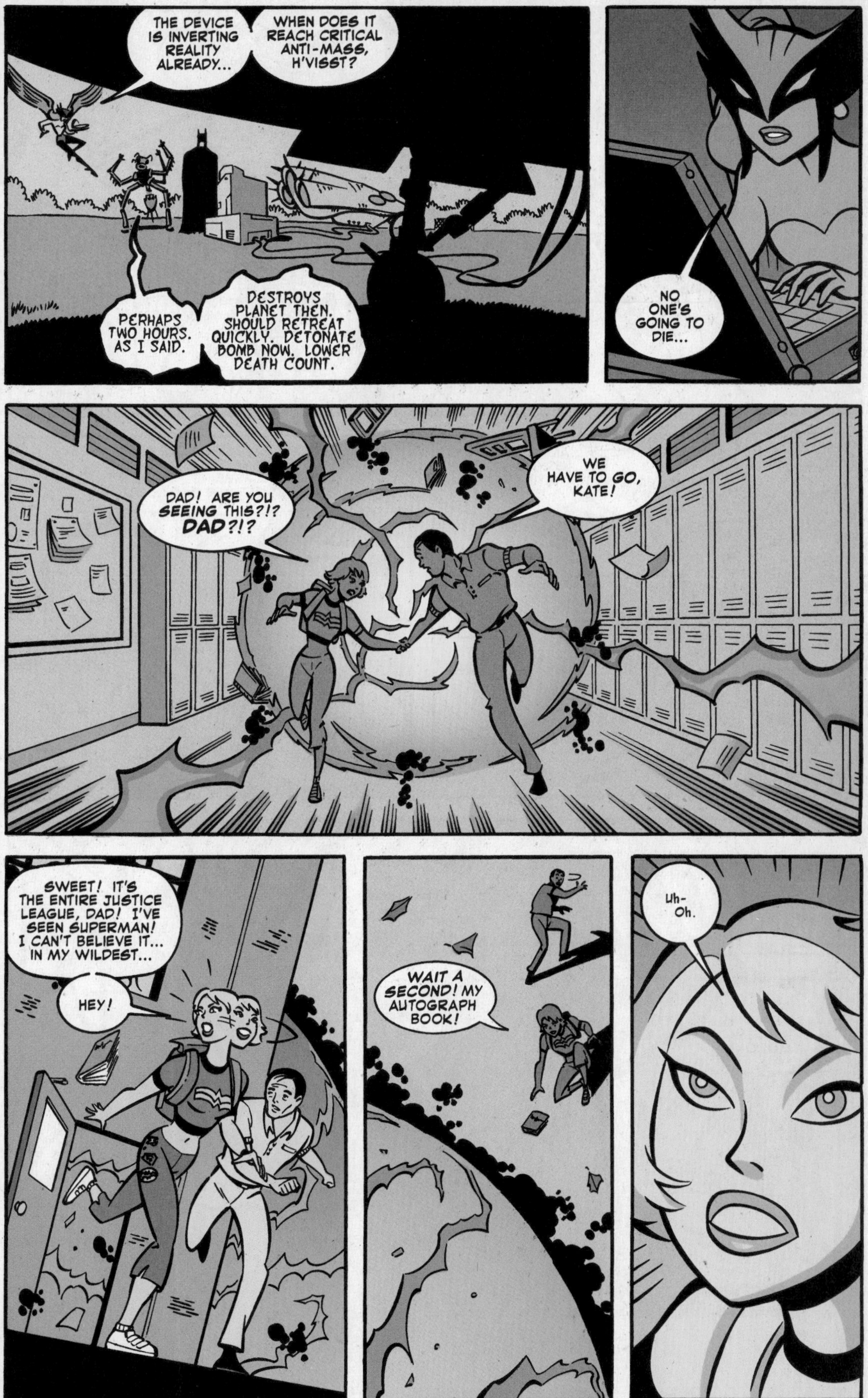
THE DEVICE IS INVERTING REALITY ALREADY...
WHEN DOES IT REACH CRITICAL ANTI-MASS, H'VISST?
PERHAPS TWO HOURS. AS I SAID.
DESTROYS PLANET THEN. SHOULD RETREAT QUICKLY. DETONATE BOMB NOW. LOWER DEATH COUNT.
NO ONE'S GOING TO DIE...
DAD! ARE YOU SEEING THIS?!? DAD?!?
WE HAVE TO GO, KATE!
SWEET! IT'S THE ENTIRE JUSTICE LEAGUE, DAD! I'VE SEEN SUPERMAN! I CAN'T BELIEVE IT... IN MY WILDEST...
HEY!
WAIT A SECOND! MY AUTOGRAPH BOOK!
Uh-Oh.

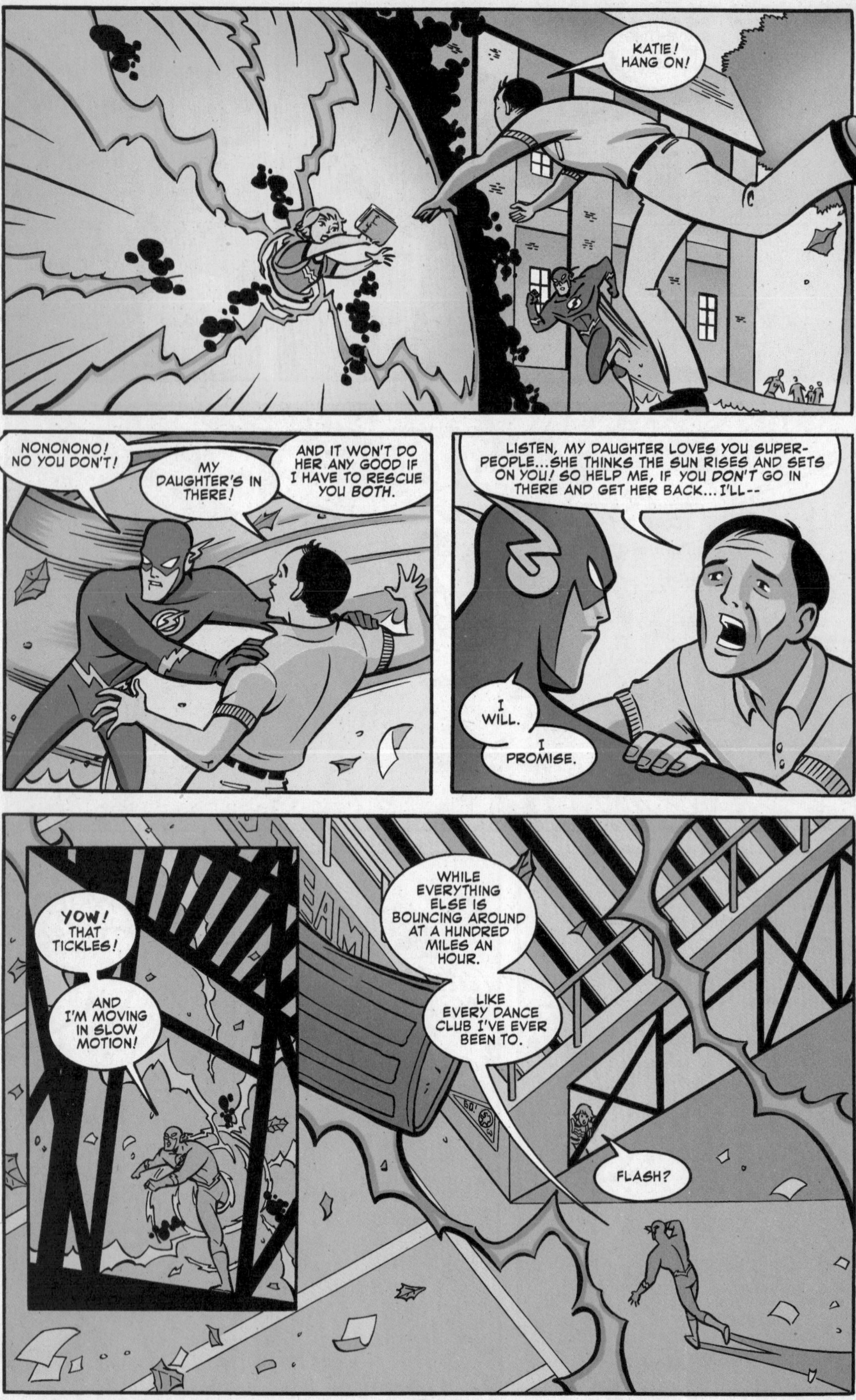
KATIE! HANG ON!
NONONONO! NO YOU DON'T!
MY DAUGHTER'S IN THERE!
AND IT WON'T DO HER ANY GOOD IF I HAVE TO RESCUE YOU BOTH.
LISTEN, MY DAUGHTER LOVES YOU SUPER-PEOPLE... SHE THINKS THE SUN RISES AND SETS ON YOU! SO HELP ME, IF YOU DON'T GO IN THERE AND GET HER BACK... I'LL--
I WILL.
I PROMISE.
YOW! THAT TICKLES!
AND I'M MOVING IN SLOW MOTION!
WHILE EVERYTHING ELSE IS BOUNCING AROUND AT A HUNDRED MILES AN HOUR.
LIKE EVERY DANCE CLUB I'VE EVER BEEN TO.
FLASH?

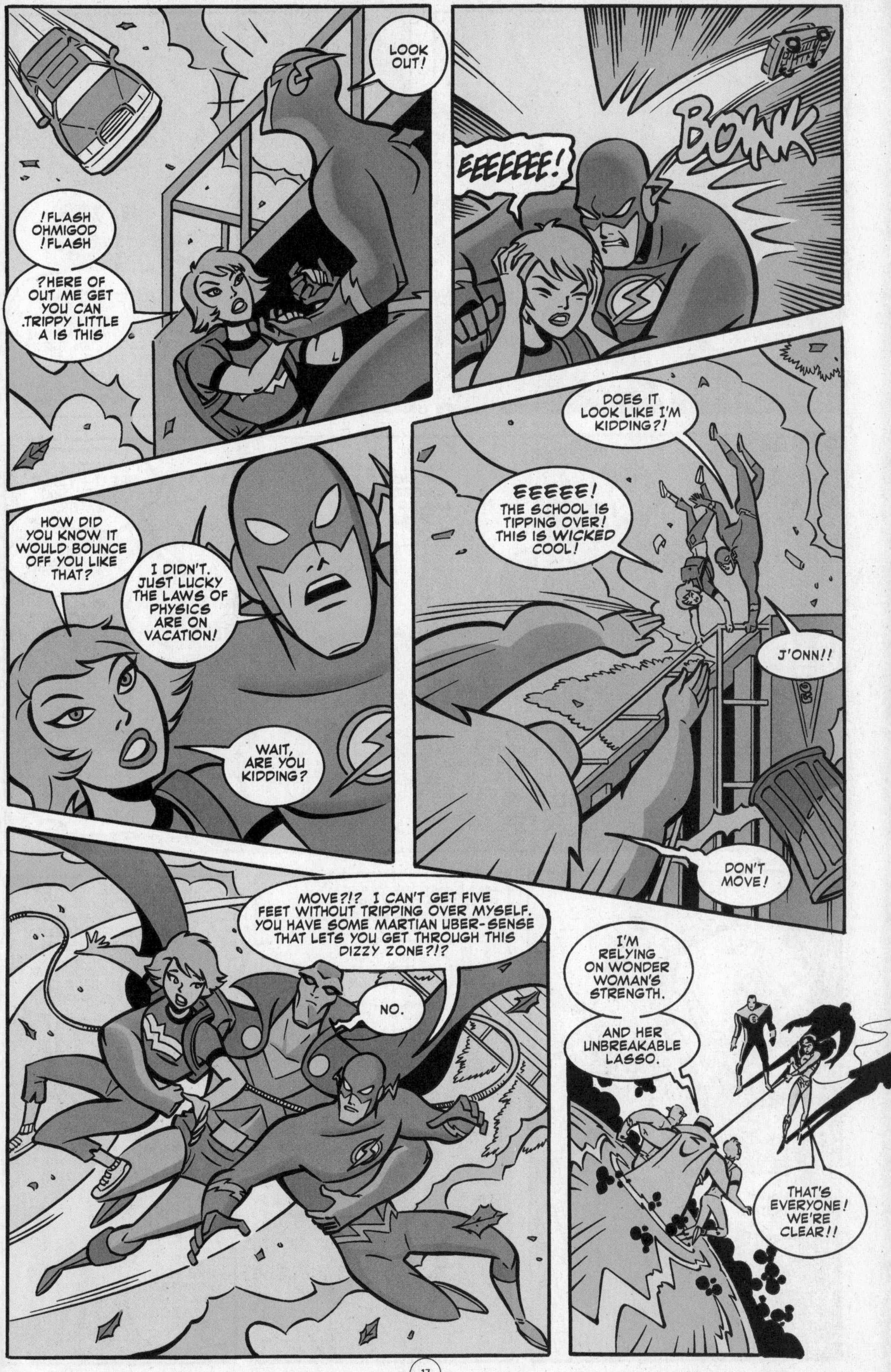

LOOK OUT!
!FLASH OHMIGOD !FLASH
?HERE OF OUT ME GET YOU CAN .TRIPPY LITTLE A IS THIS
EEEEEEE!
BONK
HOW DID YOU KNOW IT WOULD BOUNCE OFF YOU LIKE THAT?
I DIDN'T. JUST LUCKY THE LAWS OF PHYSICS ARE ON VACATION!
WAIT, ARE YOU KIDDING?
DOES IT LOOK LIKE I'M KIDDING?!
EEEEE! THE SCHOOL IS TIPPING OVER! THIS IS WICKED COOL!
J'ONN!!
DON'T MOVE!
MOVE?!? I CAN'T GET FIVE FEET WITHOUT TRIPPING OVER MYSELF. YOU HAVE SOME MARTIAN UBER-SENSE THAT LETS YOU GET THROUGH THIS DIZZY ZONE?!?
NO.
I'M RELYING ON WONDER WOMAN'S STRENGTH.
AND HER UNBREAKABLE LASSO.
THAT'S EVERYONE! WE'RE CLEAR!!

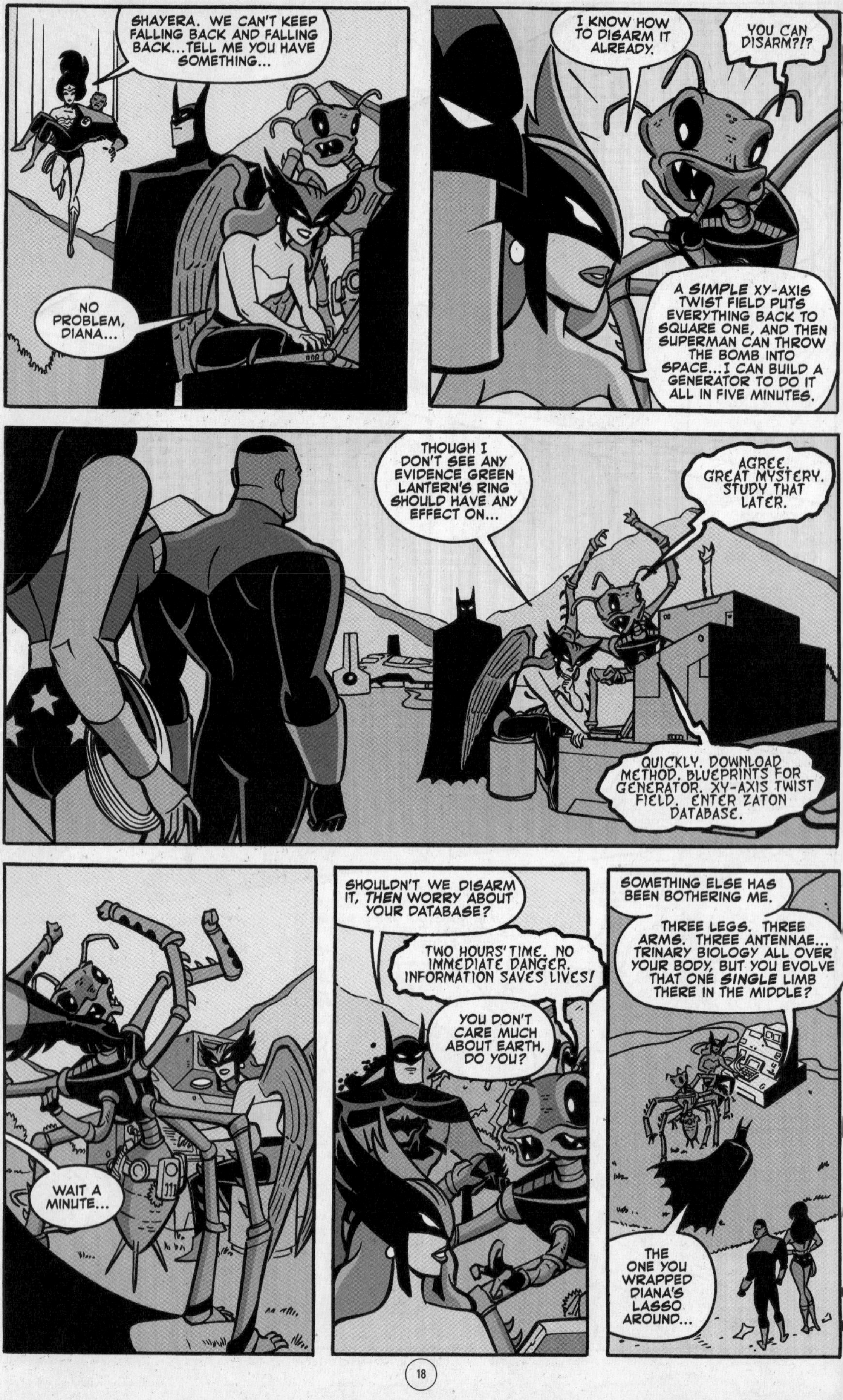
SHAYERA. WE CAN'T KEEP FALLING BACK AND FALLING BACK...TELL ME YOU HAVE SOMETHING...
NO PROBLEM, DIANA...
I KNOW HOW TO DISARM IT ALREADY.
YOU CAN DISARM?!?
A SIMPLE XY-AXIS TWIST FIELD PUTS EVERYTHING BACK TO SQUARE ONE, AND THEN SUPERMAN CAN THROW THE BOMB INTO SPACE...I CAN BUILD A GENERATOR TO DO IT ALL IN FIVE MINUTES.
THOUGH I DON'T SEE ANY EVIDENCE GREEN LANTERN'S RING SHOULD HAVE ANY EFFECT ON...
AGREE. GREAT MYSTERY. STUDY THAT LATER.
QUICKLY. DOWNLOAD METHOD. BLUEPRINTS FOR GENERATOR. XY-AXIS TWIST FIELD. ENTER ZATON DATABASE.
WAIT A MINUTE...
SHOULDN'T WE DISARM IT, THEN WORRY ABOUT YOUR DATABASE?
TWO HOURS' TIME. NO IMMEDIATE DANGER. INFORMATION SAVES LIVES!
YOU DON'T CARE MUCH ABOUT EARTH, DO YOU?
SOMETHING ELSE HAS BEEN BOTHERING ME.
THREE LEGS. THREE ARMS. THREE ANTENNAE... TRINARY BIOLOGY ALL OVER YOUR BODY, BUT YOU EVOLVE THAT ONE SINGLE LIMB THERE IN THE MIDDLE?
THE ONE YOU WRAPPED DIANA'S LASSO AROUND...

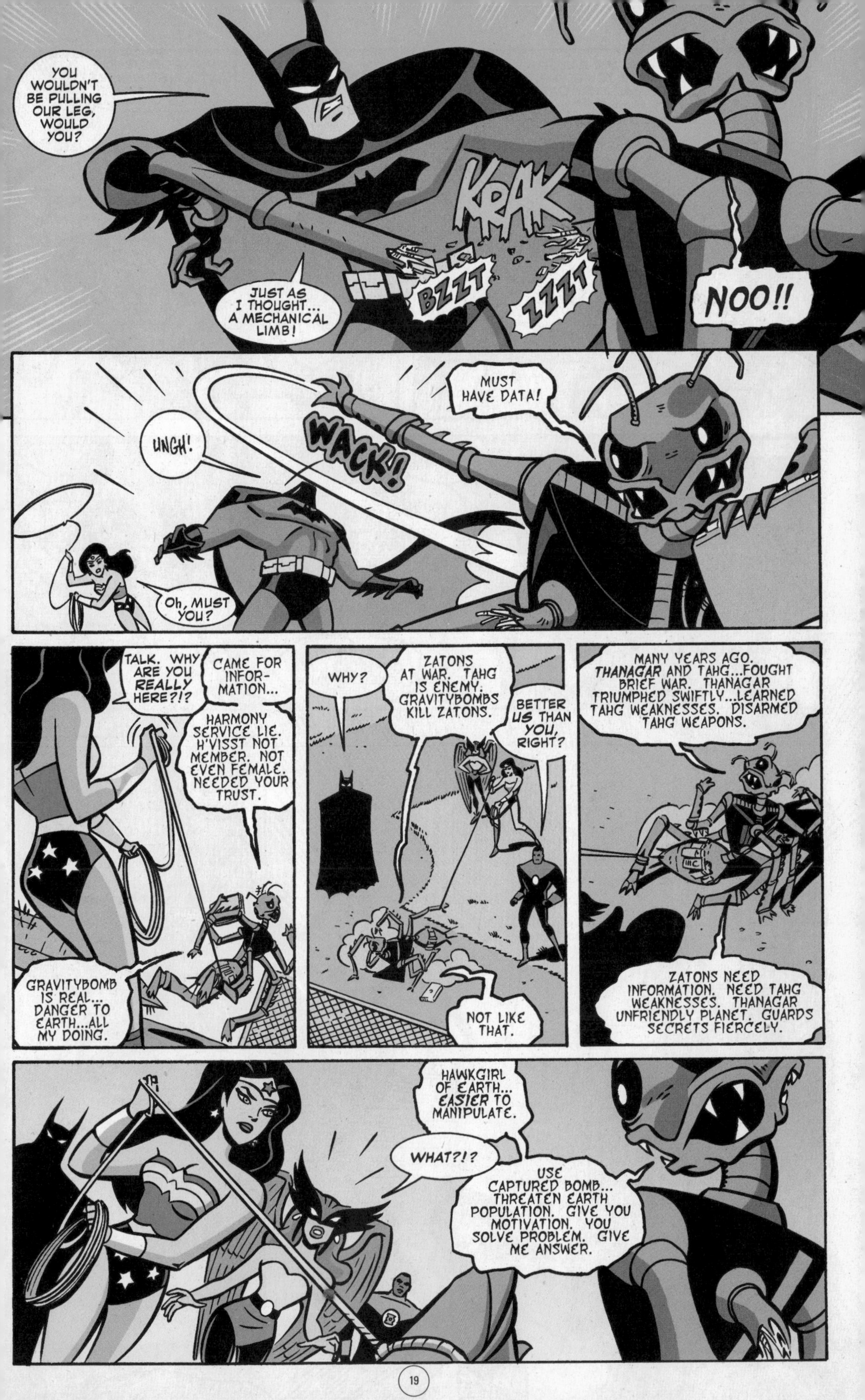
YOU WOULDN'T BE PULLING OUR LEG, WOULD YOU?
KRAK
JUST AS I THOUGHT... A MECHANICAL LIMB!
BZZZT
ZZZZT
NOO!!
MUST HAVE DATA!
UNGH!
WACK!
Oh, MUST YOU?
TALK. WHY ARE YOU REALLY HERE?!?
CAME FOR INFORMATION...
HARMONY SERVICE LIE. H'VISST NOT MEMBER. NOT EVEN FEMALE. NEEDED YOUR TRUST.
GRAVITYBOMB IS REAL... DANGER TO EARTH...ALL MY DOING.
WHY?
ZATONS AT WAR. TAHG IS ENEMY. GRAVITYBOMBS KILL ZATONS.
BETTER US THAN YOU, RIGHT?
NOT LIKE THAT.
MANY YEARS AGO. THANAGAR AND TAHG...FOUGHT BRIEF WAR. THANAGAR TRIUMPHED SWIFTLY...LEARNED TAHG WEAKNESSES. DISARMED TAHG WEAPONS.
ZATONS NEED INFORMATION. NEED TAHG WEAKNESSES. THANAGAR UNFRIENDLY PLANET. GUARDS SECRETS FIERCELY.
HAWKGIRL OF EARTH... EASIER TO MANIPULATE.
WHAT?!?
USE CAPTURED BOMB... THREATEN EARTH POPULATION. GIVE YOU MOTIVATION. YOU SOLVE PROBLEM. GIVE ME ANSWER.

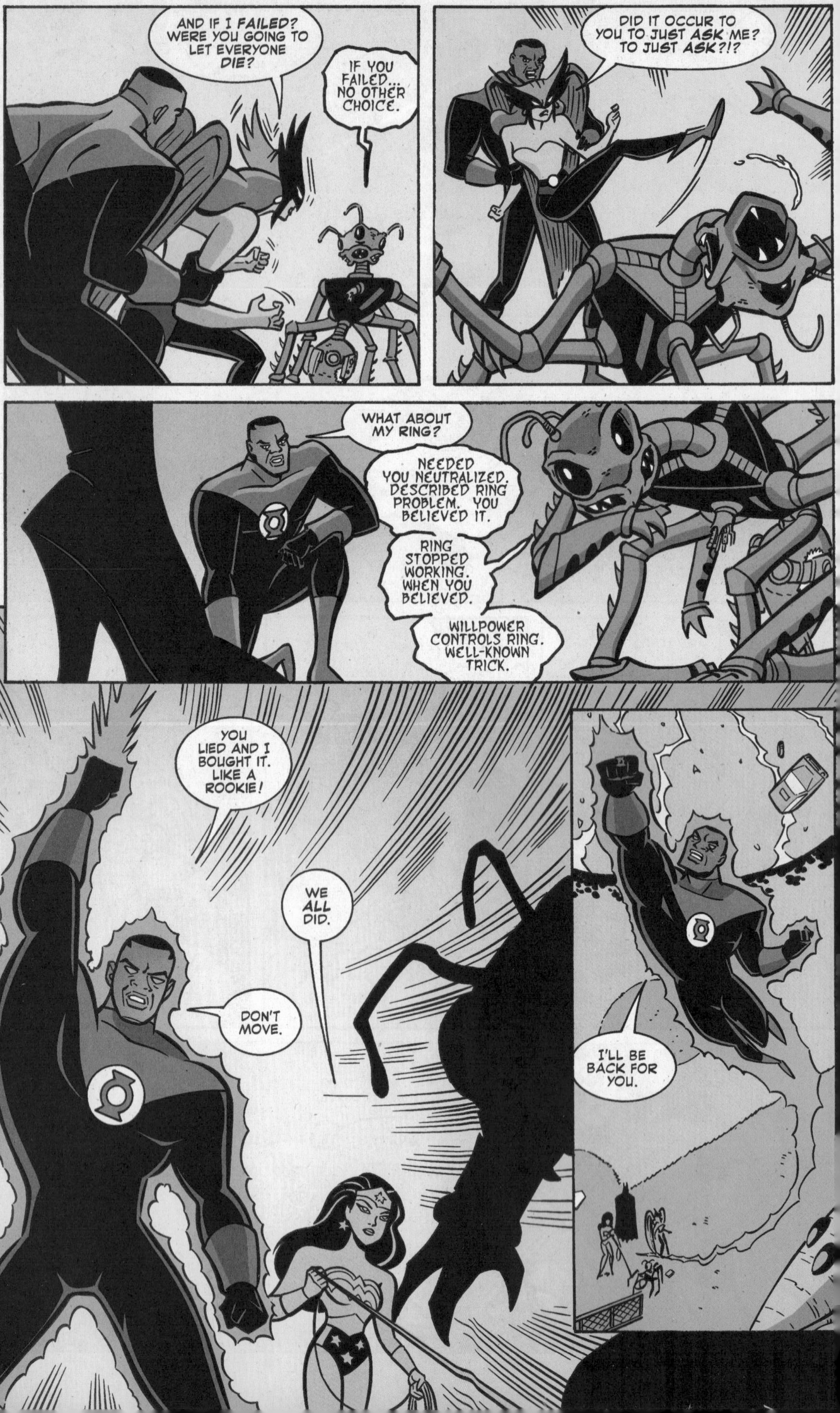
AND IF I FAILED? WERE YOU GOING TO LET EVERYONE DIE?
IF YOU FAILED... NO OTHER CHOICE.
DID IT OCCUR TO YOU TO JUST ASK ME? TO JUST ASK?!?
WHAT ABOUT MY RING?
NEEDED YOU NEUTRALIZED. DESCRIBED RING PROBLEM. YOU BELIEVED IT.
RING STOPPED WORKING. WHEN YOU BELIEVED.
WILLPOWER CONTROLS RING. WELL-KNOWN TRICK.
YOU LIED AND I BOUGHT IT. LIKE A ROOKIE!
WE ALL DID.
DON'T MOVE.
I'LL BE BACK FOR YOU.

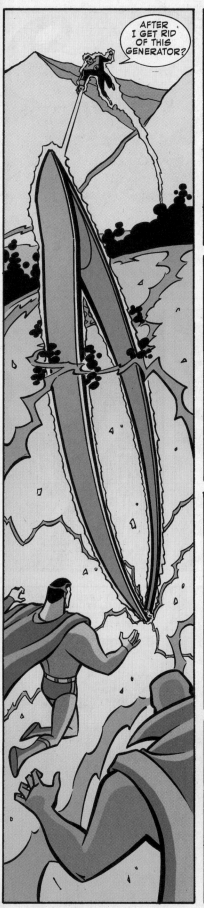

AFTER I GET RID OF THIS GENERATOR?

EARTHQUAKE!

IT'S A REACTION TO THE ANTI-FIELD BEING REMOVED FROM THE GROUND...

RRRUMMBLLE!

LUCKY DIVERSION, YES? CANNOT STAY HERE...

EZT!

EZT!

I THOUGHT YOU WEREN'T SUPPOSED TO DO THAT!

SO DID I. THAT WAS THE PROBLEM...

CONVINCE HIM NOT TO LEAVE THE PLANET, OKAY? I WANT HIM HERE WHEN I GET BACK...

HIM?

THAT ALIEN IS A CON ARTIST...HE RISKED THE LIVES OF EVERYONE ON EARTH ON A GAMBLE...

THANKS FOR HELP. ZATON SHALL TRIUMPH. TAHG IS DOOMED!

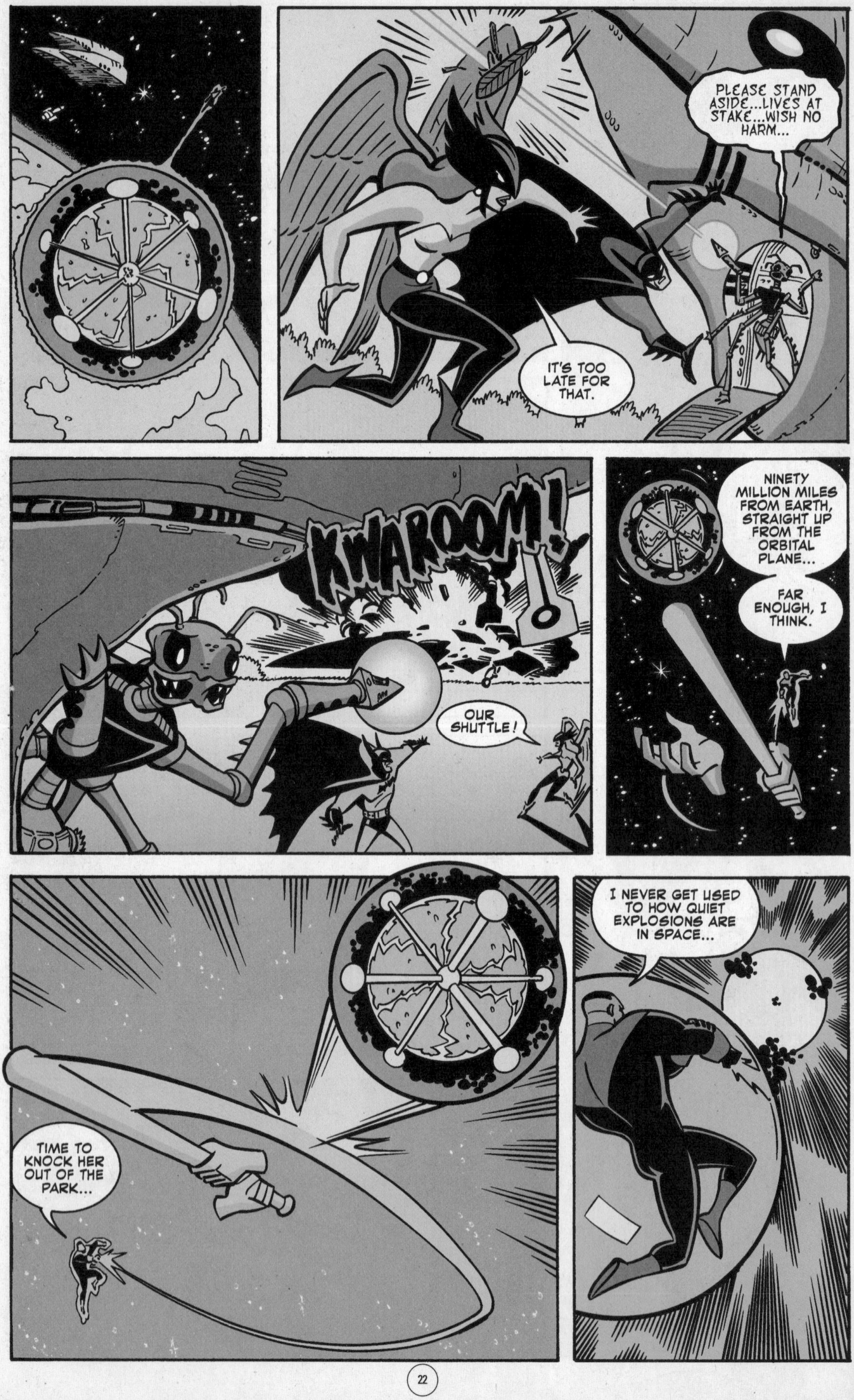
PLEASE STAND ASIDE...LIVES AT STAKE...WISH NO HARM...
IT'S TOO LATE FOR THAT.
KWAROOM!
OUR SHUTTLE!
NINETY MILLION MILES FROM EARTH, STRAIGHT UP FROM THE ORBITAL PLANE...
FAR ENOUGH, I THINK.
TIME TO KNOCK HER OUT OF THE PARK...
I NEVER GET USED TO HOW QUIET EXPLOSIONS ARE IN SPACE...

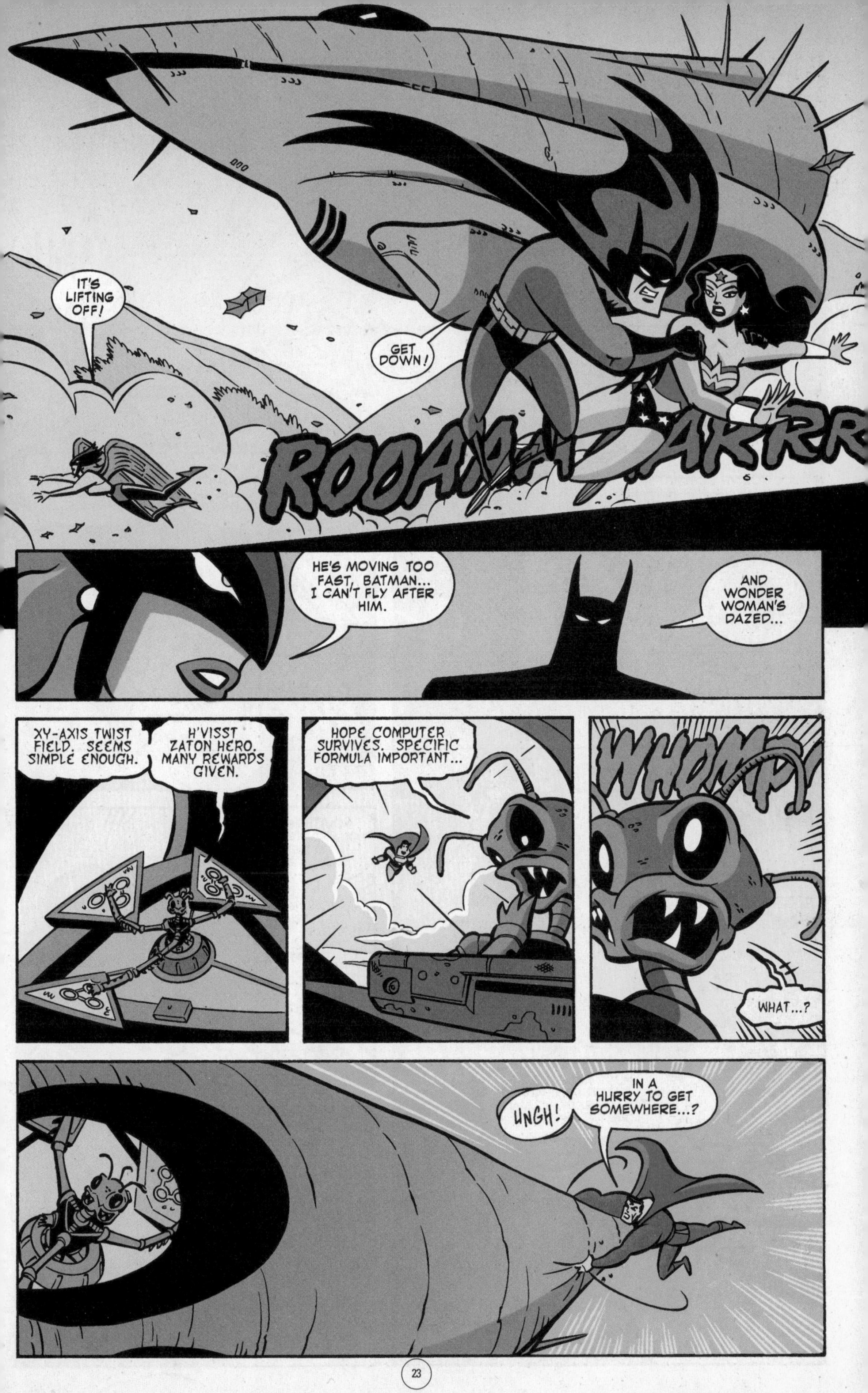
IT'S LIFTING OFF!
GET DOWN!
ROOAAAARRRR
HE'S MOVING TOO FAST, BATMAN... I CAN'T FLY AFTER HIM.
AND WONDER WOMAN'S DAZED...
XY-AXIS TWIST FIELD. SEEMS SIMPLE ENOUGH.
H'VISST ZATON HERO. MANY REWARDS GIVEN.
HOPE COMPUTER SURVIVES. SPECIFIC FORMULA IMPORTANT...
WHOM
WHAT...?
UNGH!
IN A HURRY TO GET SOMEWHERE...?

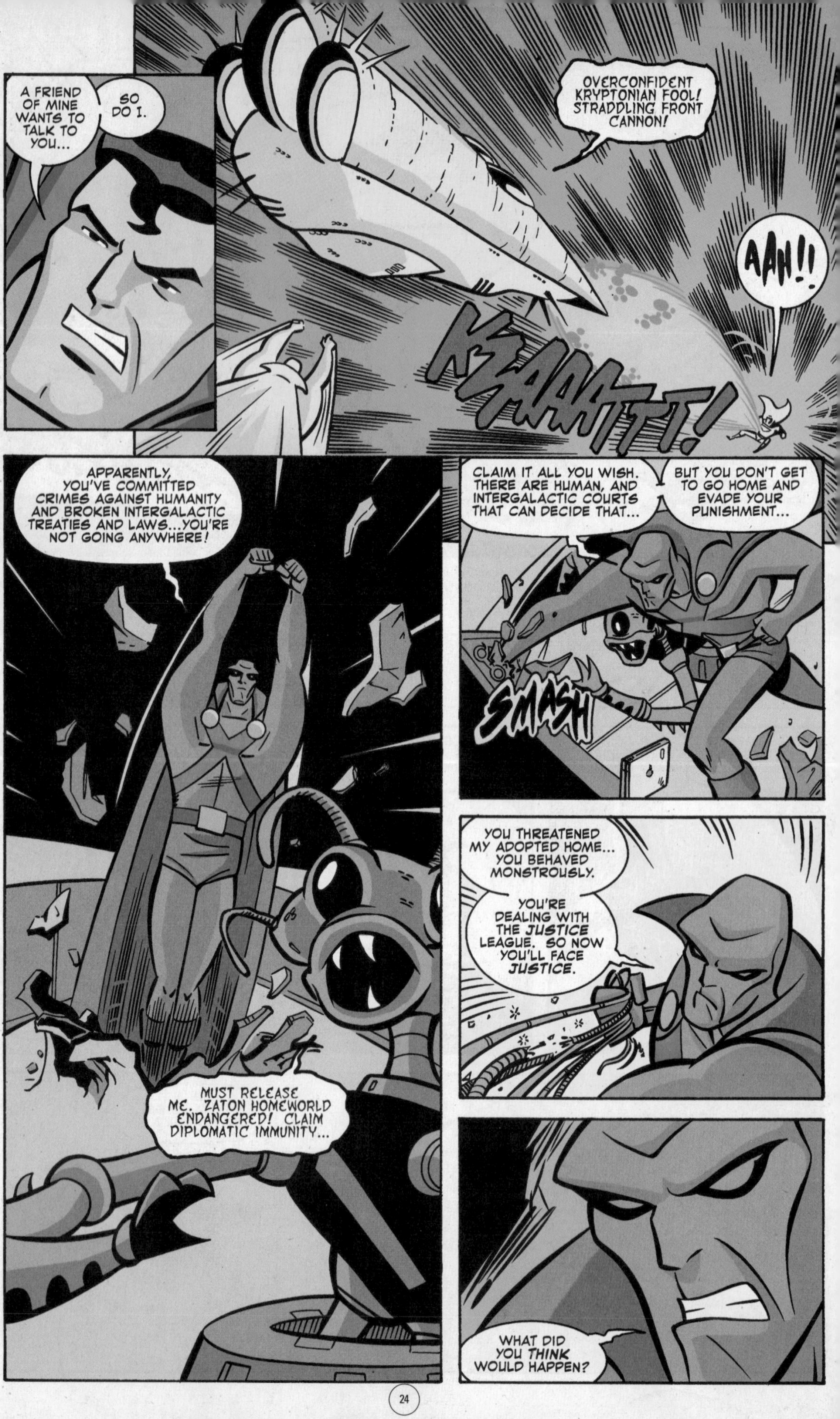
A FRIEND OF MINE WANTS TO TALK TO YOU...
SO DO I.
OVERCONFIDENT KRYPTONIAN FOOL! STRADDLING FRONT CANNON!
AAH!!
KSSAAATTT!
APPARENTLY, YOU'VE COMMITTED CRIMES AGAINST HUMANITY AND BROKEN INTERGALACTIC TREATIES AND LAWS...YOU'RE NOT GOING ANYWHERE!
MUST RELEASE ME. ZATON HOMEWORLD ENDANGERED! CLAIM DIPLOMATIC IMMUNITY...
CLAIM IT ALL YOU WISH. THERE ARE HUMAN, AND INTERGALACTIC COURTS THAT CAN DECIDE THAT...
BUT YOU DON'T GET TO GO HOME AND EVADE YOUR PUNISHMENT...
SMASH
YOU THREATENED MY ADOPTED HOME... YOU BEHAVED MONSTROUSLY.
YOU'RE DEALING WITH THE JUSTICE LEAGUE. SO NOW YOU'LL FACE JUSTICE.
WHAT DID YOU THINK WOULD HAPPEN?

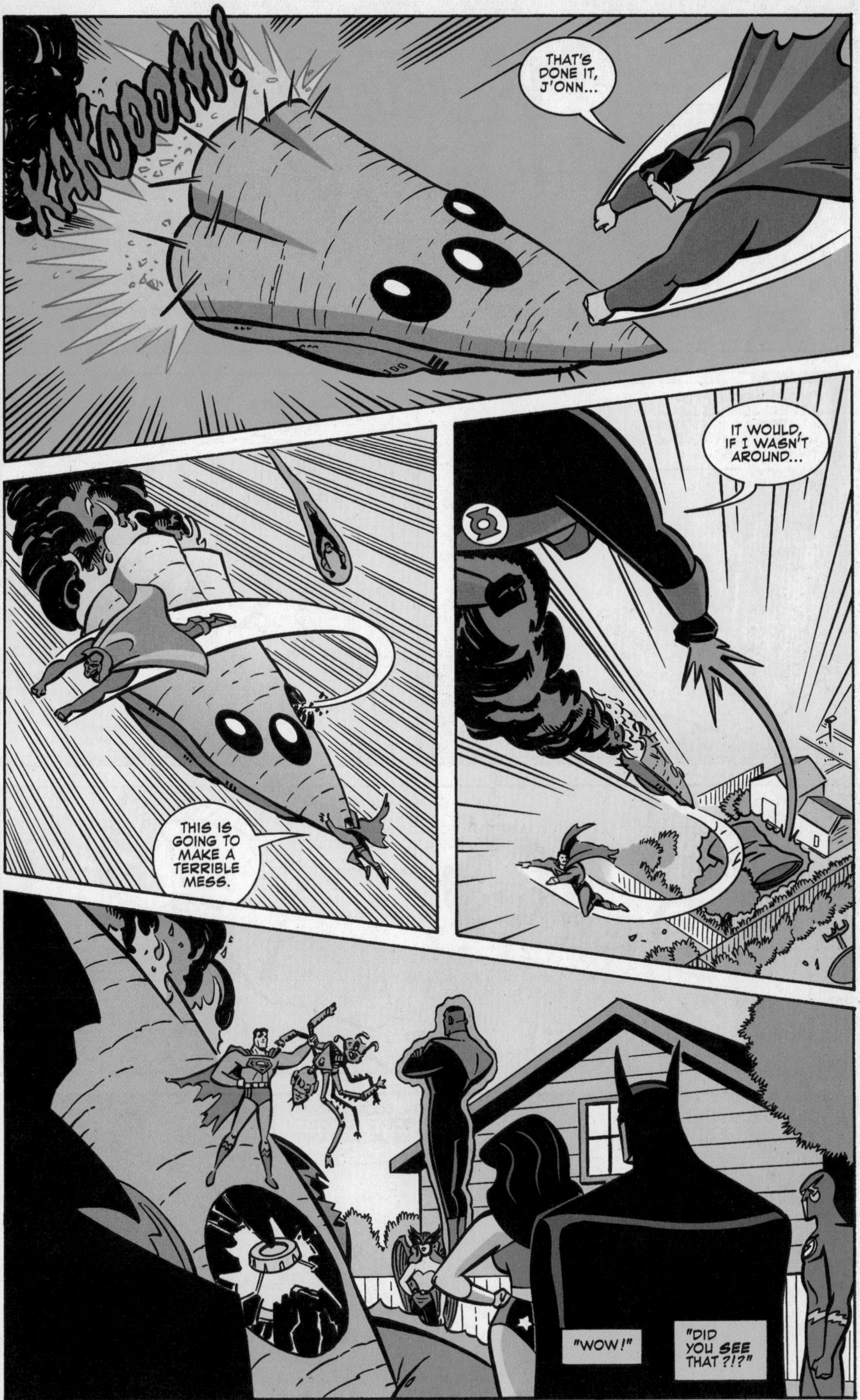

KAKOOOM!
THAT'S DONE IT, J'ONN...
THIS IS GOING TO MAKE A TERRIBLE MESS.
IT WOULD, IF I WASN'T AROUND...
"WOW!"
"DID YOU SEE THAT?!?"

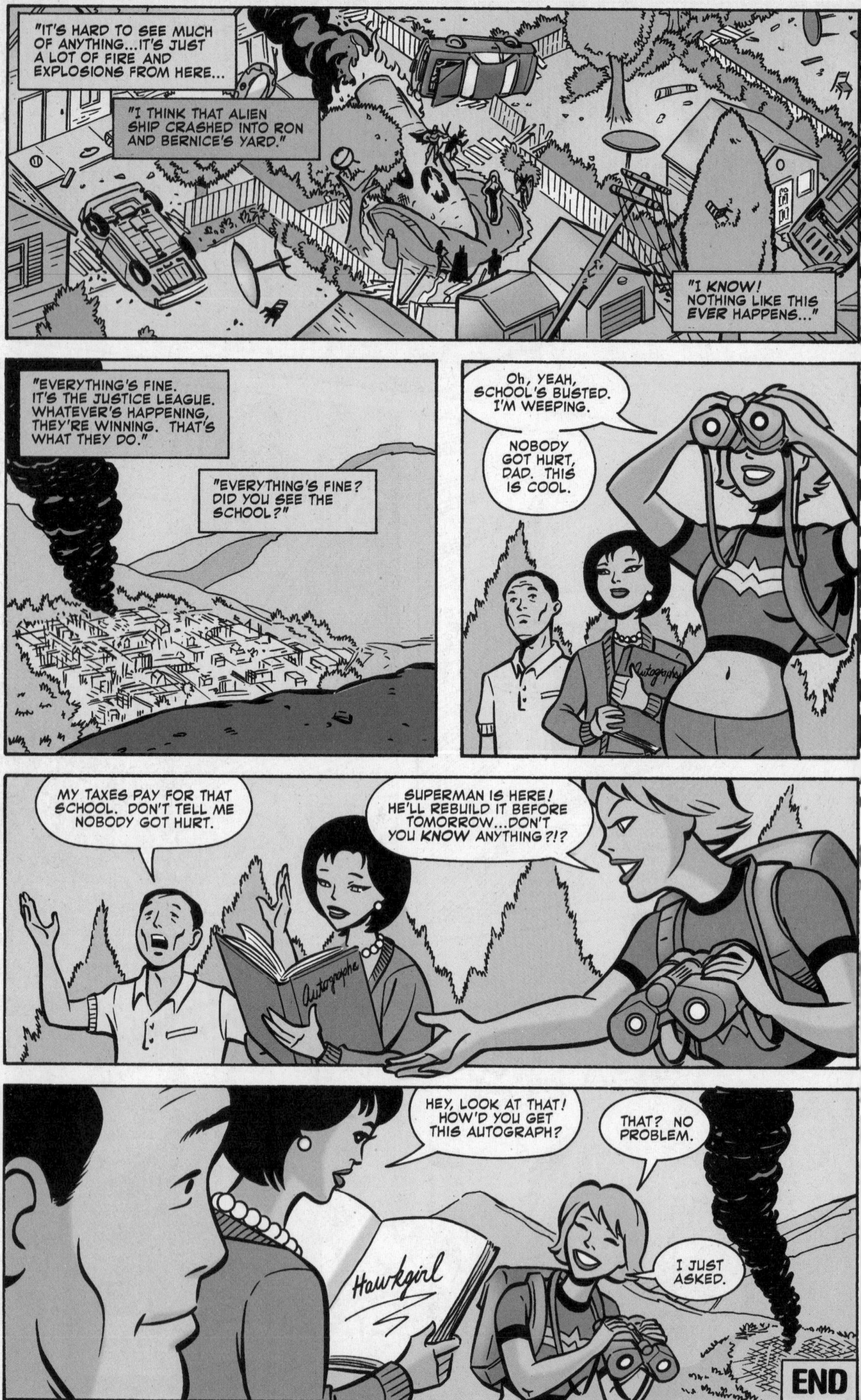
"IT'S HARD TO SEE MUCH OF ANYTHING...IT'S JUST A LOT OF FIRE AND EXPLOSIONS FROM HERE...
"I THINK THAT ALIEN SHIP CRASHED INTO RON AND BERNICE'S YARD."
"I KNOW! NOTHING LIKE THIS EVER HAPPENS..."
"EVERYTHING'S FINE. IT'S THE JUSTICE LEAGUE. WHATEVER'S HAPPENING, THEY'RE WINNING. THAT'S WHAT THEY DO."
"EVERYTHING'S FINE? DID YOU SEE THE SCHOOL?"
Oh, YEAH, SCHOOL'S BUSTED. I'M WEEPING.
NOBODY GOT HURT, DAD. THIS IS COOL.
Autographs
MY TAXES PAY FOR THAT SCHOOL. DON'T TELL ME NOBODY GOT HURT.
SUPERMAN IS HERE! HE'LL REBUILD IT BEFORE TOMORROW...DON'T YOU KNOW ANYTHING?!?
Autographs
HEY, LOOK AT THAT! HOW'D YOU GET THIS AUTOGRAPH?
THAT? NO PROBLEM.
Hawkgirl
I JUST ASKED.
END

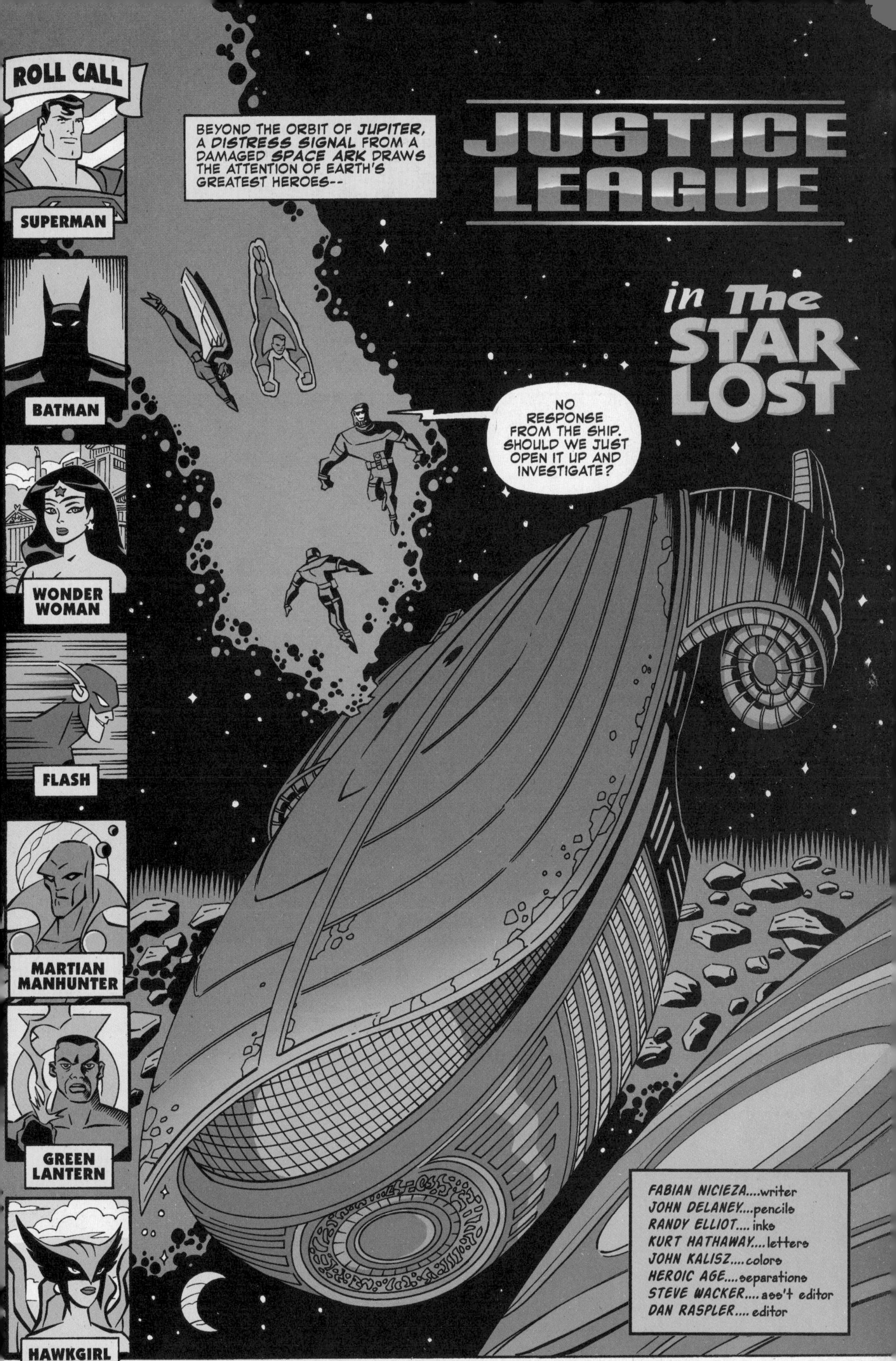
ROLL CALL
SUPERMAN
BATMAN
WONDER WOMAN
FLASH
MARTIAN MANHUNTER
GREEN LANTERN
HAWKGIRL
BEYOND THE ORBIT OF JUPITER, A DISTRESS SIGNAL FROM A DAMAGED SPACE ARK DRAWS THE ATTENTION OF EARTH'S GREATEST HEROES--
JUSTICE LEAGUE
in The STAR LOST
NO RESPONSE FROM THE SHIP. SHOULD WE JUST OPEN IT UP AND INVESTIGATE?
FABIAN NICIEZA....writer
JOHN DELANEY....pencils
RANDY ELLIOT.... inks
KURT HATHAWAY....letters
JOHN KALISZ....colors
HEROIC AGE....separations
STEVE WACKER.... ass't editor
DAN RASPLER.... editor

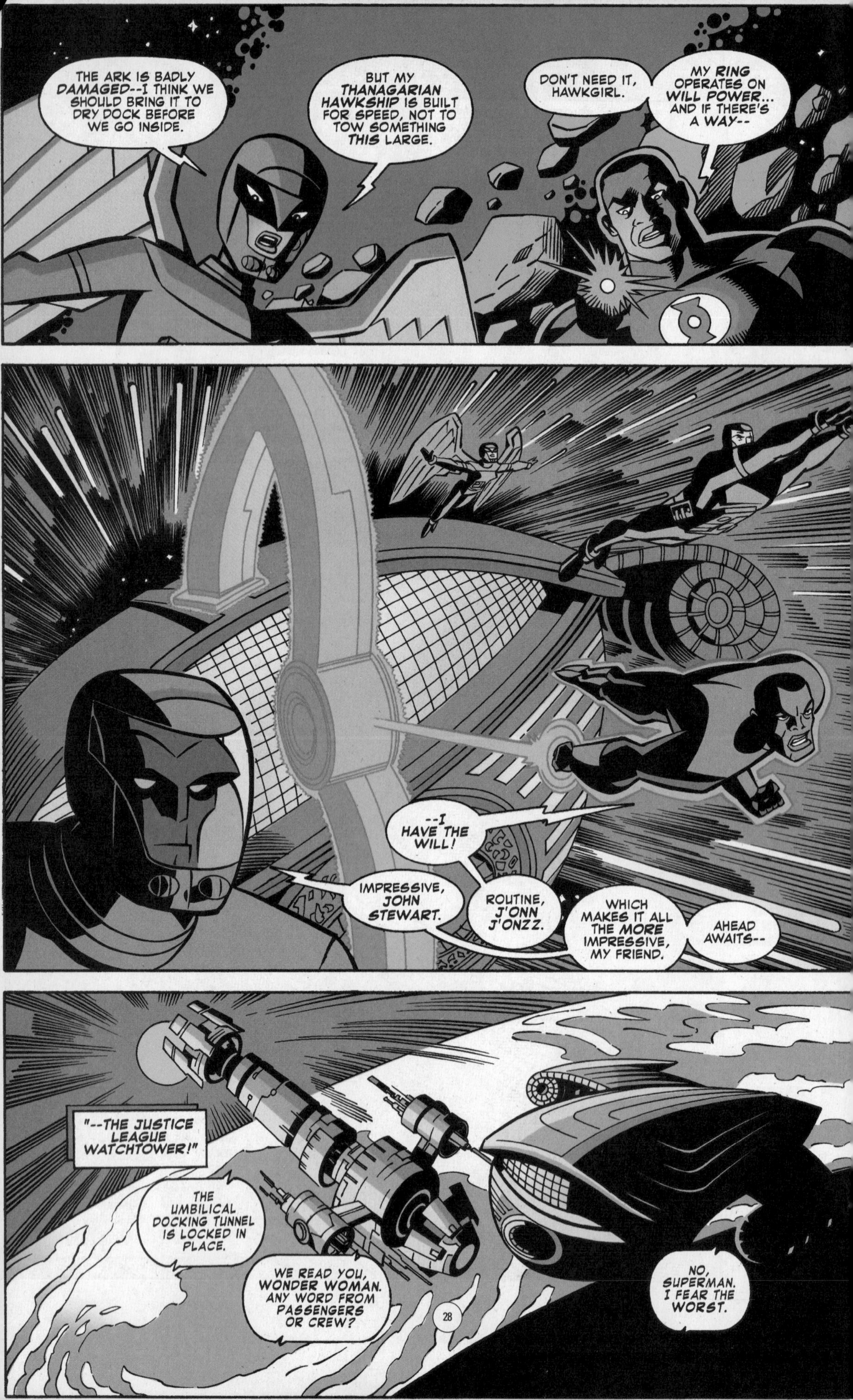
THE ARK IS BADLY DAMAGED--I THINK WE SHOULD BRING IT TO DRY DOCK BEFORE WE GO INSIDE.
BUT MY THANAGARIAN HAWKSHIP IS BUILT FOR SPEED, NOT TO TOW SOMETHING THIS LARGE.
DON'T NEED IT, HAWKGIRL.
MY RING OPERATES ON WILL POWER... AND IF THERE'S A WAY--
--I HAVE THE WILL!
IMPRESSIVE, JOHN STEWART.
ROUTINE, J'ONN J'ONZZ.
WHICH MAKES IT ALL THE MORE IMPRESSIVE, MY FRIEND.
AHEAD AWAITS--
"--THE JUSTICE LEAGUE WATCHTOWER!"
THE UMBILICAL DOCKING TUNNEL IS LOCKED IN PLACE.
WE READ YOU, WONDER WOMAN. ANY WORD FROM PASSENGERS OR CREW?
NO, SUPERMAN. I FEAR THE WORST.

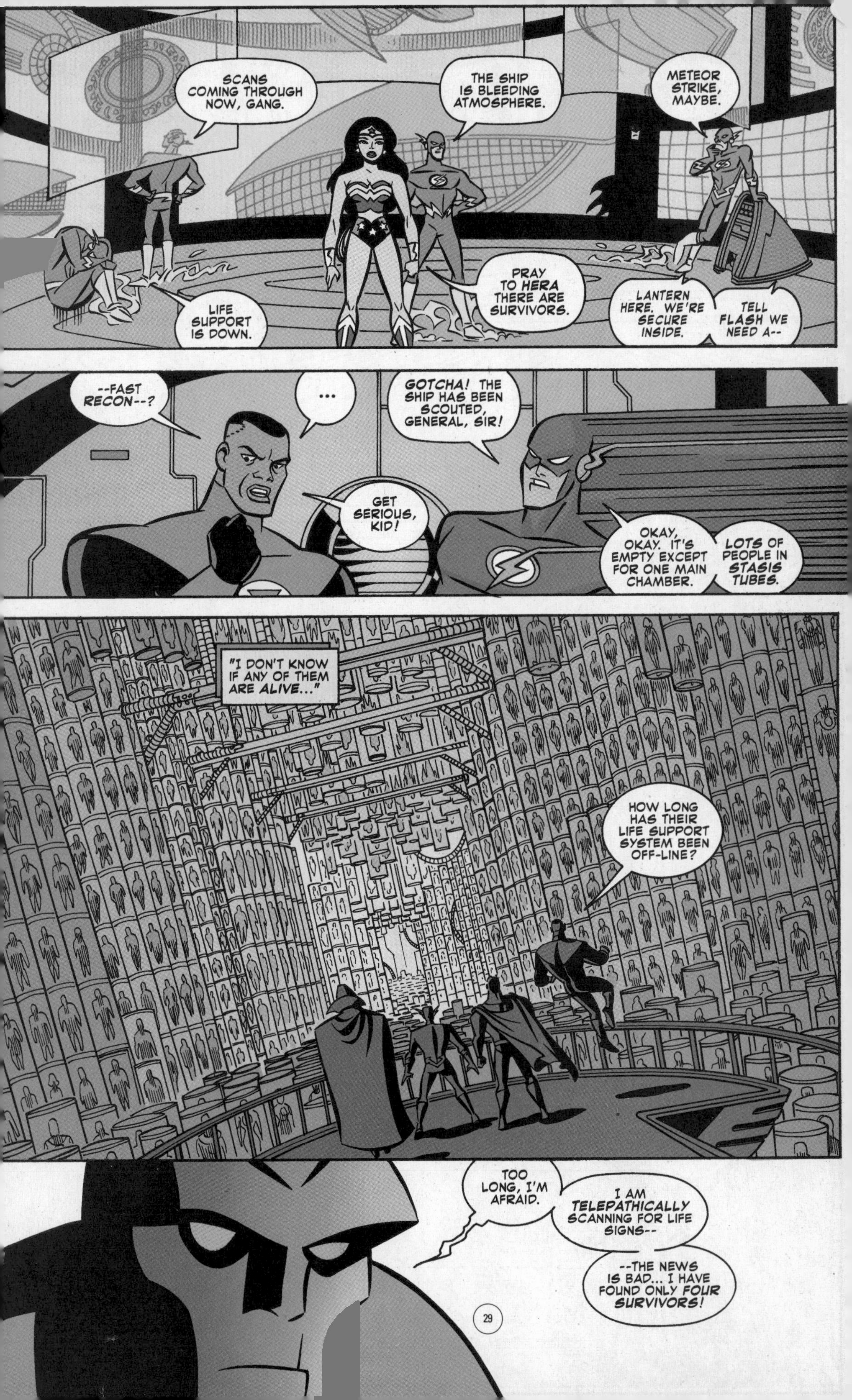
SCANS COMING THROUGH NOW, GANG.
THE SHIP IS BLEEDING ATMOSPHERE.
METEOR STRIKE, MAYBE.
LIFE SUPPORT IS DOWN.
PRAY TO HERA THERE ARE SURVIVORS.
LANTERN HERE. WE'RE SECURE INSIDE.
TELL FLASH WE NEED A--
--FAST RECON--?
...
GOTCHA! THE SHIP HAS BEEN SCOUTED, GENERAL, SIR!
GET SERIOUS, KID!
OKAY, OKAY. IT'S EMPTY EXCEPT FOR ONE MAIN CHAMBER.
LOTS OF PEOPLE IN STASIS TUBES.
"I DON'T KNOW IF ANY OF THEM ARE ALIVE..."
HOW LONG HAS THEIR LIFE SUPPORT SYSTEM BEEN OFF-LINE?
TOO LONG, I'M AFRAID.
I AM TELEPATHICALLY SCANNING FOR LIFE SIGNS--
--THE NEWS IS BAD... I HAVE FOUND ONLY FOUR SURVIVORS!

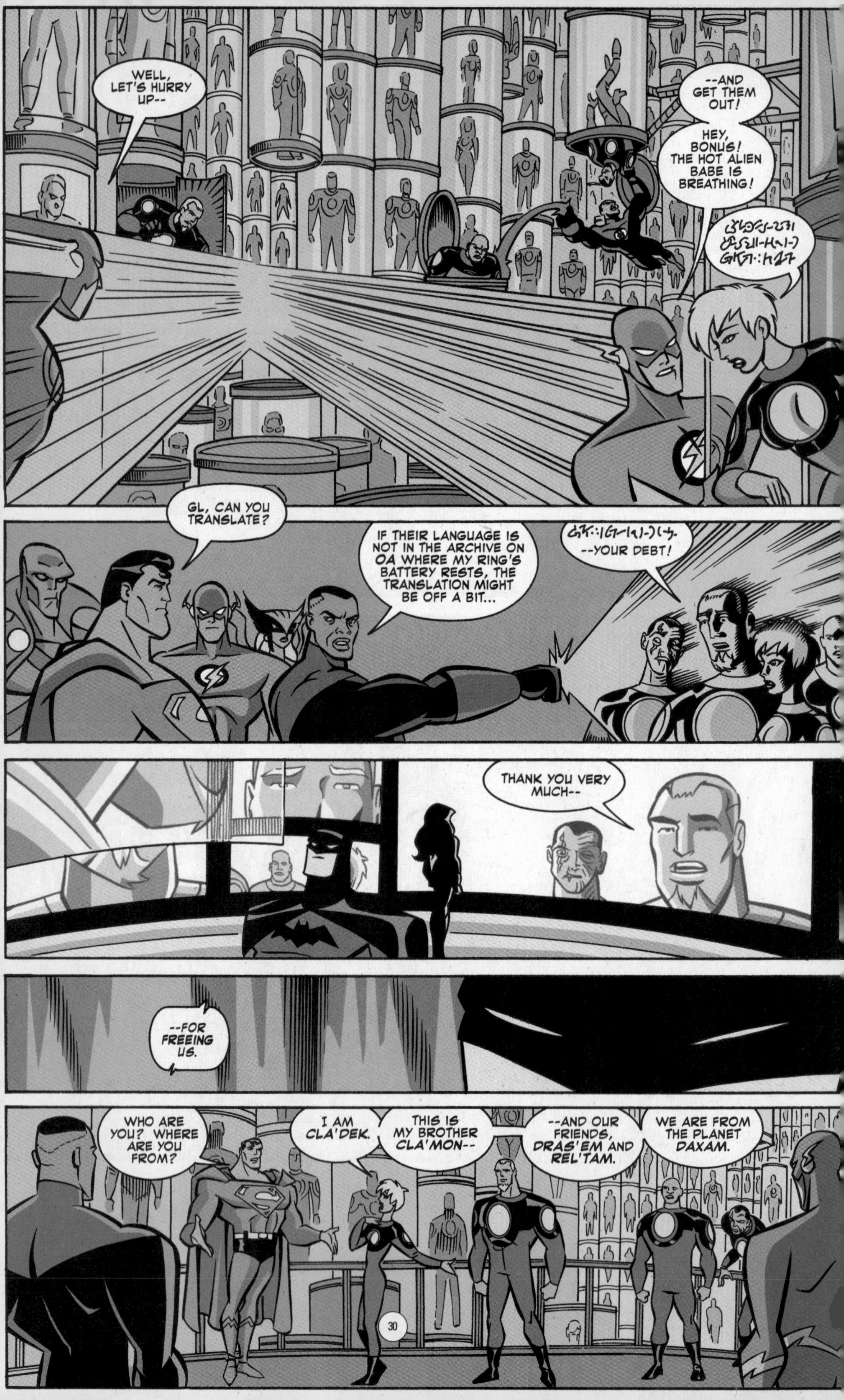
WELL, LET'S HURRY UP--
--AND GET THEM OUT!
HEY, BONUS! THE HOT ALIEN BABE IS BREATHING!
GL, CAN YOU TRANSLATE?
IF THEIR LANGUAGE IS NOT IN THE ARCHIVE ON OA WHERE MY RING'S BATTERY RESTS, THE TRANSLATION MIGHT BE OFF A BIT...
--YOUR DEBT!
THANK YOU VERY MUCH--
--FOR FREEING US.
WHO ARE YOU? WHERE ARE YOU FROM?
I AM *CLA'DEK.*
THIS IS MY BROTHER *CLA'MON*--
--AND OUR FRIENDS, *DRAS'EM* AND *REL'TAM.*
WE ARE FROM THE PLANET *DAXAM.*
30

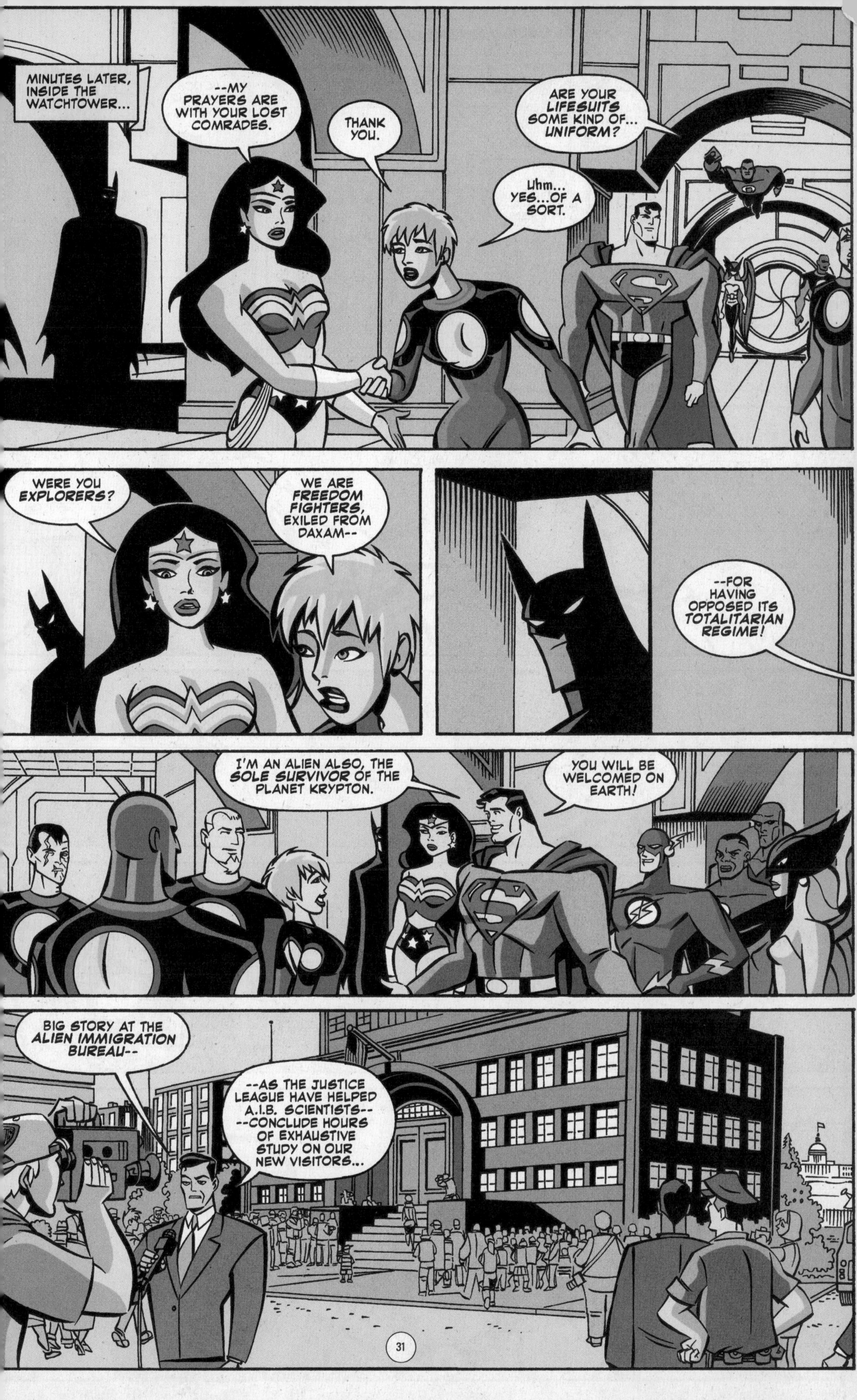

MINUTES LATER, INSIDE THE WATCHTOWER...
--MY PRAYERS ARE WITH YOUR LOST COMRADES.
THANK YOU.
ARE YOUR LIFESUITS SOME KIND OF... UNIFORM?
Uhm... YES...OF A SORT.
WERE YOU EXPLORERS?
WE ARE FREEDOM FIGHTERS, EXILED FROM DAXAM--
--FOR HAVING OPPOSED ITS TOTALITARIAN REGIME!
I'M AN ALIEN ALSO, THE SOLE SURVIVOR OF THE PLANET KRYPTON.
YOU WILL BE WELCOMED ON EARTH!
BIG STORY AT THE ALIEN IMMIGRATION BUREAU--
--AS THE JUSTICE LEAGUE HAVE HELPED A.I.B. SCIENTISTS--
--CONCLUDE HOURS OF EXHAUSTIVE STUDY ON OUR NEW VISITORS...

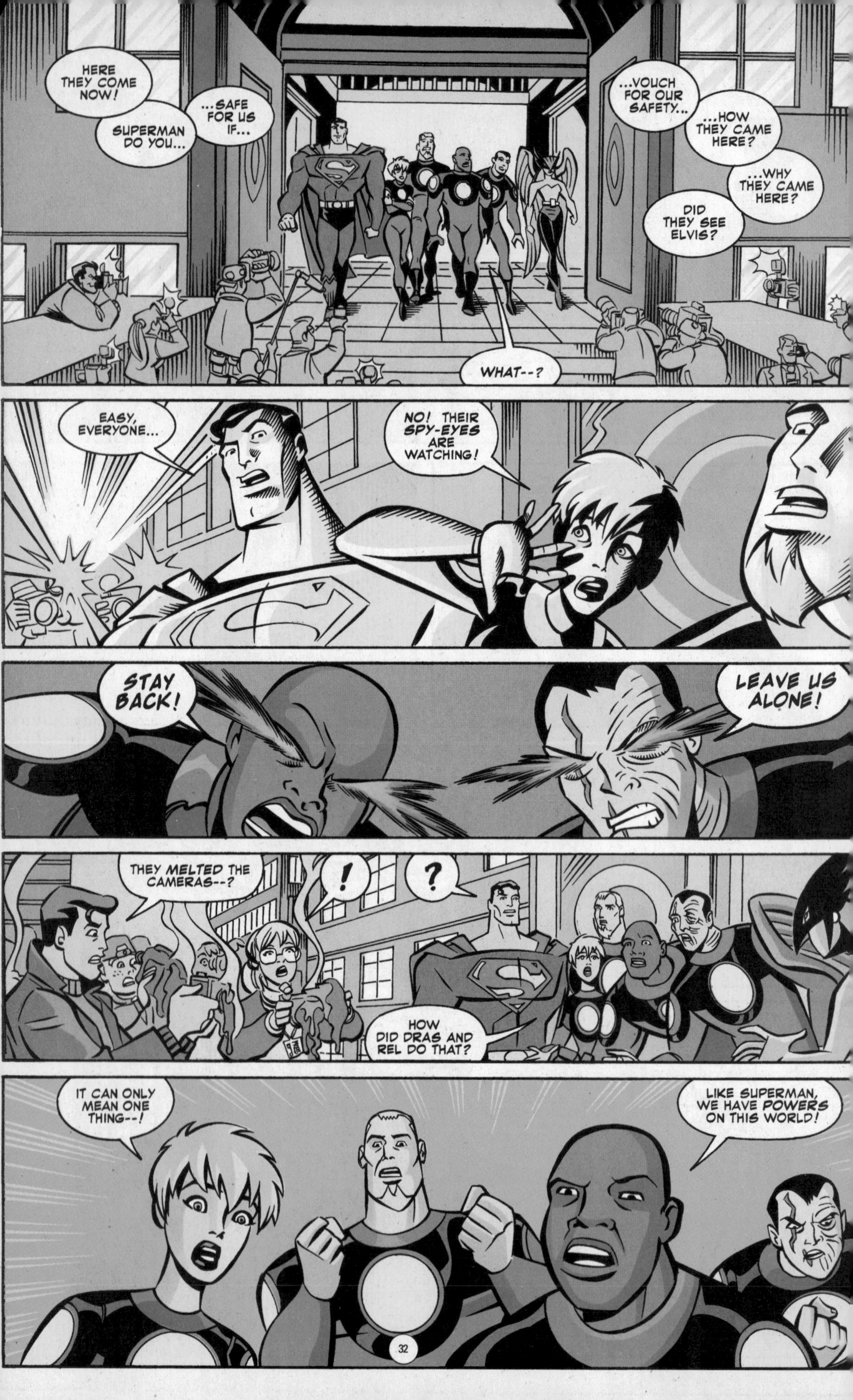
HERE THEY COME NOW!
SUPERMAN DO YOU...
...SAFE FOR US IF...
...VOUCH FOR OUR SAFETY...
...HOW THEY CAME HERE?
...WHY THEY CAME HERE?
DID THEY SEE ELVIS?
WHAT--?
EASY, EVERYONE...
NO! THEIR SPY-EYES ARE WATCHING!
STAY BACK!
LEAVE US ALONE!
THEY MELTED THE CAMERAS--?
!
?
HOW DID DRAS AND REL DO THAT?
IT CAN ONLY MEAN ONE THING--!
LIKE SUPERMAN, WE HAVE POWERS ON THIS WORLD!

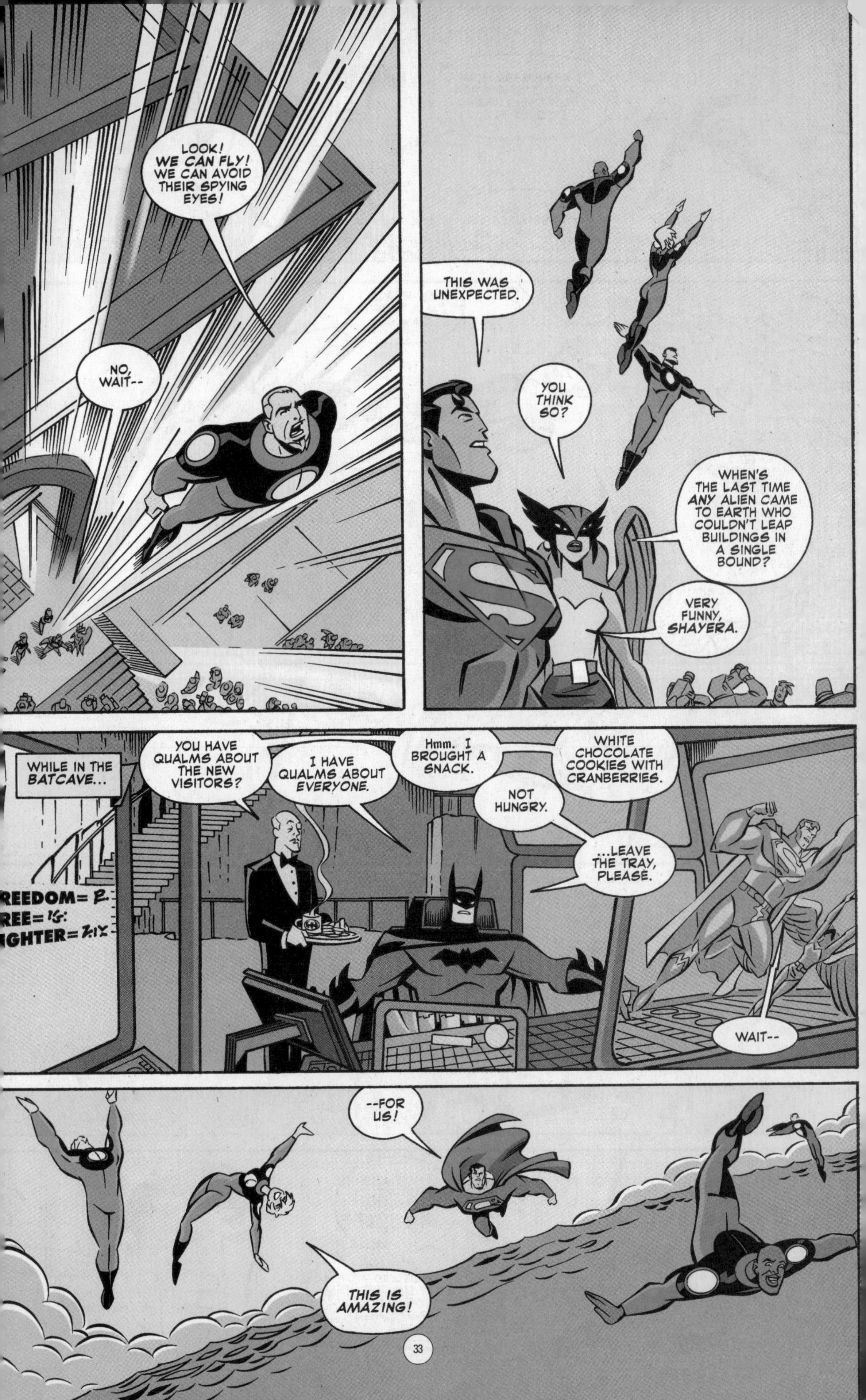
LOOK! WE CAN FLY! WE CAN AVOID THEIR SPYING EYES!
NO, WAIT--
THIS WAS UNEXPECTED.
YOU THINK SO?
WHEN'S THE LAST TIME ANY ALIEN CAME TO EARTH WHO COULDN'T LEAP BUILDINGS IN A SINGLE BOUND?
VERY FUNNY, SHAYERA.
WHILE IN THE BATCAVE...
YOU HAVE QUALMS ABOUT THE NEW VISITORS?
I HAVE QUALMS ABOUT EVERYONE.
Hmm. I BROUGHT A SNACK.
WHITE CHOCOLATE COOKIES WITH CRANBERRIES.
NOT HUNGRY.
...LEAVE THE TRAY, PLEASE.
WAIT--
--FOR US!
THIS IS AMAZING!

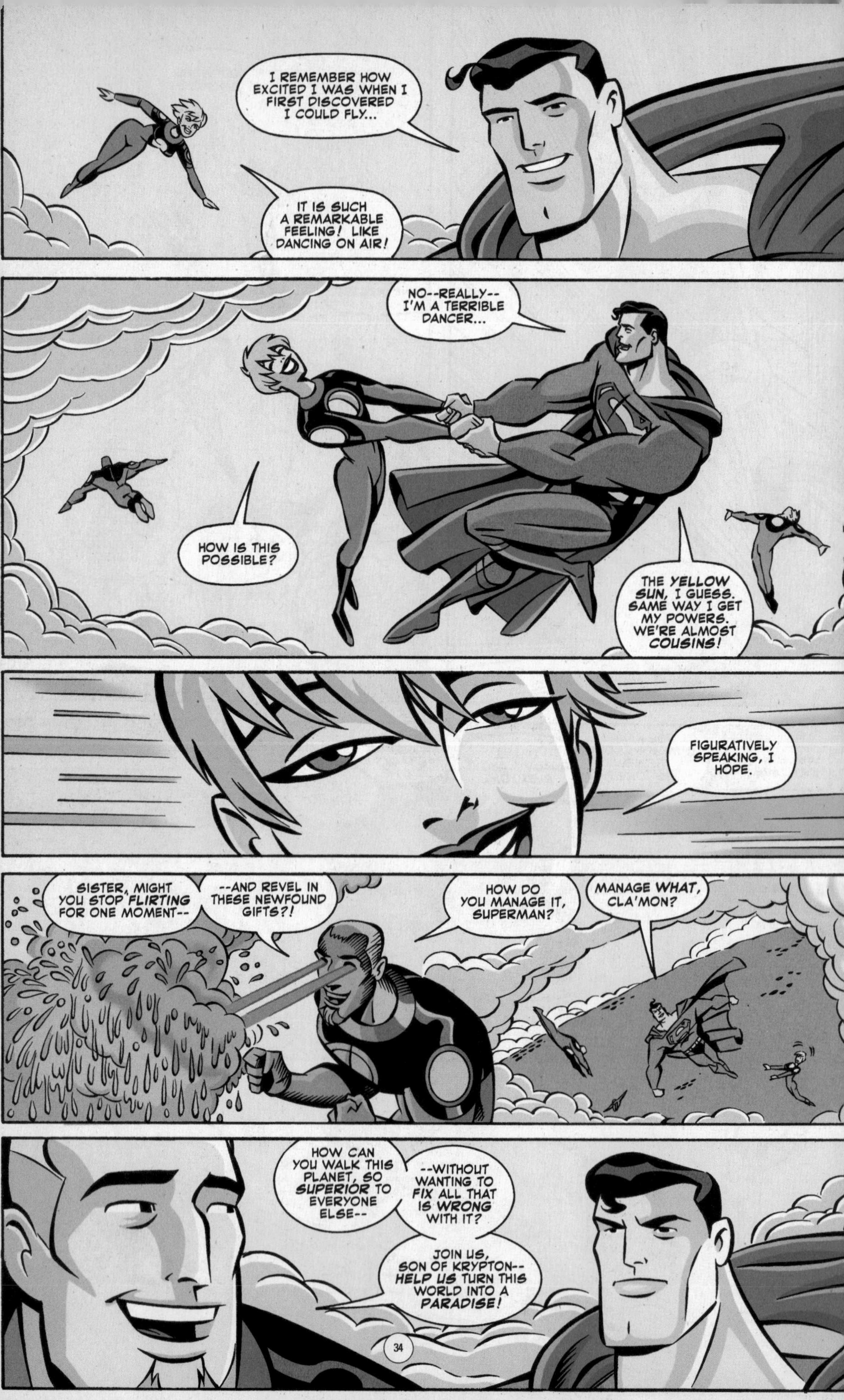
I REMEMBER HOW EXCITED I WAS WHEN I FIRST DISCOVERED I COULD FLY...
IT IS SUCH A REMARKABLE FEELING! LIKE DANCING ON AIR!
NO--REALLY-- I'M A TERRIBLE DANCER...
HOW IS THIS POSSIBLE?
THE YELLOW SUN, I GUESS. SAME WAY I GET MY POWERS. WE'RE ALMOST COUSINS!
FIGURATIVELY SPEAKING, I HOPE.
SISTER, MIGHT YOU STOP FLIRTING FOR ONE MOMENT--
--AND REVEL IN THESE NEWFOUND GIFTS?!
HOW DO YOU MANAGE IT, SUPERMAN?
MANAGE WHAT, CLA'MON?
HOW CAN YOU WALK THIS PLANET, SO SUPERIOR TO EVERYONE ELSE--
--WITHOUT WANTING TO FIX ALL THAT IS WRONG WITH IT?
JOIN US, SON OF KRYPTON-- HELP US TURN THIS WORLD INTO A PARADISE!

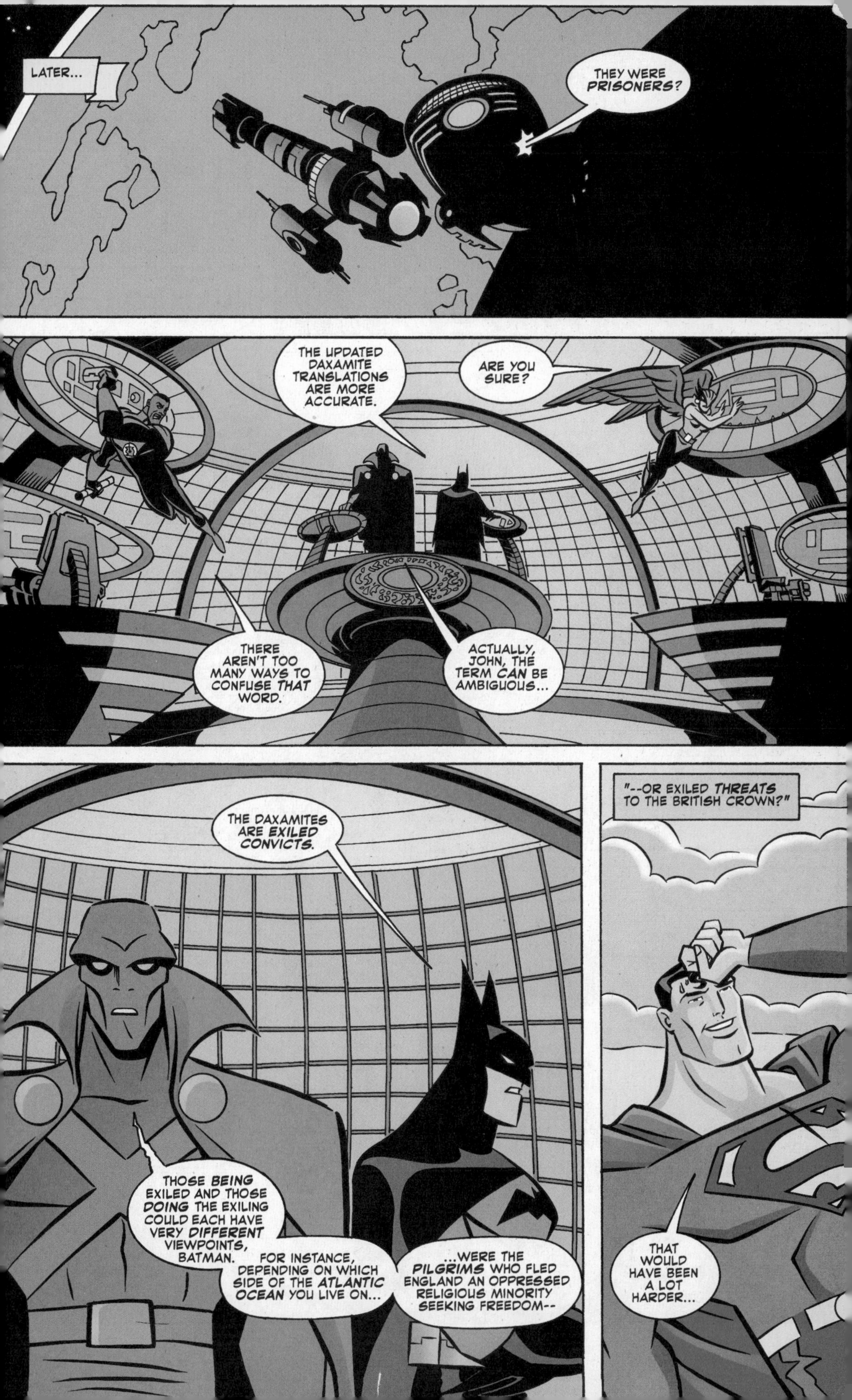
LATER...
THEY WERE PRISONERS?
THE UPDATED DAXAMITE TRANSLATIONS ARE MORE ACCURATE.
ARE YOU SURE?
THERE AREN'T TOO MANY WAYS TO CONFUSE THAT WORD.
ACTUALLY, JOHN, THE TERM CAN BE AMBIGUOUS...
THE DAXAMITES ARE EXILED CONVICTS.
THOSE BEING EXILED AND THOSE DOING THE EXILING COULD EACH HAVE VERY DIFFERENT VIEWPOINTS, BATMAN.
FOR INSTANCE, DEPENDING ON WHICH SIDE OF THE ATLANTIC OCEAN YOU LIVE ON...
...WERE THE PILGRIMS WHO FLED ENGLAND AN OPPRESSED RELIGIOUS MINORITY SEEKING FREEDOM--
"--OR EXILED THREATS TO THE BRITISH CROWN?"
THAT WOULD HAVE BEEN A LOT HARDER...

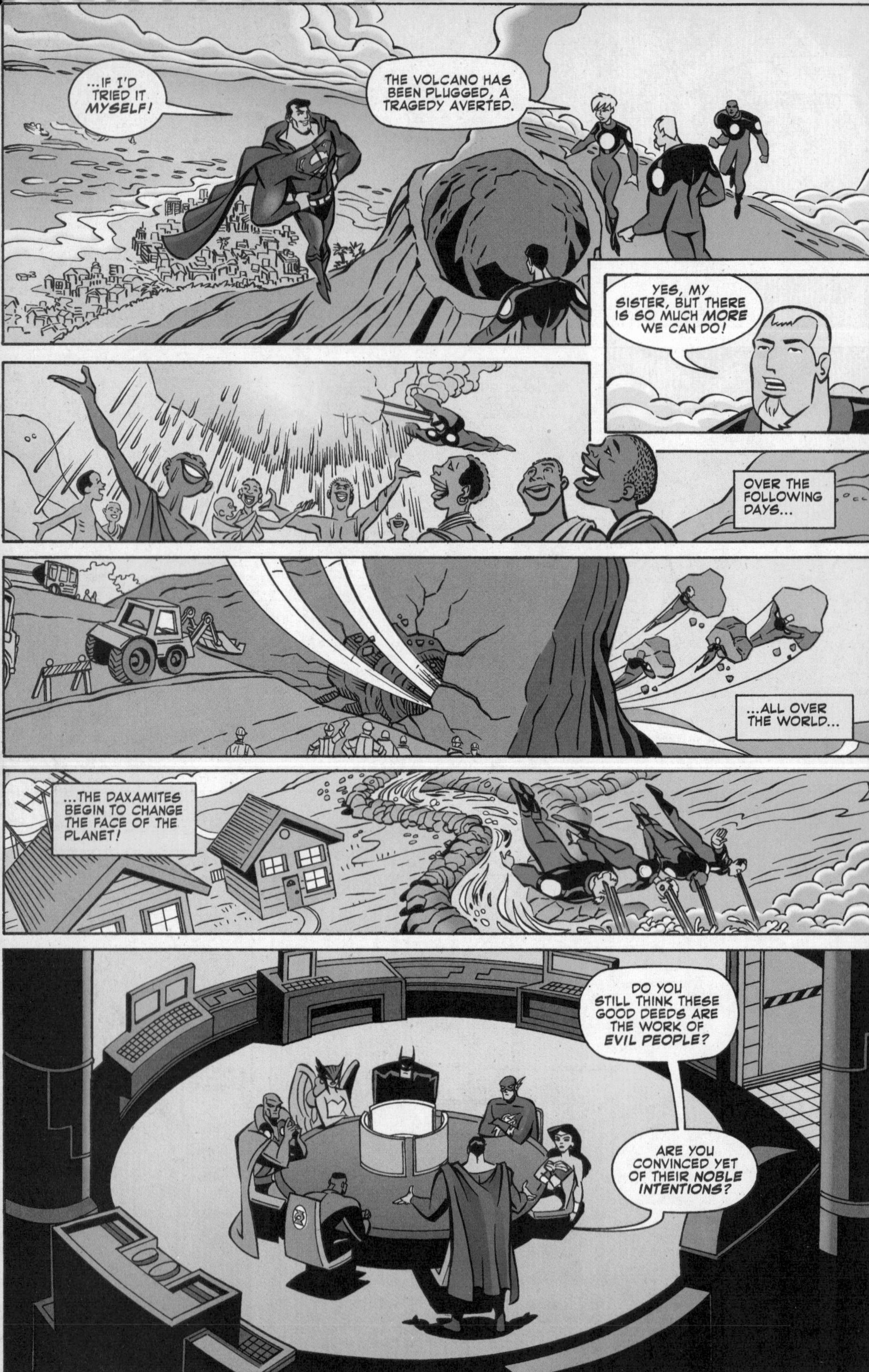
...IF I'D TRIED IT MYSELF!
THE VOLCANO HAS BEEN PLUGGED, A TRAGEDY AVERTED.
YES, MY SISTER, BUT THERE IS SO MUCH MORE WE CAN DO!
OVER THE FOLLOWING DAYS...
...ALL OVER THE WORLD...
...THE DAXAMITES BEGIN TO CHANGE THE FACE OF THE PLANET!
DO YOU STILL THINK THESE GOOD DEEDS ARE THE WORK OF EVIL PEOPLE?
ARE YOU CONVINCED YET OF THEIR NOBLE INTENTIONS?

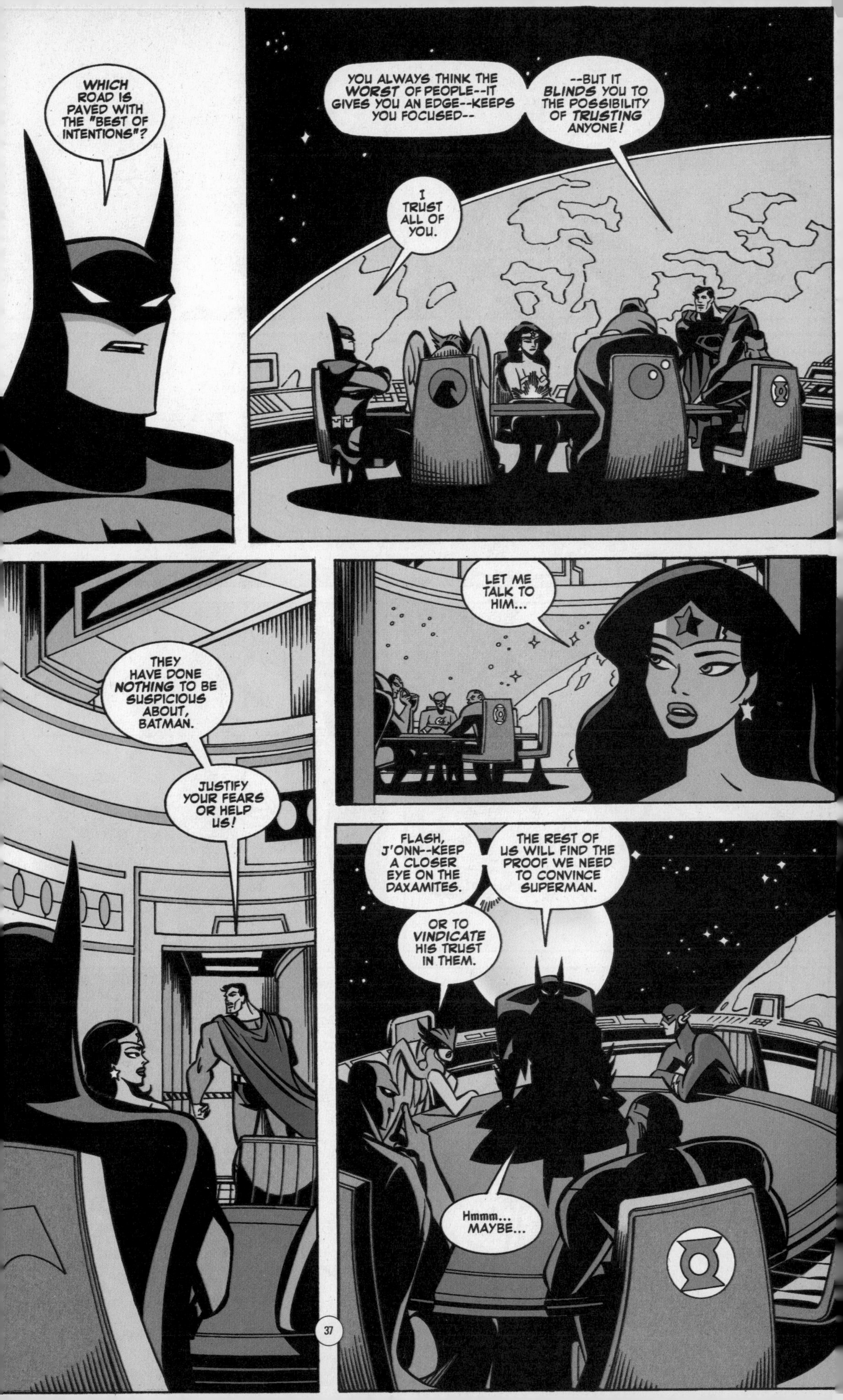
WHICH ROAD IS PAVED WITH THE "BEST OF INTENTIONS"?
YOU ALWAYS THINK THE WORST OF PEOPLE--IT GIVES YOU AN EDGE--KEEPS YOU FOCUSED--
--BUT IT BLINDS YOU TO THE POSSIBILITY OF TRUSTING ANYONE!
I TRUST ALL OF YOU.
THEY HAVE DONE NOTHING TO BE SUSPICIOUS ABOUT, BATMAN.
JUSTIFY YOUR FEARS OR HELP US!
LET ME TALK TO HIM...
FLASH, J'ONN--KEEP A CLOSER EYE ON THE DAXAMITES.
THE REST OF US WILL FIND THE PROOF WE NEED TO CONVINCE SUPERMAN.
OR TO VINDICATE HIS TRUST IN THEM.
Hmmm... MAYBE...

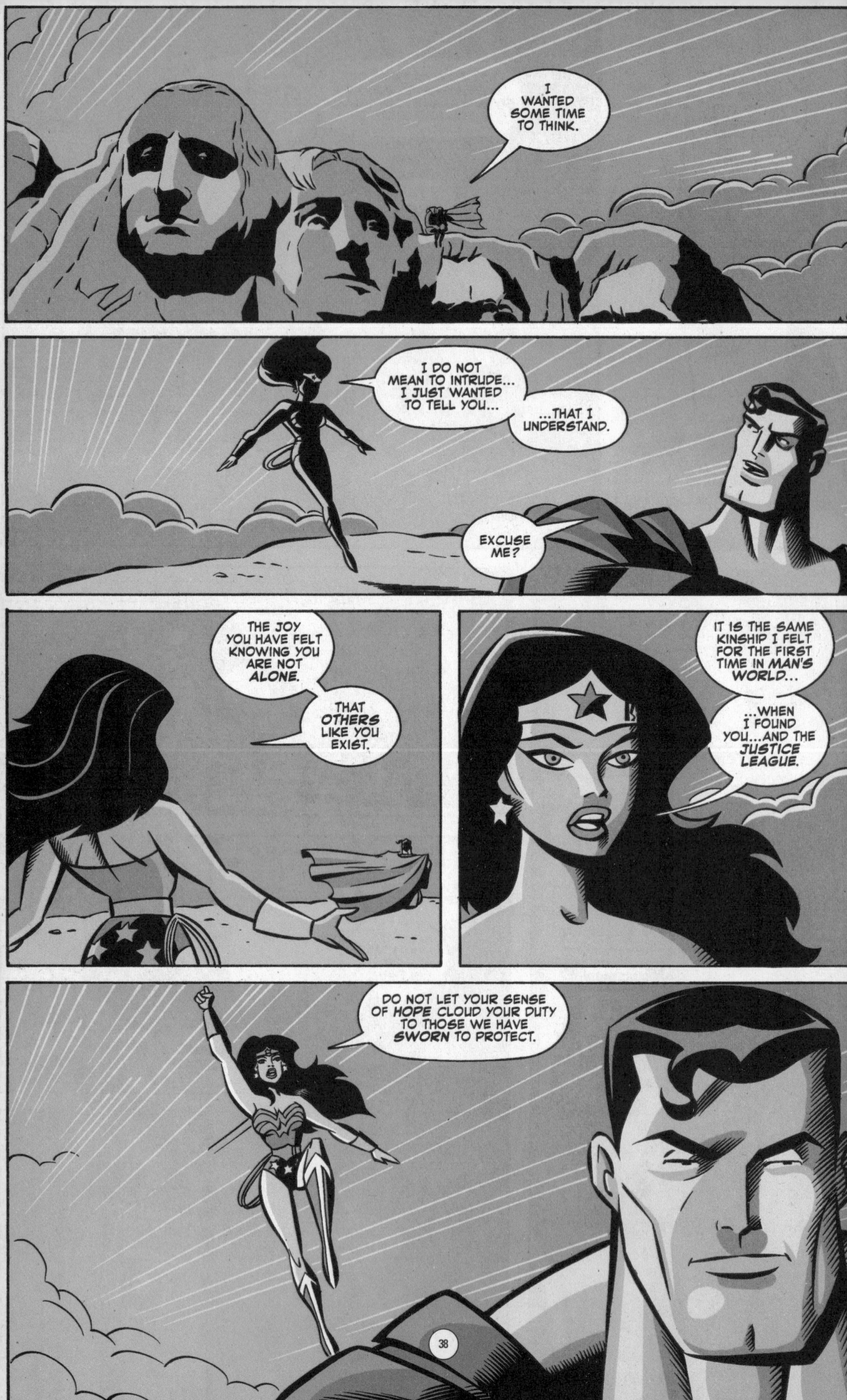
I WANTED SOME TIME TO THINK.
I DO NOT MEAN TO INTRUDE... I JUST WANTED TO TELL YOU...
...THAT I UNDERSTAND.
EXCUSE ME?
THE JOY YOU HAVE FELT KNOWING YOU ARE NOT ALONE.
THAT OTHERS LIKE YOU EXIST.
IT IS THE SAME KINSHIP I FELT FOR THE FIRST TIME IN MAN'S WORLD...
...WHEN I FOUND YOU...AND THE JUSTICE LEAGUE.
DO NOT LET YOUR SENSE OF HOPE CLOUD YOUR DUTY TO THOSE WE HAVE SWORN TO PROTECT.

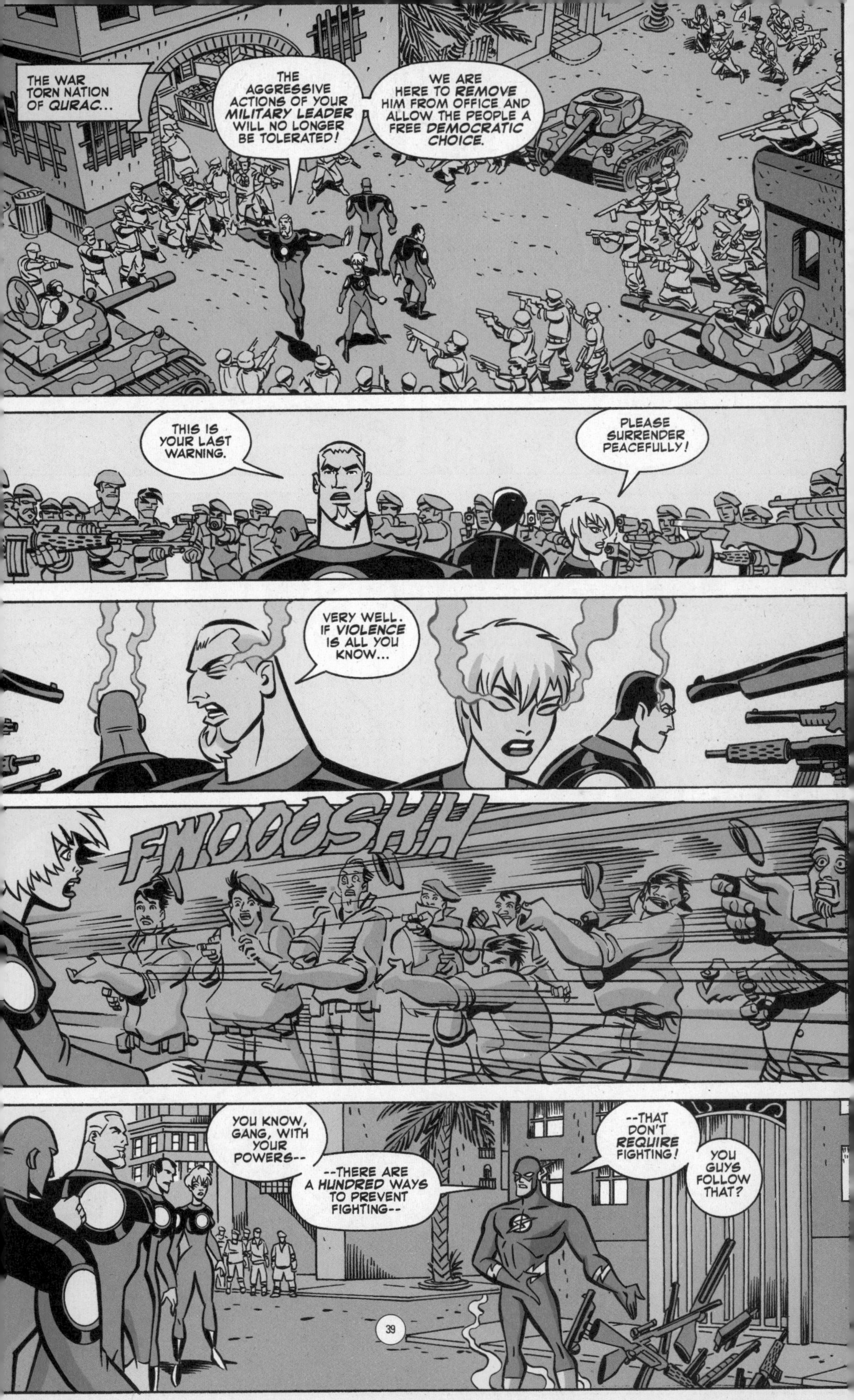
THE WAR TORN NATION OF QURAC...
THE AGGRESSIVE ACTIONS OF YOUR MILITARY LEADER WILL NO LONGER BE TOLERATED!
WE ARE HERE TO REMOVE HIM FROM OFFICE AND ALLOW THE PEOPLE A FREE DEMOCRATIC CHOICE.
THIS IS YOUR LAST WARNING.
PLEASE SURRENDER PEACEFULLY!
VERY WELL. IF VIOLENCE IS ALL YOU KNOW...
FWOOOSHH
YOU KNOW, GANG, WITH YOUR POWERS--
--THERE ARE A HUNDRED WAYS TO PREVENT FIGHTING--
--THAT DON'T REQUIRE FIGHTING!
YOU GUYS FOLLOW THAT?

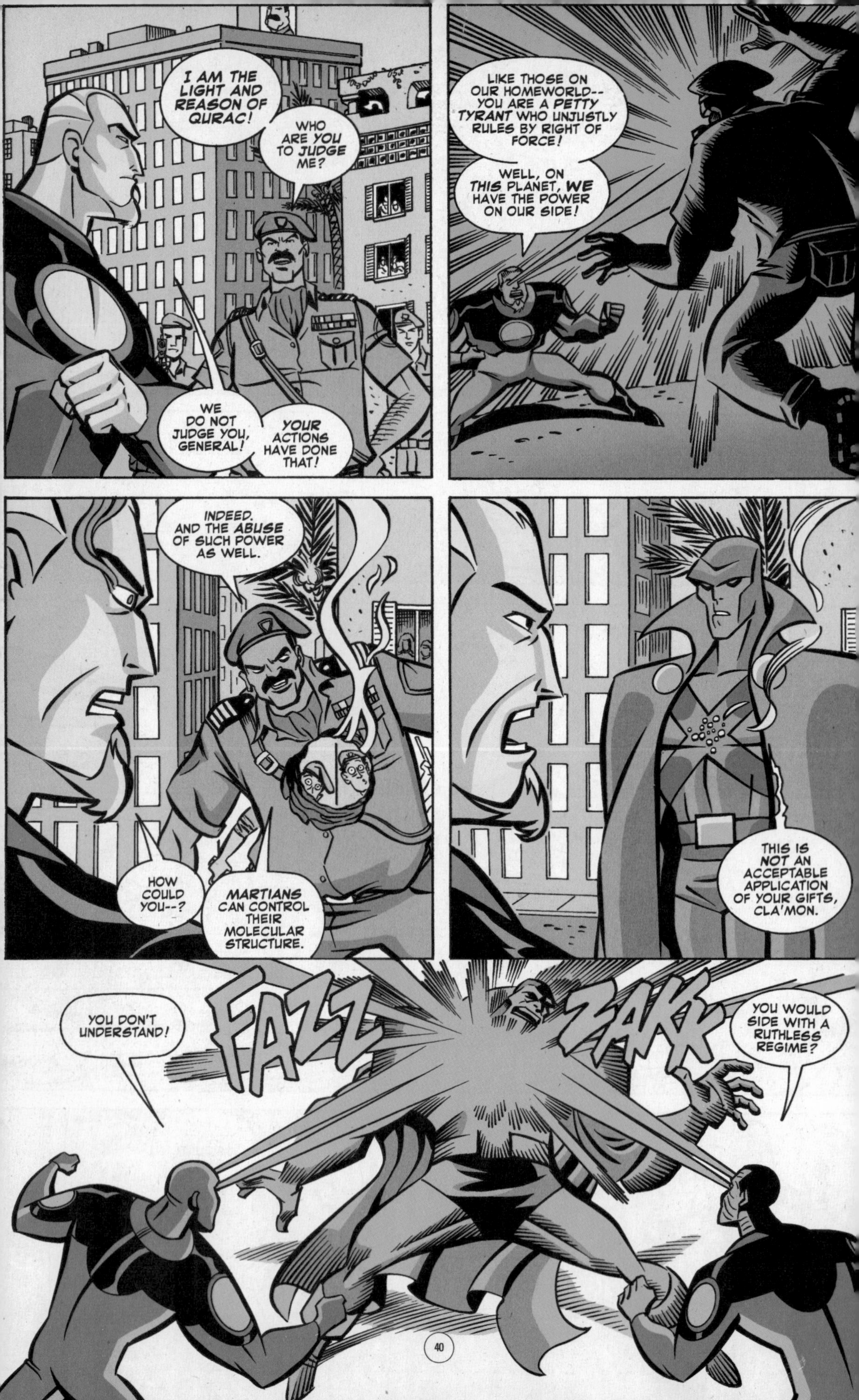
I AM THE LIGHT AND REASON OF QURAC!
WHO ARE YOU TO JUDGE ME?
WE DO NOT JUDGE YOU, GENERAL!
YOUR ACTIONS HAVE DONE THAT!
LIKE THOSE ON OUR HOMEWORLD-- YOU ARE A PETTY TYRANT WHO UNJUSTLY RULES BY RIGHT OF FORCE!
WELL, ON THIS PLANET, WE HAVE THE POWER ON OUR SIDE!
INDEED. AND THE ABUSE OF SUCH POWER AS WELL.
HOW COULD YOU--?
MARTIANS CAN CONTROL THEIR MOLECULAR STRUCTURE.
THIS IS NOT AN ACCEPTABLE APPLICATION OF YOUR GIFTS, CLA'MON.
YOU DON'T UNDERSTAND!
FAZZ
ZAKK
YOU WOULD SIDE WITH A RUTHLESS REGIME?

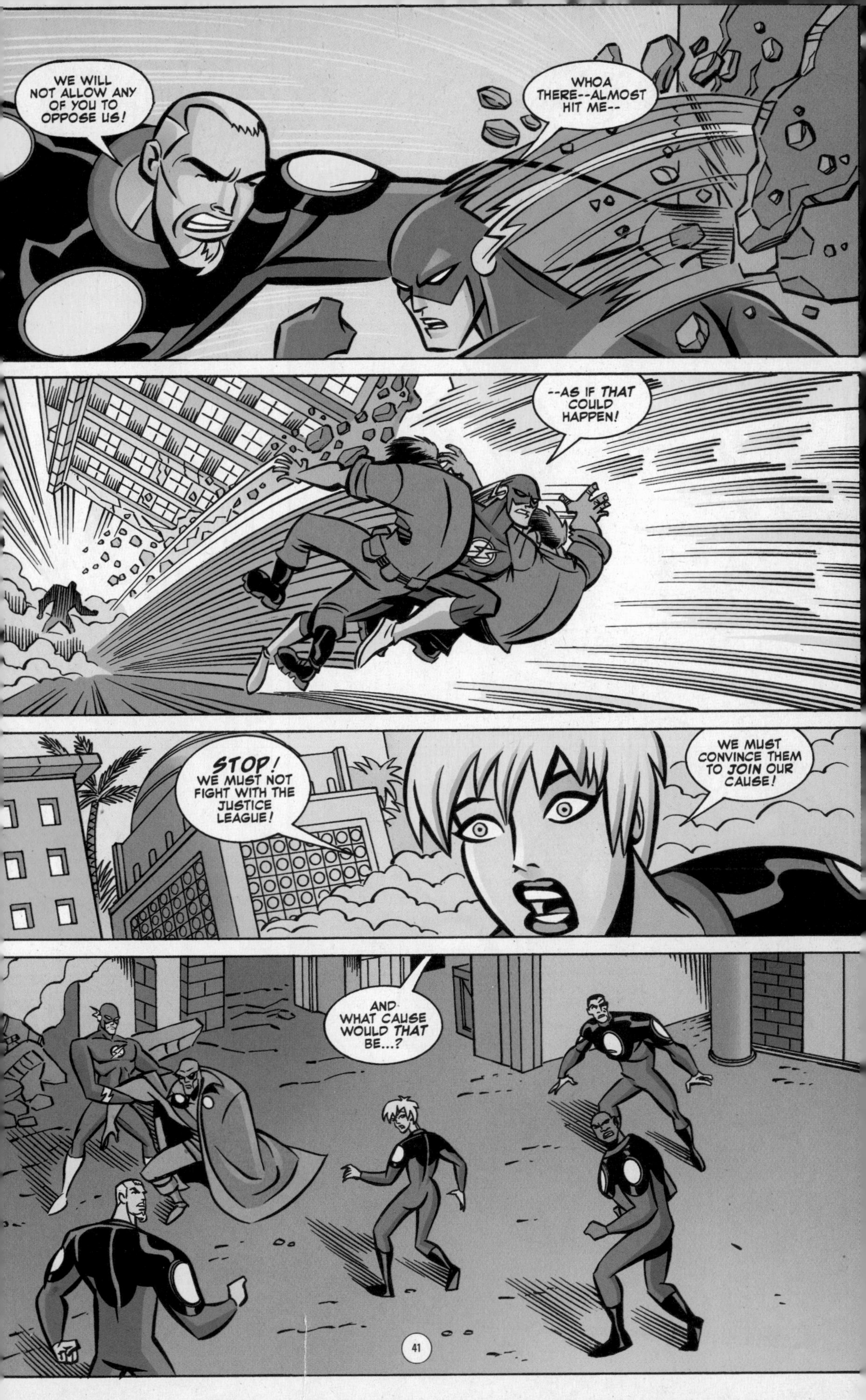
WE WILL NOT ALLOW ANY OF YOU TO OPPOSE US!
WHOA THERE--ALMOST HIT ME--
--AS IF THAT COULD HAPPEN!
STOP! WE MUST NOT FIGHT WITH THE JUSTICE LEAGUE!
WE MUST CONVINCE THEM TO JOIN OUR CAUSE!
AND WHAT CAUSE WOULD THAT BE...?

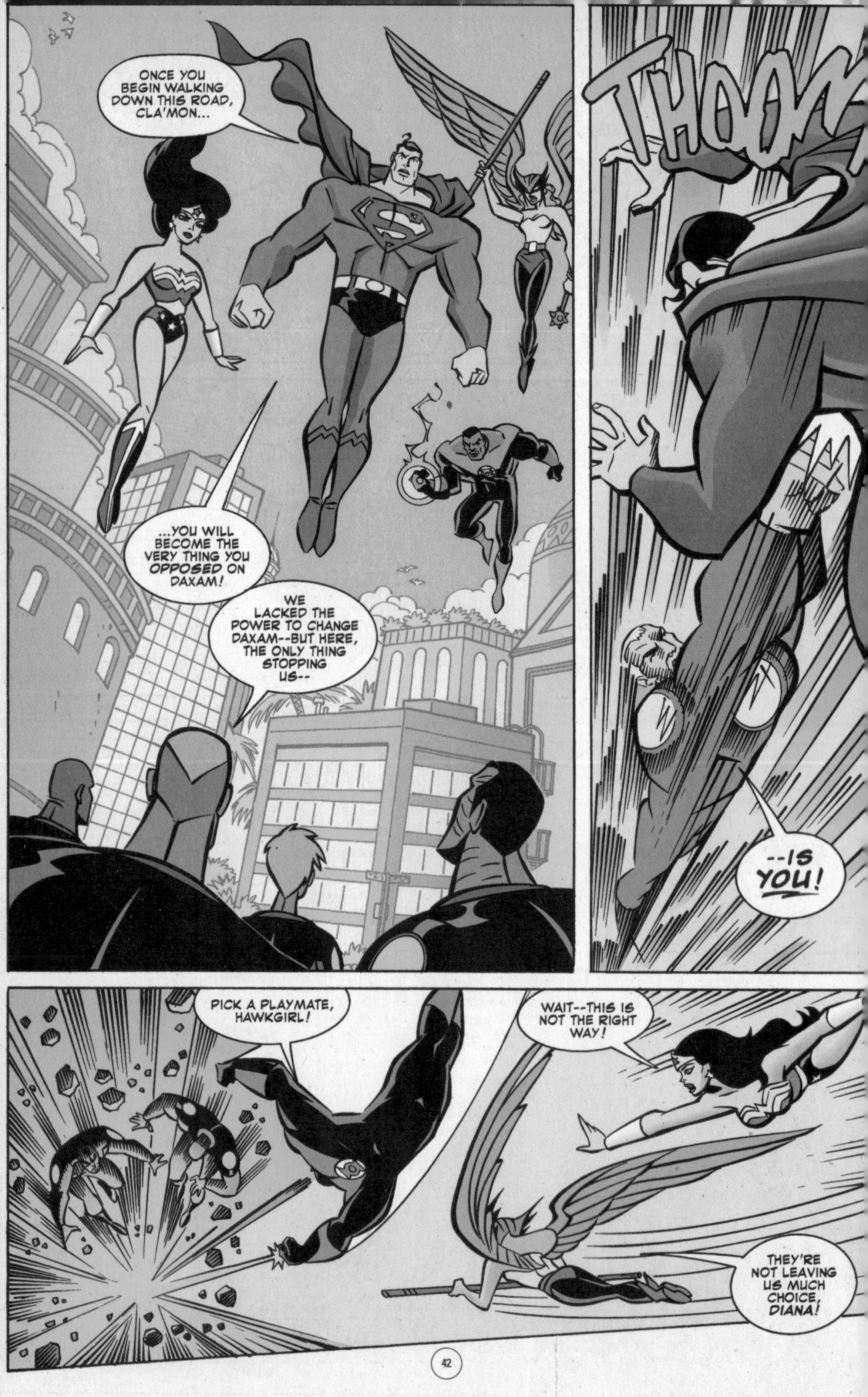
ONCE YOU BEGIN WALKING DOWN THIS ROAD, CLA'MON...
...YOU WILL BECOME THE VERY THING YOU OPPOSED ON DAXAM!
WE LACKED THE POWER TO CHANGE DAXAM--BUT HERE, THE ONLY THING STOPPING US--
THOOM
--IS YOU!
PICK A PLAYMATE, HAWKGIRL!
WAIT--THIS IS NOT THE RIGHT WAY!
THEY'RE NOT LEAVING US MUCH CHOICE, DIANA!

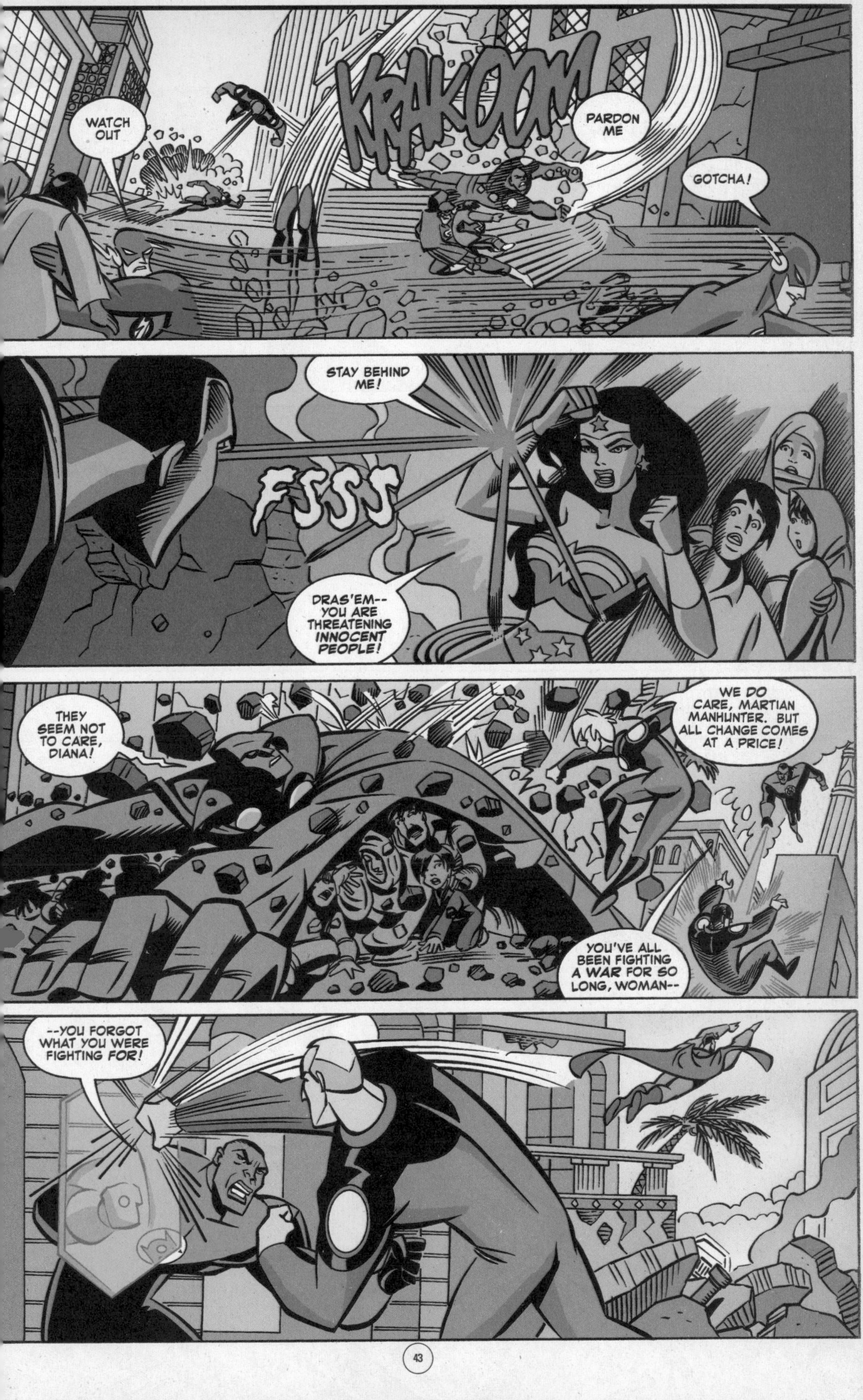
WATCH OUT
KRAKOOM
PARDON ME
GOTCHA!
STAY BEHIND ME!
FSSS
DRAS'EM-- YOU ARE THREATENING INNOCENT PEOPLE!
THEY SEEM NOT TO CARE, DIANA!
WE DO CARE, MARTIAN MANHUNTER. BUT ALL CHANGE COMES AT A PRICE!
YOU'VE ALL BEEN FIGHTING A WAR FOR SO LONG, WOMAN--
--YOU FORGOT WHAT YOU WERE FIGHTING FOR!

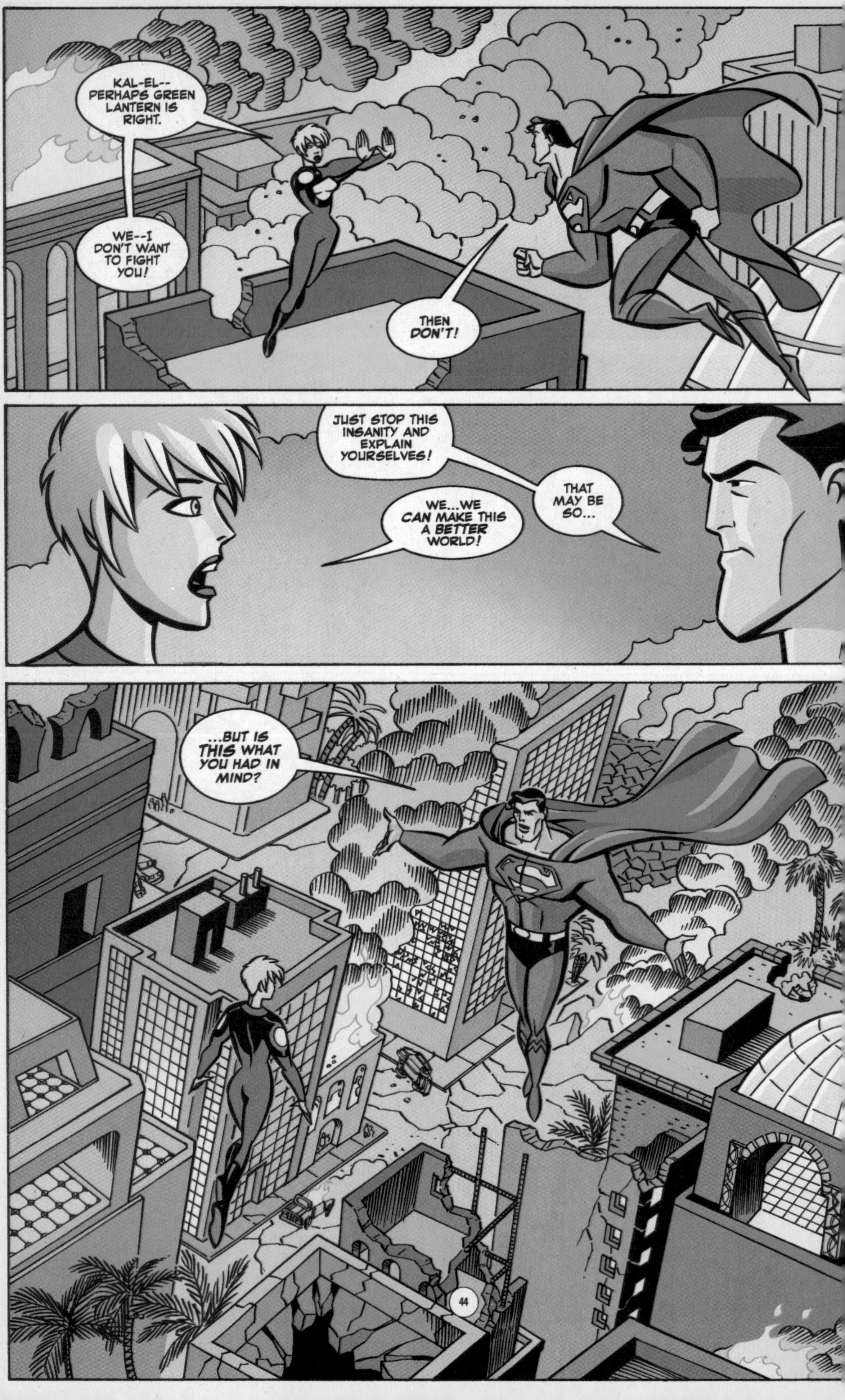
KAL-EL-- PERHAPS GREEN LANTERN IS RIGHT.
WE--I DON'T WANT TO FIGHT YOU!
THEN DON'T!
JUST STOP THIS INSANITY AND EXPLAIN YOURSELVES!
WE...WE CAN MAKE THIS A BETTER WORLD!
THAT MAY BE SO...
...BUT IS THIS WHAT YOU HAD IN MIND?

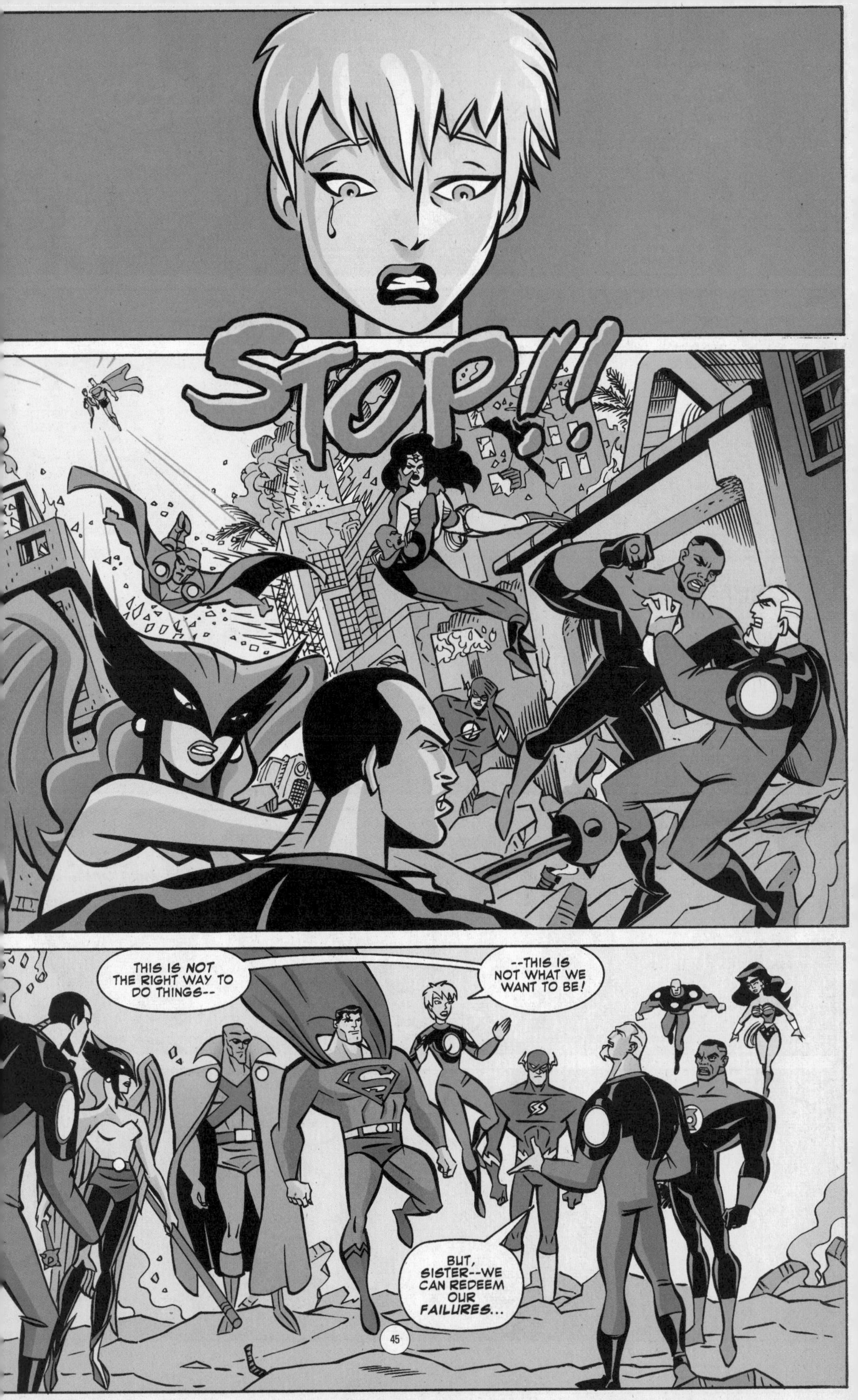
STOP!!
THIS IS NOT THE RIGHT WAY TO DO THINGS--
--THIS IS NOT WHAT WE WANT TO BE!
BUT, SISTER--WE CAN REDEEM OUR FAILURES...

ᗷᒎᑊᗩ ᗷᑌᑐ ᒎᗝᗩ.

WHAT--?

ᗷᒎ ᒎᗝᗩᗝ᙭ᗝᗝ.

IT'S ALWAYS SO COOL WHEN HE DOES THIS...

ᑫᗷ ᒎᑊᗪ᙭ᒎ ᙭ᗝᗪᑊᗪ.

"WE CONSIGN THESE SEDITIONISTS TO A LIFE SENTENCE IN SPACE...

"...FOR THE CRIMES THEY HAVE COMMITTED AGAINST THE STATE."

THAT WAS THE COMPLETED TRANSLATION FROM YOUR SHIP'S CHARTER.

BUT AFTER INSPECTING YOUR PLANET'S HISTORY I REALIZED--

--DAXAM'S NAME FOR A SEDITIONIST--FOR A REBEL...

...IS OUR DEFINITION OF "FREEDOM FIGHTERS."

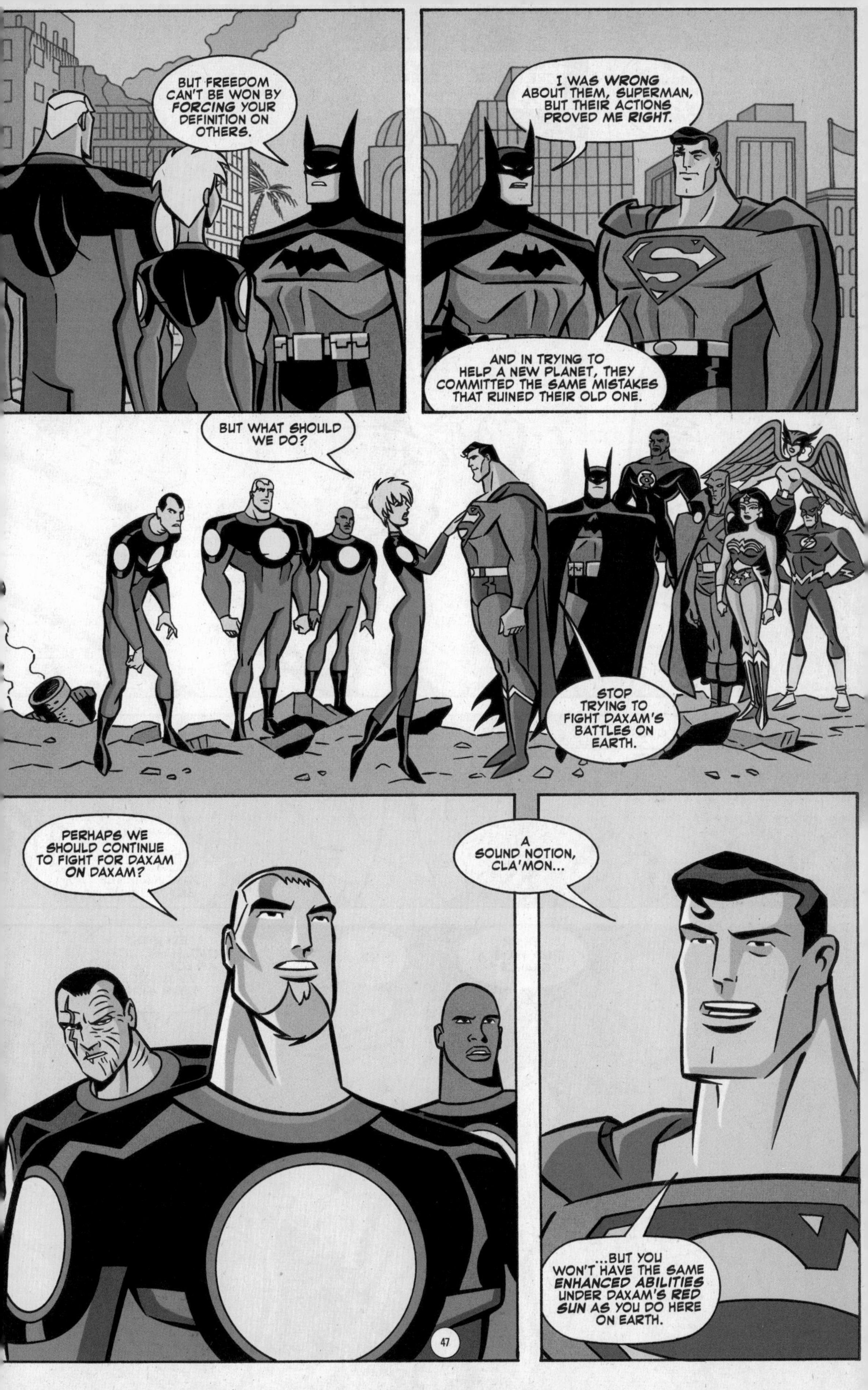
BUT FREEDOM CAN'T BE WON BY FORCING YOUR DEFINITION ON OTHERS.
I WAS WRONG ABOUT THEM, SUPERMAN, BUT THEIR ACTIONS PROVED ME RIGHT.
AND IN TRYING TO HELP A NEW PLANET, THEY COMMITTED THE SAME MISTAKES THAT RUINED THEIR OLD ONE.
BUT WHAT SHOULD WE DO?
STOP TRYING TO FIGHT DAXAM'S BATTLES ON EARTH.
PERHAPS WE SHOULD CONTINUE TO FIGHT FOR DAXAM ON DAXAM?
A SOUND NOTION, CLA'MON...
...BUT YOU WON'T HAVE THE SAME ENHANCED ABILITIES UNDER DAXAM'S RED SUN AS YOU DO HERE ON EARTH.

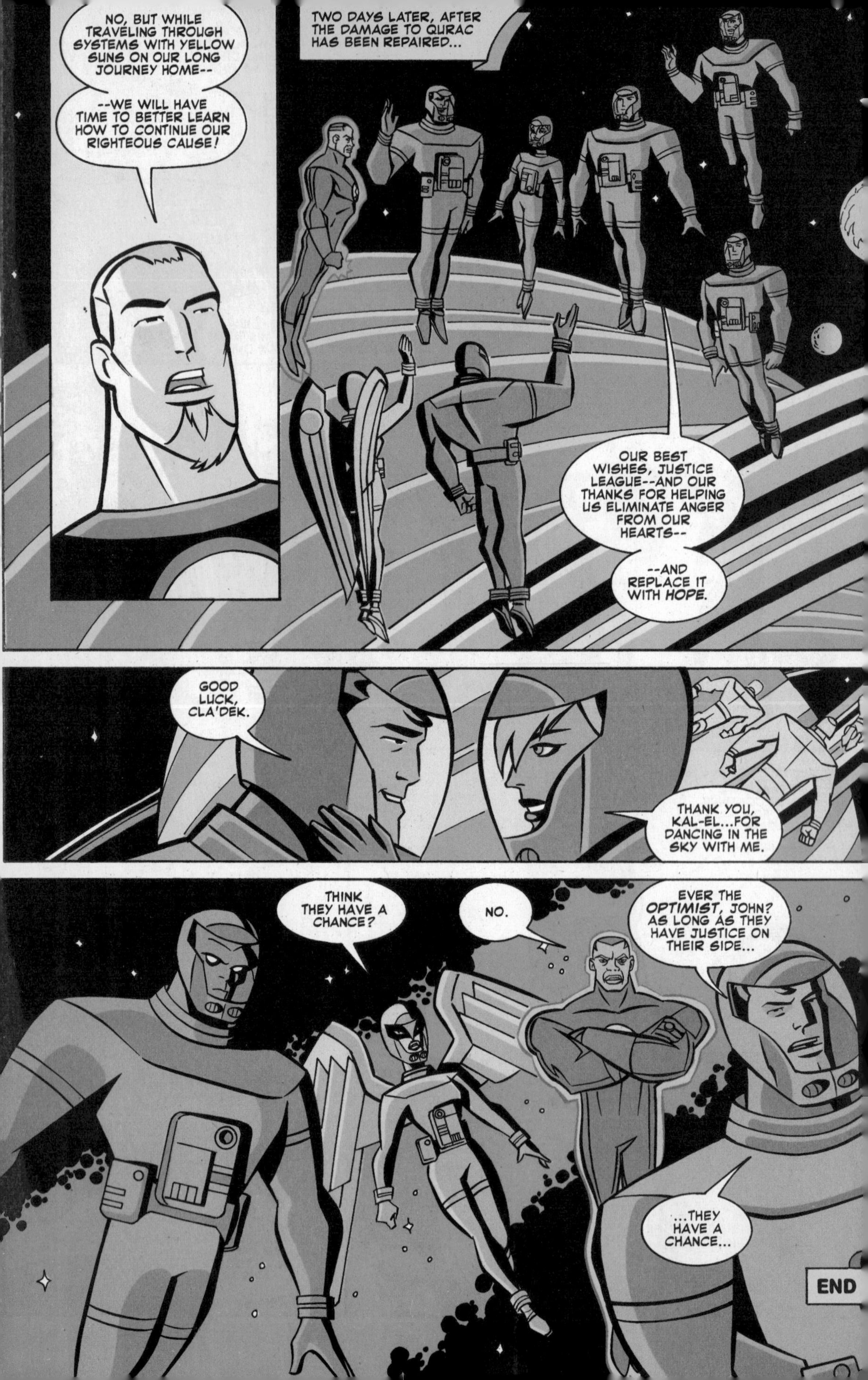

NO, BUT WHILE TRAVELING THROUGH SYSTEMS WITH YELLOW SUNS ON OUR LONG JOURNEY HOME--
--WE WILL HAVE TIME TO BETTER LEARN HOW TO CONTINUE OUR RIGHTEOUS CAUSE!
TWO DAYS LATER, AFTER THE DAMAGE TO QURAC HAS BEEN REPAIRED...
OUR BEST WISHES, JUSTICE LEAGUE--AND OUR THANKS FOR HELPING US ELIMINATE ANGER FROM OUR HEARTS--
--AND REPLACE IT WITH HOPE.
GOOD LUCK, CLA'DEK.
THANK YOU, KAL-EL...FOR DANCING IN THE SKY WITH ME.
THINK THEY HAVE A CHANCE?
NO.
EVER THE OPTIMIST, JOHN? AS LONG AS THEY HAVE JUSTICE ON THEIR SIDE...
...THEY HAVE A CHANCE...
END

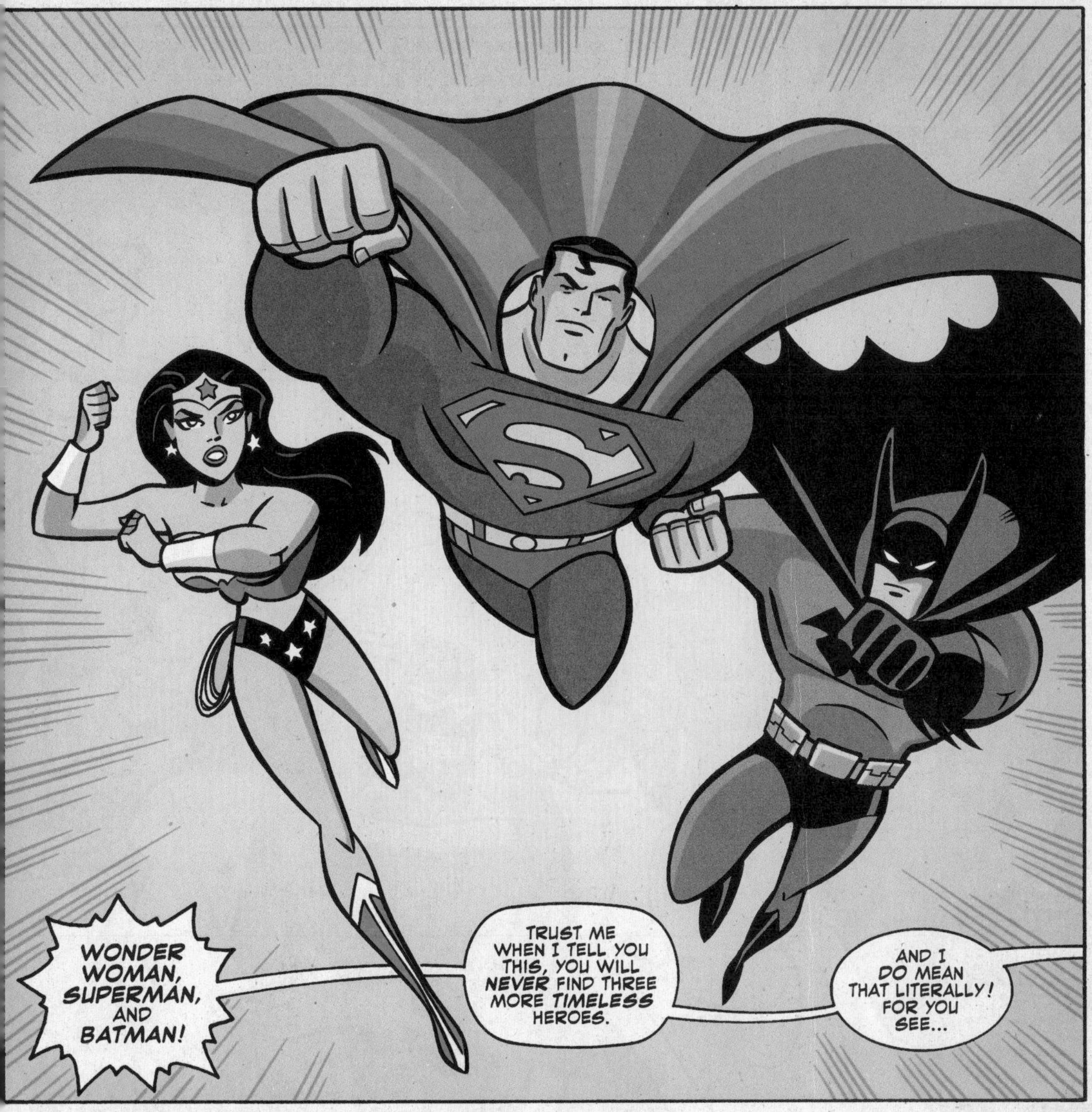
WONDER WOMAN, SUPERMAN, AND BATMAN!
TRUST ME WHEN I TELL YOU THIS, YOU WILL NEVER FIND THREE MORE TIMELESS HEROES.
AND I DO MEAN THAT LITERALLY! FOR YOU SEE...

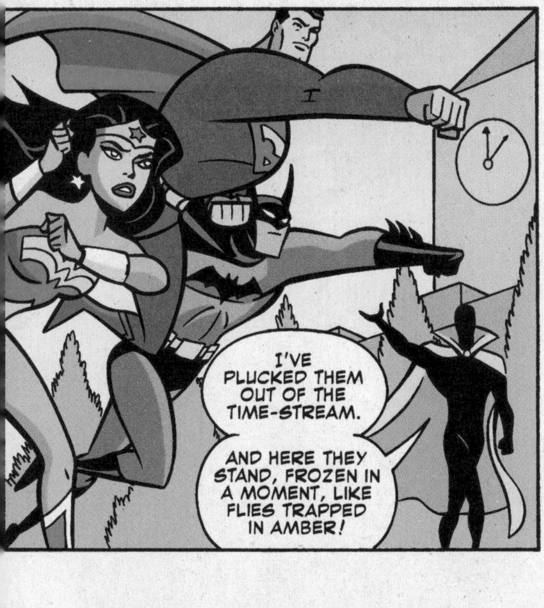
I'VE PLUCKED THEM OUT OF THE TIME-STREAM.
AND HERE THEY STAND, FROZEN IN A MOMENT, LIKE FLIES TRAPPED IN AMBER!

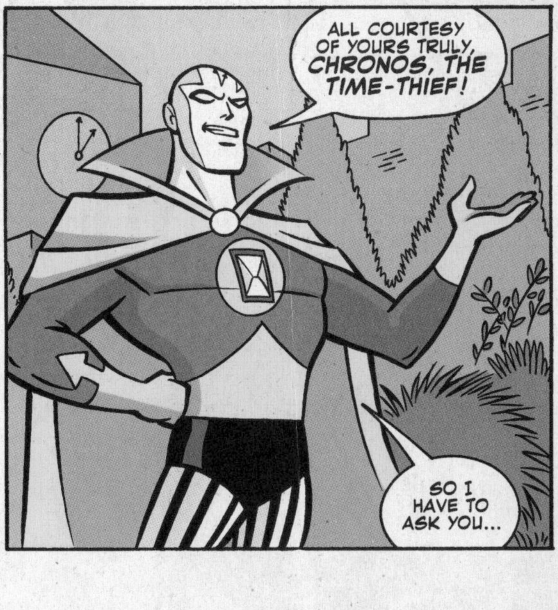
ALL COURTESY OF YOURS TRULY, CHRONOS, THE TIME-THIEF!
SO I HAVE TO ASK YOU...

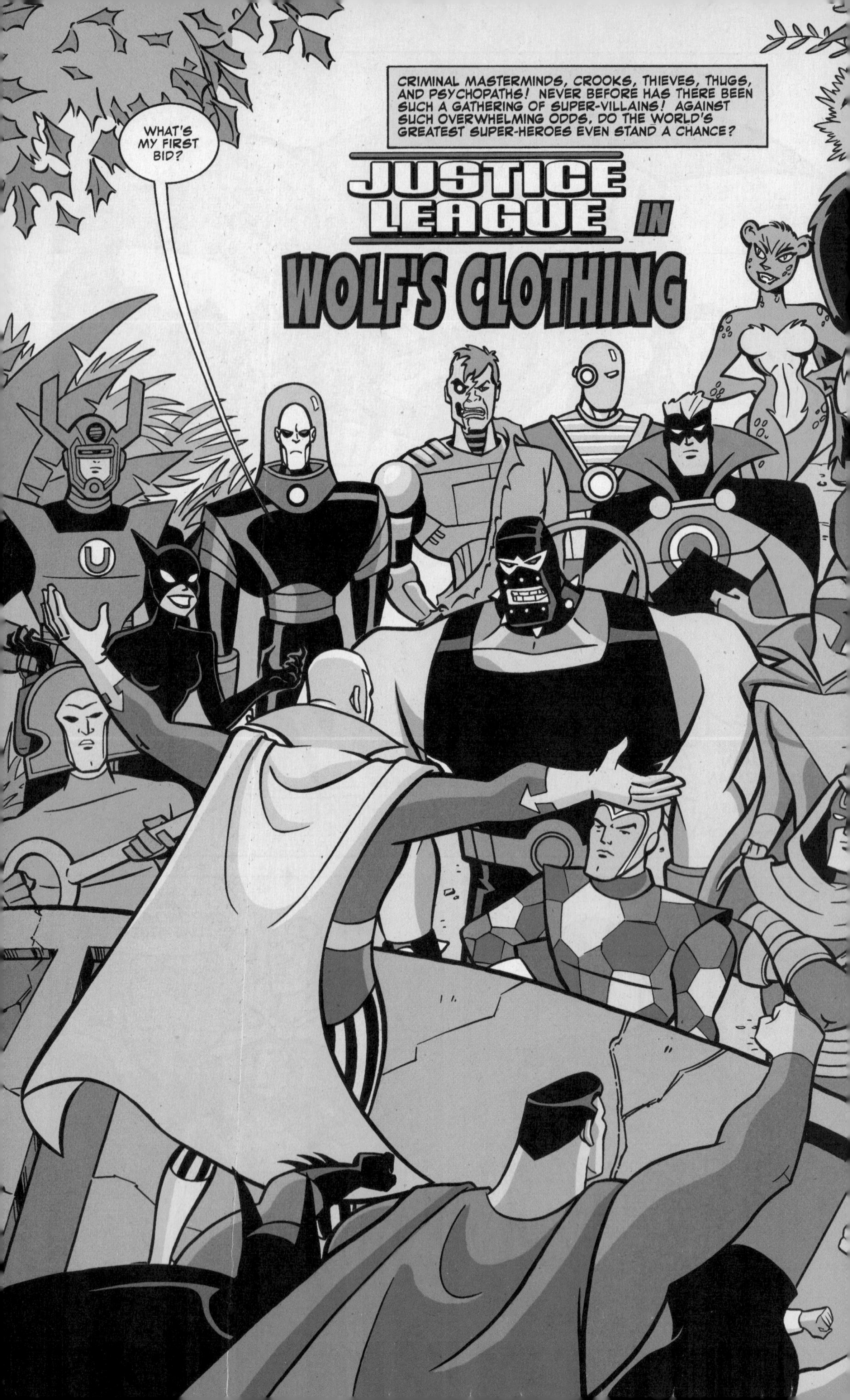
CRIMINAL MASTERMINDS, CROOKS, THIEVES, THUGS, AND PSYCHOPATHS! NEVER BEFORE HAS THERE BEEN SUCH A GATHERING OF SUPER-VILLAINS! AGAINST SUCH OVERWHELMING ODDS, DO THE WORLD'S GREATEST SUPER-HEROES EVEN STAND A CHANCE?
WHAT'S MY FIRST BID?
JUSTICE LEAGUE IN
WOLF'S CLOTHING

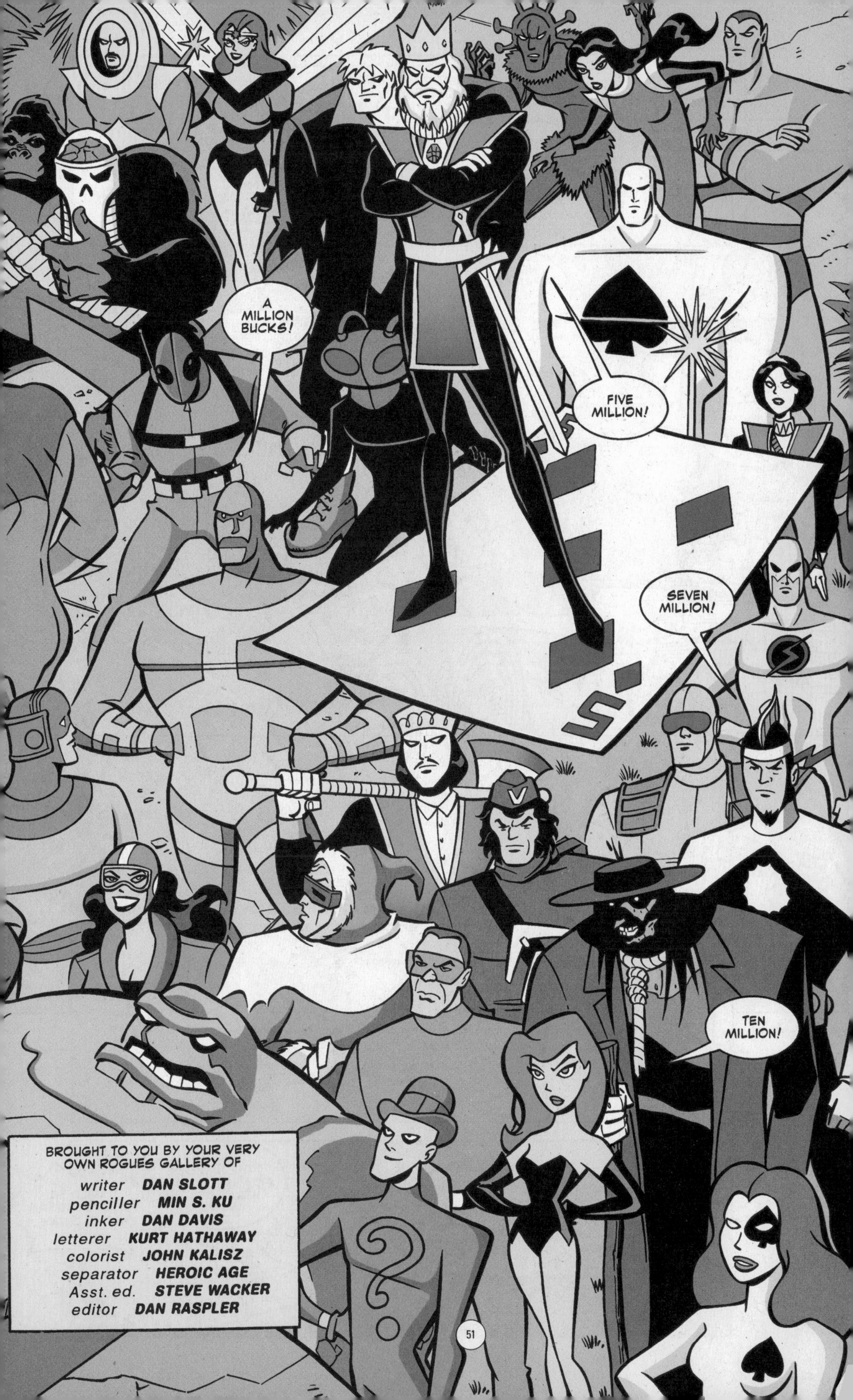
A MILLION BUCKS!
FIVE MILLION!
SEVEN MILLION!
TEN MILLION!
BROUGHT TO YOU BY YOUR VERY OWN ROGUES GALLERY OF
writer DAN SLOTT
penciller MIN S. KU
inker DAN DAVIS
letterer KURT HATHAWAY
colorist JOHN KALISZ
separator HEROIC AGE
Asst. ed. STEVE WACKER
editor DAN RASPLER

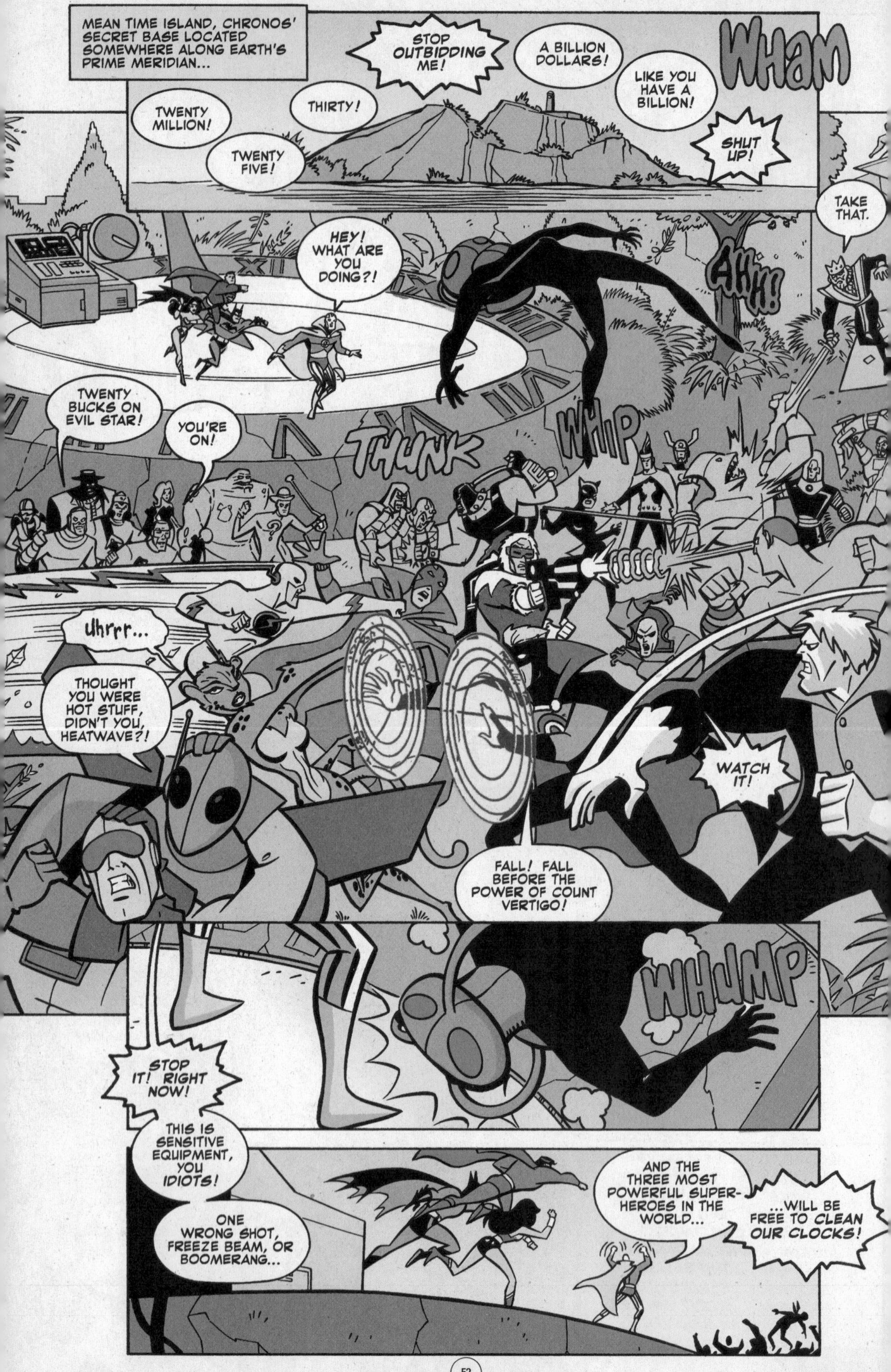

MEAN TIME ISLAND, CHRONOS' SECRET BASE LOCATED SOMEWHERE ALONG EARTH'S PRIME MERIDIAN...
TWENTY MILLION!
TWENTY FIVE!
THIRTY!
STOP OUTBIDDING ME!
A BILLION DOLLARS!
LIKE YOU HAVE A BILLION!
WHAM
SHUT UP!
TAKE THAT.
AHHH!
HEY! WHAT ARE YOU DOING?!
TWENTY BUCKS ON EVIL STAR!
YOU'RE ON!
THUNK
WHIP
Uhrrr...
THOUGHT YOU WERE HOT STUFF, DIDN'T YOU, HEATWAVE?!
WATCH IT!
FALL! FALL BEFORE THE POWER OF COUNT VERTIGO!
WHUMP
STOP IT! RIGHT NOW!
THIS IS SENSITIVE EQUIPMENT, YOU IDIOTS!
ONE WRONG SHOT, FREEZE BEAM, OR BOOMERANG...
AND THE THREE MOST POWERFUL SUPER-HEROES IN THE WORLD...
...WILL BE FREE TO CLEAN OUR CLOCKS!

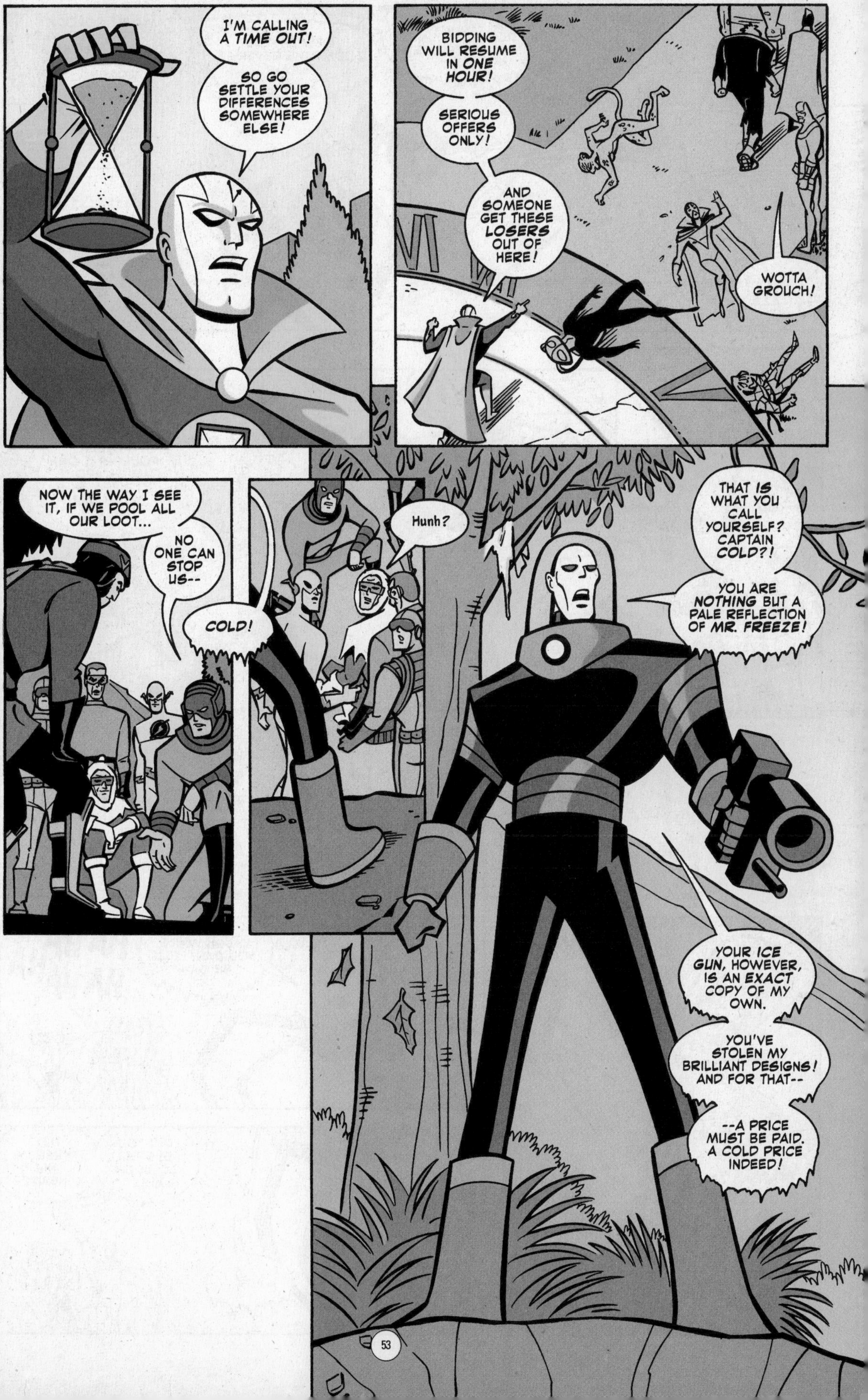

I'M CALLING A TIME OUT!
SO GO SETTLE YOUR DIFFERENCES SOMEWHERE ELSE!
BIDDING WILL RESUME IN ONE HOUR!
SERIOUS OFFERS ONLY!
AND SOMEONE GET THESE LOSERS OUT OF HERE!
WOTTA GROUCH!
NOW THE WAY I SEE IT, IF WE POOL ALL OUR LOOT...
NO ONE CAN STOP US--
COLD!
Hunh?
THAT IS WHAT YOU CALL YOURSELF? CAPTAIN COLD?!
YOU ARE NOTHING BUT A PALE REFLECTION OF MR. FREEZE!
YOUR ICE GUN, HOWEVER, IS AN EXACT COPY OF MY OWN.
YOU'VE STOLEN MY BRILLIANT DESIGNS! AND FOR THAT--
--A PRICE MUST BE PAID. A COLD PRICE INDEED!

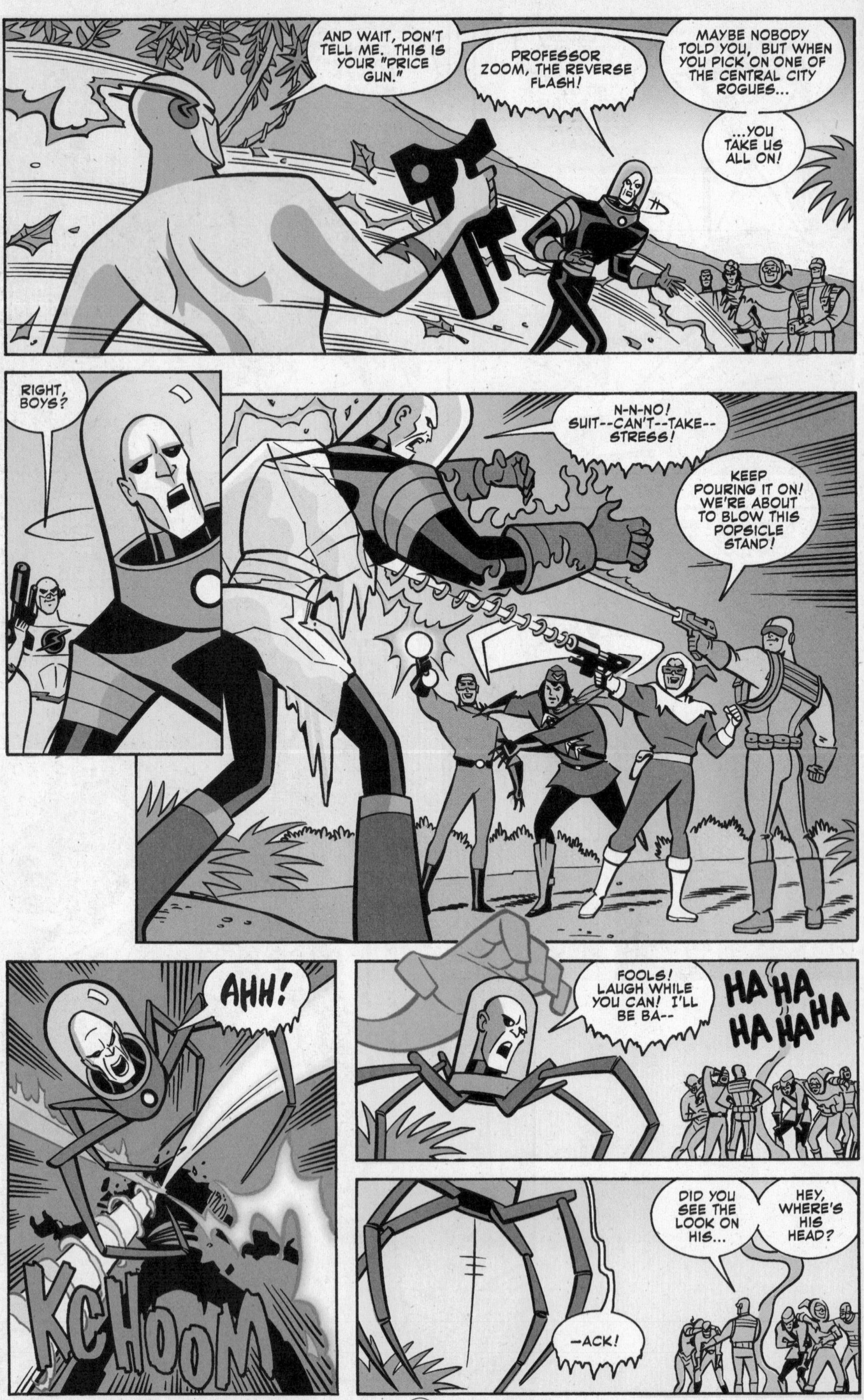
AND WAIT, DON'T TELL ME. THIS IS YOUR "PRICE GUN."
PROFESSOR ZOOM, THE REVERSE FLASH!
MAYBE NOBODY TOLD YOU, BUT WHEN YOU PICK ON ONE OF THE CENTRAL CITY ROGUES...
...YOU TAKE US ALL ON!
RIGHT, BOYS?
N-N-NO! SUIT--CAN'T--TAKE--STRESS!
KEEP POURING IT ON! WE'RE ABOUT TO BLOW THIS POPSICLE STAND!
AHH!
KCHOOM
FOOLS! LAUGH WHILE YOU CAN! I'LL BE BA--
HA HA HA HA HA HA
DID YOU SEE THE LOOK ON HIS...
HEY, WHERE'S HIS HEAD?
--ACK!

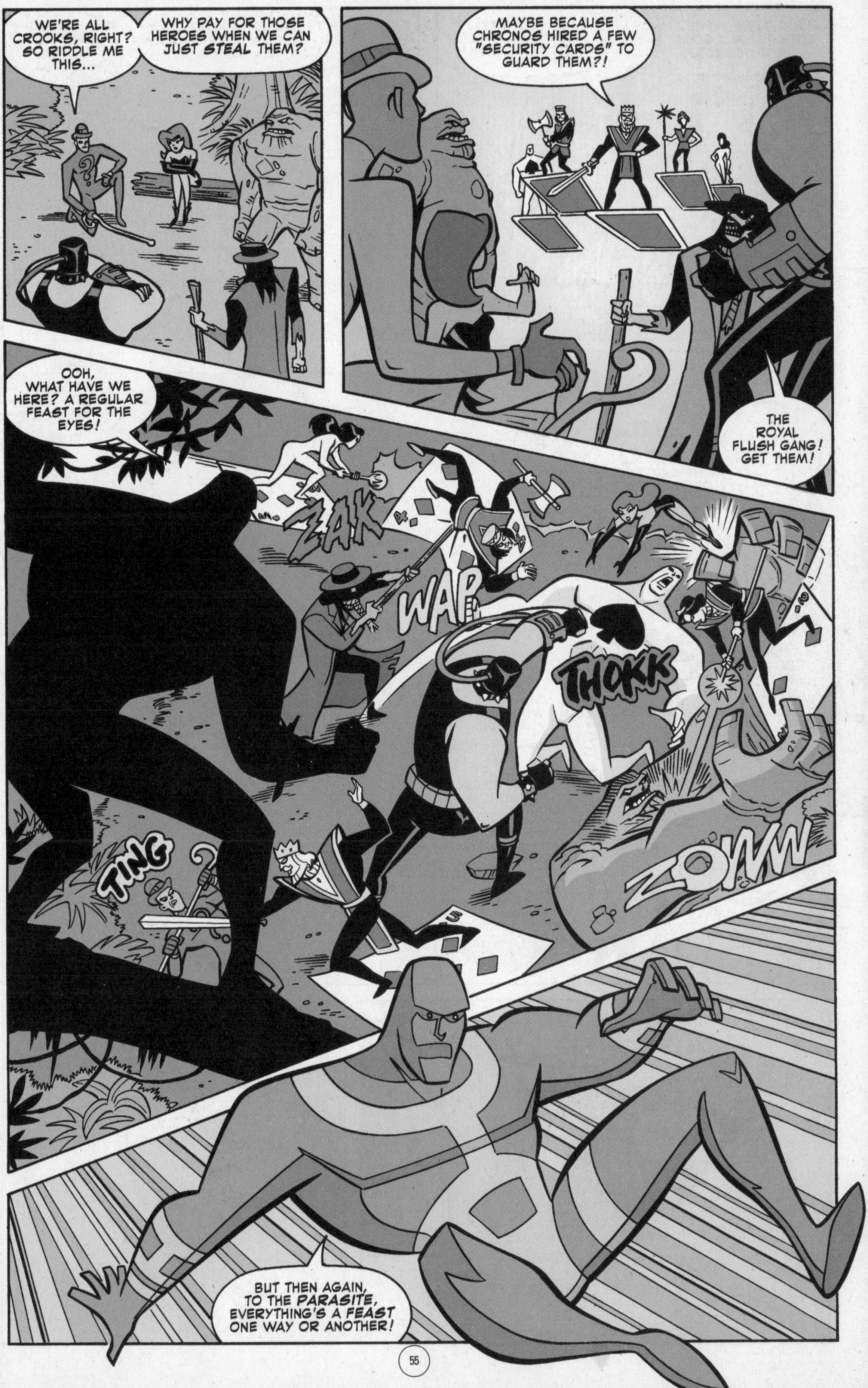
WE'RE ALL CROOKS, RIGHT? SO RIDDLE ME THIS...
WHY PAY FOR THOSE HEROES WHEN WE CAN JUST *STEAL* THEM?
MAYBE BECAUSE CHRONOS HIRED A FEW "SECURITY CARDS" TO GUARD THEM?!
THE ROYAL FLUSH GANG! GET THEM!
OOH, WHAT HAVE WE HERE? A REGULAR FEAST FOR THE EYES!
ZAK
WAP
THOKK
TING
ZOWW
BUT THEN AGAIN, TO THE *PARASITE*, EVERYTHING'S A *FEAST* ONE WAY OR ANOTHER!

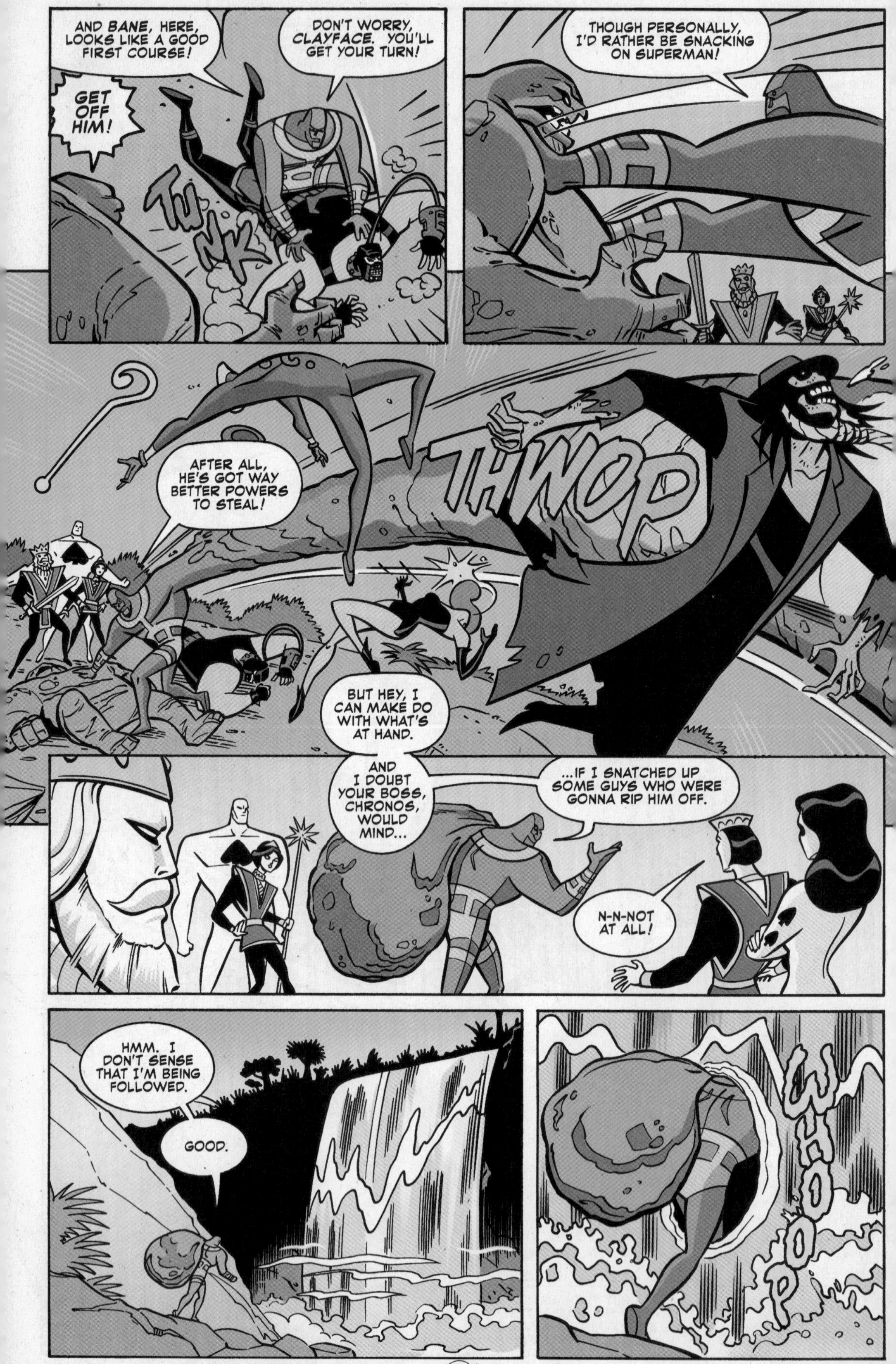
AND BANE, HERE, LOOKS LIKE A GOOD FIRST COURSE!
GET OFF HIM!
DON'T WORRY, CLAYFACE. YOU'LL GET YOUR TURN!
TUNK
THOUGH PERSONALLY, I'D RATHER BE SNACKING ON SUPERMAN!
AFTER ALL, HE'S GOT WAY BETTER POWERS TO STEAL!
THWOP
BUT HEY, I CAN MAKE DO WITH WHAT'S AT HAND.
AND I DOUBT YOUR BOSS, CHRONOS, WOULD MIND...
...IF I SNATCHED UP SOME GUYS WHO WERE GONNA RIP HIM OFF.
N-N-NOT AT ALL!
HMM. I DON'T SENSE THAT I'M BEING FOLLOWED.
GOOD.
WHOOP

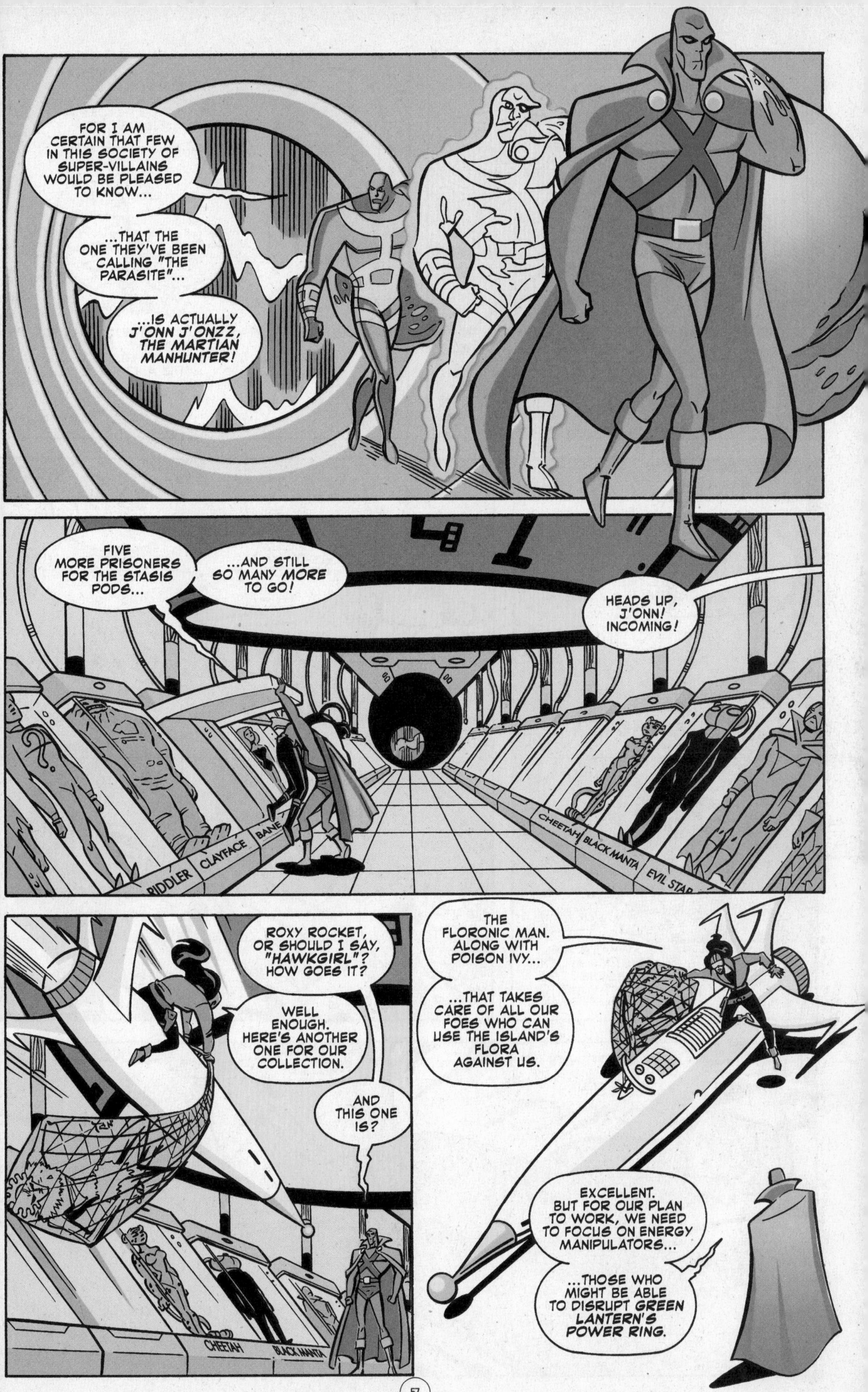
FOR I AM CERTAIN THAT FEW IN THIS SOCIETY OF SUPER-VILLAINS WOULD BE PLEASED TO KNOW...
...THAT THE ONE THEY'VE BEEN CALLING "THE PARASITE"...
...IS ACTUALLY J'ONN J'ONZZ, THE MARTIAN MANHUNTER!
FIVE MORE PRISONERS FOR THE STASIS PODS...
...AND STILL SO MANY MORE TO GO!
HEADS UP, J'ONN! INCOMING!
RIDDLER
CLAYFACE
BANE
CHEETAH
BLACK MANTA
EVIL STAR
ROXY ROCKET, OR SHOULD I SAY, "HAWKGIRL"? HOW GOES IT?
WELL ENOUGH. HERE'S ANOTHER ONE FOR OUR COLLECTION.
AND THIS ONE IS?
CHEETAH
BLACK MANTA
THE FLORONIC MAN. ALONG WITH POISON IVY...
...THAT TAKES CARE OF ALL OUR FOES WHO CAN USE THE ISLAND'S FLORA AGAINST US.
EXCELLENT. BUT FOR OUR PLAN TO WORK, WE NEED TO FOCUS ON ENERGY MANIPULATORS...
...THOSE WHO MIGHT BE ABLE TO DISRUPT GREEN LANTERN'S POWER RING.

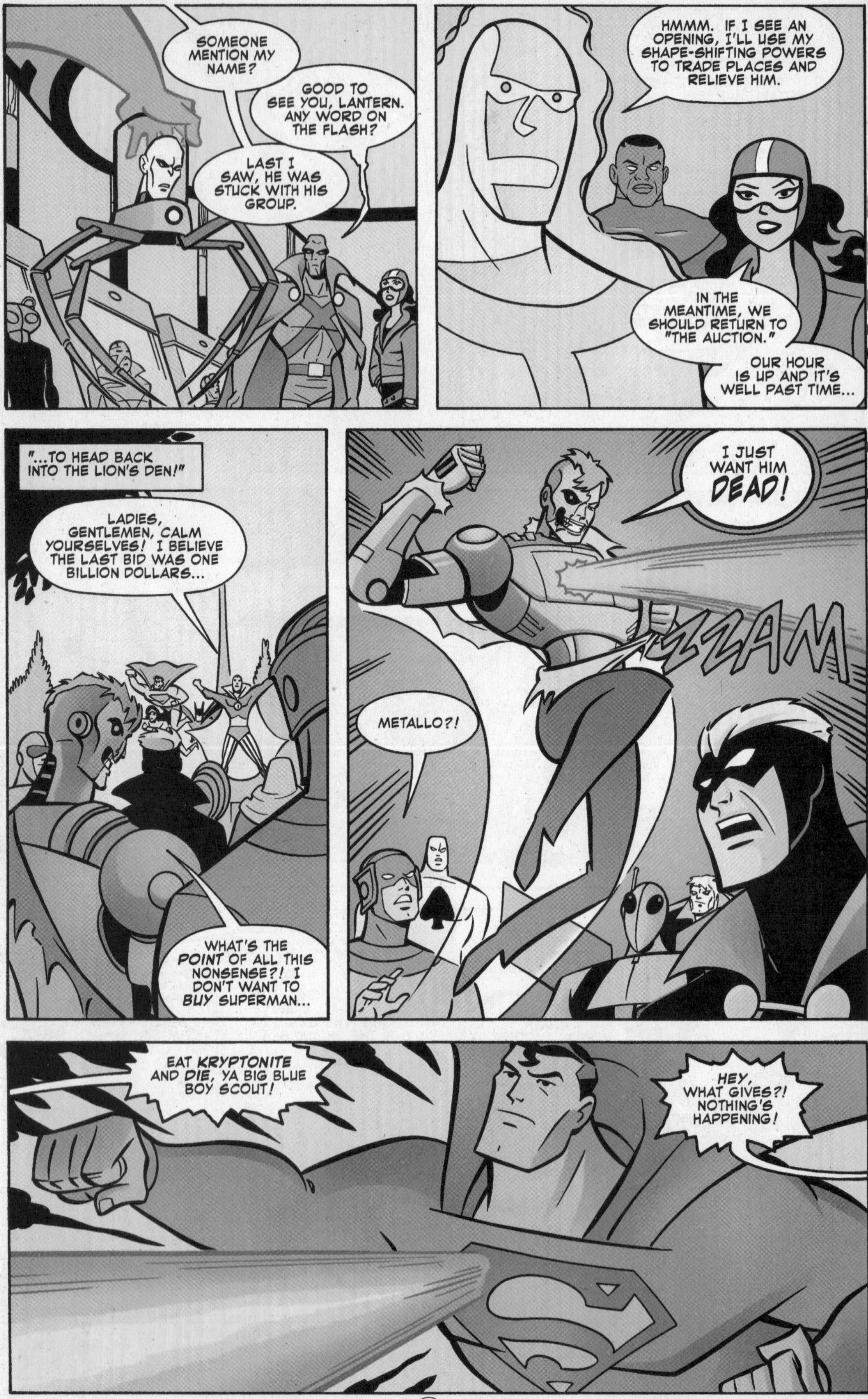
SOMEONE MENTION MY NAME?
GOOD TO SEE YOU, LANTERN. ANY WORD ON THE FLASH?
LAST I SAW, HE WAS STUCK WITH HIS GROUP.
HMMM. IF I SEE AN OPENING, I'LL USE MY SHAPE-SHIFTING POWERS TO TRADE PLACES AND RELIEVE HIM.
IN THE MEANTIME, WE SHOULD RETURN TO "THE AUCTION."
OUR HOUR IS UP AND IT'S WELL PAST TIME...
"...TO HEAD BACK INTO THE LION'S DEN!"
LADIES, GENTLEMEN, CALM YOURSELVES! I BELIEVE THE LAST BID WAS ONE BILLION DOLLARS...
WHAT'S THE POINT OF ALL THIS NONSENSE?! I DON'T WANT TO BUY SUPERMAN...
I JUST WANT HIM DEAD!
ZZZAM
METALLO?!
EAT KRYPTONITE AND DIE, YA BIG BLUE BOY SCOUT!
HEY, WHAT GIVES?! NOTHING'S HAPPENING!

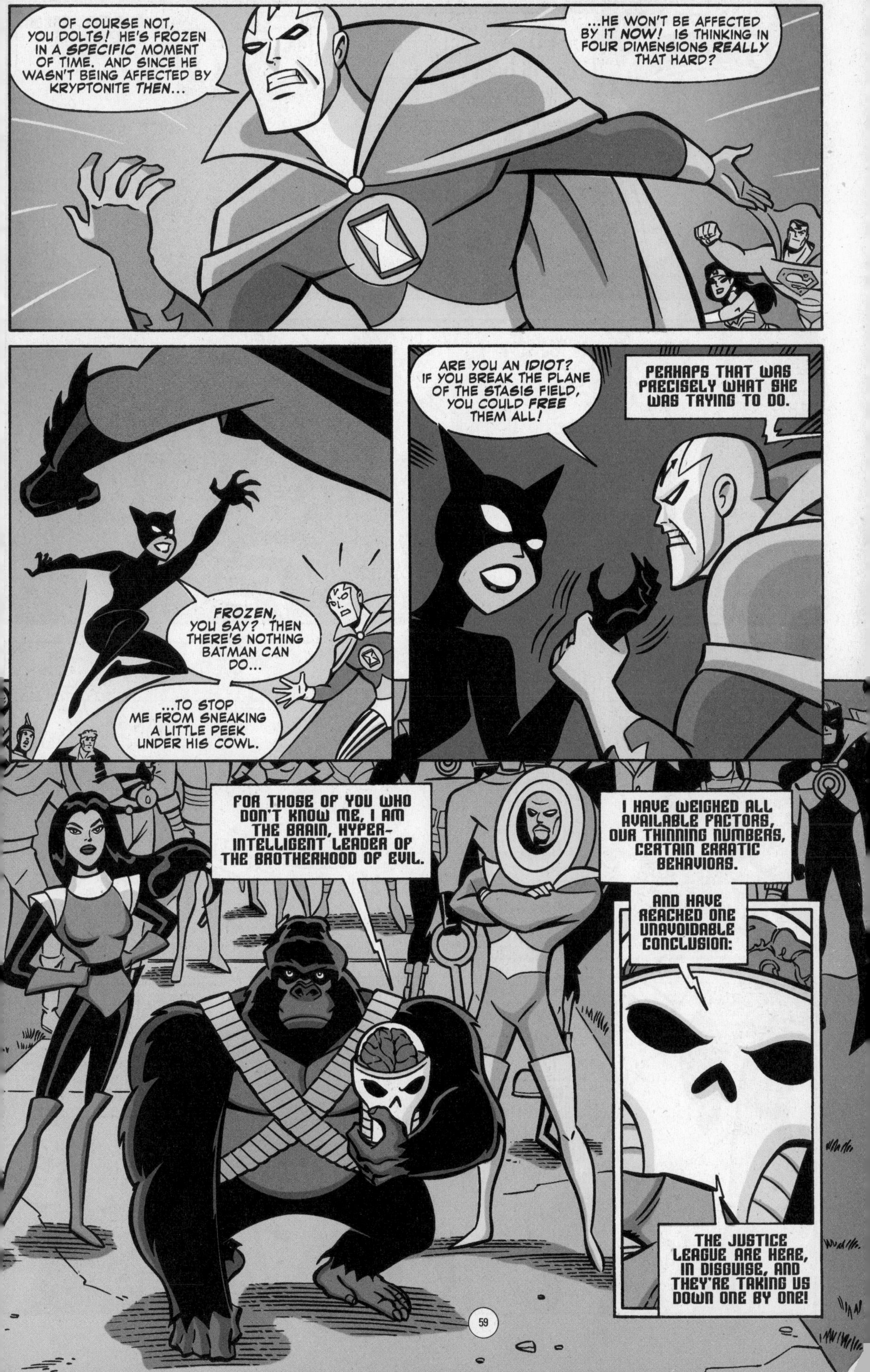
OF COURSE NOT, YOU DOLTS! HE'S FROZEN IN A SPECIFIC MOMENT OF TIME. AND SINCE HE WASN'T BEING AFFECTED BY KRYPTONITE THEN...
...HE WON'T BE AFFECTED BY IT NOW! IS THINKING IN FOUR DIMENSIONS REALLY THAT HARD?
FROZEN, YOU SAY? THEN THERE'S NOTHING BATMAN CAN DO...
...TO STOP ME FROM SNEAKING A LITTLE PEEK UNDER HIS COWL.
ARE YOU AN IDIOT? IF YOU BREAK THE PLANE OF THE STASIS FIELD, YOU COULD FREE THEM ALL!
PERHAPS THAT WAS PRECISELY WHAT SHE WAS TRYING TO DO.
FOR THOSE OF YOU WHO DON'T KNOW ME, I AM THE BRAIN, HYPER-INTELLIGENT LEADER OF THE BROTHERHOOD OF EVIL.
I HAVE WEIGHED ALL AVAILABLE FACTORS, OUR THINNING NUMBERS, CERTAIN ERRATIC BEHAVIORS.
AND HAVE REACHED ONE UNAVOIDABLE CONCLUSION:
THE JUSTICE LEAGUE ARE HERE, IN DISGUISE, AND THEY'RE TAKING US DOWN ONE BY ONE!

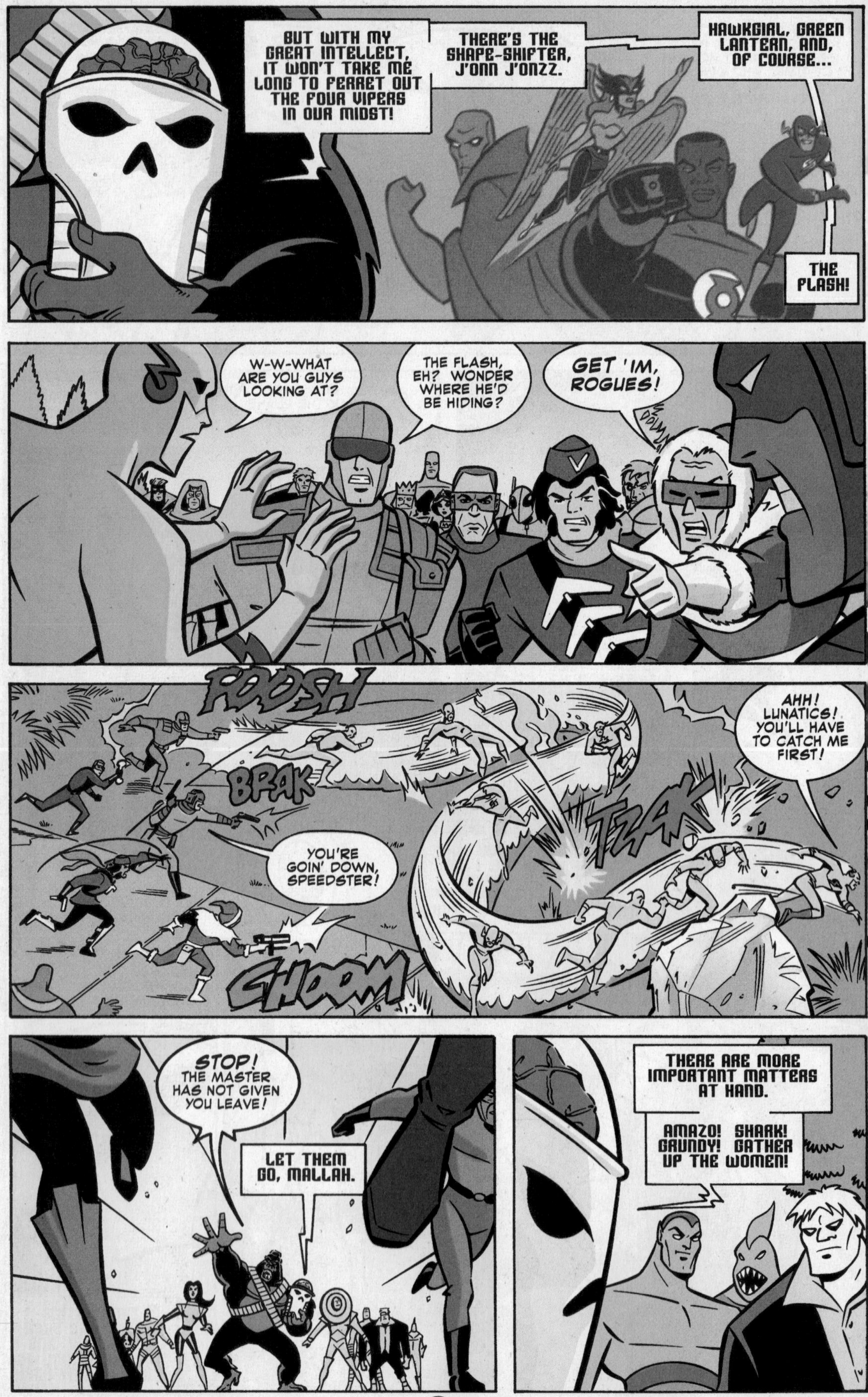

BUT WITH MY GREAT INTELLECT, IT WON'T TAKE ME LONG TO FERRET OUT THE FOUR VIPERS IN OUR MIDST!
THERE'S THE SHAPE-SHIFTER, J'ONN J'ONZZ.
HAWKGIRL, GREEN LANTERN, AND, OF COURSE...
THE FLASH!
W-W-WHAT ARE YOU GUYS LOOKING AT?
THE FLASH, EH? WONDER WHERE HE'D BE HIDING?
GET 'IM, ROGUES!
FOOSH
BRAK
AHH! LUNATICS! YOU'LL HAVE TO CATCH ME FIRST!
TZAK
YOU'RE GOIN' DOWN, SPEEDSTER!
CHOOM
STOP! THE MASTER HAS NOT GIVEN YOU LEAVE!
LET THEM GO, MALLAH.
THERE ARE MORE IMPORTANT MATTERS AT HAND.
AMAZO! SHARK! GAUNDY! GATHER UP THE WOMEN!

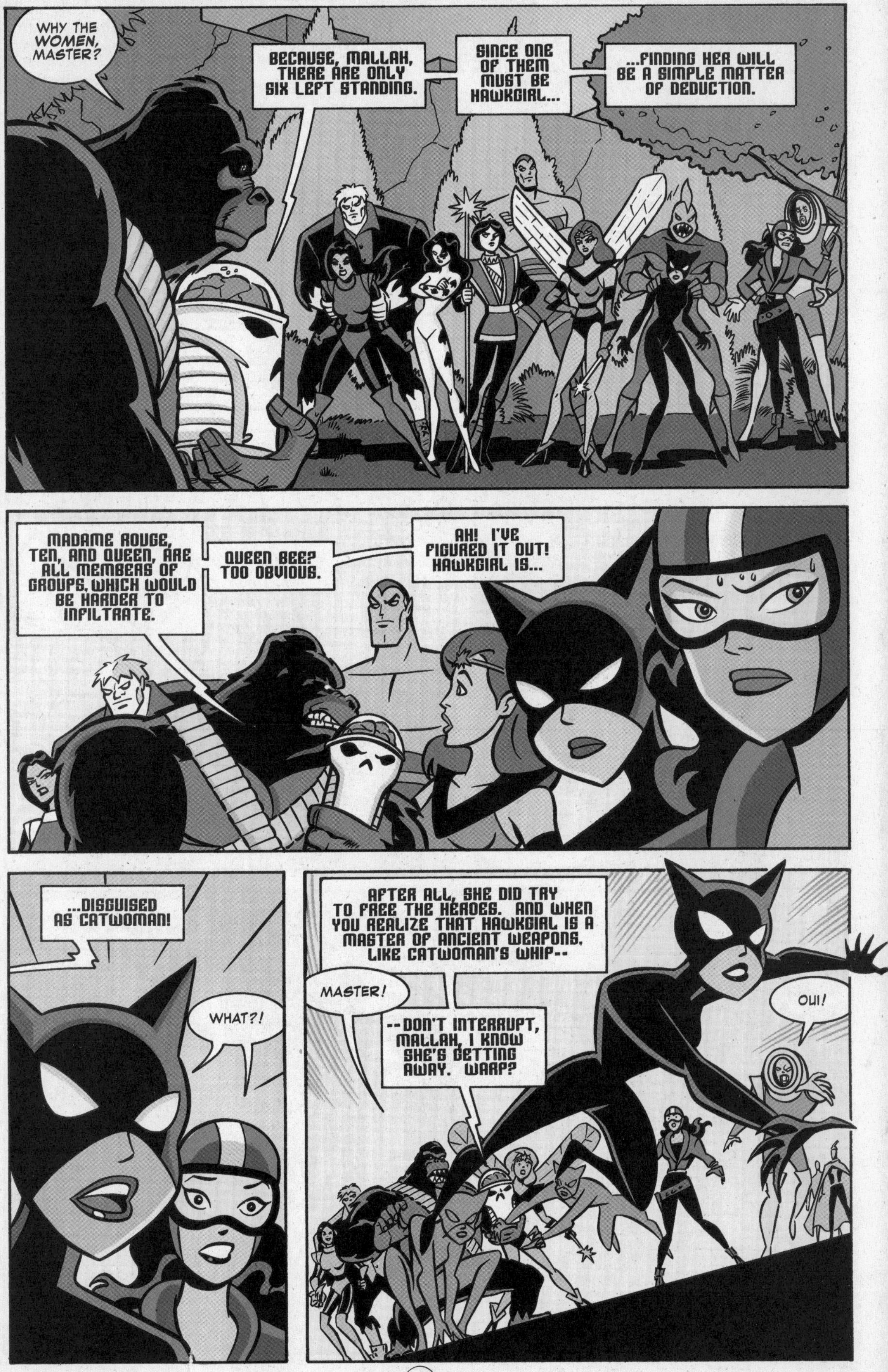
WHY THE WOMEN, MASTER?
BECAUSE, MALLAH, THERE ARE ONLY SIX LEFT STANDING.
SINCE ONE OF THEM MUST BE HAWKGIRL...
...FINDING HER WILL BE A SIMPLE MATTER OF DEDUCTION.
MADAME ROUGE, TEN, AND QUEEN, ARE ALL MEMBERS OF GROUPS, WHICH WOULD BE HARDER TO INFILTRATE.
QUEEN BEE? TOO OBVIOUS.
AH! I'VE FIGURED IT OUT! HAWKGIRL IS...
...DISGUISED AS CATWOMAN!
WHAT?!
AFTER ALL, SHE DID TRY TO FREE THE HEROES. AND WHEN YOU REALIZE THAT HAWKGIRL IS A MASTER OF ANCIENT WEAPONS, LIKE CATWOMAN'S WHIP--
MASTER!
--DON'T INTERRUPT, MALLAH, I KNOW SHE'S GETTING AWAY. WARP?
OUI!

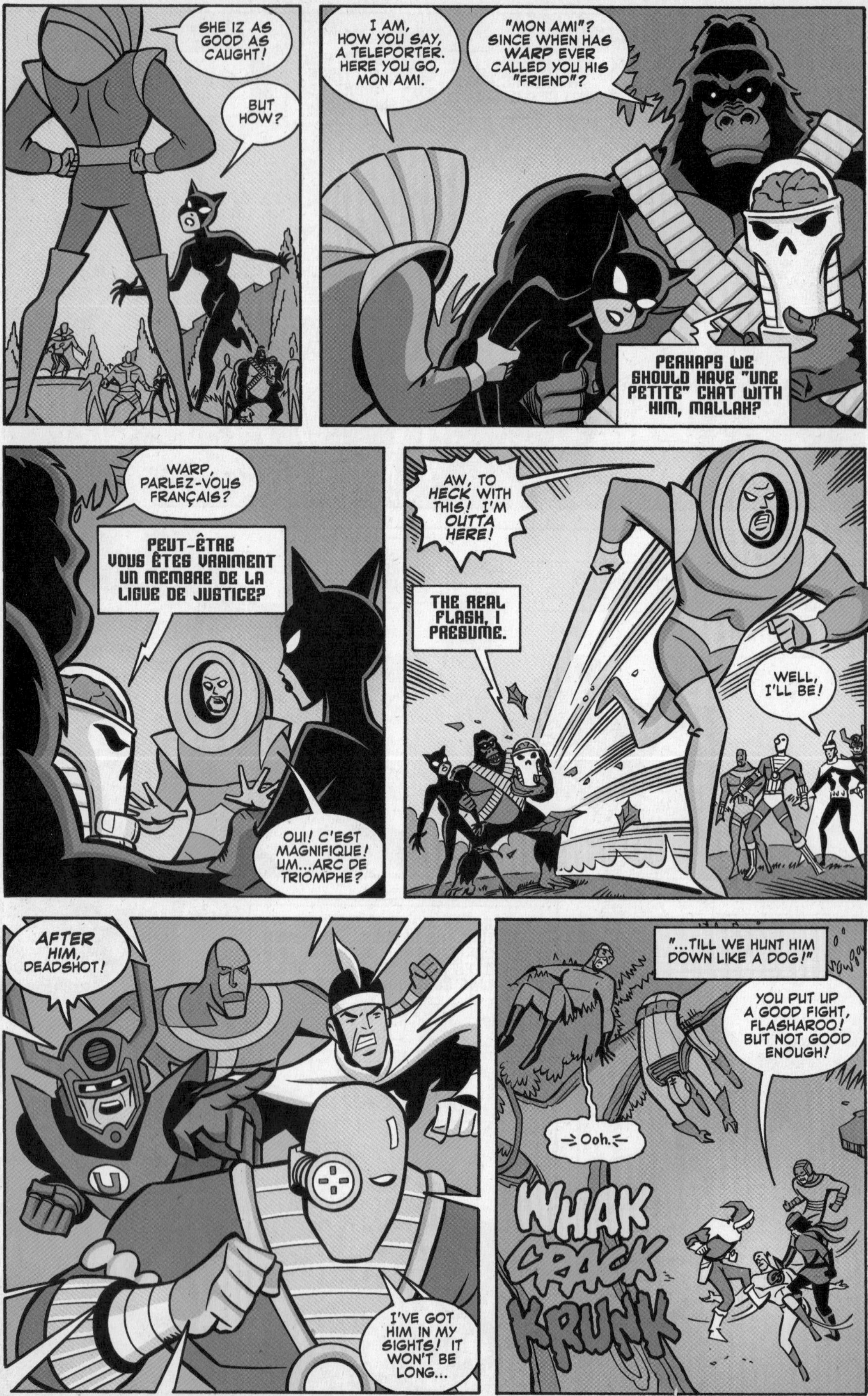

SHE IZ AS GOOD AS CAUGHT!
BUT HOW?
I AM, HOW YOU SAY, A TELEPORTER. HERE YOU GO, MON AMI.
"MON AMI"? SINCE WHEN HAS WARP EVER CALLED YOU HIS "FRIEND"?
PERHAPS WE SHOULD HAVE "UNE PETITE" CHAT WITH HIM, MALLAH?
WARP, PARLEZ-VOUS FRANÇAIS?
PEUT-ÊTRE VOUS ÊTES VRAIMENT UN MEMBRE DE LA LIGUE DE JUSTICE?
OUI! C'EST MAGNIFIQUE! UM...ARC DE TRIOMPHE?
AW, TO HECK WITH THIS! I'M OUTTA HERE!
THE REAL FLASH, I PRESUME.
WELL, I'LL BE!
AFTER HIM, DEADSHOT!
I'VE GOT HIM IN MY SIGHTS! IT WON'T BE LONG...
"...TILL WE HUNT HIM DOWN LIKE A DOG!"
YOU PUT UP A GOOD FIGHT, FLASHAROO! BUT NOT GOOD ENOUGH!
Ooh.
WHAK
CRACK
KRUNK

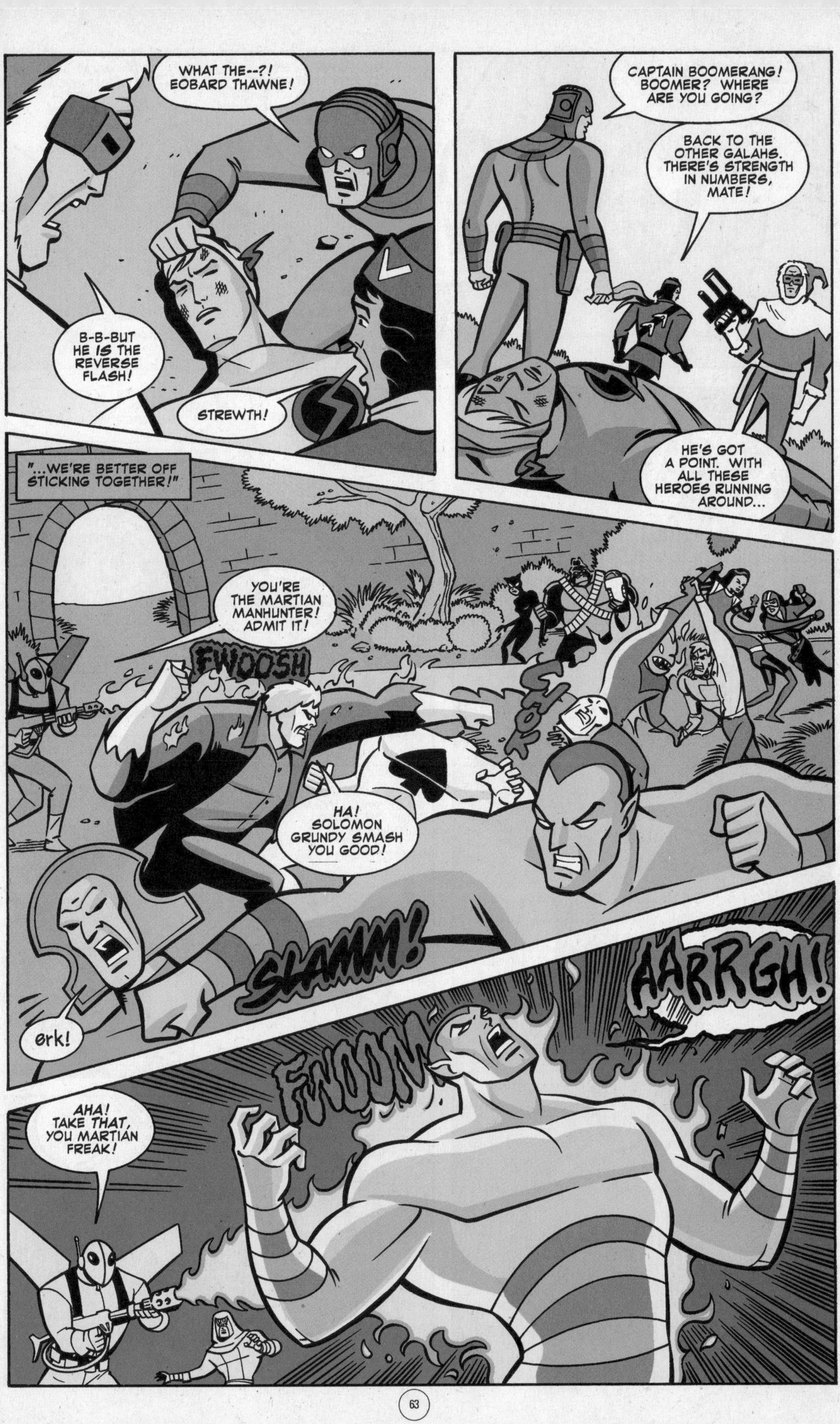
WHAT THE--?! EOBARD THAWNE!
B-B-BUT HE IS THE REVERSE FLASH!
STREWTH!
CAPTAIN BOOMERANG! BOOMER? WHERE ARE YOU GOING?
BACK TO THE OTHER GALAHS. THERE'S STRENGTH IN NUMBERS, MATE!
HE'S GOT A POINT. WITH ALL THESE HEROES RUNNING AROUND...
"...WE'RE BETTER OFF STICKING TOGETHER!"
YOU'RE THE MARTIAN MANHUNTER! ADMIT IT!
FWOOSH
HA! SOLOMON GRUNDY SMASH YOU GOOD!
SLAMM!
ERK!
AARRGH!
FWOOM
AHA! TAKE THAT, YOU MARTIAN FREAK!

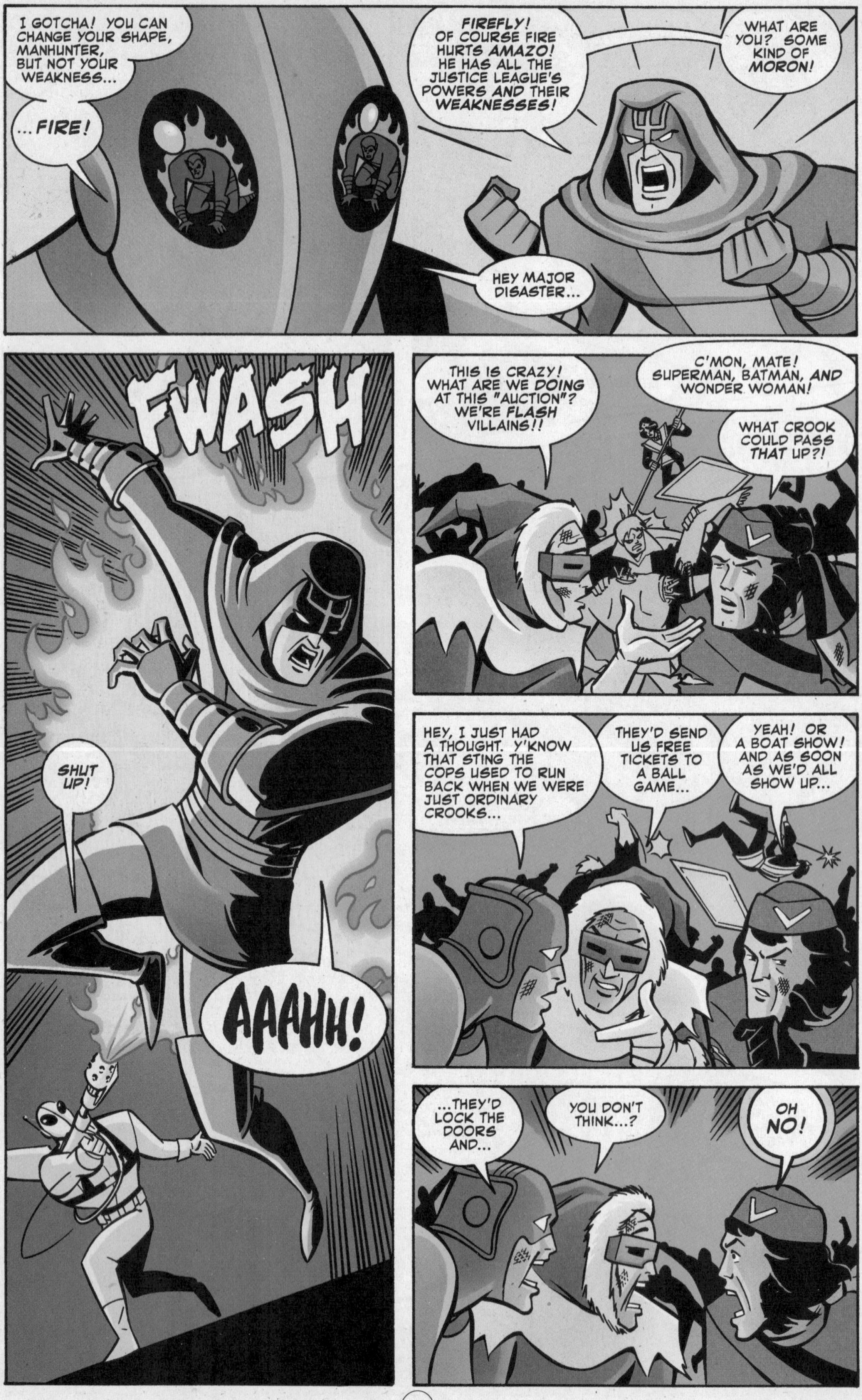
I GOTCHA! YOU CAN CHANGE YOUR SHAPE, MANHUNTER, BUT NOT YOUR WEAKNESS...
...FIRE!
FIREFLY! OF COURSE FIRE HURTS AMAZO! HE HAS ALL THE JUSTICE LEAGUE'S POWERS AND THEIR WEAKNESSES!
WHAT ARE YOU? SOME KIND OF MORON!
HEY MAJOR DISASTER...
FWASH
SHUT UP!
AAAHH!
THIS IS CRAZY! WHAT ARE WE DOING AT THIS "AUCTION"? WE'RE FLASH VILLAINS!!
C'MON, MATE! SUPERMAN, BATMAN, AND WONDER WOMAN!
WHAT CROOK COULD PASS THAT UP?!
HEY, I JUST HAD A THOUGHT. Y'KNOW THAT STING THE COPS USED TO RUN BACK WHEN WE WERE JUST ORDINARY CROOKS...
THEY'D SEND US FREE TICKETS TO A BALL GAME...
YEAH! OR A BOAT SHOW! AND AS SOON AS WE'D ALL SHOW UP...
...THEY'D LOCK THE DOORS AND...
YOU DON'T THINK...?
OH NO!

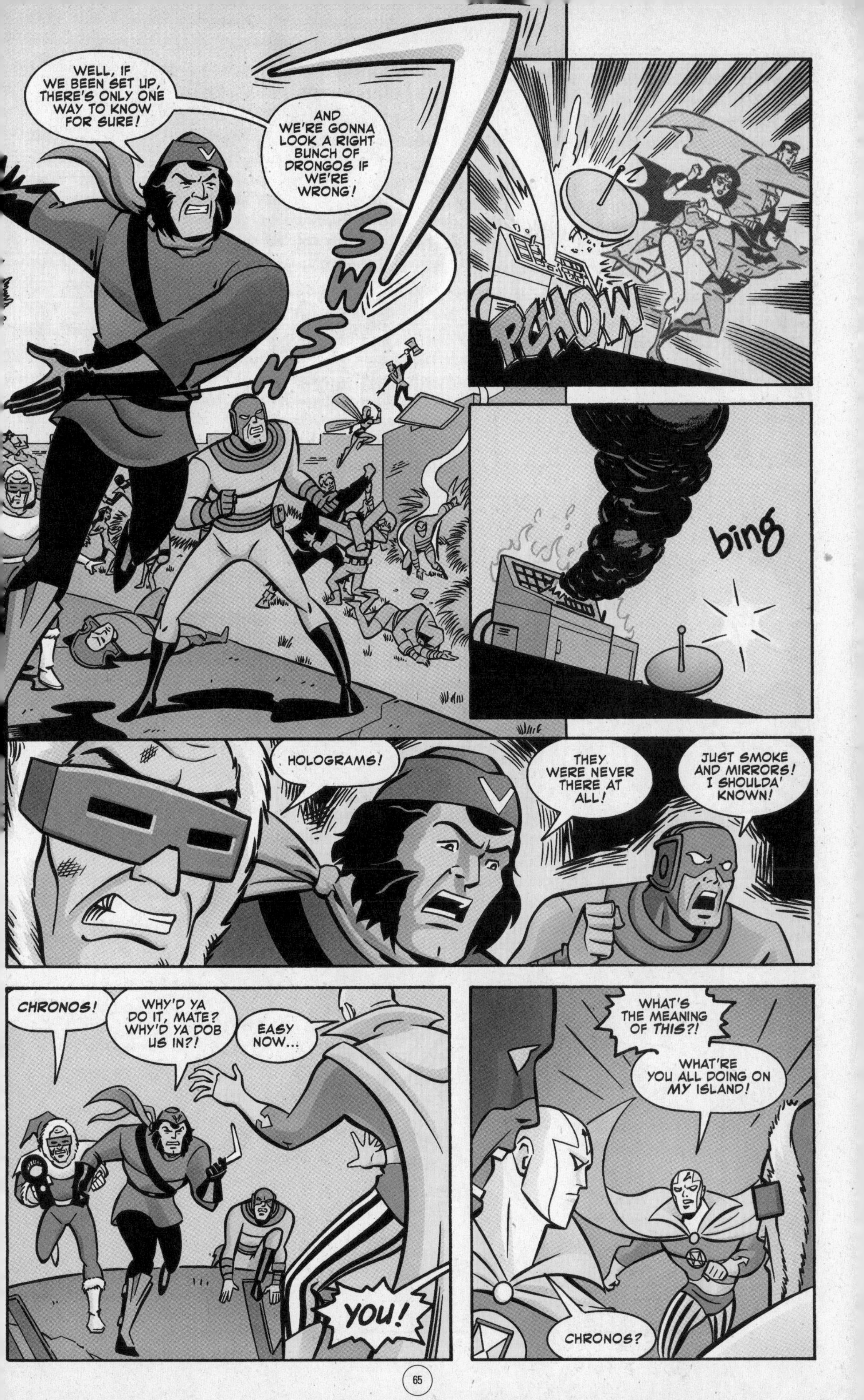
WELL, IF WE BEEN SET UP, THERE'S ONLY ONE WAY TO KNOW FOR SURE!
AND WE'RE GONNA LOOK A RIGHT BUNCH OF DRONGOS IF WE'RE WRONG!
SWSH
PCHOW
bing
HOLOGRAMS!
THEY WERE NEVER THERE AT ALL!
JUST SMOKE AND MIRRORS! I SHOULDA' KNOWN!
CHRONOS!
WHY'D YA DO IT, MATE? WHY'D YA DOB US IN?!
EASY NOW...
YOU!
WHAT'S THE MEANING OF THIS?!
WHAT'RE YOU ALL DOING ON MY ISLAND!
CHRONOS?

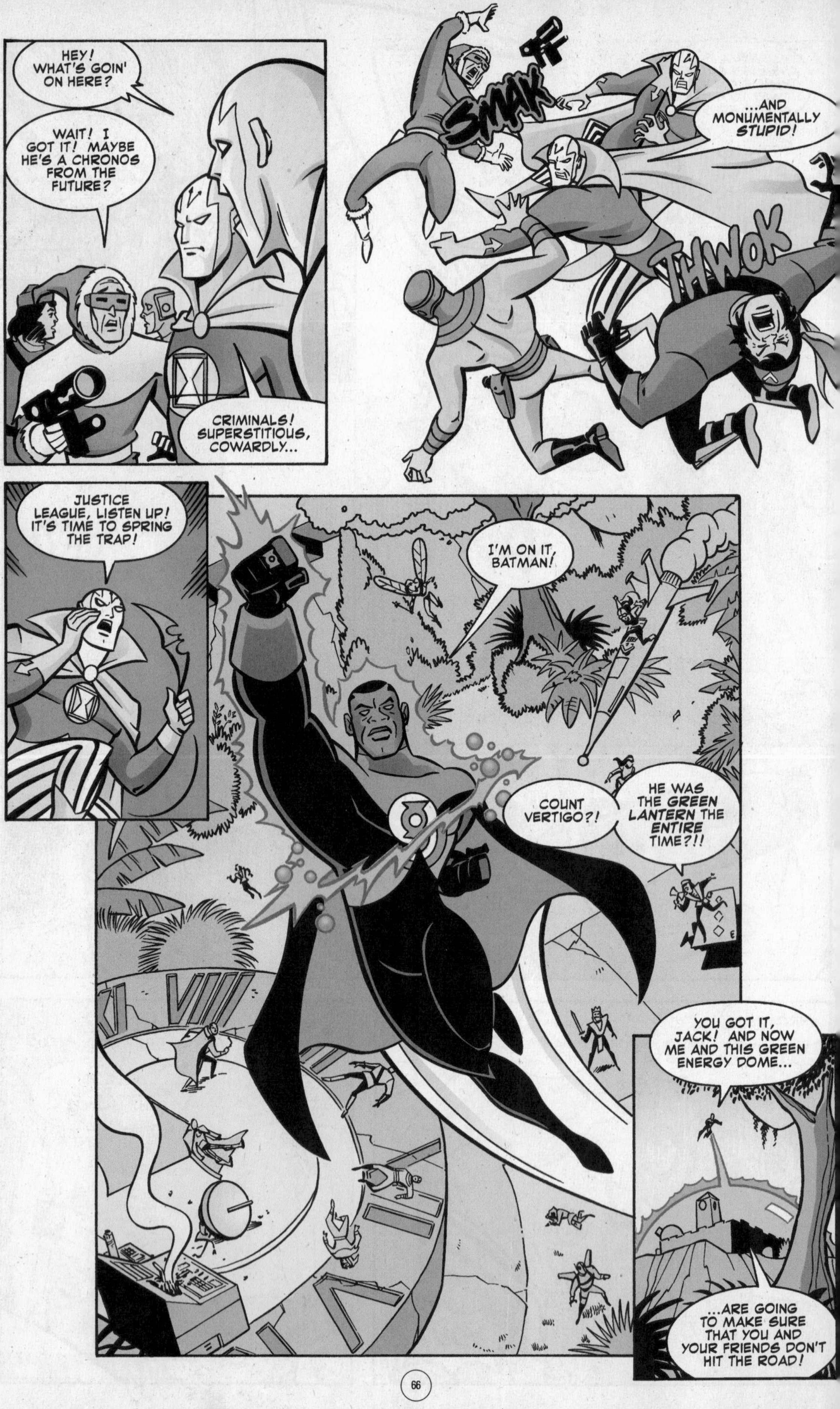
HEY! WHAT'S GOIN' ON HERE?
WAIT! I GOT IT! MAYBE HE'S A CHRONOS FROM THE FUTURE?
CRIMINALS! SUPERSTITIOUS, COWARDLY...
SMAK
...AND MONUMENTALLY STUPID!
THWOK
JUSTICE LEAGUE, LISTEN UP! IT'S TIME TO SPRING THE TRAP!
I'M ON IT, BATMAN!
COUNT VERTIGO?!
HE WAS THE GREEN LANTERN THE ENTIRE TIME?!!
YOU GOT IT, JACK! AND NOW ME AND THIS GREEN ENERGY DOME...
...ARE GOING TO MAKE SURE THAT YOU AND YOUR FRIENDS DON'T HIT THE ROAD!

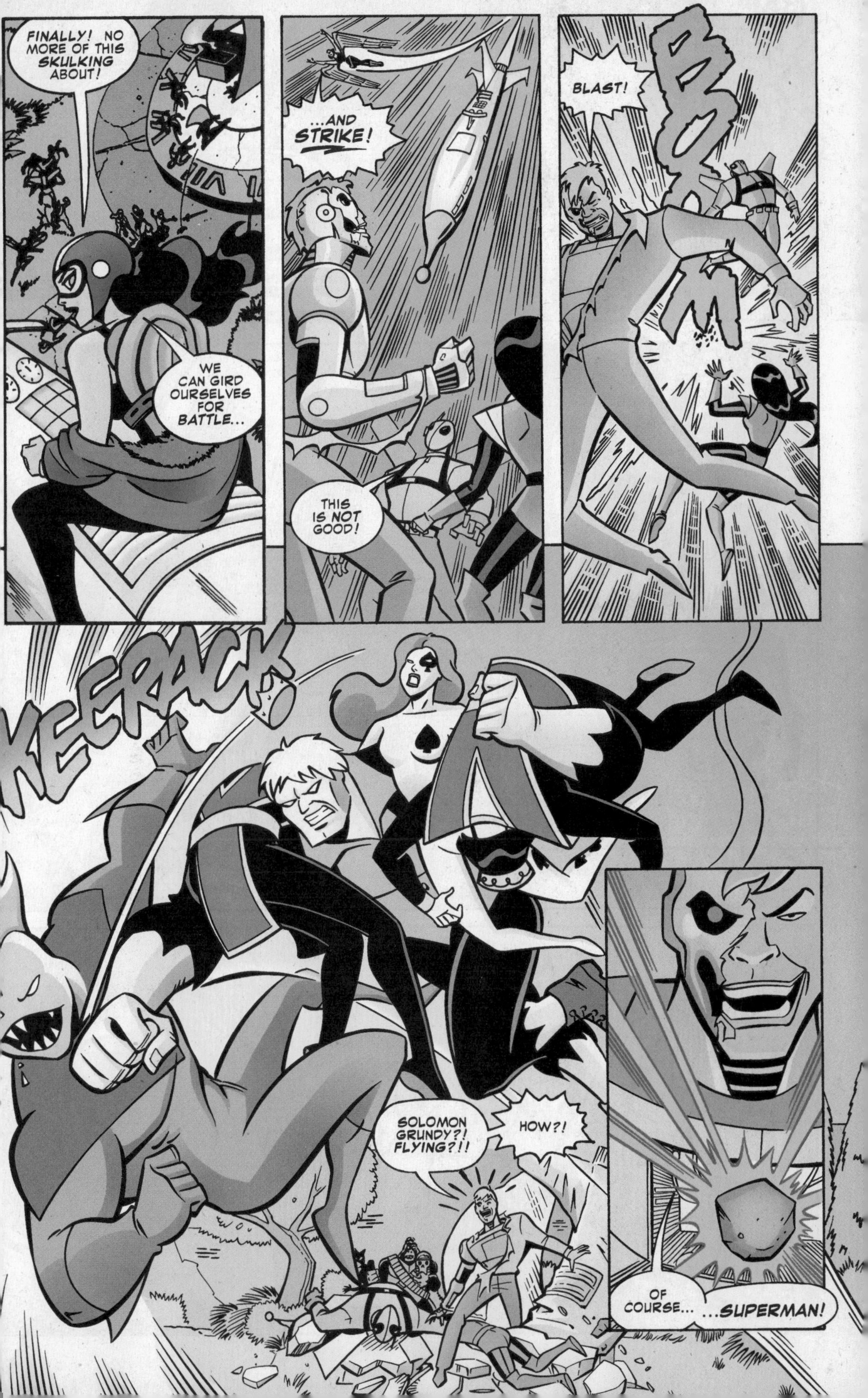

FINALLY! NO MORE OF THIS SKULKING ABOUT!
WE CAN GIRD OURSELVES FOR BATTLE...
...AND STRIKE!
THIS IS NOT GOOD!
BLAST!
BOOM
KEERACK
SOLOMON GRUNDY?! FLYING?!!
HOW?!
OF COURSE...
...SUPERMAN!

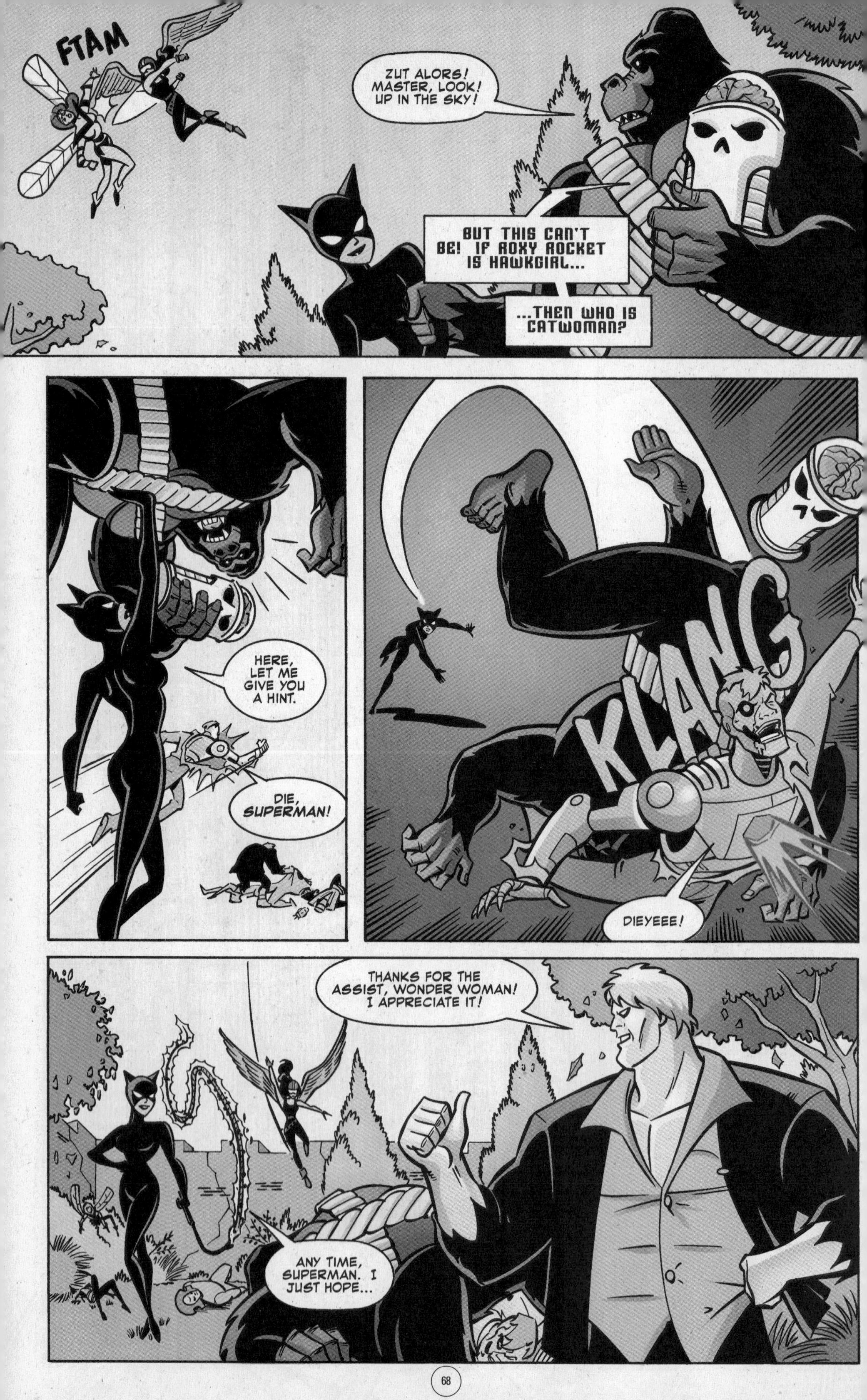
FTAM
ZUT ALORS! MASTER, LOOK! UP IN THE SKY!
BUT THIS CAN'T BE! IF ROXY ROCKET IS HAWKGIRL...
...THEN WHO IS CATWOMAN?
HERE, LET ME GIVE YOU A HINT.
DIE, SUPERMAN!
KLANG
DIEYEEE!
THANKS FOR THE ASSIST, WONDER WOMAN! I APPRECIATE IT!
ANY TIME, SUPERMAN. I JUST HOPE...

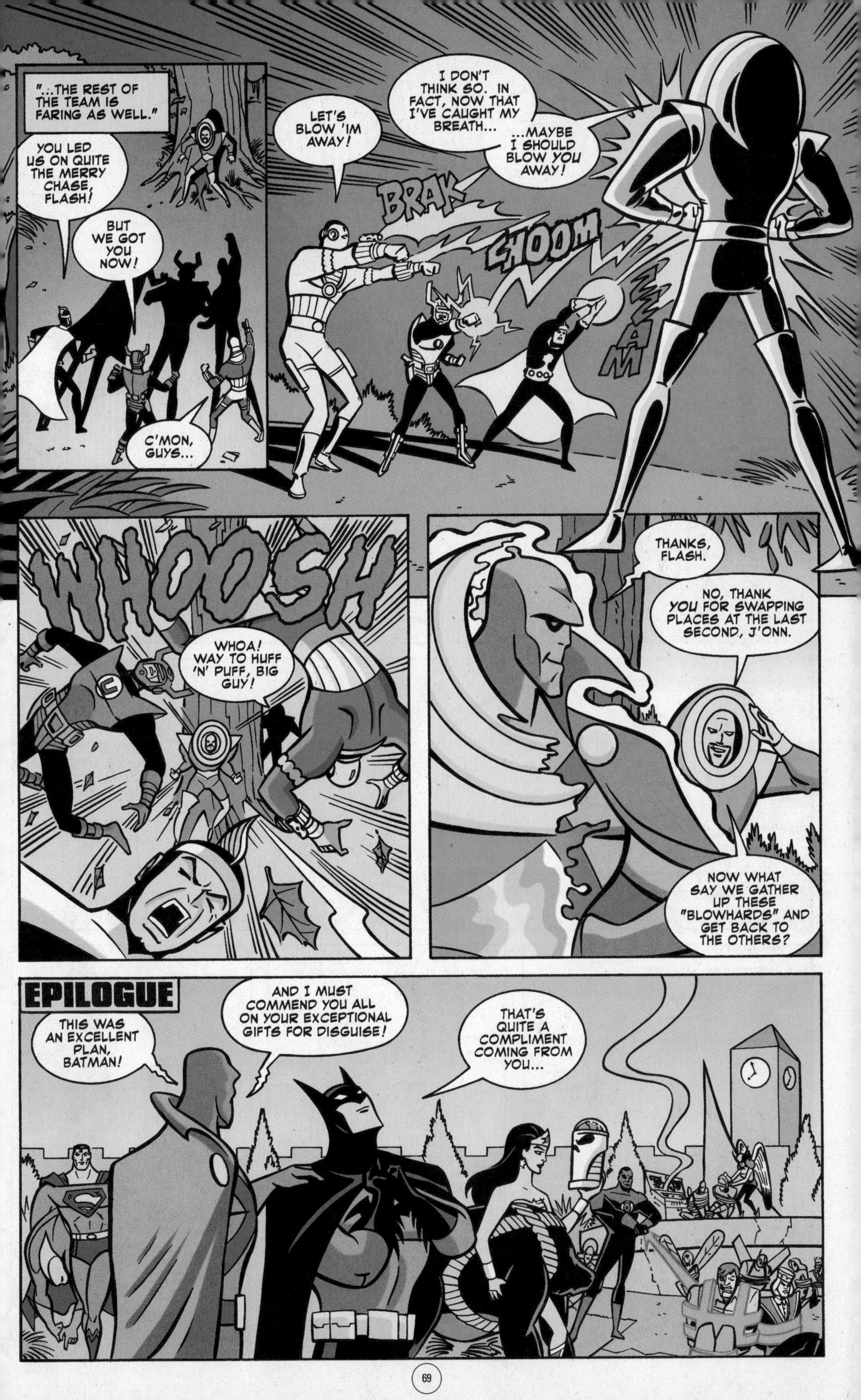
"...THE REST OF THE TEAM IS FARING AS WELL."
YOU LED US ON QUITE THE MERRY CHASE, FLASH!
BUT WE GOT YOU NOW!
C'MON, GUYS...
LET'S BLOW 'IM AWAY!
I DON'T THINK SO. IN FACT, NOW THAT I'VE CAUGHT MY BREATH...
...MAYBE I SHOULD BLOW YOU AWAY!
BRAK
CHOOM
ZZAM
WHOOSH
WHOA! WAY TO HUFF 'N' PUFF, BIG GUY!
THANKS, FLASH.
NO, THANK YOU FOR SWAPPING PLACES AT THE LAST SECOND, J'ONN.
NOW WHAT SAY WE GATHER UP THESE "BLOWHARDS" AND GET BACK TO THE OTHERS?
EPILOGUE
THIS WAS AN EXCELLENT PLAN, BATMAN!
AND I MUST COMMEND YOU ALL ON YOUR EXCEPTIONAL GIFTS FOR DISGUISE!
THAT'S QUITE A COMPLIMENT COMING FROM YOU...

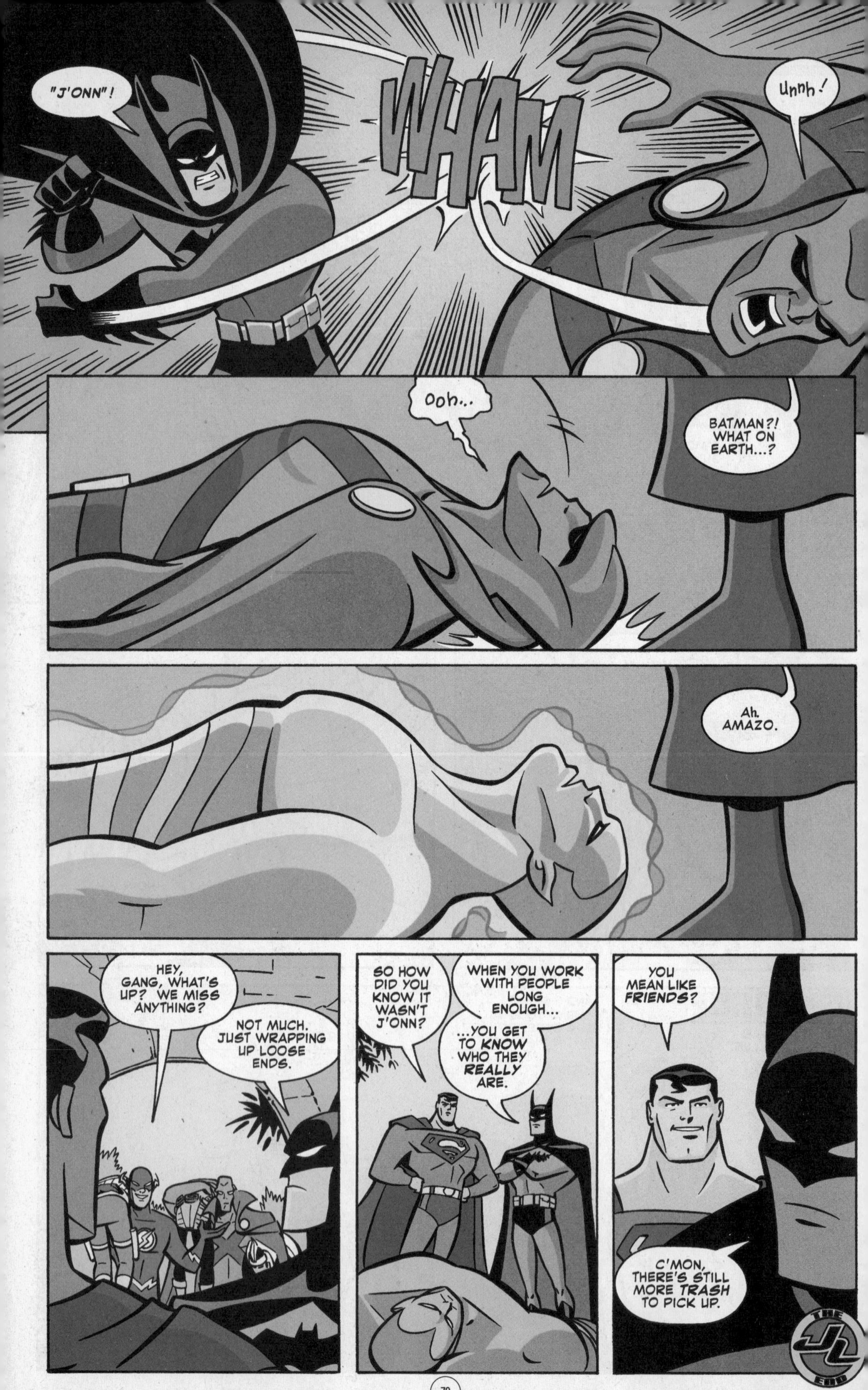
"J'ONN"!
WHAM
Unnh!
Ooh..
BATMAN?! WHAT ON EARTH...?
Ah. AMAZO.
HEY, GANG, WHAT'S UP? WE MISS ANYTHING?
NOT MUCH. JUST WRAPPING UP LOOSE ENDS.
SO HOW DID YOU KNOW IT WASN'T J'ONN?
WHEN YOU WORK WITH PEOPLE LONG ENOUGH...
...YOU GET TO KNOW WHO THEY REALLY ARE.
YOU MEAN LIKE FRIENDS?
C'MON, THERE'S STILL MORE TRASH TO PICK UP.
THE END

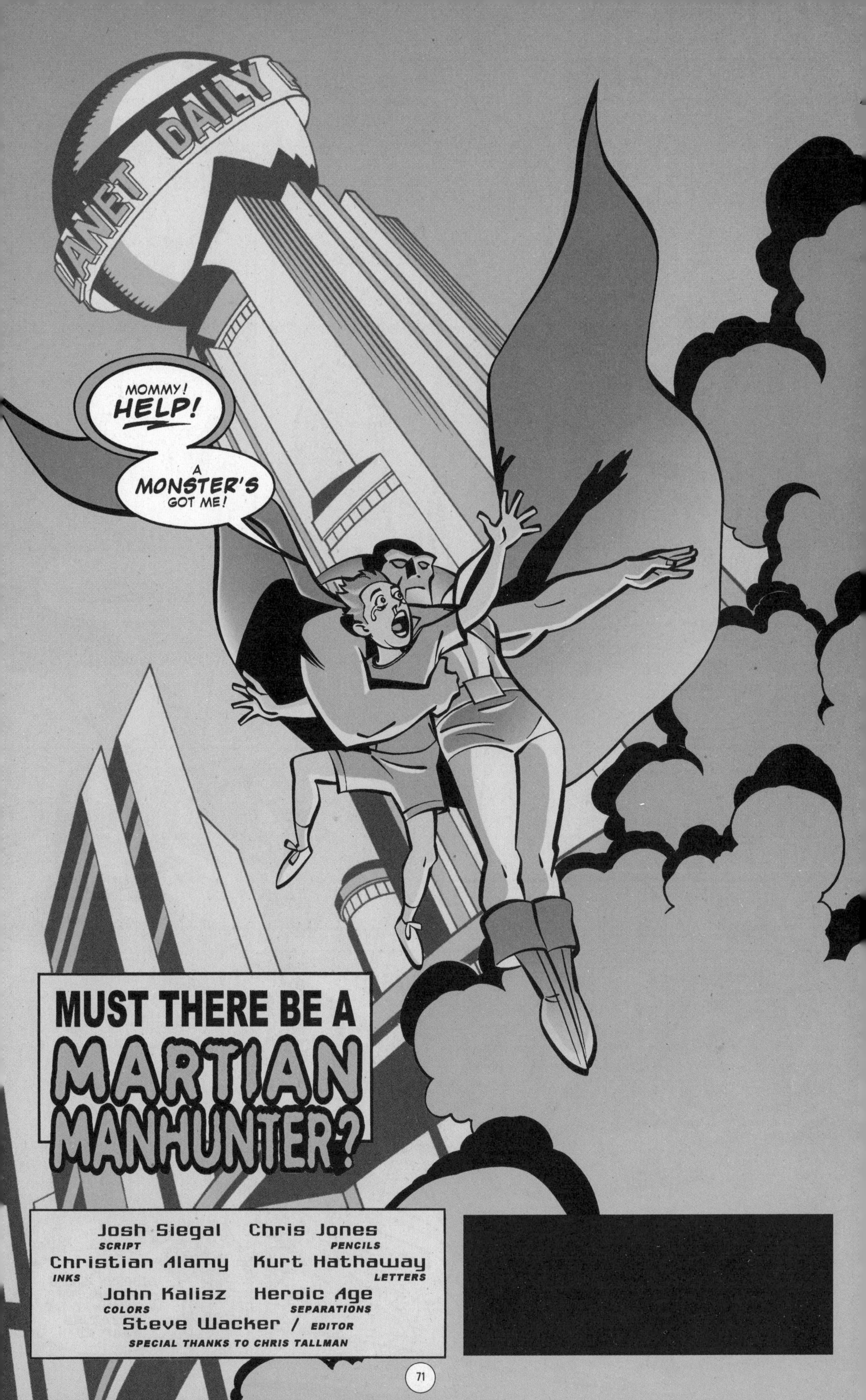
MOMMY! HELP!
A MONSTER'S GOT ME!
MUST THERE BE A MARTIAN MANHUNTER?
Josh Siegal SCRIPT
Chris Jones PENCILS
Christian Alamy INKS
Kurt Hathaway LETTERS
John Kalisz COLORS
Heroic Age SEPARATIONS
Steve Wacker / EDITOR
SPECIAL THANKS TO CHRIS TALLMAN

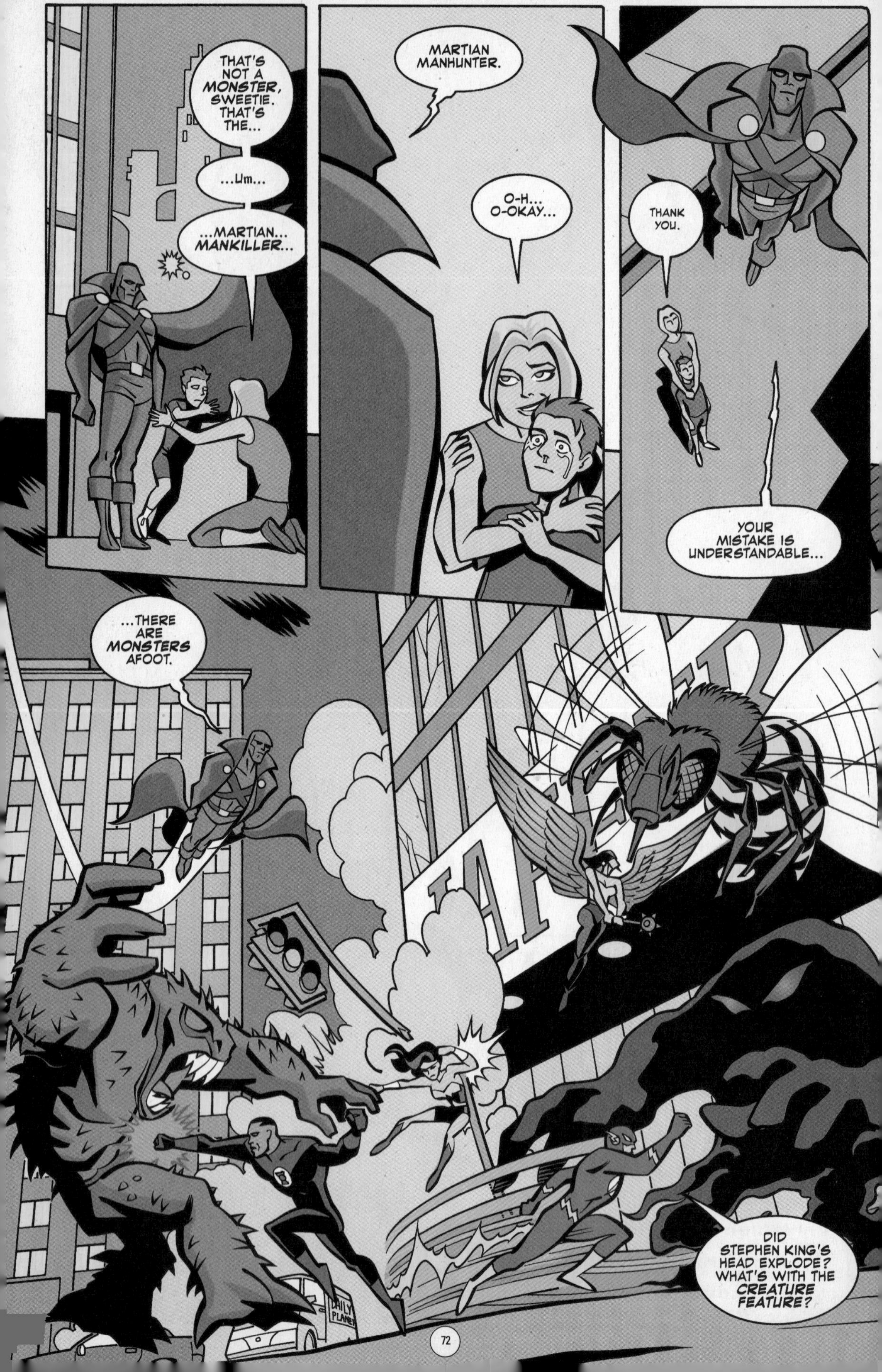
THAT'S NOT A MONSTER, SWEETIE. THAT'S THE...
...UM...
...MARTIAN... MANKILLER...
MARTIAN MANHUNTER.
O-H... O-OKAY...
THANK YOU.
YOUR MISTAKE IS UNDERSTANDABLE...
...THERE ARE MONSTERS AFOOT.
DAILY PLANET
DID STEPHEN KING'S HEAD EXPLODE? WHAT'S WITH THE CREATURE FEATURE?

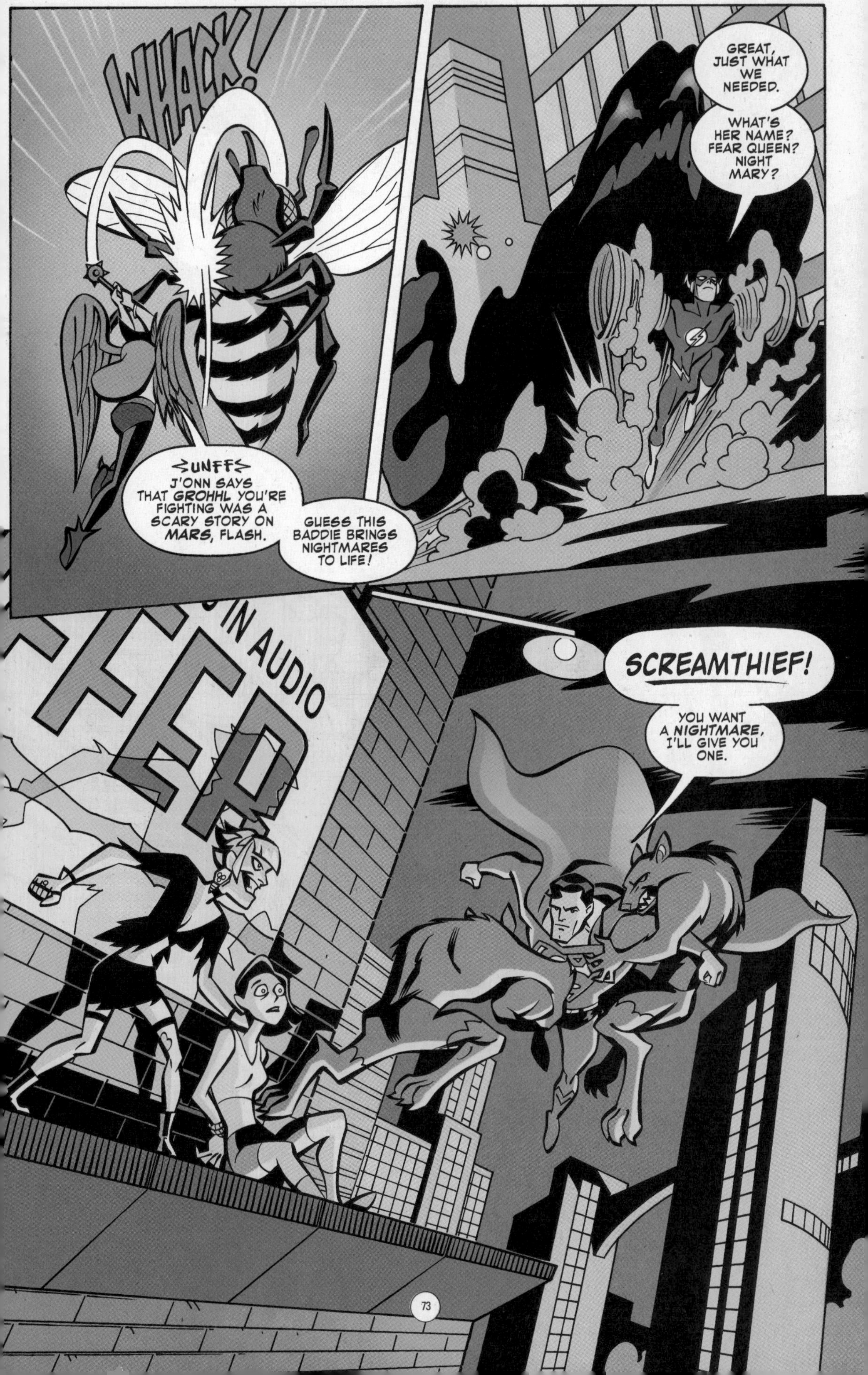

WHACK!
GREAT, JUST WHAT WE NEEDED.
WHAT'S HER NAME? FEAR QUEEN? NIGHT MARY?
UNFF
J'ONN SAYS THAT GROHHL YOU'RE FIGHTING WAS A SCARY STORY ON MARS, FLASH.
GUESS THIS BADDIE BRINGS NIGHTMARES TO LIFE!
IN AUDIO
SCREAMTHIEF!
YOU WANT A NIGHTMARE, I'LL GIVE YOU ONE.

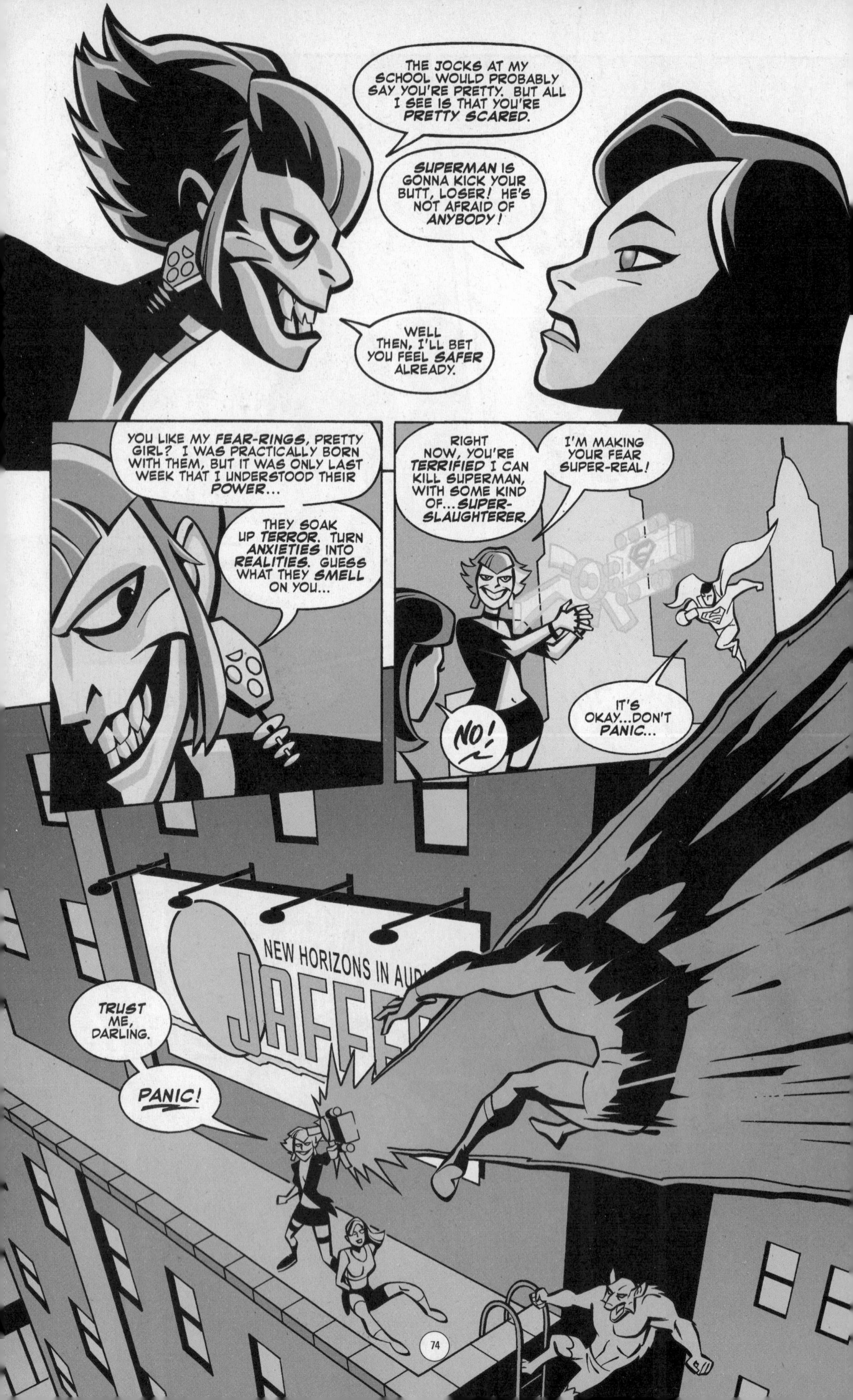
THE JOCKS AT MY SCHOOL WOULD PROBABLY SAY YOU'RE PRETTY. BUT ALL I SEE IS THAT YOU'RE PRETTY SCARED.
SUPERMAN IS GONNA KICK YOUR BUTT, LOSER! HE'S NOT AFRAID OF ANYBODY!
WELL THEN, I'LL BET YOU FEEL SAFER ALREADY.
YOU LIKE MY FEAR-RINGS, PRETTY GIRL? I WAS PRACTICALLY BORN WITH THEM, BUT IT WAS ONLY LAST WEEK THAT I UNDERSTOOD THEIR POWER...
THEY SOAK UP TERROR. TURN ANXIETIES INTO REALITIES. GUESS WHAT THEY SMELL ON YOU...
RIGHT NOW, YOU'RE TERRIFIED I CAN KILL SUPERMAN, WITH SOME KIND OF...SUPER-SLAUGHTERER.
I'M MAKING YOUR FEAR SUPER-REAL!
NO!
IT'S OKAY...DON'T PANIC...
NEW HORIZONS IN AUD
JAFFE
TRUST ME, DARLING.
PANIC!

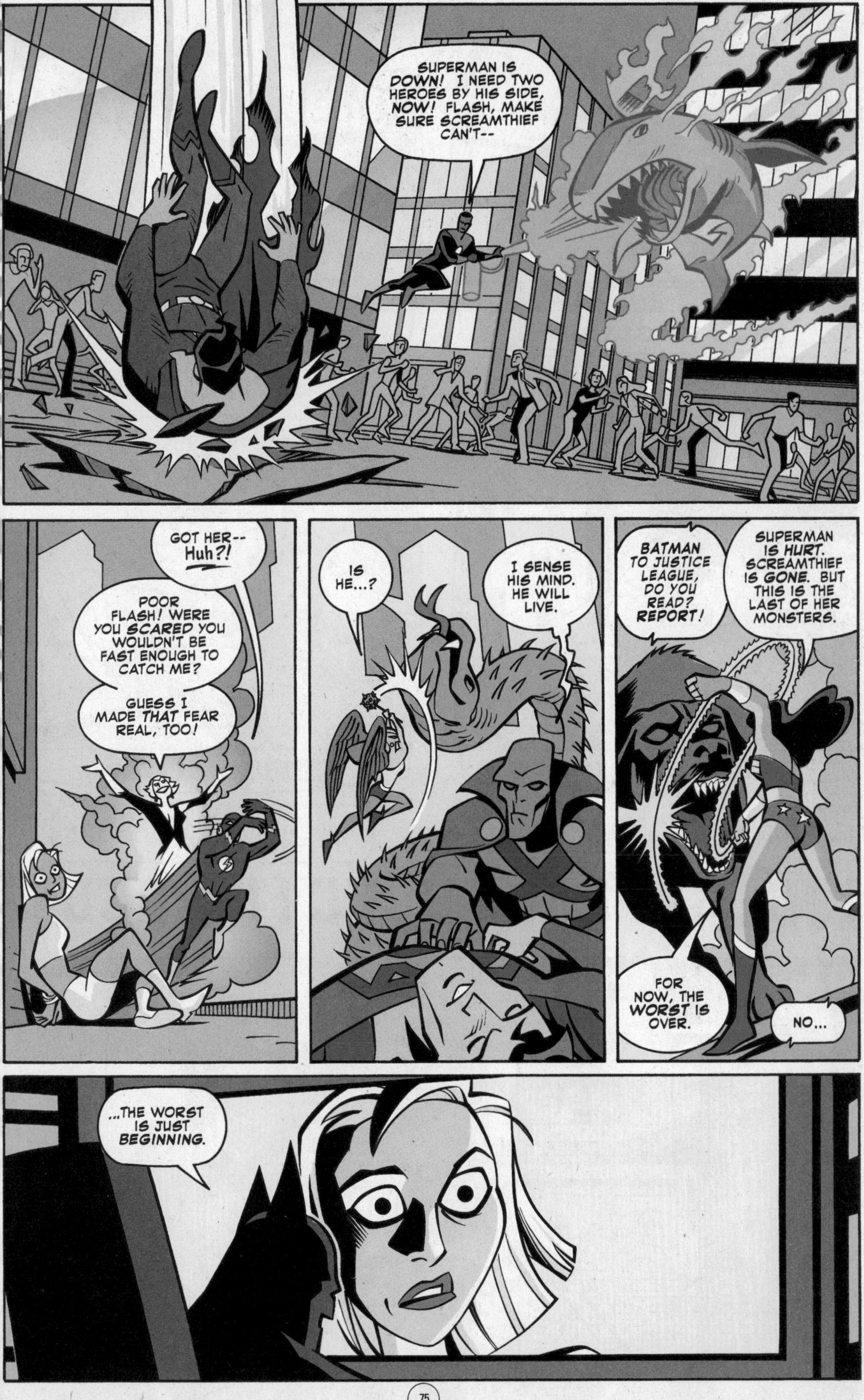
SUPERMAN IS DOWN! I NEED TWO HEROES BY HIS SIDE, NOW! FLASH, MAKE SURE SCREAMTHIEF CAN'T--
GOT HER-- Huh?!
POOR FLASH! WERE YOU SCARED YOU WOULDN'T BE FAST ENOUGH TO CATCH ME?
GUESS I MADE THAT FEAR REAL, TOO!
IS HE...?
I SENSE HIS MIND. HE WILL LIVE.
BATMAN TO JUSTICE LEAGUE, DO YOU READ? REPORT!
SUPERMAN IS HURT. SCREAMTHIEF IS GONE. BUT THIS IS THE LAST OF HER MONSTERS.
FOR NOW, THE WORST IS OVER.
NO...
...THE WORST IS JUST BEGINNING.

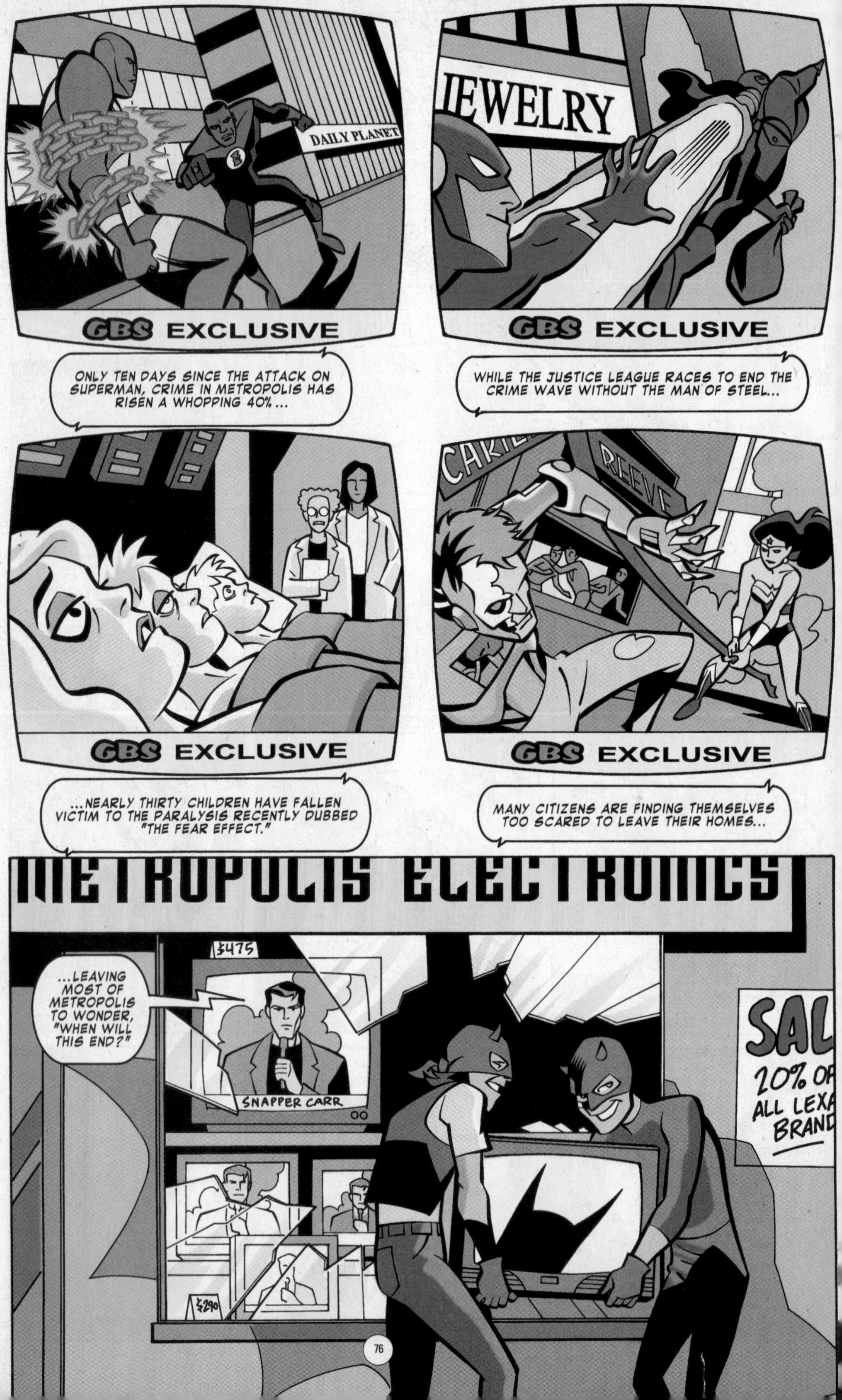
DAILY PLANET
GBS EXCLUSIVE
JEWELRY
GBS EXCLUSIVE
ONLY TEN DAYS SINCE THE ATTACK ON SUPERMAN, CRIME IN METROPOLIS HAS RISEN A WHOPPING 40%...
WHILE THE JUSTICE LEAGUE RACES TO END THE CRIME WAVE WITHOUT THE MAN OF STEEL...
GBS EXCLUSIVE
GBS EXCLUSIVE
...NEARLY THIRTY CHILDREN HAVE FALLEN VICTIM TO THE PARALYSIS RECENTLY DUBBED "THE FEAR EFFECT."
MANY CITIZENS ARE FINDING THEMSELVES TOO SCARED TO LEAVE THEIR HOMES...
METROPOLIS ELECTRONICS
$475
...LEAVING MOST OF METROPOLIS TO WONDER, "WHEN WILL THIS END?"
SNAPPER CARR
$290

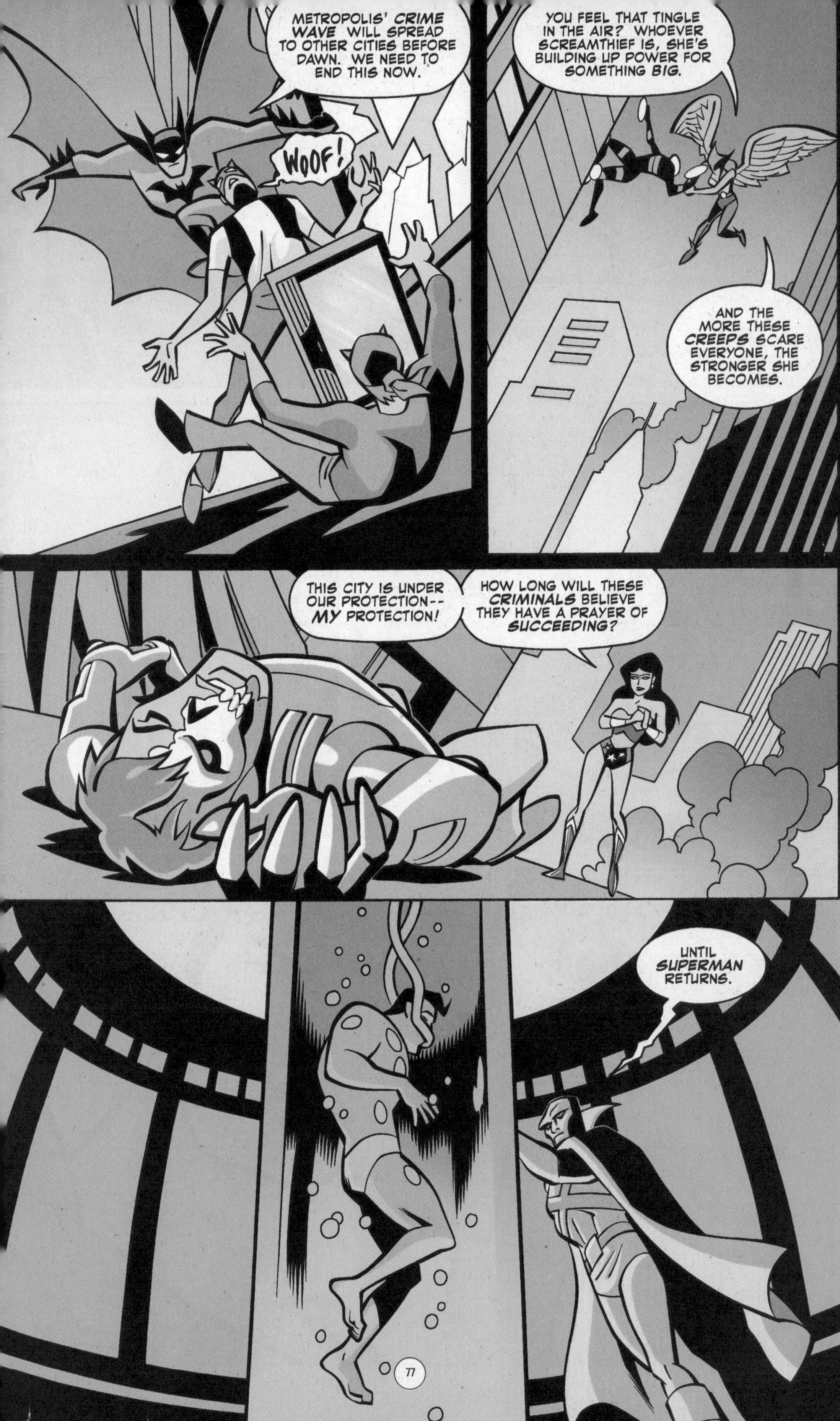
METROPOLIS' CRIME WAVE WILL SPREAD TO OTHER CITIES BEFORE DAWN. WE NEED TO END THIS NOW.
WOOF!
YOU FEEL THAT TINGLE IN THE AIR? WHOEVER SCREAMTHIEF IS, SHE'S BUILDING UP POWER FOR SOMETHING BIG.
AND THE MORE THESE CREEPS SCARE EVERYONE, THE STRONGER SHE BECOMES.
THIS CITY IS UNDER OUR PROTECTION-- MY PROTECTION!
HOW LONG WILL THESE CRIMINALS BELIEVE THEY HAVE A PRAYER OF SUCCEEDING?
UNTIL SUPERMAN RETURNS.

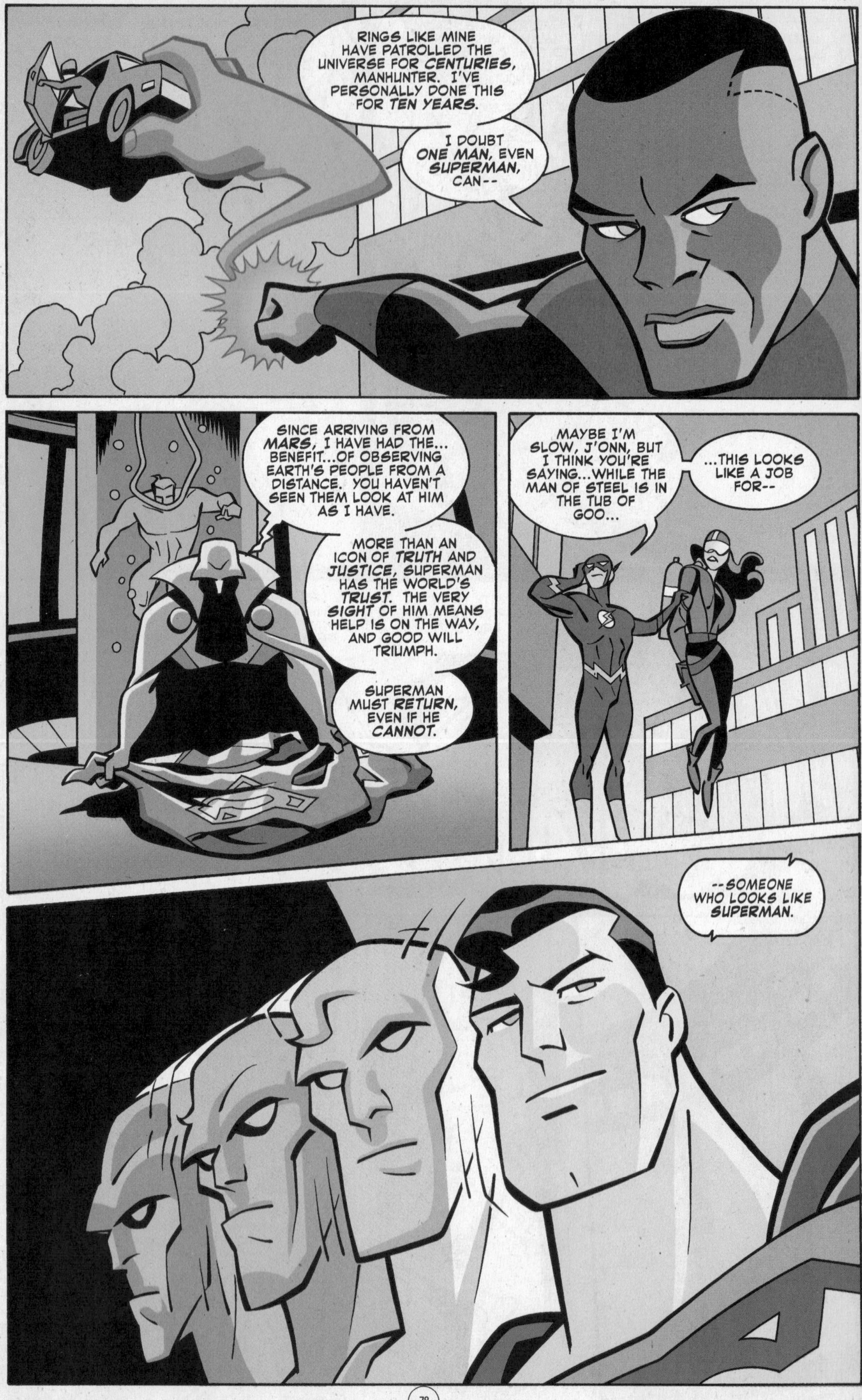
RINGS LIKE MINE HAVE PATROLLED THE UNIVERSE FOR CENTURIES, MANHUNTER. I'VE PERSONALLY DONE THIS FOR TEN YEARS.
I DOUBT ONE MAN, EVEN SUPERMAN, CAN--
SINCE ARRIVING FROM MARS, I HAVE HAD THE... BENEFIT...OF OBSERVING EARTH'S PEOPLE FROM A DISTANCE. YOU HAVEN'T SEEN THEM LOOK AT HIM AS I HAVE.
MORE THAN AN ICON OF TRUTH AND JUSTICE, SUPERMAN HAS THE WORLD'S TRUST. THE VERY SIGHT OF HIM MEANS HELP IS ON THE WAY, AND GOOD WILL TRIUMPH.
SUPERMAN MUST RETURN, EVEN IF HE CANNOT.
MAYBE I'M SLOW, J'ONN, BUT I THINK YOU'RE SAYING...WHILE THE MAN OF STEEL IS IN THE TUB OF GOO...
...THIS LOOKS LIKE A JOB FOR--
--SOMEONE WHO LOOKS LIKE SUPERMAN.

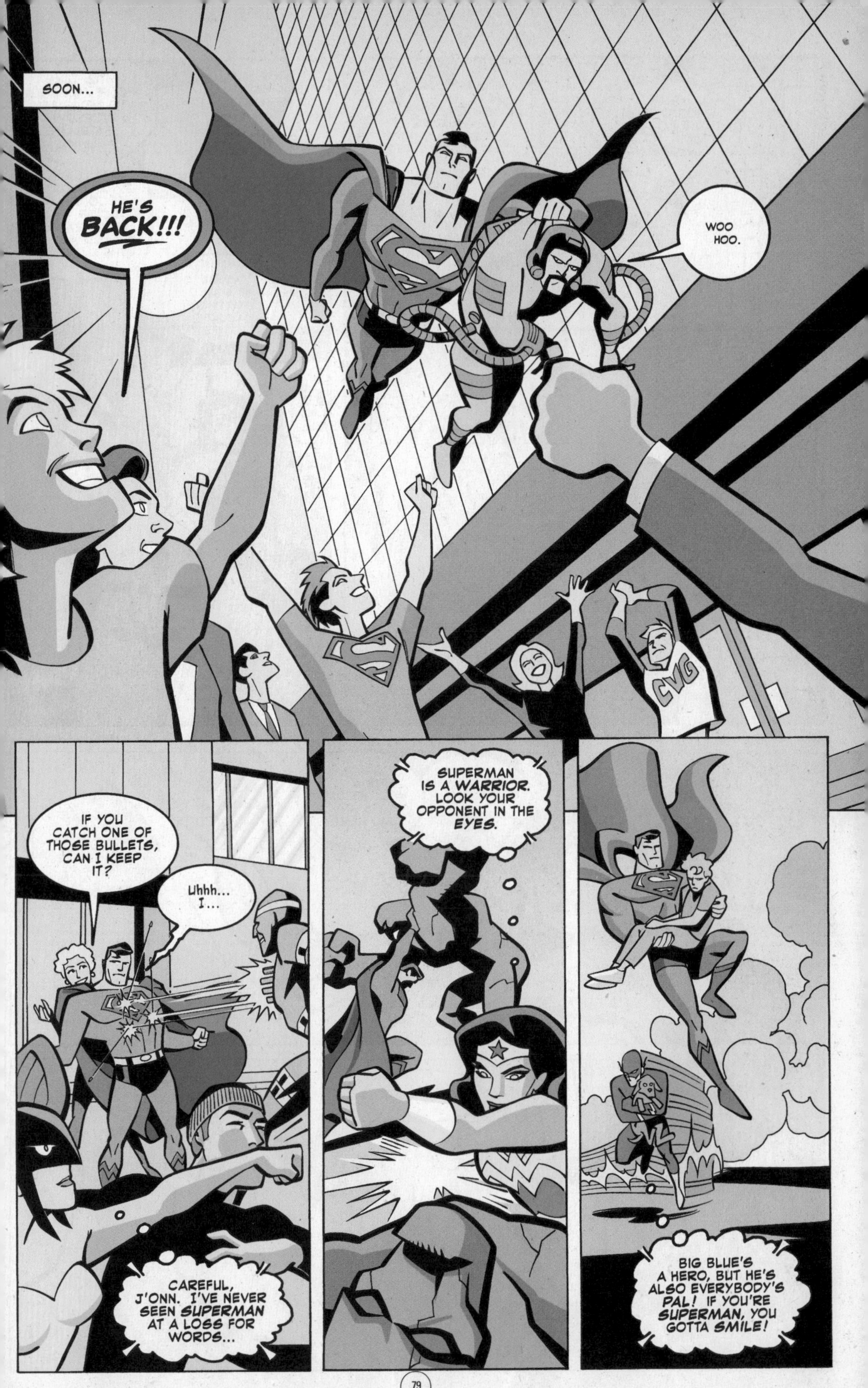
SOON...
HE'S BACK!!!
WOO HOO.
IF YOU CATCH ONE OF THOSE BULLETS, CAN I KEEP IT?
Uhhh... I...
CAREFUL, J'ONN. I'VE NEVER SEEN SUPERMAN AT A LOSS FOR WORDS...
SUPERMAN IS A WARRIOR. LOOK YOUR OPPONENT IN THE EYES.
BIG BLUE'S A HERO, BUT HE'S ALSO EVERYBODY'S PAL! IF YOU'RE SUPERMAN, YOU GOTTA SMILE!

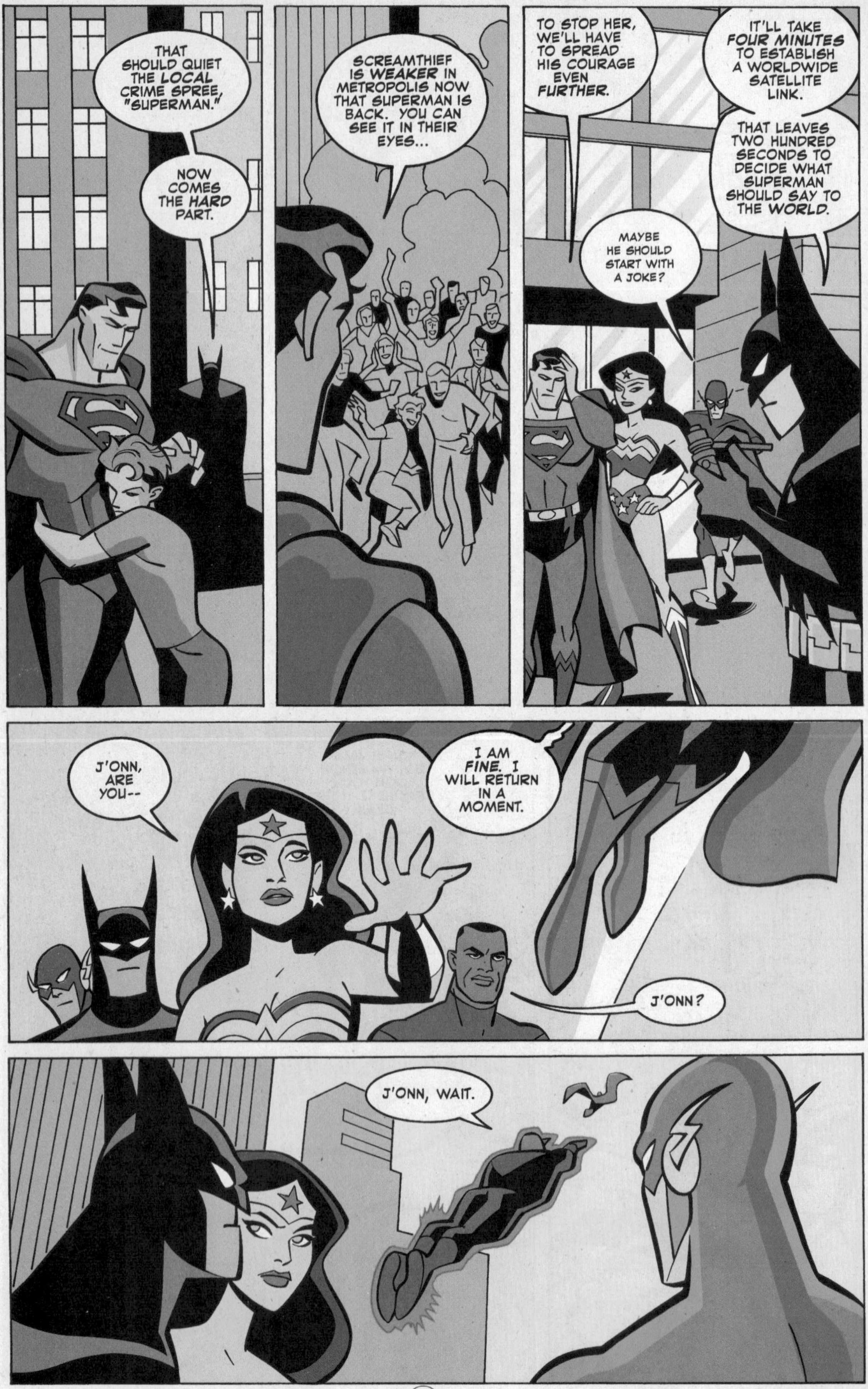
THAT SHOULD QUIET THE LOCAL CRIME SPREE, "SUPERMAN."
NOW COMES THE HARD PART.
SCREAMTHIEF IS WEAKER IN METROPOLIS NOW THAT SUPERMAN IS BACK. YOU CAN SEE IT IN THEIR EYES...
TO STOP HER, WE'LL HAVE TO SPREAD HIS COURAGE EVEN FURTHER.
IT'LL TAKE FOUR MINUTES TO ESTABLISH A WORLDWIDE SATELLITE LINK.
THAT LEAVES TWO HUNDRED SECONDS TO DECIDE WHAT SUPERMAN SHOULD SAY TO THE WORLD.
MAYBE HE SHOULD START WITH A JOKE?
J'ONN, ARE YOU--
I AM FINE. I WILL RETURN IN A MOMENT.
J'ONN?
J'ONN, WAIT.

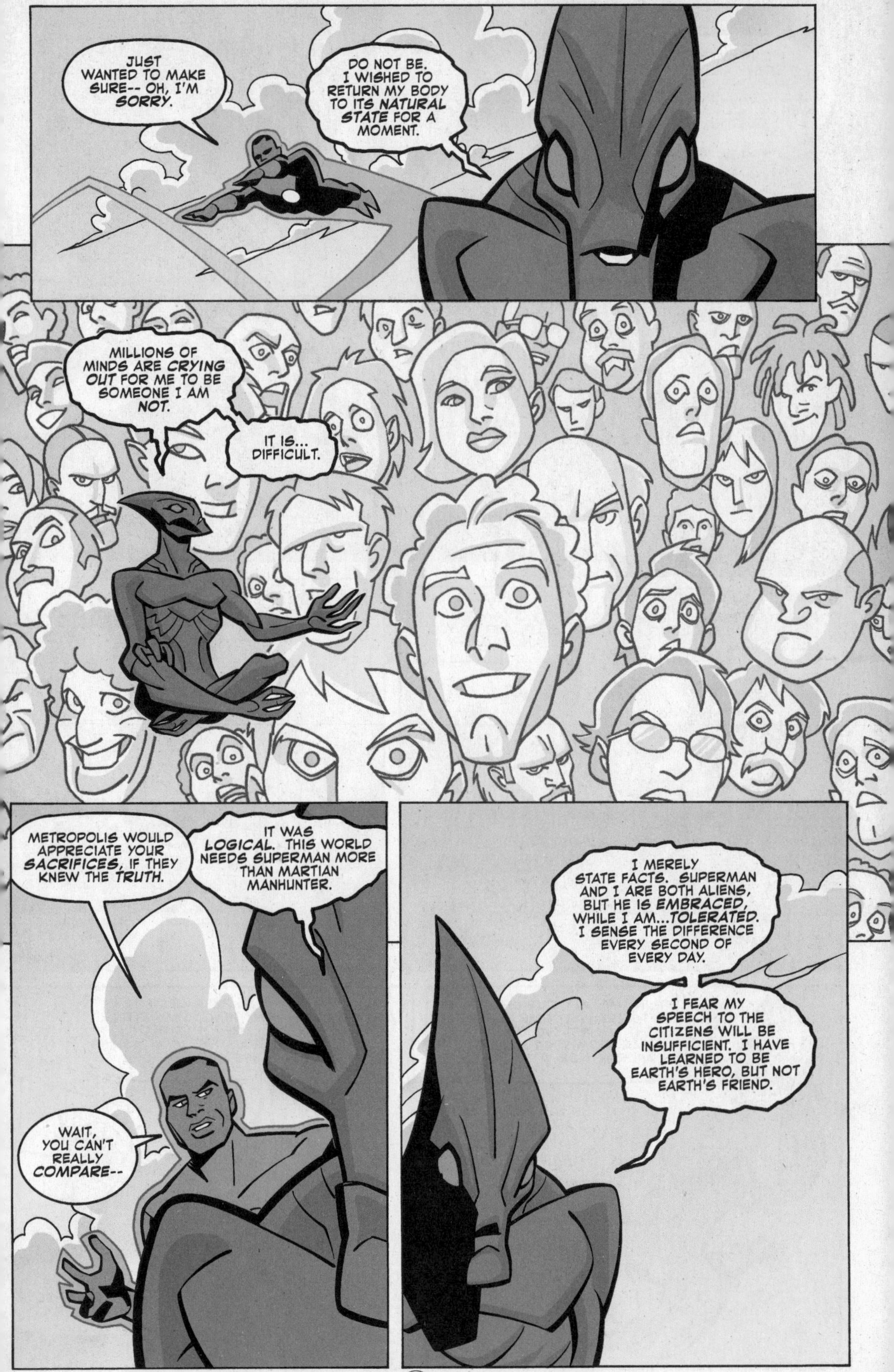
JUST WANTED TO MAKE SURE-- OH, I'M *SORRY*.
DO NOT BE. I WISHED TO RETURN MY BODY TO ITS *NATURAL STATE* FOR A MOMENT.
MILLIONS OF MINDS ARE *CRYING OUT* FOR ME TO BE SOMEONE I AM *NOT*.
IT IS... DIFFICULT.
METROPOLIS WOULD APPRECIATE YOUR *SACRIFICES*, IF THEY KNEW THE *TRUTH*.
IT WAS *LOGICAL*. THIS WORLD NEEDS SUPERMAN MORE THAN MARTIAN MANHUNTER.
WAIT, YOU CAN'T REALLY *COMPARE*--
I MERELY STATE FACTS. SUPERMAN AND I ARE BOTH ALIENS, BUT HE IS *EMBRACED*, WHILE I AM...*TOLERATED*. I SENSE THE DIFFERENCE EVERY SECOND OF EVERY DAY.
I FEAR MY SPEECH TO THE CITIZENS WILL BE INSUFFICIENT. I HAVE LEARNED TO BE EARTH'S HERO, BUT NOT EARTH'S FRIEND.

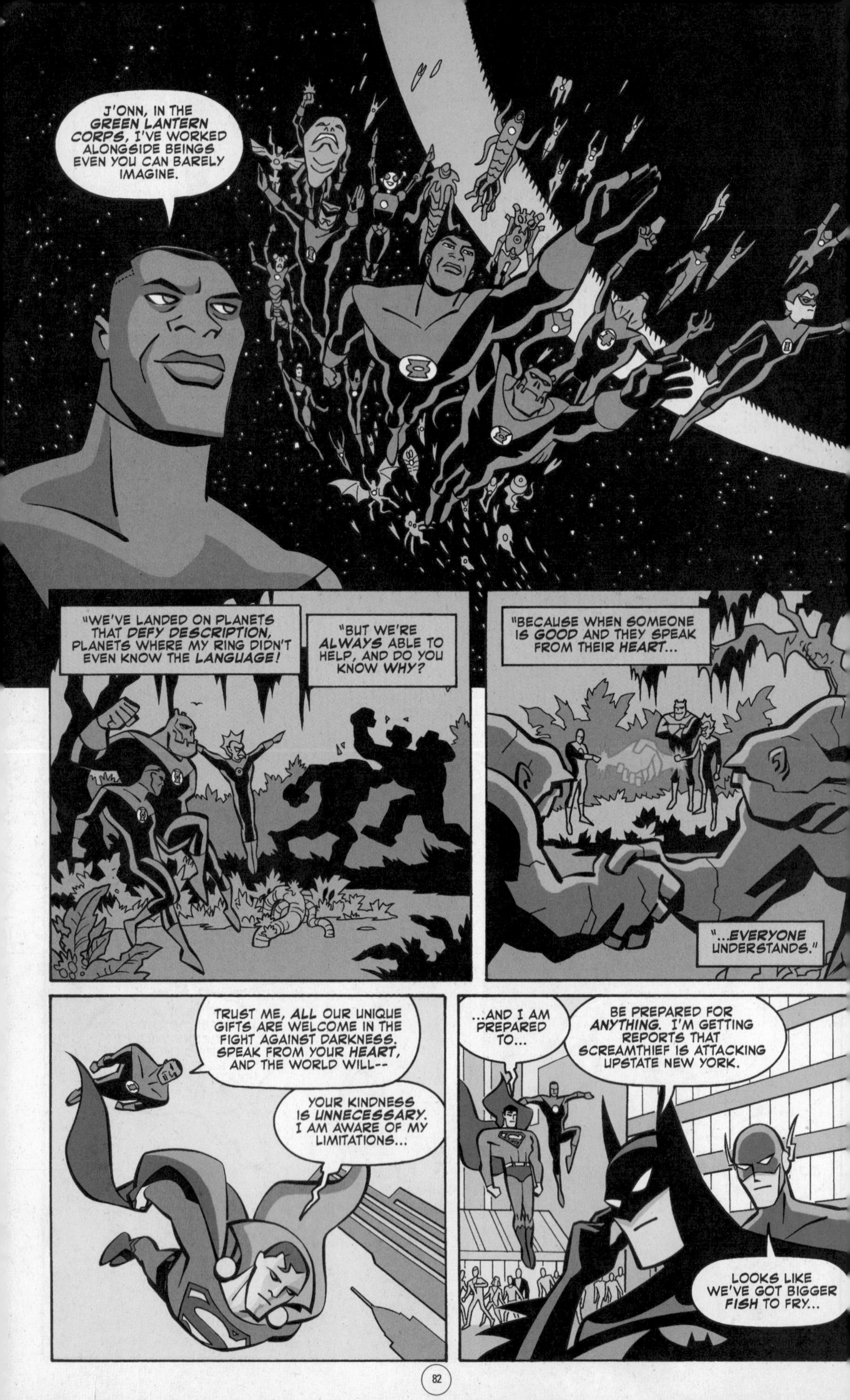

J'ONN, IN THE GREEN LANTERN CORPS, I'VE WORKED ALONGSIDE BEINGS EVEN YOU CAN BARELY IMAGINE.
"WE'VE LANDED ON PLANETS THAT DEFY DESCRIPTION, PLANETS WHERE MY RING DIDN'T EVEN KNOW THE LANGUAGE!
"BUT WE'RE ALWAYS ABLE TO HELP, AND DO YOU KNOW WHY?
"BECAUSE WHEN SOMEONE IS GOOD AND THEY SPEAK FROM THEIR HEART...
"...EVERYONE UNDERSTANDS."
TRUST ME, ALL OUR UNIQUE GIFTS ARE WELCOME IN THE FIGHT AGAINST DARKNESS. SPEAK FROM YOUR HEART, AND THE WORLD WILL--
YOUR KINDNESS IS UNNECESSARY. I AM AWARE OF MY LIMITATIONS...
...AND I AM PREPARED TO...
BE PREPARED FOR ANYTHING. I'M GETTING REPORTS THAT SCREAMTHIEF IS ATTACKING UPSTATE NEW YORK.
LOOKS LIKE WE'VE GOT BIGGER FISH TO FRY...

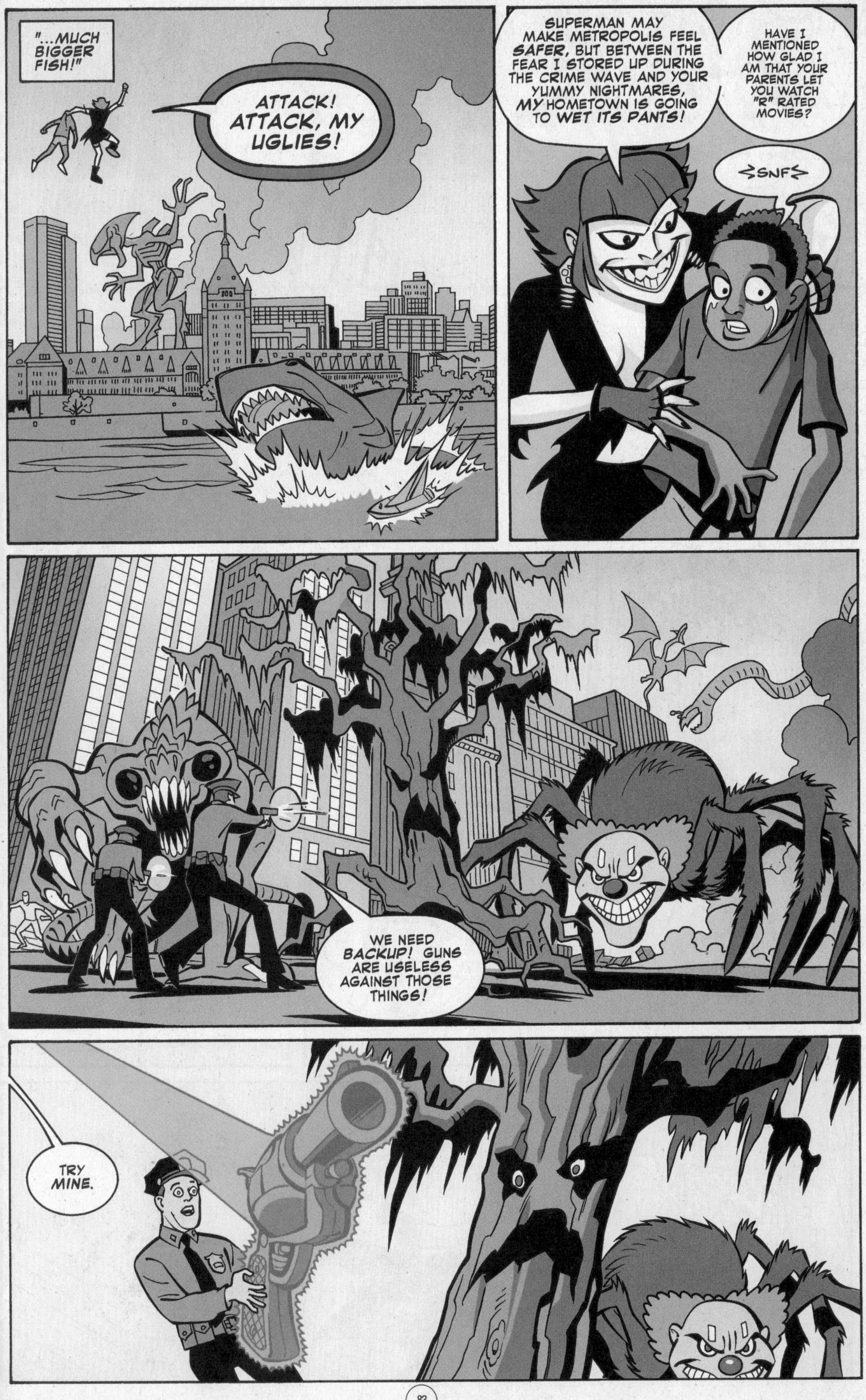
"...MUCH BIGGER FISH!"
ATTACK! ATTACK, MY UGLIES!
SUPERMAN MAY MAKE METROPOLIS FEEL SAFER, BUT BETWEEN THE FEAR I STORED UP DURING THE CRIME WAVE AND YOUR YUMMY NIGHTMARES, MY HOMETOWN IS GOING TO WET ITS PANTS!
HAVE I MENTIONED HOW GLAD I AM THAT YOUR PARENTS LET YOU WATCH "R" RATED MOVIES?
SNF
WE NEED BACKUP! GUNS ARE USELESS AGAINST THOSE THINGS!
TRY MINE.

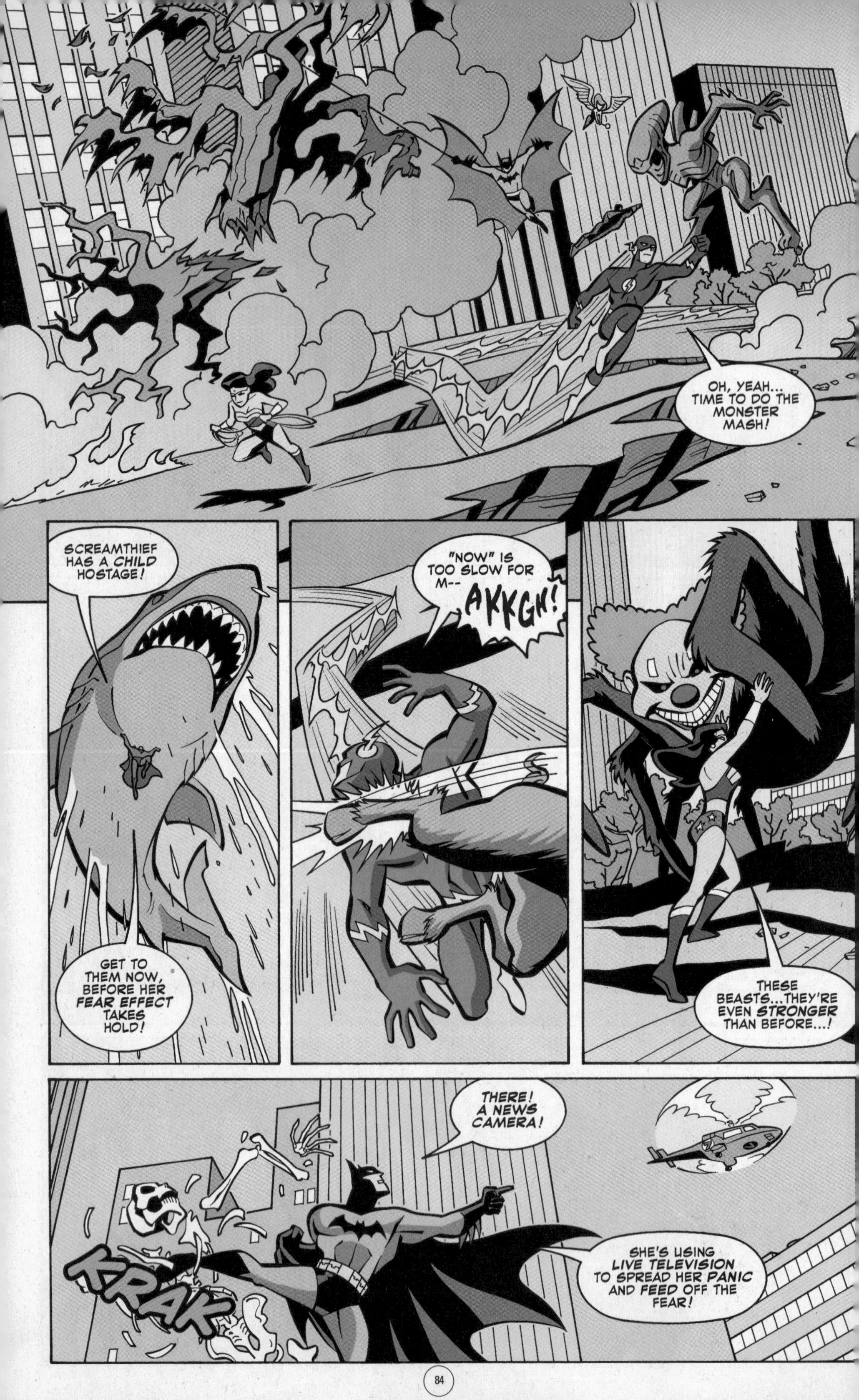
OH, YEAH... TIME TO DO THE MONSTER MASH!
SCREAMTHIEF HAS A *CHILD* HOSTAGE!
GET TO THEM NOW, BEFORE HER *FEAR EFFECT* TAKES HOLD!
"NOW" IS TOO SLOW FOR M--
AKKGH!
THESE BEASTS...THEY'RE EVEN *STRONGER* THAN BEFORE...!
THERE! A NEWS CAMERA!
KRAK
SHE'S USING *LIVE TELEVISION* TO SPREAD HER *PANIC* AND *FEED* OFF THE FEAR!

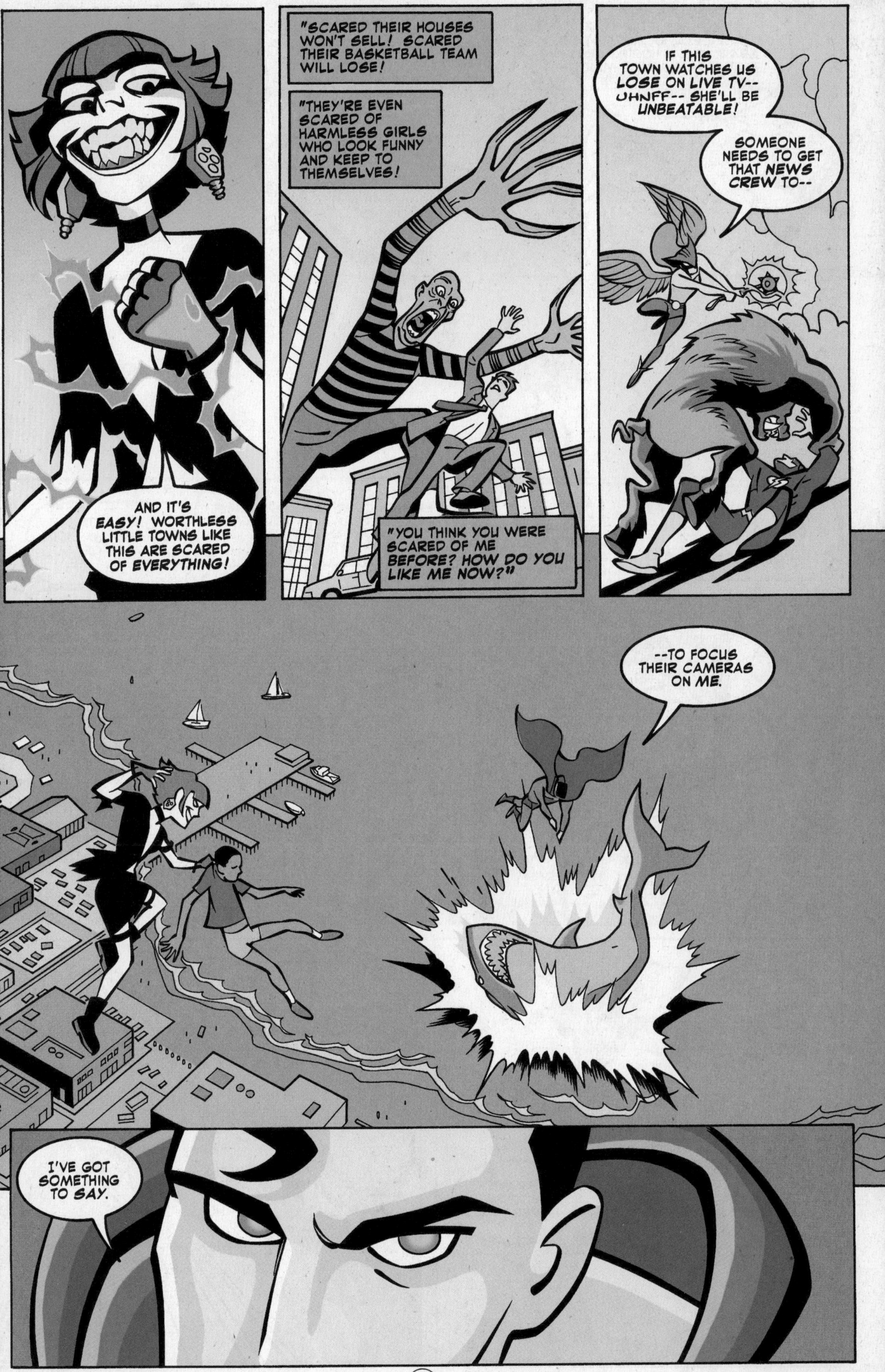
AND IT'S EASY! WORTHLESS LITTLE TOWNS LIKE THIS ARE SCARED OF EVERYTHING!
"SCARED THEIR HOUSES WON'T SELL! SCARED THEIR BASKETBALL TEAM WILL LOSE!
"THEY'RE EVEN SCARED OF HARMLESS GIRLS WHO LOOK FUNNY AND KEEP TO THEMSELVES!
"YOU THINK YOU WERE SCARED OF ME BEFORE? HOW DO YOU LIKE ME NOW?"
IF THIS TOWN WATCHES US LOSE ON LIVE TV-- UHNFF-- SHE'LL BE UNBEATABLE!
SOMEONE NEEDS TO GET THAT NEWS CREW TO--
--TO FOCUS THEIR CAMERAS ON ME.
I'VE GOT SOMETHING TO SAY.

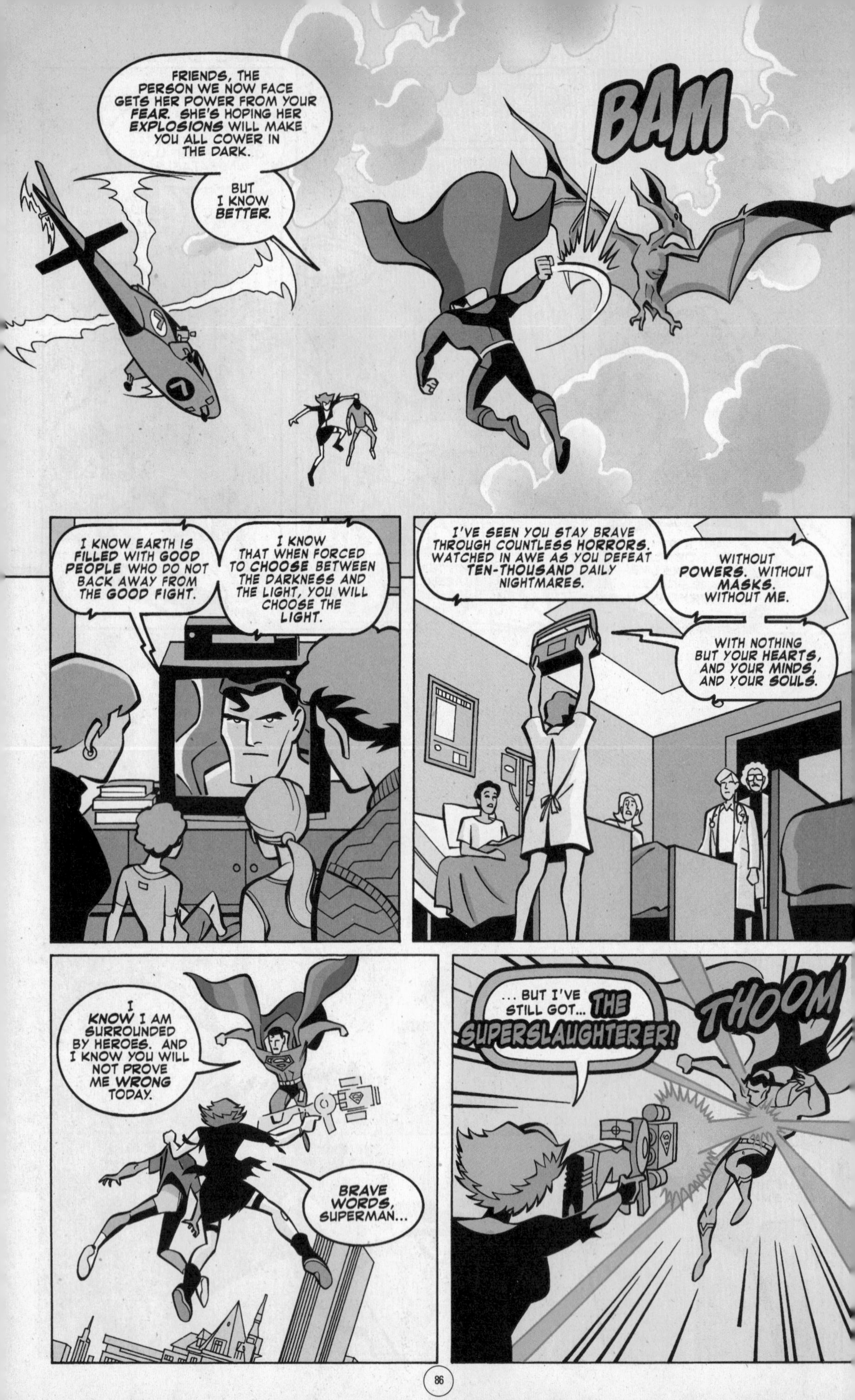
FRIENDS, THE PERSON WE NOW FACE GETS HER POWER FROM YOUR FEAR. SHE'S HOPING HER EXPLOSIONS WILL MAKE YOU ALL COWER IN THE DARK.
BUT I KNOW BETTER.
BAM
I KNOW EARTH IS FILLED WITH GOOD PEOPLE WHO DO NOT BACK AWAY FROM THE GOOD FIGHT.
I KNOW THAT WHEN FORCED TO CHOOSE BETWEEN THE DARKNESS AND THE LIGHT, YOU WILL CHOOSE THE LIGHT.
I'VE SEEN YOU STAY BRAVE THROUGH COUNTLESS HORRORS. WATCHED IN AWE AS YOU DEFEAT TEN-THOUSAND DAILY NIGHTMARES.
WITHOUT POWERS. WITHOUT MASKS. WITHOUT ME.
WITH NOTHING BUT YOUR HEARTS, AND YOUR MINDS, AND YOUR SOULS.
I KNOW I AM SURROUNDED BY HEROES. AND I KNOW YOU WILL NOT PROVE ME WRONG TODAY.
BRAVE WORDS, SUPERMAN...
... BUT I'VE STILL GOT... THE SUPERSLAUGHTERER!
THOOM

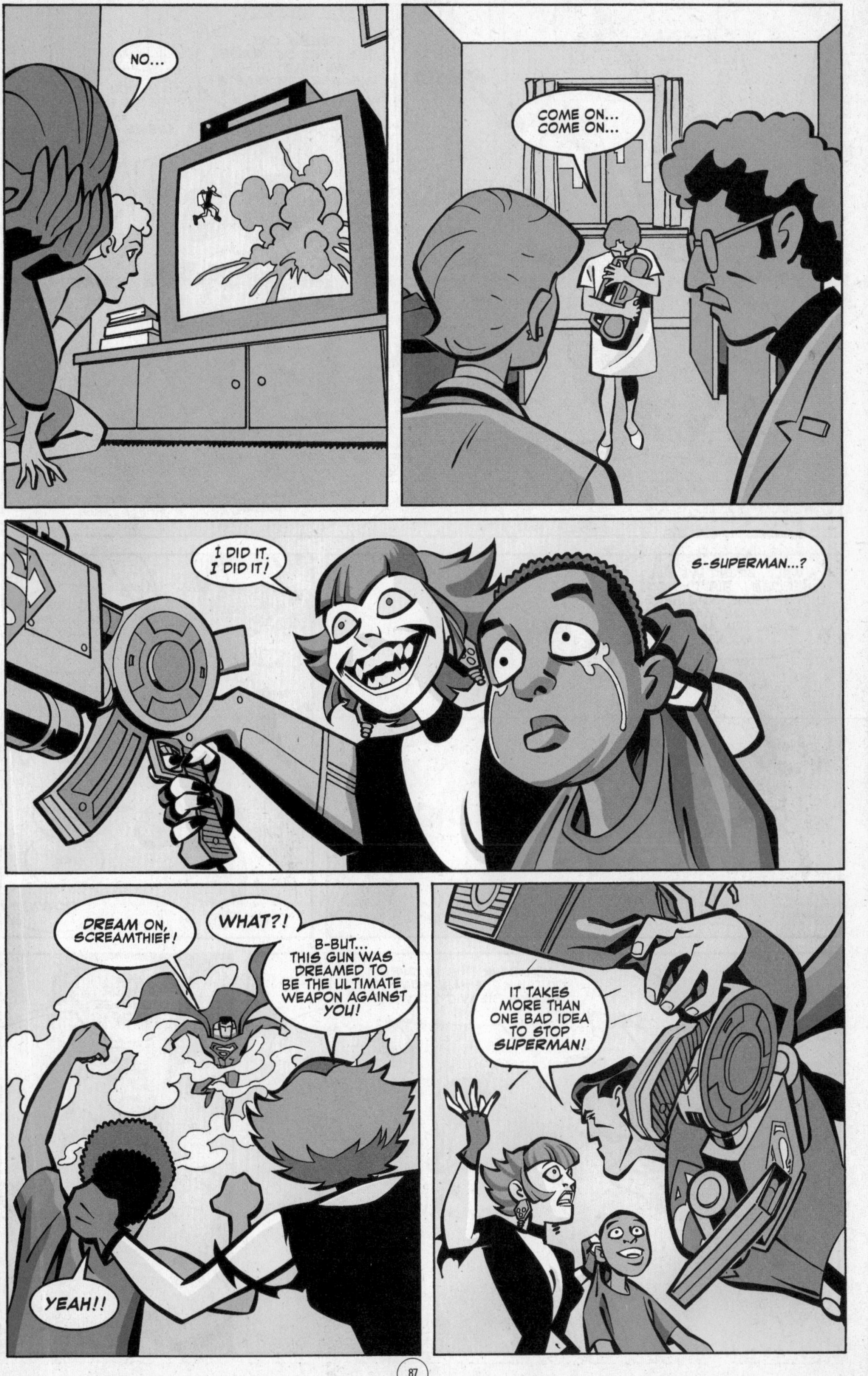
NO...
COME ON... COME ON...
I DID IT. I DID IT!
S-SUPERMAN...?
DREAM ON, SCREAMTHIEF!
WHAT?!
B-BUT... THIS GUN WAS DREAMED TO BE THE ULTIMATE WEAPON AGAINST YOU!
YEAH!!
IT TAKES MORE THAN ONE BAD IDEA TO STOP SUPERMAN!

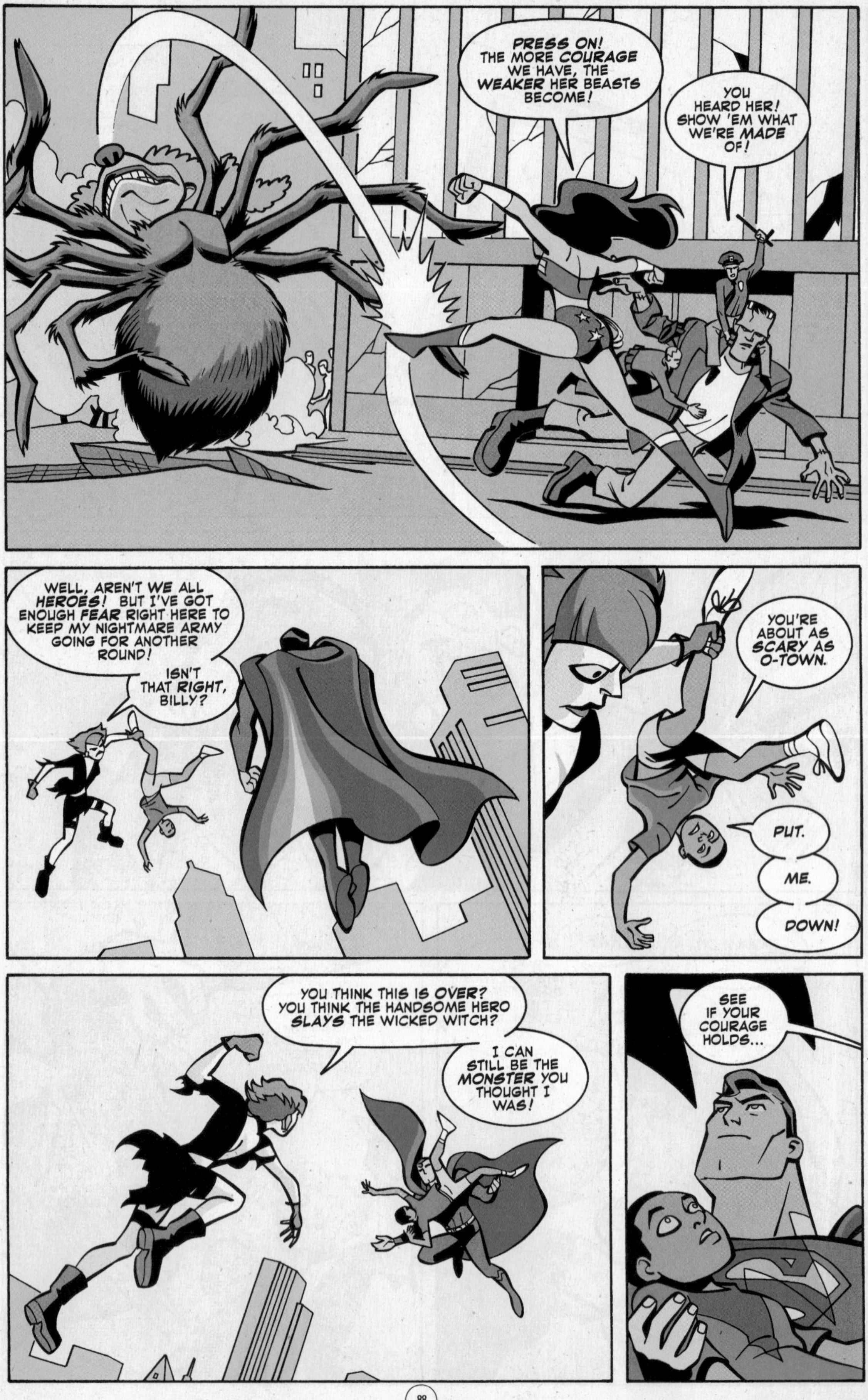
PRESS ON! THE MORE COURAGE WE HAVE, THE WEAKER HER BEASTS BECOME!
YOU HEARD HER! SHOW 'EM WHAT WE'RE MADE OF!
WELL, AREN'T WE ALL HEROES! BUT I'VE GOT ENOUGH FEAR RIGHT HERE TO KEEP MY NIGHTMARE ARMY GOING FOR ANOTHER ROUND!
ISN'T THAT RIGHT, BILLY?
YOU'RE ABOUT AS SCARY AS O-TOWN.
PUT.
ME.
DOWN!
YOU THINK THIS IS OVER? YOU THINK THE HANDSOME HERO SLAYS THE WICKED WITCH?
I CAN STILL BE THE MONSTER YOU THOUGHT I WAS!
SEE IF YOUR COURAGE HOLDS...

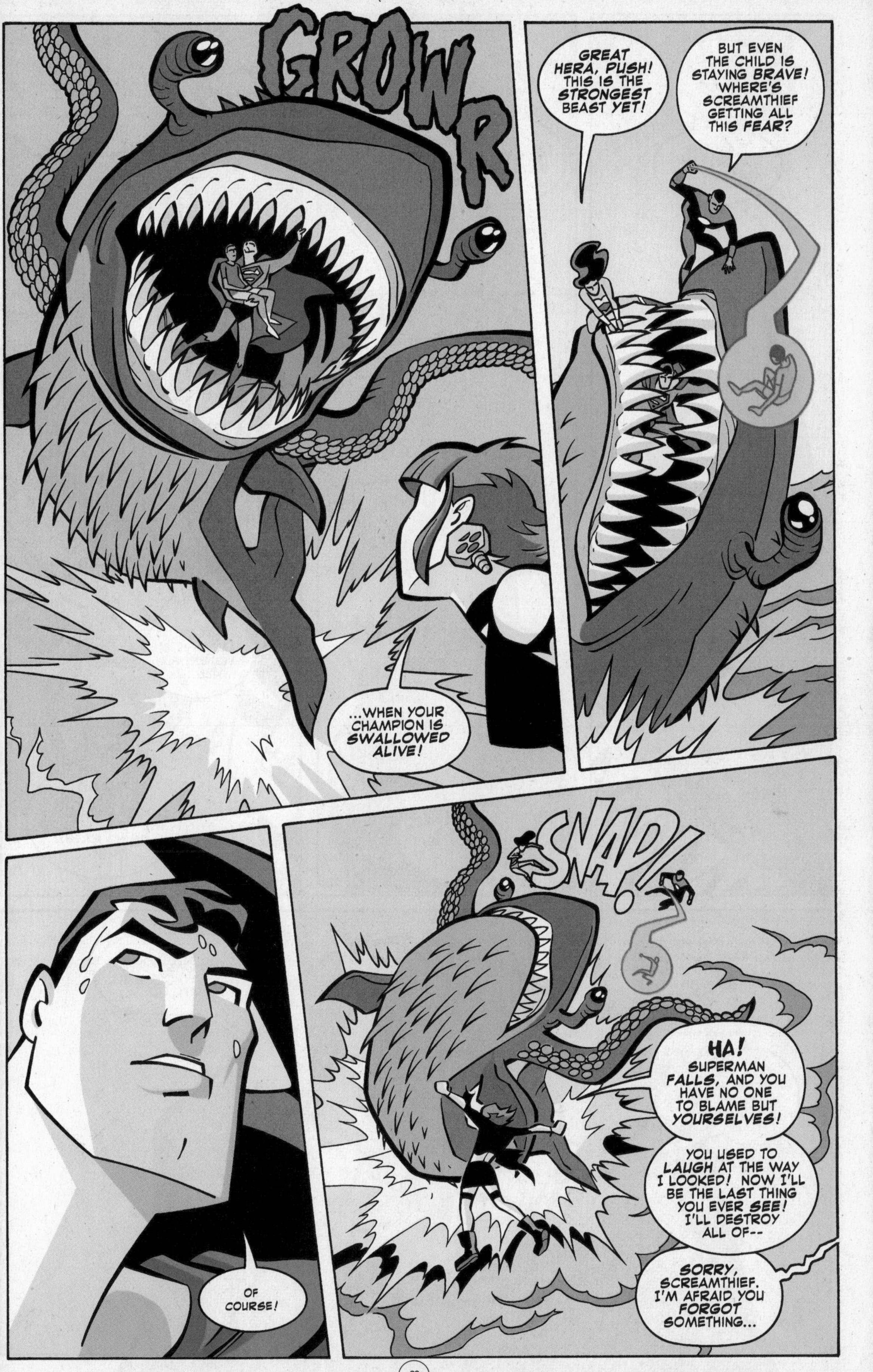
GROWR
GREAT HERA, PUSH! THIS IS THE STRONGEST BEAST YET!
BUT EVEN THE CHILD IS STAYING BRAVE! WHERE'S SCREAMTHIEF GETTING ALL THIS FEAR?
...WHEN YOUR CHAMPION IS SWALLOWED ALIVE!
OF COURSE!
SNAP!
HA! SUPERMAN FALLS, AND YOU HAVE NO ONE TO BLAME BUT YOURSELVES!
YOU USED TO LAUGH AT THE WAY I LOOKED! NOW I'LL BE THE LAST THING YOU EVER SEE! I'LL DESTROY ALL OF--
SORRY, SCREAMTHIEF. I'M AFRAID YOU FORGOT SOMETHING...

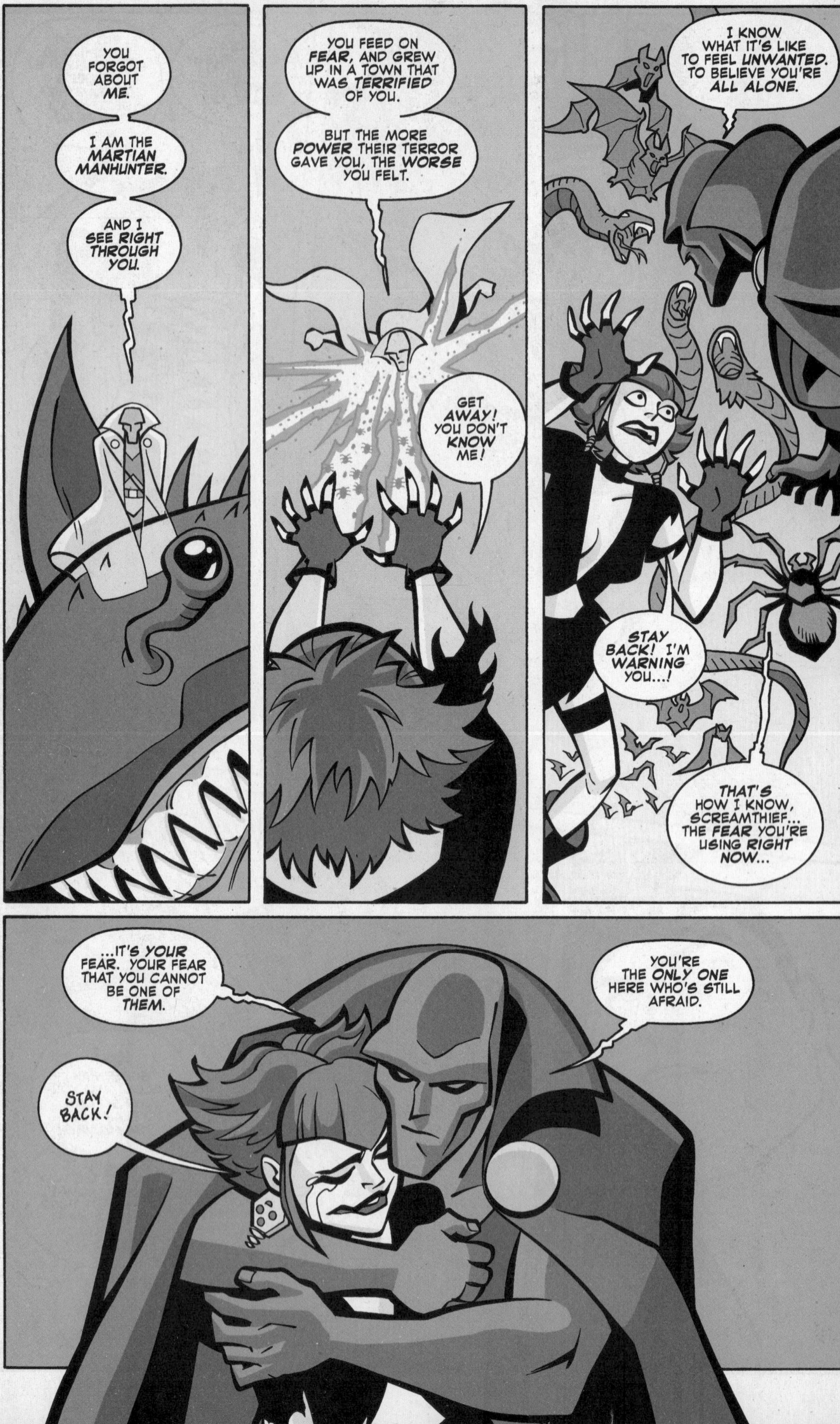
YOU FORGOT ABOUT ME.
I AM THE MARTIAN MANHUNTER.
AND I SEE RIGHT THROUGH YOU.
YOU FEED ON FEAR, AND GREW UP IN A TOWN THAT WAS TERRIFIED OF YOU.
BUT THE MORE POWER THEIR TERROR GAVE YOU, THE WORSE YOU FELT.
GET AWAY! YOU DON'T KNOW ME!
I KNOW WHAT IT'S LIKE TO FEEL UNWANTED. TO BELIEVE YOU'RE ALL ALONE.
STAY BACK! I'M WARNING YOU...!
THAT'S HOW I KNOW, SCREAMTHIEF... THE FEAR YOU'RE USING RIGHT NOW...
...IT'S YOUR FEAR. YOUR FEAR THAT YOU CANNOT BE ONE OF THEM.
STAY BACK!
YOU'RE THE ONLY ONE HERE WHO'S STILL AFRAID.

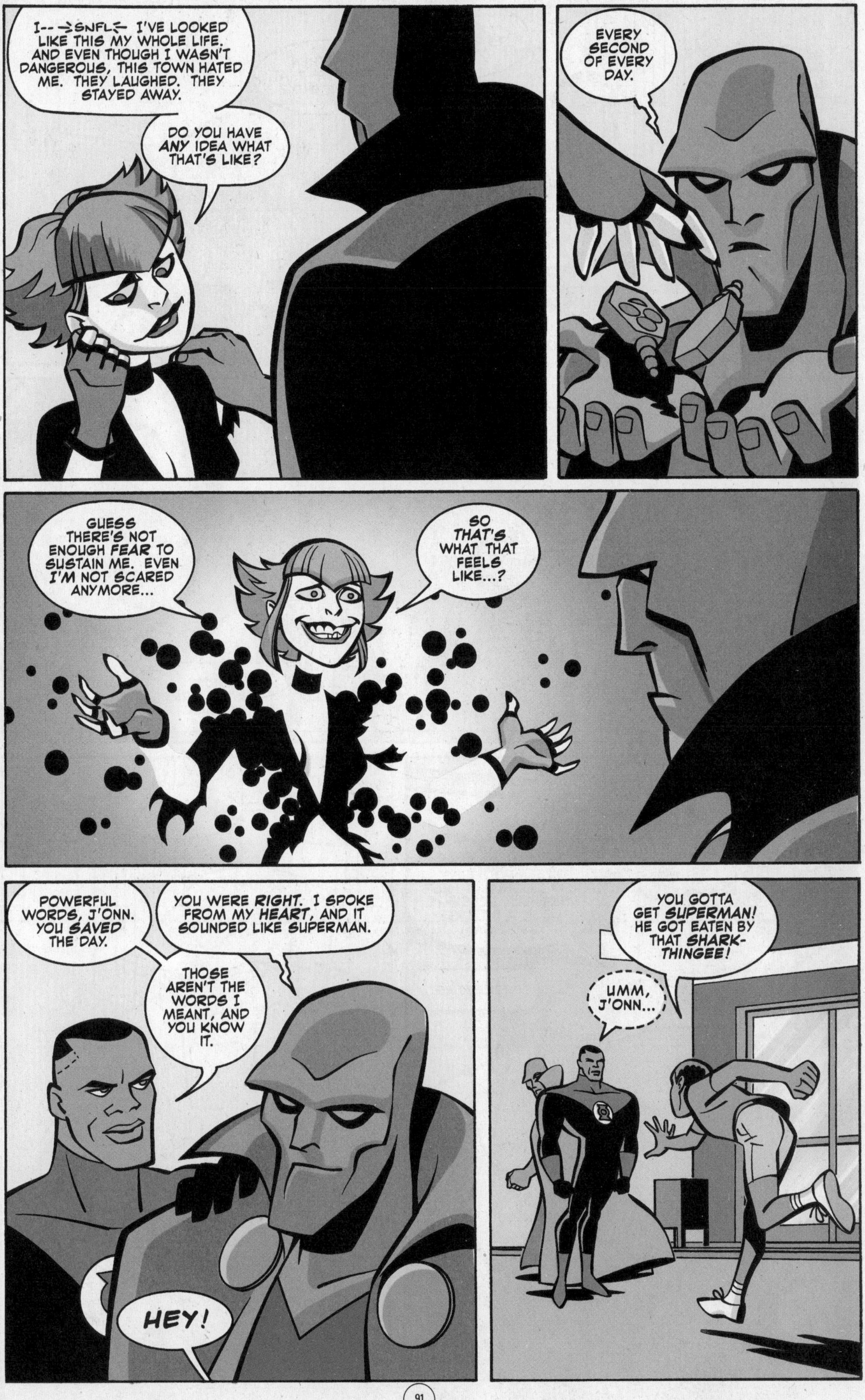

I-- ⇝SNFL⇜ I'VE LOOKED LIKE THIS MY WHOLE LIFE. AND EVEN THOUGH I WASN'T DANGEROUS, THIS TOWN HATED ME. THEY LAUGHED. THEY STAYED AWAY.
DO YOU HAVE ANY IDEA WHAT THAT'S LIKE?
EVERY SECOND OF EVERY DAY.
GUESS THERE'S NOT ENOUGH FEAR TO SUSTAIN ME. EVEN I'M NOT SCARED ANYMORE...
SO THAT'S WHAT THAT FEELS LIKE...?
POWERFUL WORDS, J'ONN. YOU SAVED THE DAY.
YOU WERE RIGHT. I SPOKE FROM MY HEART, AND IT SOUNDED LIKE SUPERMAN.
THOSE AREN'T THE WORDS I MEANT, AND YOU KNOW IT.
HEY!
YOU GOTTA GET SUPERMAN! HE GOT EATEN BY THAT SHARK-THINGEE!
UMM, J'ONN...

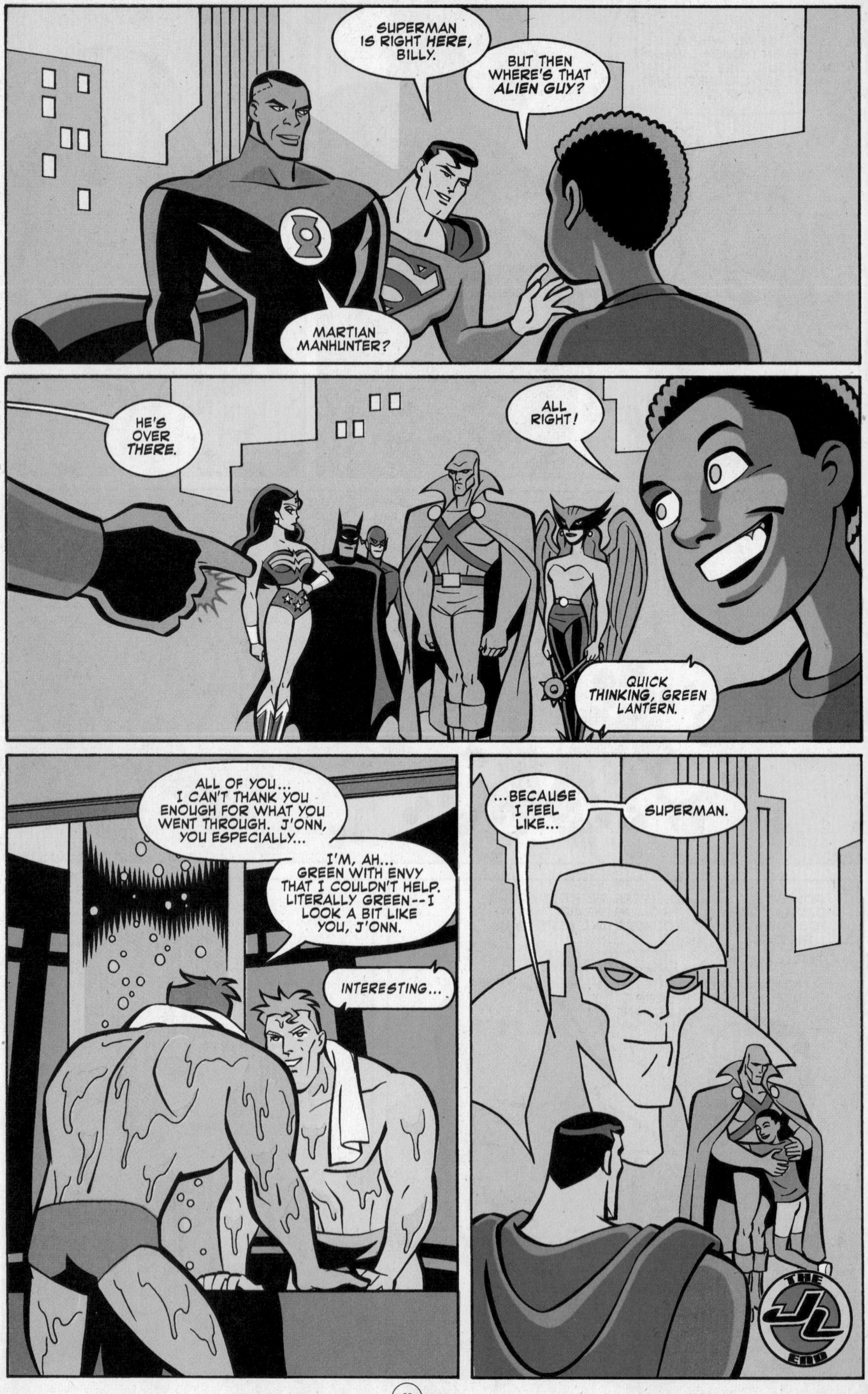
SUPERMAN IS RIGHT HERE, BILLY.
BUT THEN WHERE'S THAT ALIEN GUY?
MARTIAN MANHUNTER?
HE'S OVER THERE.
ALL RIGHT!
QUICK THINKING, GREEN LANTERN.
ALL OF YOU... I CAN'T THANK YOU ENOUGH FOR WHAT YOU WENT THROUGH. J'ONN, YOU ESPECIALLY...
I'M, AH... GREEN WITH ENVY THAT I COULDN'T HELP. LITERALLY GREEN--I LOOK A BIT LIKE YOU, J'ONN.
INTERESTING...
...BECAUSE I FEEL LIKE...
SUPERMAN.
THE END

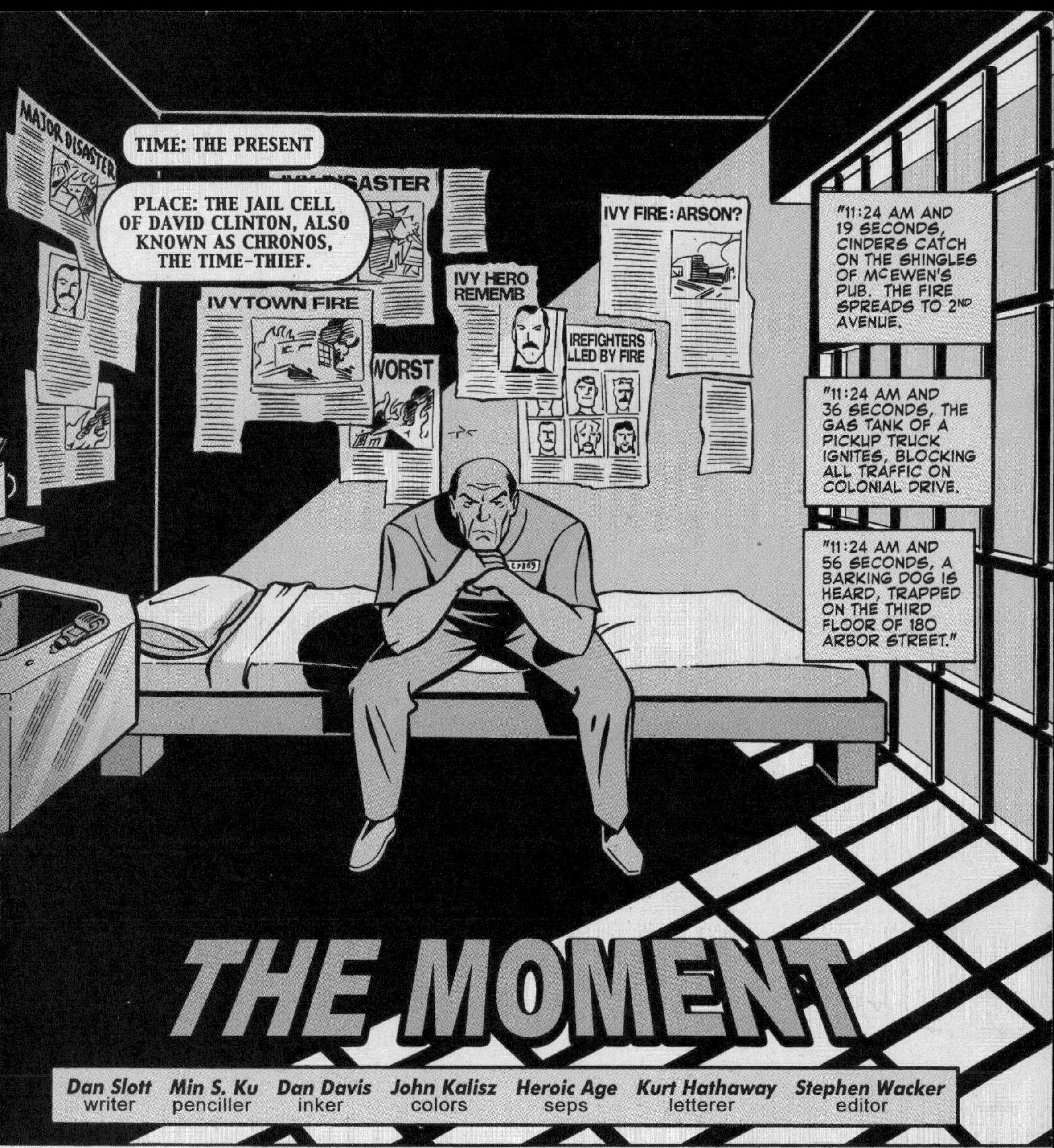
TIME: THE PRESENT
PLACE: THE JAIL CELL OF DAVID CLINTON, ALSO KNOWN AS CHRONOS, THE TIME-THIEF.
MAJOR DISASTER
IVYTOWN FIRE
IVY HERO REMEMB
IVY FIRE: ARSON?
WORST
IREFIGHTERS LLED BY FIRE
"11:24 AM AND 19 SECONDS, CINDERS CATCH ON THE SHINGLES OF McEWEN'S PUB. THE FIRE SPREADS TO 2ND AVENUE.
"11:24 AM AND 36 SECONDS, THE GAS TANK OF A PICKUP TRUCK IGNITES, BLOCKING ALL TRAFFIC ON COLONIAL DRIVE.
"11:24 AM AND 56 SECONDS, A BARKING DOG IS HEARD, TRAPPED ON THE THIRD FLOOR OF 180 ARBOR STREET."
THE MOMENT
Dan Slott writer
Min S. Ku penciller
Dan Davis inker
John Kalisz colors
Heroic Age seps
Kurt Hathaway letterer
Stephen Wacker editor

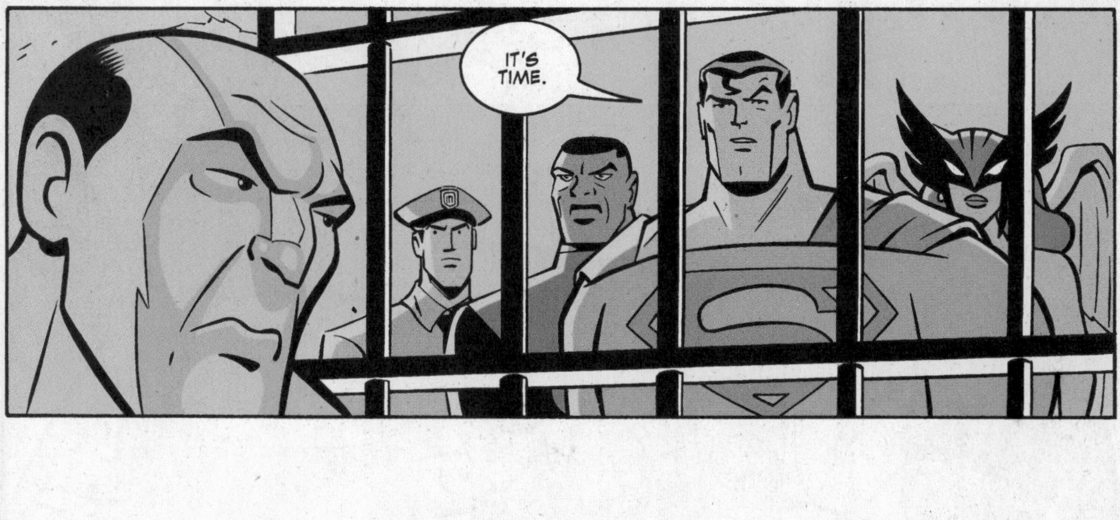
IT'S TIME.

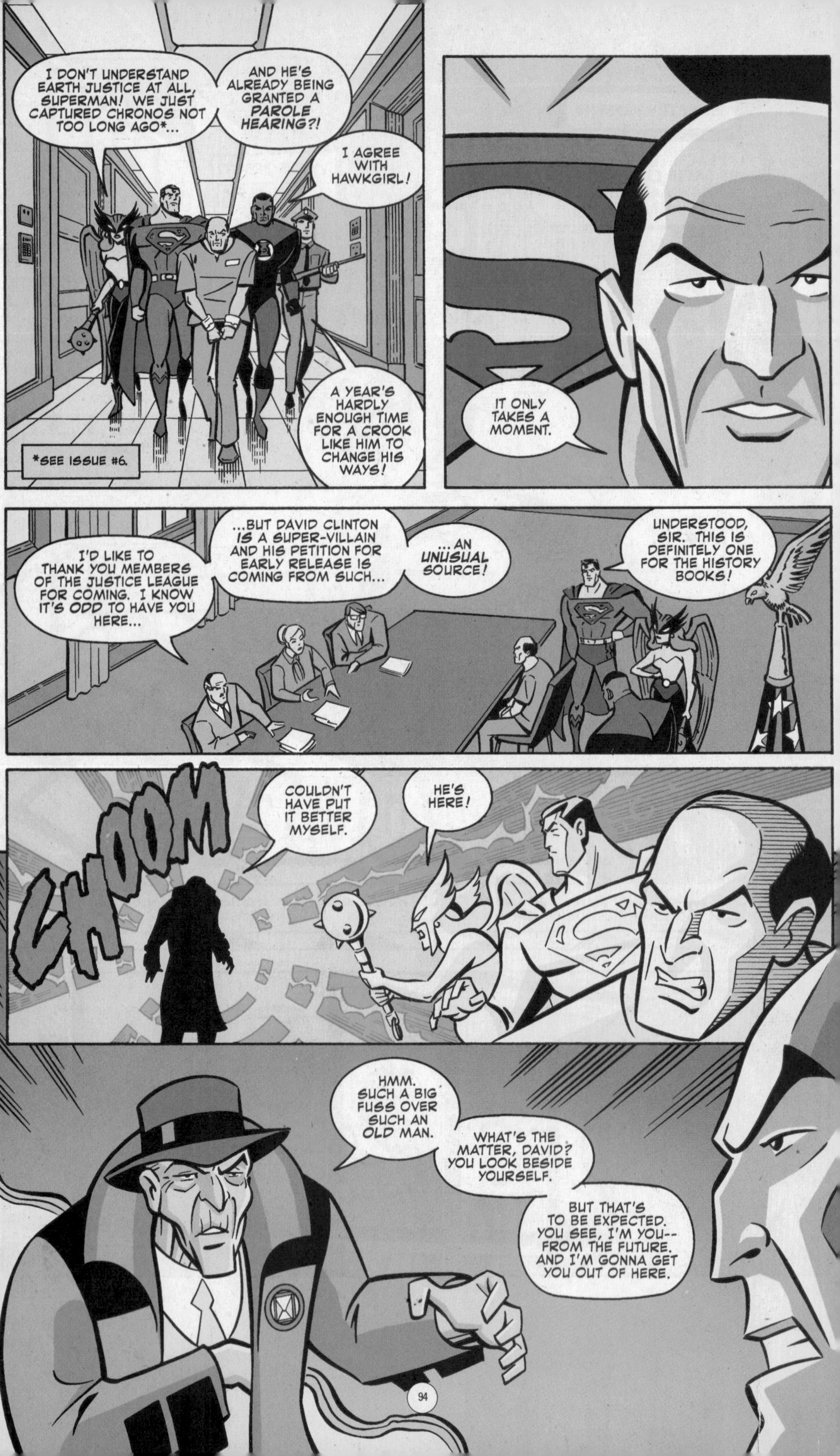
I DON'T UNDERSTAND EARTH JUSTICE AT ALL, SUPERMAN! WE JUST CAPTURED CHRONOS NOT TOO LONG AGO*...
AND HE'S ALREADY BEING GRANTED A PAROLE HEARING?!
I AGREE WITH HAWKGIRL!
A YEAR'S HARDLY ENOUGH TIME FOR A CROOK LIKE HIM TO CHANGE HIS WAYS!
*SEE ISSUE #6.
IT ONLY TAKES A MOMENT.
I'D LIKE TO THANK YOU MEMBERS OF THE JUSTICE LEAGUE FOR COMING. I KNOW IT'S ODD TO HAVE YOU HERE...
...BUT DAVID CLINTON IS A SUPER-VILLAIN AND HIS PETITION FOR EARLY RELEASE IS COMING FROM SUCH...
...AN UNUSUAL SOURCE!
UNDERSTOOD, SIR. THIS IS DEFINITELY ONE FOR THE HISTORY BOOKS!
CHOOM
COULDN'T HAVE PUT IT BETTER MYSELF.
HE'S HERE!
HMM. SUCH A BIG FUSS OVER SUCH AN OLD MAN.
WHAT'S THE MATTER, DAVID? YOU LOOK BESIDE YOURSELF.
BUT THAT'S TO BE EXPECTED. YOU SEE, I'M YOU--FROM THE FUTURE. AND I'M GONNA GET YOU OUT OF HERE.

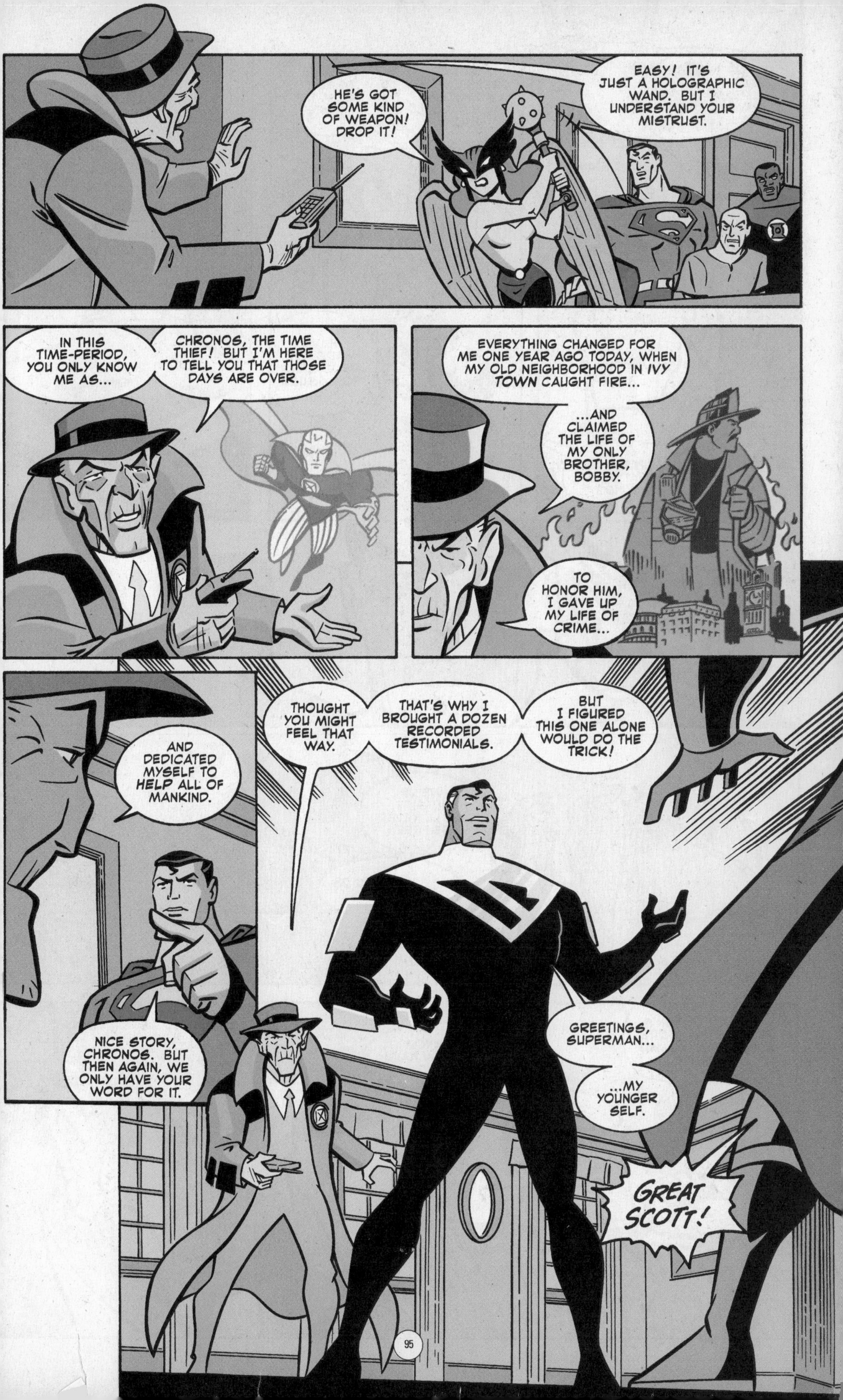
HE'S GOT SOME KIND OF WEAPON! DROP IT!
EASY! IT'S JUST A HOLOGRAPHIC WAND. BUT I UNDERSTAND YOUR MISTRUST.
IN THIS TIME-PERIOD, YOU ONLY KNOW ME AS...
CHRONOS, THE TIME THIEF! BUT I'M HERE TO TELL YOU THAT THOSE DAYS ARE OVER.
EVERYTHING CHANGED FOR ME ONE YEAR AGO TODAY, WHEN MY OLD NEIGHBORHOOD IN IVY TOWN CAUGHT FIRE...
...AND CLAIMED THE LIFE OF MY ONLY BROTHER, BOBBY.
TO HONOR HIM, I GAVE UP MY LIFE OF CRIME...
AND DEDICATED MYSELF TO HELP ALL OF MANKIND.
NICE STORY, CHRONOS. BUT THEN AGAIN, WE ONLY HAVE YOUR WORD FOR IT.
THOUGHT YOU MIGHT FEEL THAT WAY.
THAT'S WHY I BROUGHT A DOZEN RECORDED TESTIMONIALS.
BUT I FIGURED THIS ONE ALONE WOULD DO THE TRICK!
GREETINGS, SUPERMAN...
...MY YOUNGER SELF.
GREAT SCOTT!

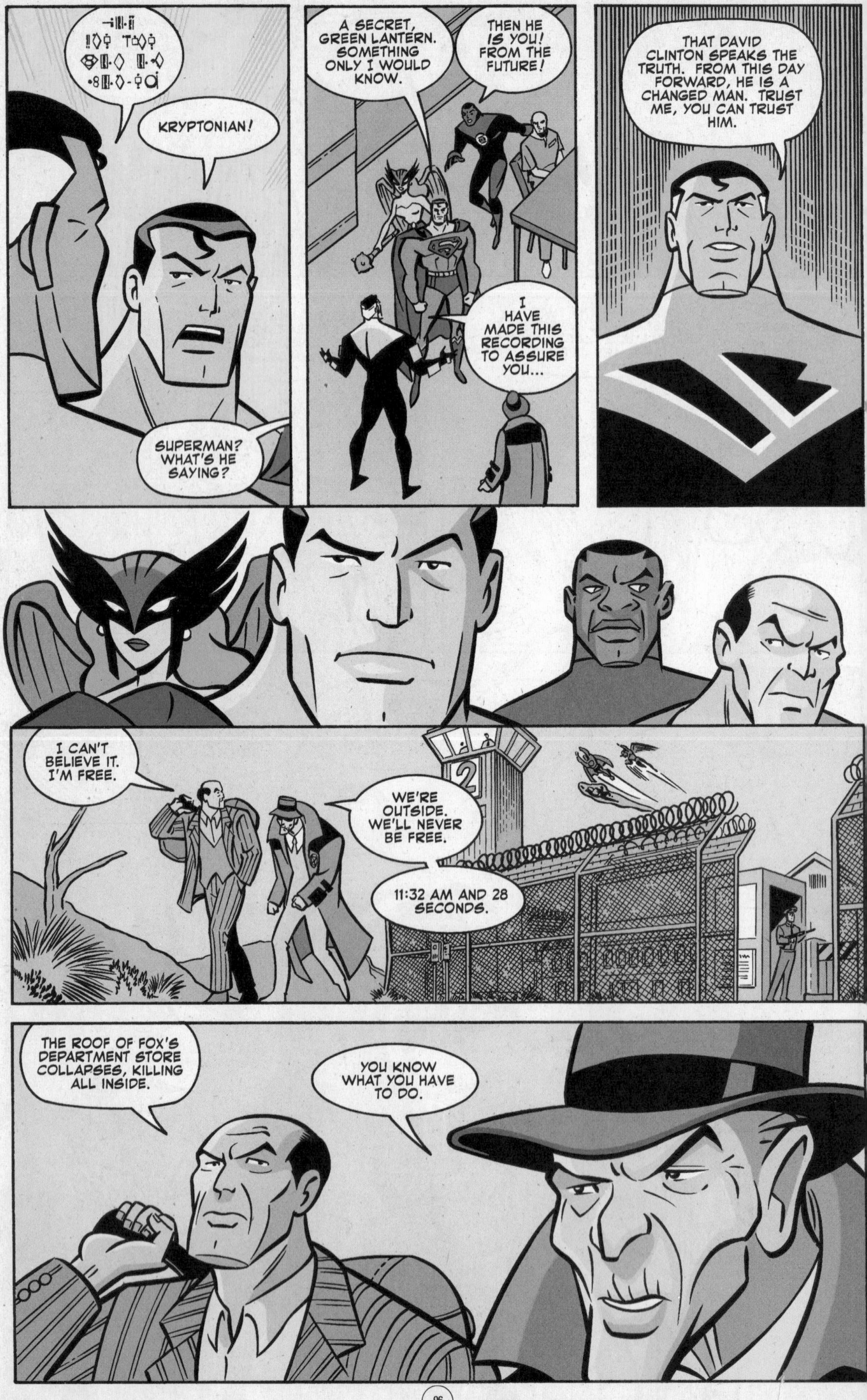
KRYPTONIAN!
SUPERMAN? WHAT'S HE SAYING?
A SECRET, GREEN LANTERN. SOMETHING ONLY I WOULD KNOW.
THEN HE IS YOU! FROM THE FUTURE!
I HAVE MADE THIS RECORDING TO ASSURE YOU...
THAT DAVID CLINTON SPEAKS THE TRUTH. FROM THIS DAY FORWARD, HE IS A CHANGED MAN. TRUST ME, YOU CAN TRUST HIM.
I CAN'T BELIEVE IT. I'M FREE.
WE'RE OUTSIDE. WE'LL NEVER BE FREE.
11:32 AM AND 28 SECONDS.
THE ROOF OF FOX'S DEPARTMENT STORE COLLAPSES, KILLING ALL INSIDE.
YOU KNOW WHAT YOU HAVE TO DO.

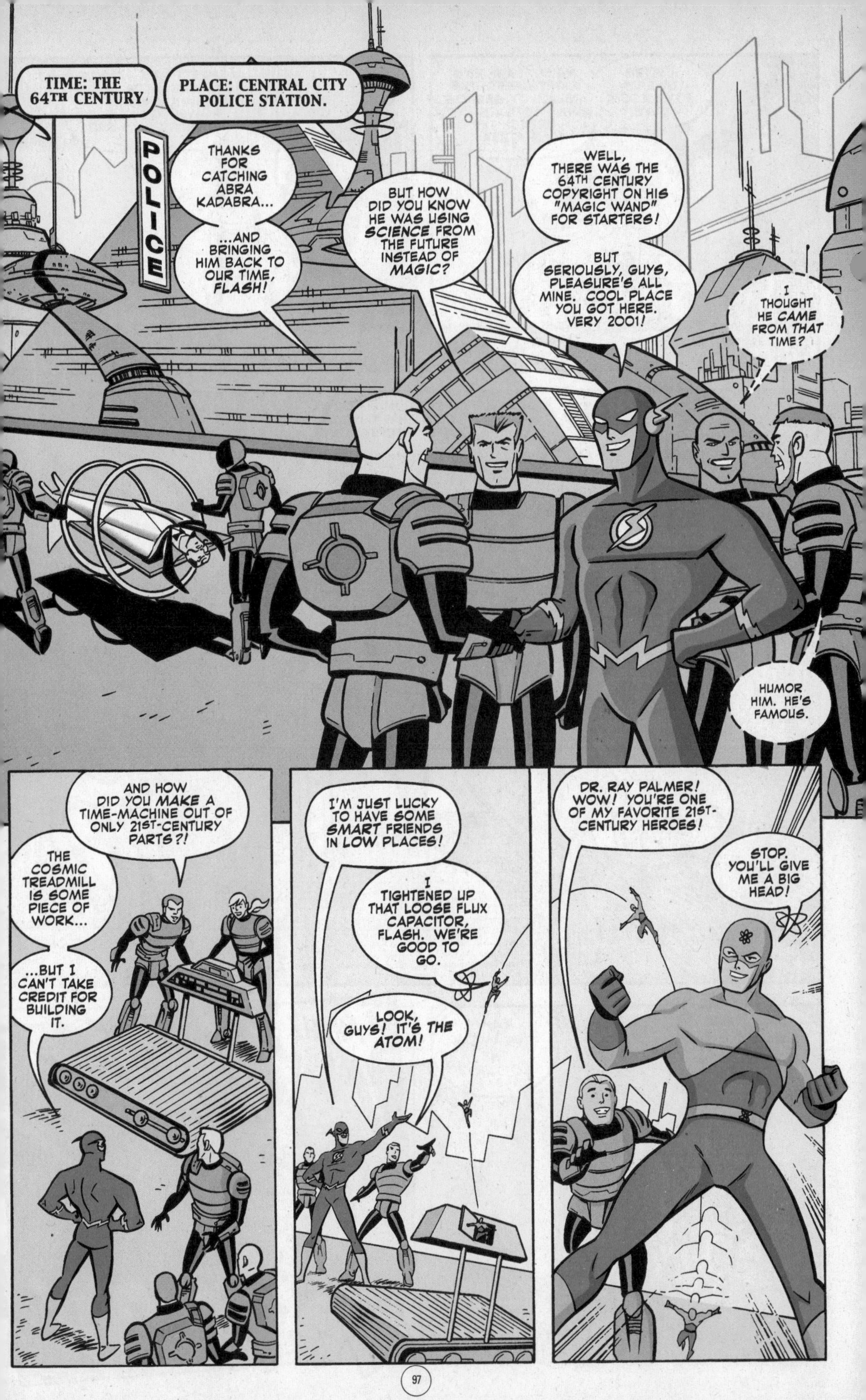
TIME: THE 64TH CENTURY
PLACE: CENTRAL CITY POLICE STATION.
POLICE
THANKS FOR CATCHING ABRA KADABRA...
...AND BRINGING HIM BACK TO OUR TIME, FLASH!
BUT HOW DID YOU KNOW HE WAS USING SCIENCE FROM THE FUTURE INSTEAD OF MAGIC?
WELL, THERE WAS THE 64TH CENTURY COPYRIGHT ON HIS "MAGIC WAND" FOR STARTERS!
BUT SERIOUSLY, GUYS, PLEASURE'S ALL MINE. COOL PLACE YOU GOT HERE. VERY 2001!
I THOUGHT HE CAME FROM THAT TIME?
HUMOR HIM. HE'S FAMOUS.
AND HOW DID YOU MAKE A TIME-MACHINE OUT OF ONLY 21ST-CENTURY PARTS?!
THE COSMIC TREADMILL IS SOME PIECE OF WORK...
...BUT I CAN'T TAKE CREDIT FOR BUILDING IT.
I'M JUST LUCKY TO HAVE SOME SMART FRIENDS IN LOW PLACES!
I TIGHTENED UP THAT LOOSE FLUX CAPACITOR, FLASH. WE'RE GOOD TO GO.
LOOK, GUYS! IT'S THE ATOM!
DR. RAY PALMER! WOW! YOU'RE ONE OF MY FAVORITE 21ST-CENTURY HEROES!
STOP. YOU'LL GIVE ME A BIG HEAD!

BETTER GIVE US SOME ROOM, GUYS.

WHEN FLASH HITS LIGHT-SPEED, THE RELATIVITY SERVOS WILL ACTIVATE AND BREACH THE TIME-STREAM!

PRETTY BIG WORDS THERE, ATOM, FOR SOMETHING THAT'S POWERED LIKE FRED FLINTSTONE'S CAR.

WALLY, DON'T EMBARRASS ME IN FRONT OF THE FUTURE MEN.

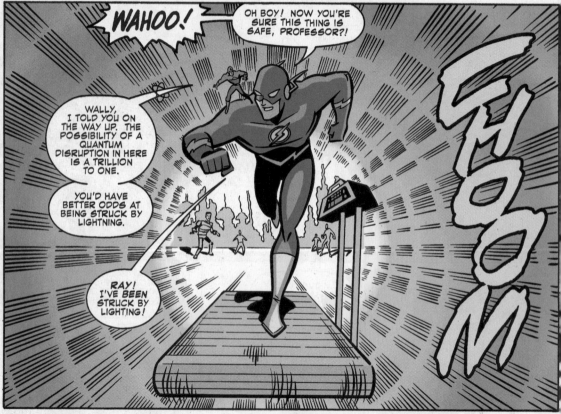

WAHOO!

OH BOY! NOW YOU'RE SURE THIS THING IS SAFE, PROFESSOR?!

WALLY, I TOLD YOU ON THE WAY UP. THE POSSIBILITY OF A QUANTUM DISRUPTION IN HERE IS A TRILLION TO ONE.

YOU'D HAVE BETTER ODDS AT BEING STRUCK BY LIGHTNING.

RAY! I'VE BEEN STRUCK BY LIGHTING!

GHOOM

OKAY, THEN YOU'D HAVE A BETTER CHANCE AT WINNING THE LOTTERY.

RAY! I'VE WON THE LOTTERY!

AHHH!

KRAKKOW

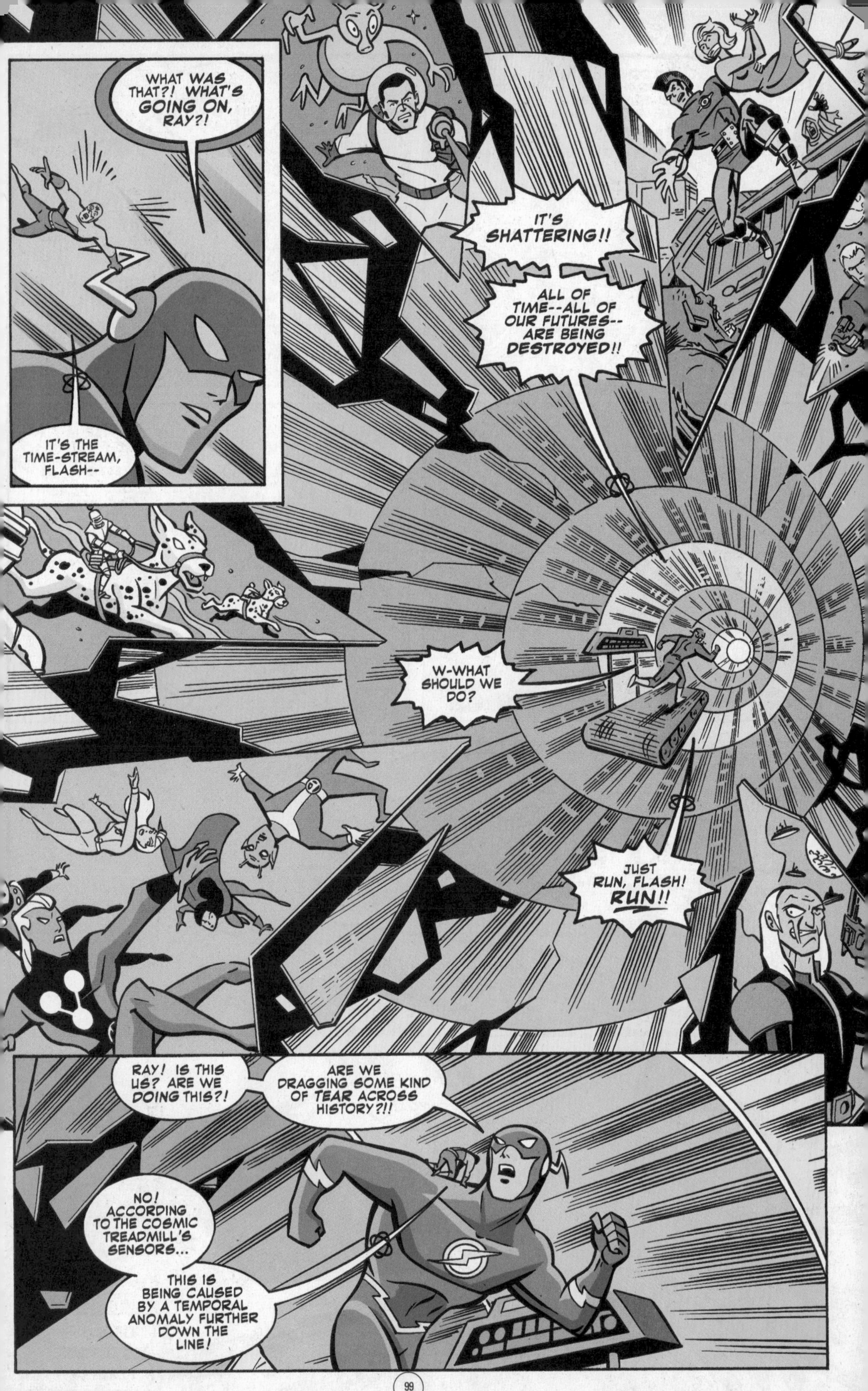
WHAT WAS THAT?! WHAT'S GOING ON, RAY?!
IT'S THE TIME-STREAM, FLASH--
IT'S SHATTERING!!
ALL OF TIME--ALL OF OUR FUTURES--ARE BEING DESTROYED!!
W-WHAT SHOULD WE DO?
JUST RUN, FLASH! RUN!!
RAY! IS THIS US? ARE WE DOING THIS?!
ARE WE DRAGGING SOME KIND OF TEAR ACROSS HISTORY?!!
NO! ACCORDING TO THE COSMIC TREADMILL'S SENSORS...
THIS IS BEING CAUSED BY A TEMPORAL ANOMALY FURTHER DOWN THE LINE!

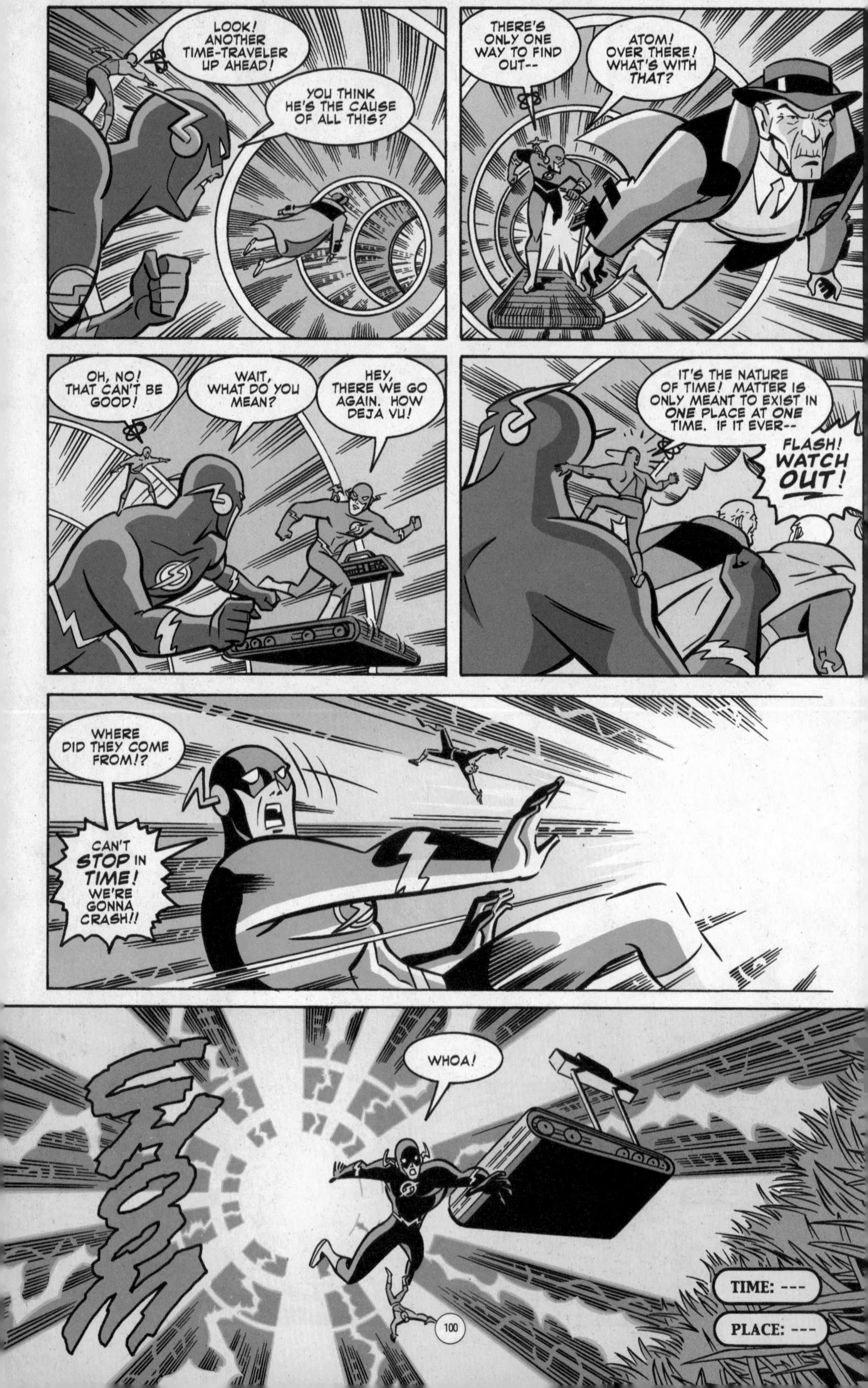
LOOK! ANOTHER TIME-TRAVELER UP AHEAD!
YOU THINK HE'S THE CAUSE OF ALL THIS?
THERE'S ONLY ONE WAY TO FIND OUT--
ATOM! OVER THERE! WHAT'S WITH THAT?
OH, NO! THAT CAN'T BE GOOD!
WAIT, WHAT DO YOU MEAN?
HEY, THERE WE GO AGAIN. HOW DEJA VU!
IT'S THE NATURE OF TIME! MATTER IS ONLY MEANT TO EXIST IN ONE PLACE AT ONE TIME. IF IT EVER--
FLASH! WATCH OUT!
WHERE DID THEY COME FROM!?
CAN'T STOP IN TIME! WE'RE GONNA CRASH!!
WHOA!
TIME: ---
PLACE: ---

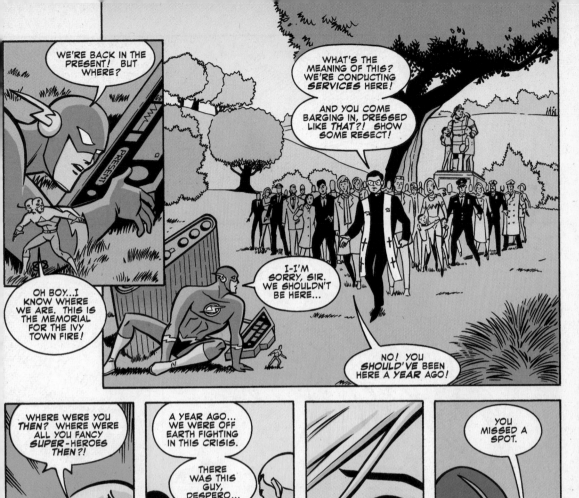

WE'RE BACK IN THE PRESENT! BUT WHERE?

WHAT'S THE MEANING OF THIS? WE'RE CONDUCTING SERVICES HERE!

AND YOU COME BARGING IN, DRESSED LIKE THAT?! SHOW SOME RESECT!

I-I'M SORRY, SIR. WE SHOULDN'T BE HERE...

OH BOY...I KNOW WHERE WE ARE. THIS IS THE MEMORIAL FOR THE IVY TOWN FIRE!

NO! YOU SHOULD'VE BEEN HERE A YEAR AGO!

WHERE WERE YOU THEN? WHERE WERE ALL YOU FANCY SUPER-HEROES THEN?!

A YEAR AGO... WE WERE OFF EARTH FIGHTING IN THIS CRISIS.

THERE WAS THIS GUY, DESPERO...

AND... WELL...WE SAVED THE WHOLE UNIVERSE.

YOU MISSED A SPOT.

WAIT A MINUTE...IT'S THAT TIME-TRAVELER AGAIN.

WHAT'S HE DOING HERE? AND WHO'S THAT WITH HIM?

READY?

JUST PAYING MY RESPECTS. IN CASE WE FAIL.

SINCE WHEN DID I GET SO CYNICAL...

HEROES OF IVY TOWN

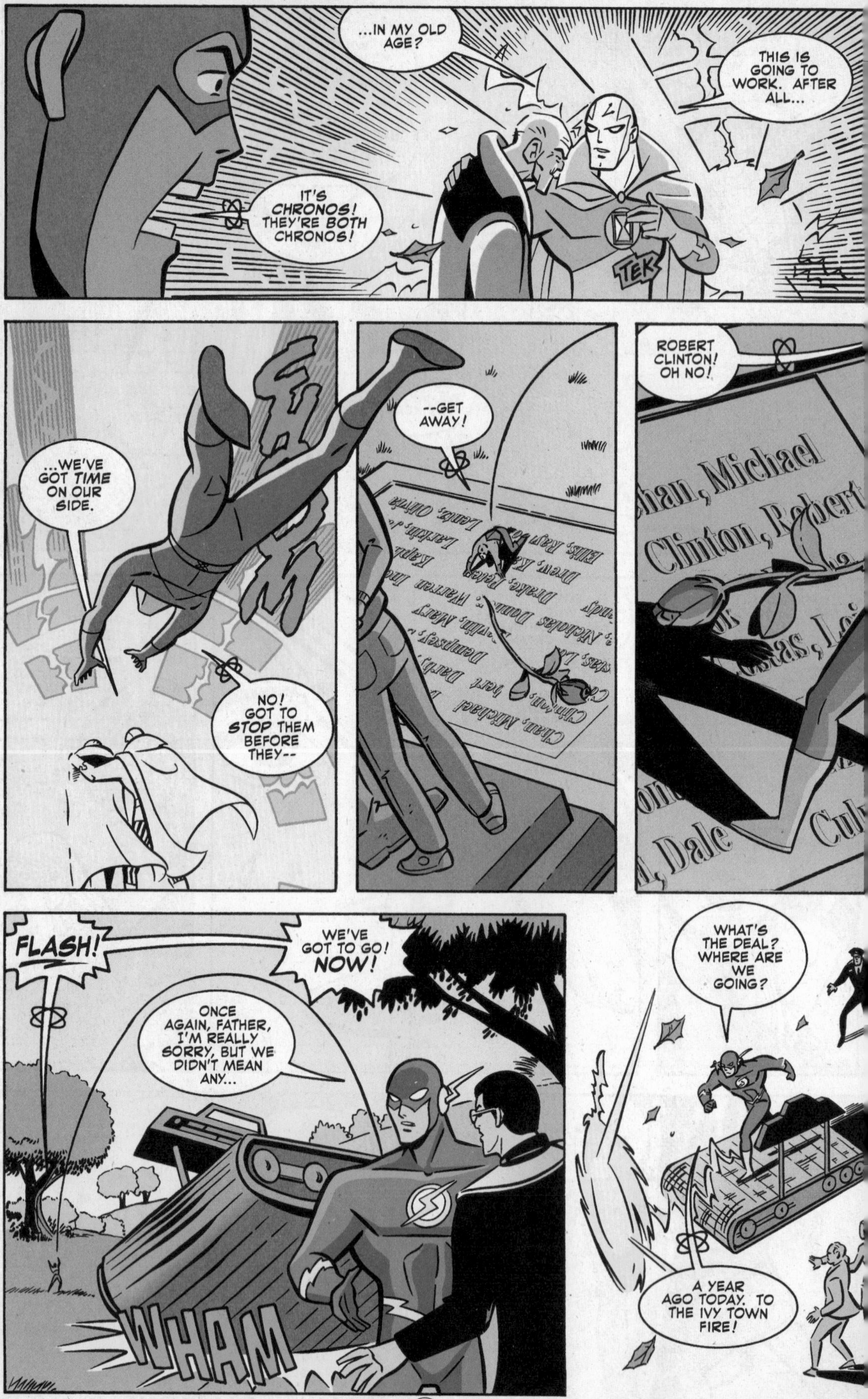
...IN MY OLD AGE?
THIS IS GOING TO WORK. AFTER ALL...
IT'S CHRONOS! THEY'RE BOTH CHRONOS!
TEK
...WE'VE GOT TIME ON OUR SIDE.
NO! GOT TO STOP THEM BEFORE THEY--
--GET AWAY!
ROBERT CLINTON! OH NO!
Chan, Michael
Clinton, Robert
Dale
FLASH!
WE'VE GOT TO GO! NOW!
ONCE AGAIN, FATHER, I'M REALLY SORRY, BUT WE DIDN'T MEAN ANY...
WHAM
WHAT'S THE DEAL? WHERE ARE WE GOING?
A YEAR AGO TODAY. TO THE IVY TOWN FIRE!

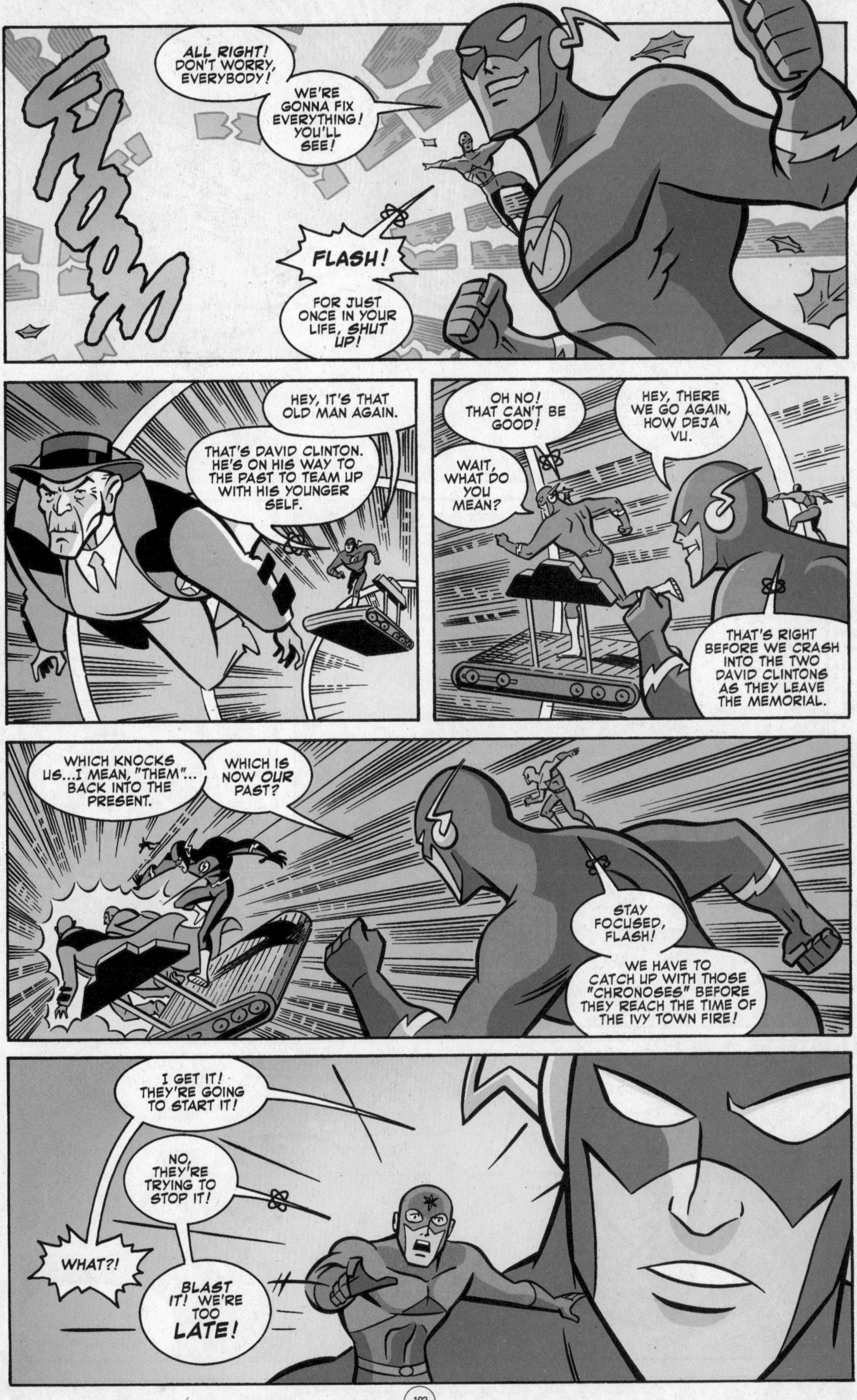
FWOOM
ALL RIGHT! DON'T WORRY, EVERYBODY!
WE'RE GONNA FIX EVERYTHING! YOU'LL SEE!
FLASH!
FOR JUST ONCE IN YOUR LIFE, SHUT UP!
HEY, IT'S THAT OLD MAN AGAIN.
THAT'S DAVID CLINTON. HE'S ON HIS WAY TO THE PAST TO TEAM UP WITH HIS YOUNGER SELF.
OH NO! THAT CAN'T BE GOOD!
HEY, THERE WE GO AGAIN, HOW DEJA VU.
WAIT, WHAT DO YOU MEAN?
THAT'S RIGHT BEFORE WE CRASH INTO THE TWO DAVID CLINTONS AS THEY LEAVE THE MEMORIAL.
WHICH KNOCKS US...I MEAN, "THEM"... BACK INTO THE PRESENT.
WHICH IS NOW OUR PAST?
STAY FOCUSED, FLASH!
WE HAVE TO CATCH UP WITH THOSE "CHRONOSES" BEFORE THEY REACH THE TIME OF THE IVY TOWN FIRE!
I GET IT! THEY'RE GOING TO START IT!
NO, THEY'RE TRYING TO STOP IT!
WHAT?!
BLAST IT! WE'RE TOO LATE!

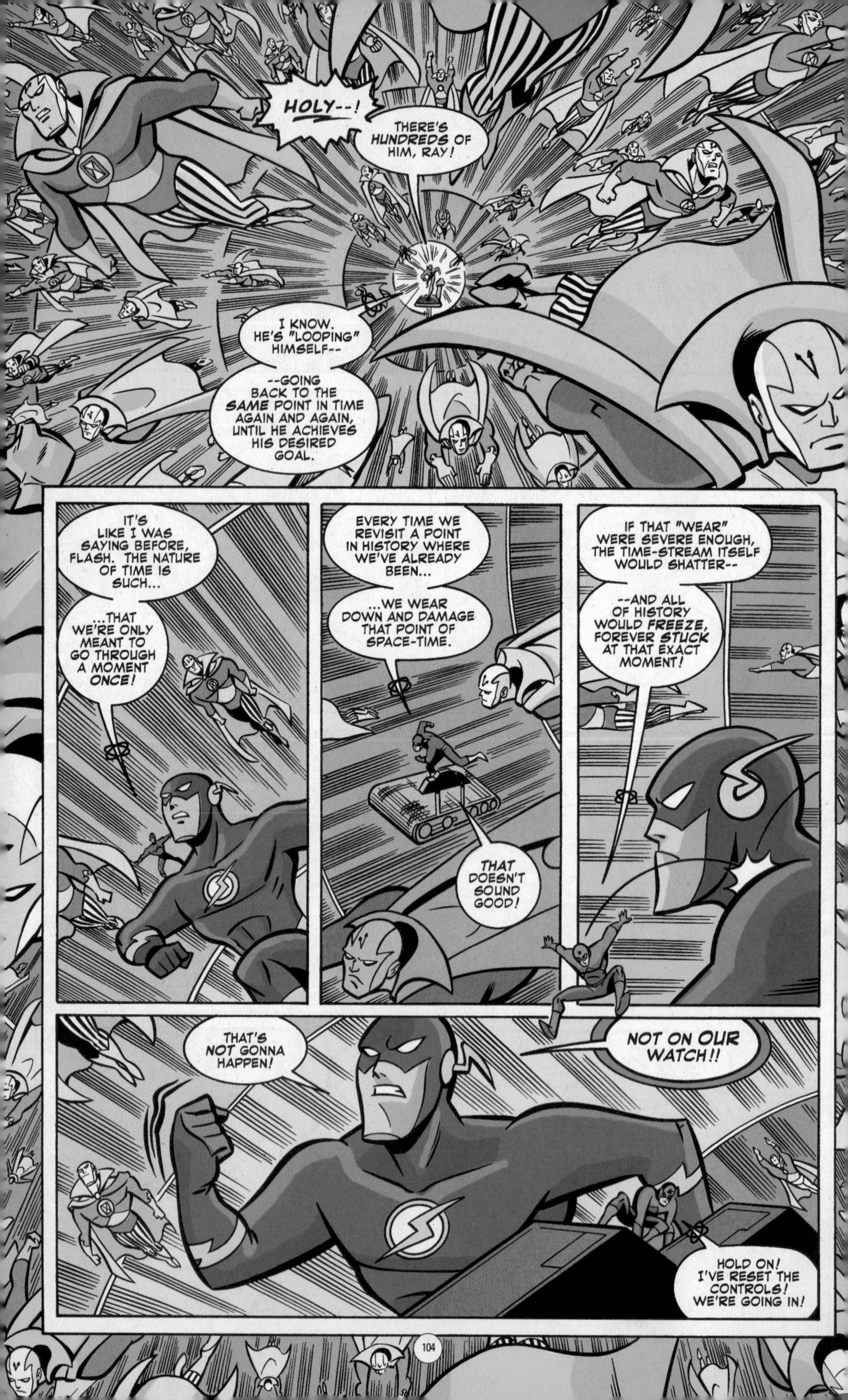
HOLY--!
THERE'S HUNDREDS OF HIM, RAY!
I KNOW. HE'S "LOOPING" HIMSELF--
--GOING BACK TO THE SAME POINT IN TIME AGAIN AND AGAIN, UNTIL HE ACHIEVES HIS DESIRED GOAL.
IT'S LIKE I WAS SAYING BEFORE, FLASH. THE NATURE OF TIME IS SUCH...
...THAT WE'RE ONLY MEANT TO GO THROUGH A MOMENT ONCE!
EVERY TIME WE REVISIT A POINT IN HISTORY WHERE WE'VE ALREADY BEEN...
...WE WEAR DOWN AND DAMAGE THAT POINT OF SPACE-TIME.
THAT DOESN'T SOUND GOOD!
IF THAT "WEAR" WERE SEVERE ENOUGH, THE TIME-STREAM ITSELF WOULD SHATTER--
--AND ALL OF HISTORY WOULD FREEZE, FOREVER STUCK AT THAT EXACT MOMENT!
THAT'S NOT GONNA HAPPEN!
NOT ON OUR WATCH!!
HOLD ON! I'VE RESET THE CONTROLS! WE'RE GOING IN!

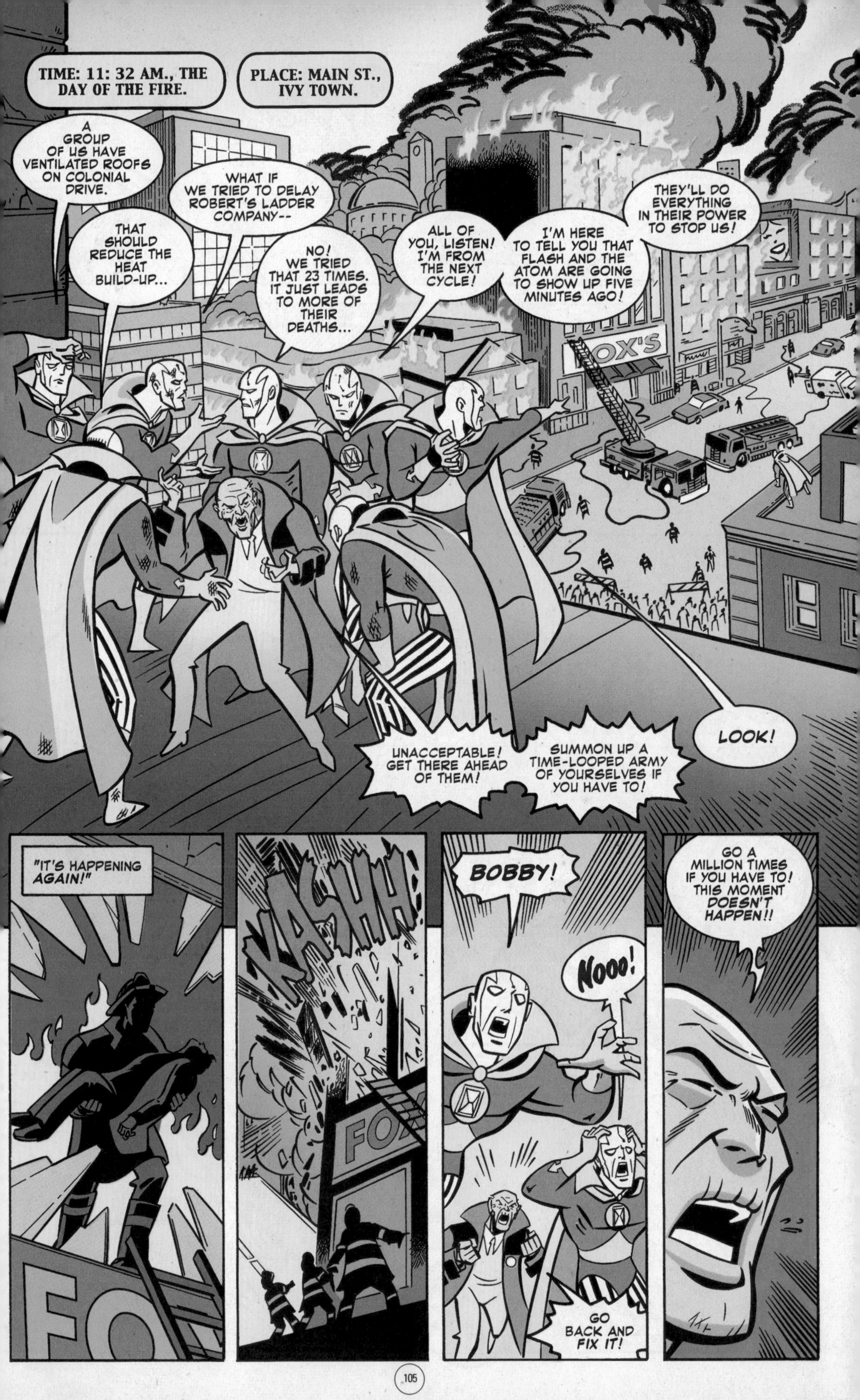
TIME: 11: 32 AM., THE DAY OF THE FIRE.
PLACE: MAIN ST., IVY TOWN.
A GROUP OF US HAVE VENTILATED ROOFS ON COLONIAL DRIVE.
THAT SHOULD REDUCE THE HEAT BUILD-UP...
WHAT IF WE TRIED TO DELAY ROBERT'S LADDER COMPANY--
NO! WE TRIED THAT 23 TIMES. IT JUST LEADS TO MORE OF THEIR DEATHS...
ALL OF YOU, LISTEN! I'M FROM THE NEXT CYCLE!
I'M HERE TO TELL YOU THAT FLASH AND THE ATOM ARE GOING TO SHOW UP FIVE MINUTES AGO!
THEY'LL DO EVERYTHING IN THEIR POWER TO STOP US!
OX'S
UNACCEPTABLE! GET THERE AHEAD OF THEM!
SUMMON UP A TIME-LOOPED ARMY OF YOURSELVES IF YOU HAVE TO!
LOOK!
"IT'S HAPPENING AGAIN!"
FO
KASHH
FO
BOBBY!
NOOO!
GO BACK AND FIX IT!
GO A MILLION TIMES IF YOU HAVE TO! THIS MOMENT DOESN'T HAPPEN!!

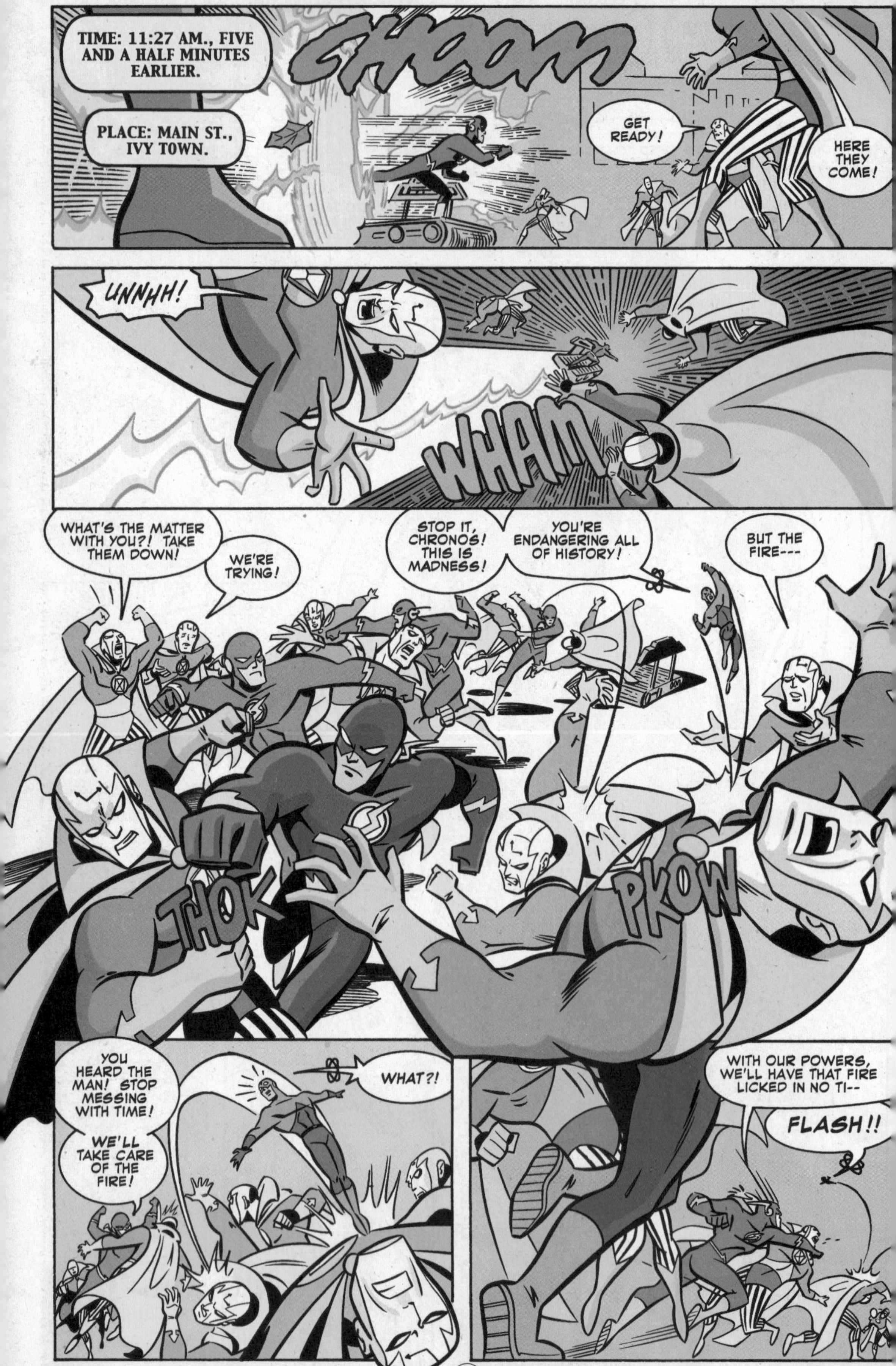
TIME: 11:27 AM., FIVE AND A HALF MINUTES EARLIER.
PLACE: MAIN ST., IVY TOWN.
CHOOM
GET READY!
HERE THEY COME!
UNNHH!
WHAM
WHAT'S THE MATTER WITH YOU?! TAKE THEM DOWN!
WE'RE TRYING!
STOP IT, CHRONOS! THIS IS MADNESS!
YOU'RE ENDANGERING ALL OF HISTORY!
BUT THE FIRE---
THOK
PKOW
YOU HEARD THE MAN! STOP MESSING WITH TIME!
WE'LL TAKE CARE OF THE FIRE!
WHAT?!
WITH OUR POWERS, WE'LL HAVE THAT FIRE LICKED IN NO TI--
FLASH!!

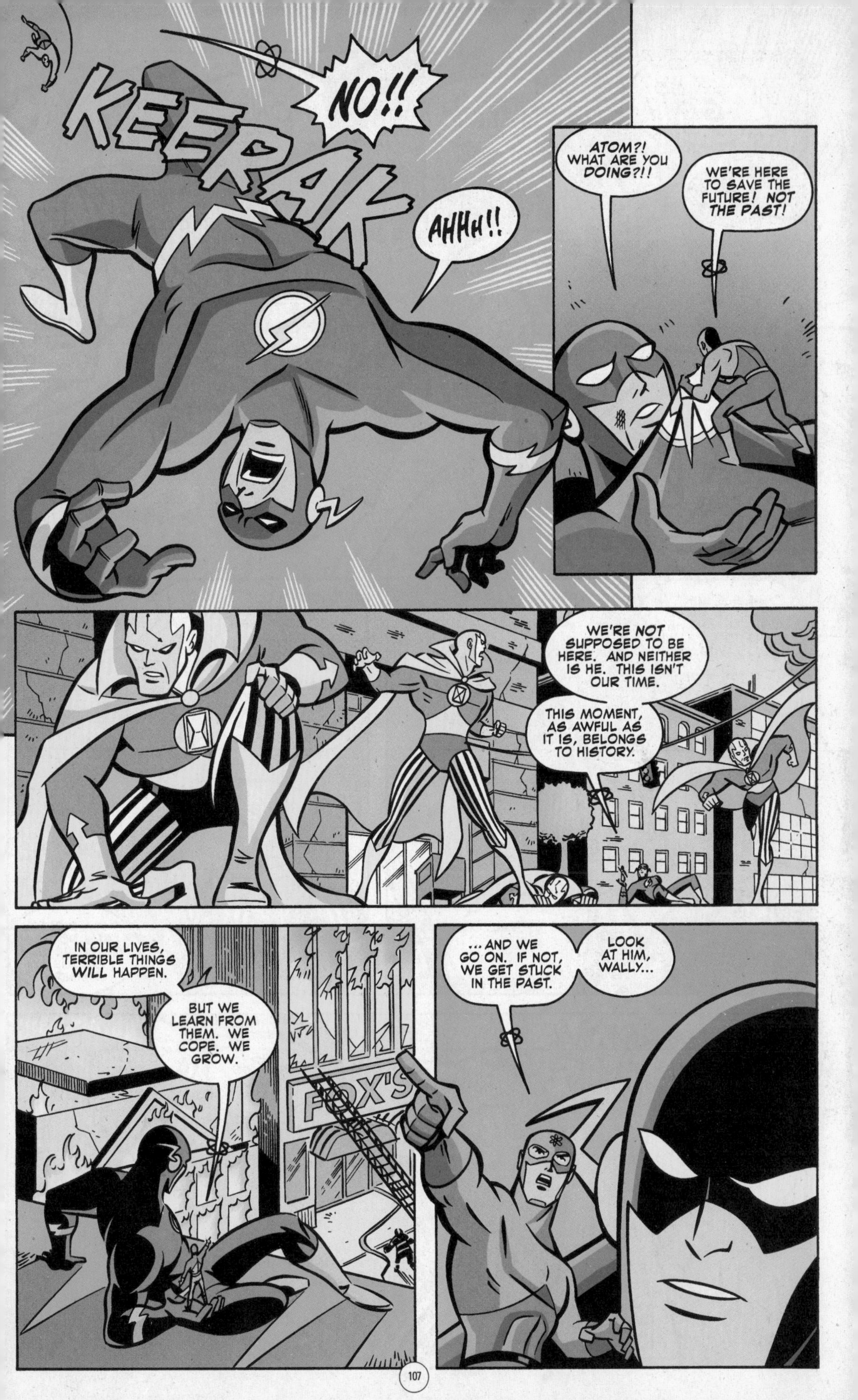
NO!!
KEERAK
AHHH!!
ATOM?! WHAT ARE YOU DOING?!!
WE'RE HERE TO SAVE THE FUTURE! NOT THE PAST!
WE'RE NOT SUPPOSED TO BE HERE. AND NEITHER IS HE. THIS ISN'T OUR TIME.
THIS MOMENT, AS AWFUL AS IT IS, BELONGS TO HISTORY.
IN OUR LIVES, TERRIBLE THINGS WILL HAPPEN.
BUT WE LEARN FROM THEM. WE COPE. WE GROW.
FOX'S
...AND WE GO ON. IF NOT, WE GET STUCK IN THE PAST.
LOOK AT HIM, WALLY...

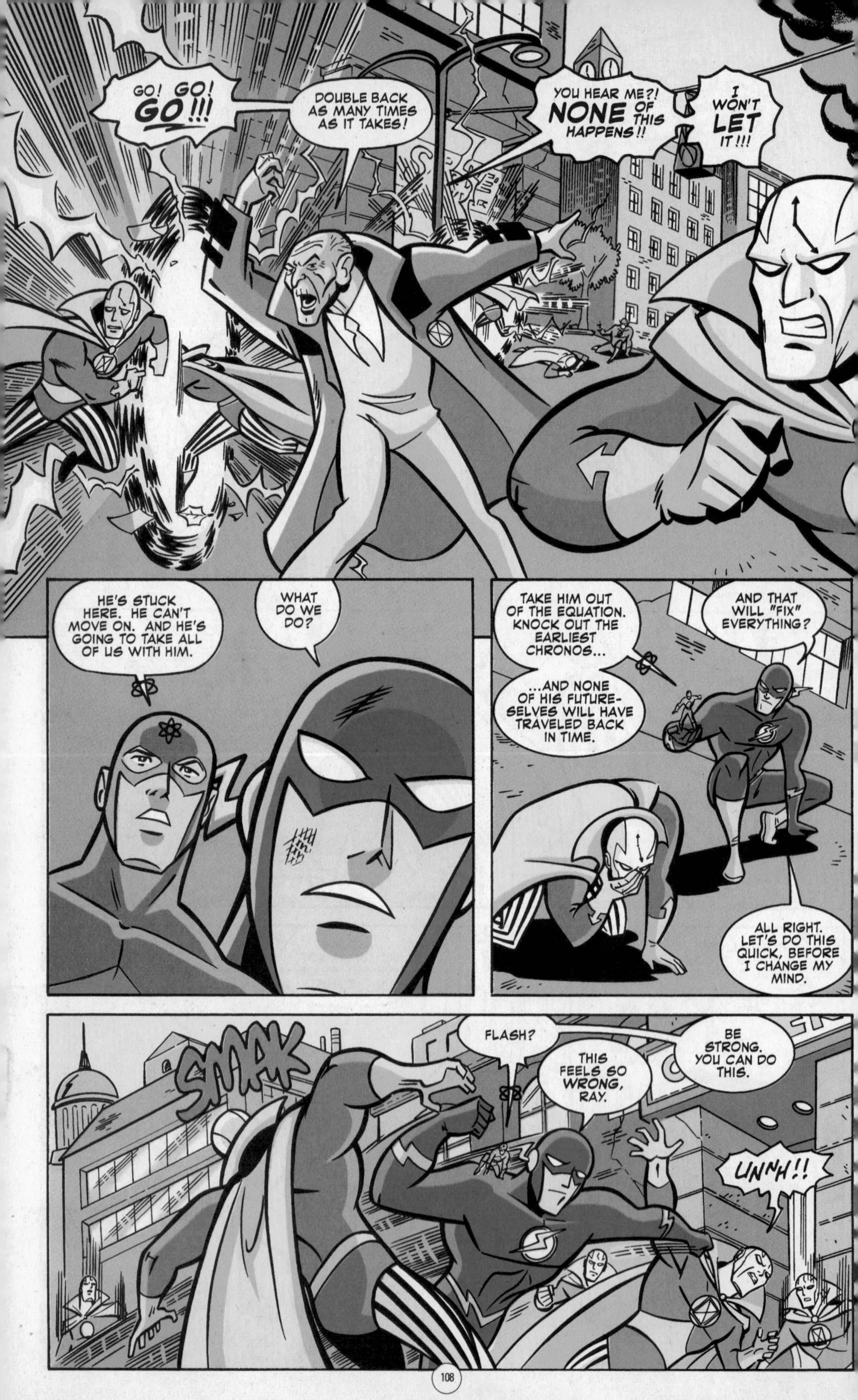

GO! GO! GO!!!
DOUBLE BACK AS MANY TIMES AS IT TAKES!
YOU HEAR ME?! NONE OF THIS HAPPENS!!
I WON'T LET IT!!!
HE'S STUCK HERE. HE CAN'T MOVE ON. AND HE'S GOING TO TAKE ALL OF US WITH HIM.
WHAT DO WE DO?
TAKE HIM OUT OF THE EQUATION. KNOCK OUT THE EARLIEST CHRONOS...
...AND NONE OF HIS FUTURE-SELVES WILL HAVE TRAVELED BACK IN TIME.
AND THAT WILL "FIX" EVERYTHING?
ALL RIGHT. LET'S DO THIS QUICK, BEFORE I CHANGE MY MIND.
SMAK
FLASH?
THIS FEELS SO WRONG, RAY.
BE STRONG. YOU CAN DO THIS.
UNNH!!

WHAT'S HAPPENING? I'M--

OUR LATER SELVES ARE DISAPPEARING!

THIS IS THE FLASH AND ATOM'S DOING!

I TRIED TO WARN YOU! I--

LOX'S

LOOK!

DON'T JUST STAND THERE! MAKE EARLIER LOOPS! CREATE REINFORCEMENTS!

"IT'S HAPPENING AGAIN!"

KASHH

AAHHH!!

FOX

GO! ALL OF YOU! DOUBLE BACK AND DOUBLE BACK AGAIN!

GO!!

SHOOM

SHOOM

CHRONOS, STOP! YOU'RE GOING TO OVERLOAD THE TIME-STREAM!

THINK OF THE FUTURE, MAN!

HANG THE FUTURE! I WANT MY PAST!

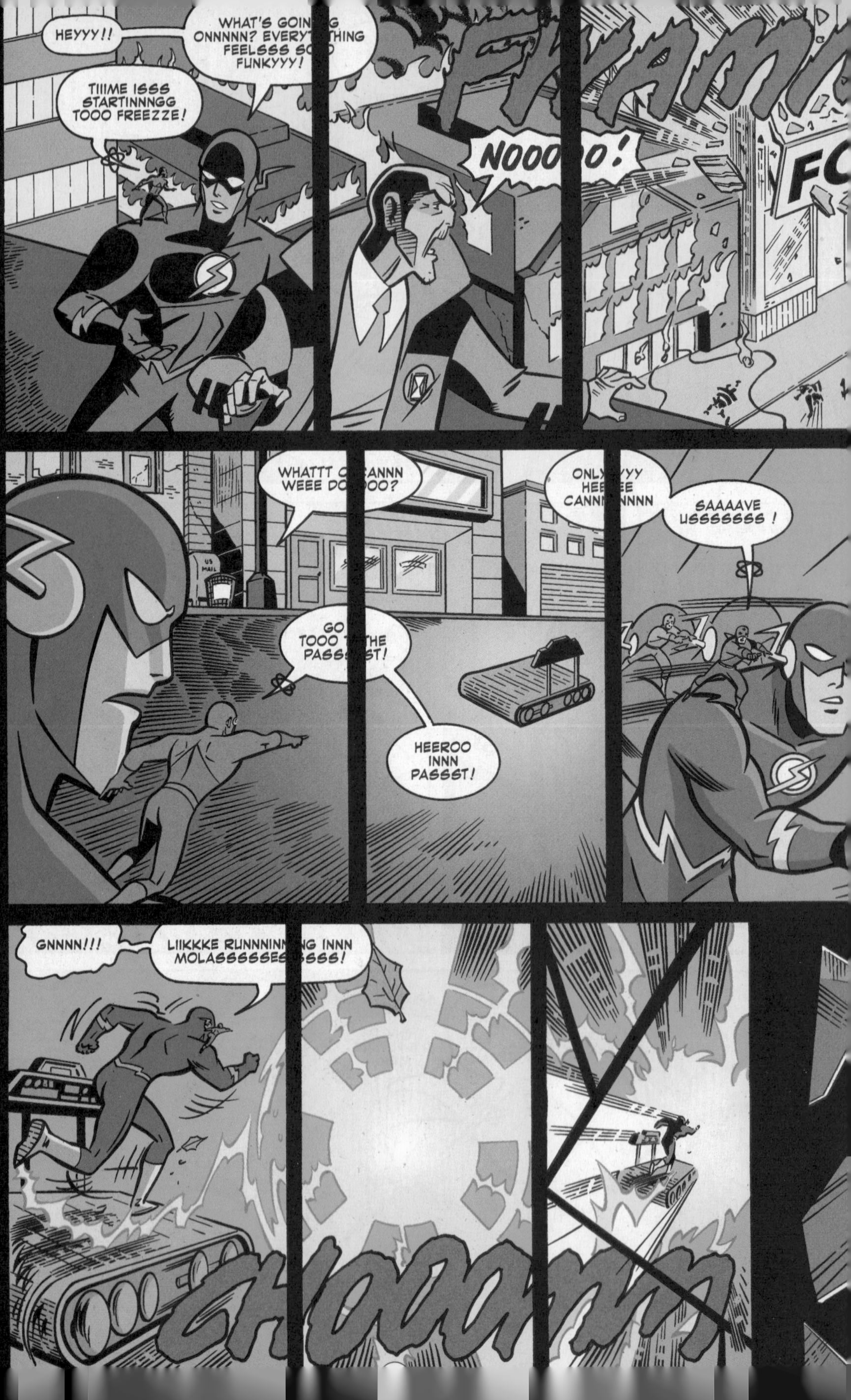
HEYYY!!
WHAT'S GOIN G ONNNNN? EVERY THING FEELSSS SO FUNKYYY!
TIIIME ISSS STARTINNNGG TOOO FREEZZE!
FWAM
NOOO O!
FO
WHATTT C ANNN WEEE DO OO?
US MAIL
ONLY YY HEE EE CANN NNN
SAAAAVE USSSSSSS!
GO TOOO T THE PASS ST!
HEEROO INNN PASSST!
GNNNN!!!
LIIKKKE RUNNNINN NG INNN MOLASSSSSES SSSS!

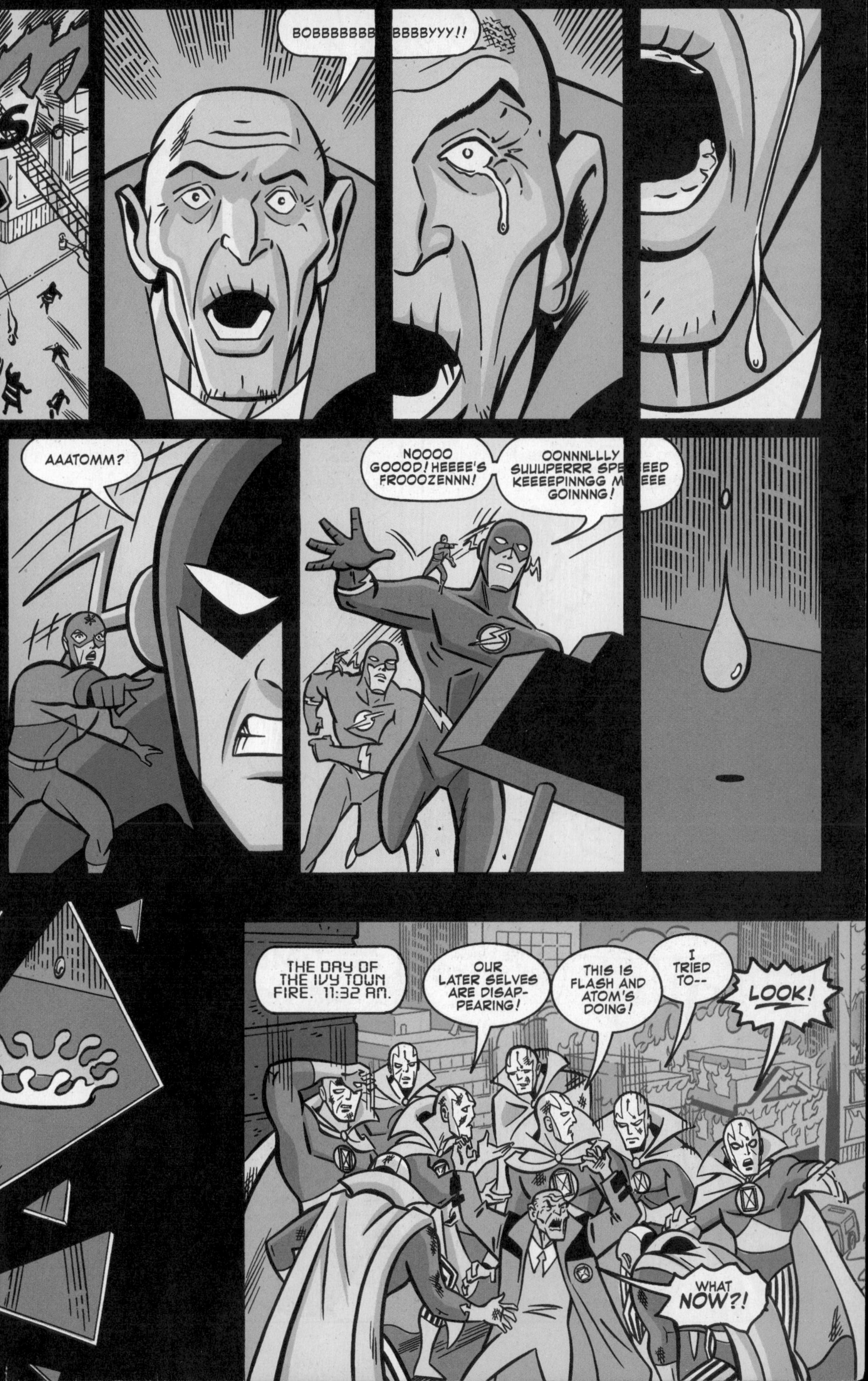
BOBBBBBBBBBBBBBYYY!!
AAATOMM?
NOOOO GOOOD! HEEEE'S FROOOZENNN!
OONNNLLLY SUUUPERRR SPEEEEED KEEEEPINNGG MEEEE GOINNNG!
THE DAY OF THE IVY TOWN FIRE. 11:32 AM.
OUR LATER SELVES ARE DISAP-PEARING!
THIS IS FLASH AND ATOM'S DOING!
I TRIED TO--
LOOK!
WHAT NOW?!

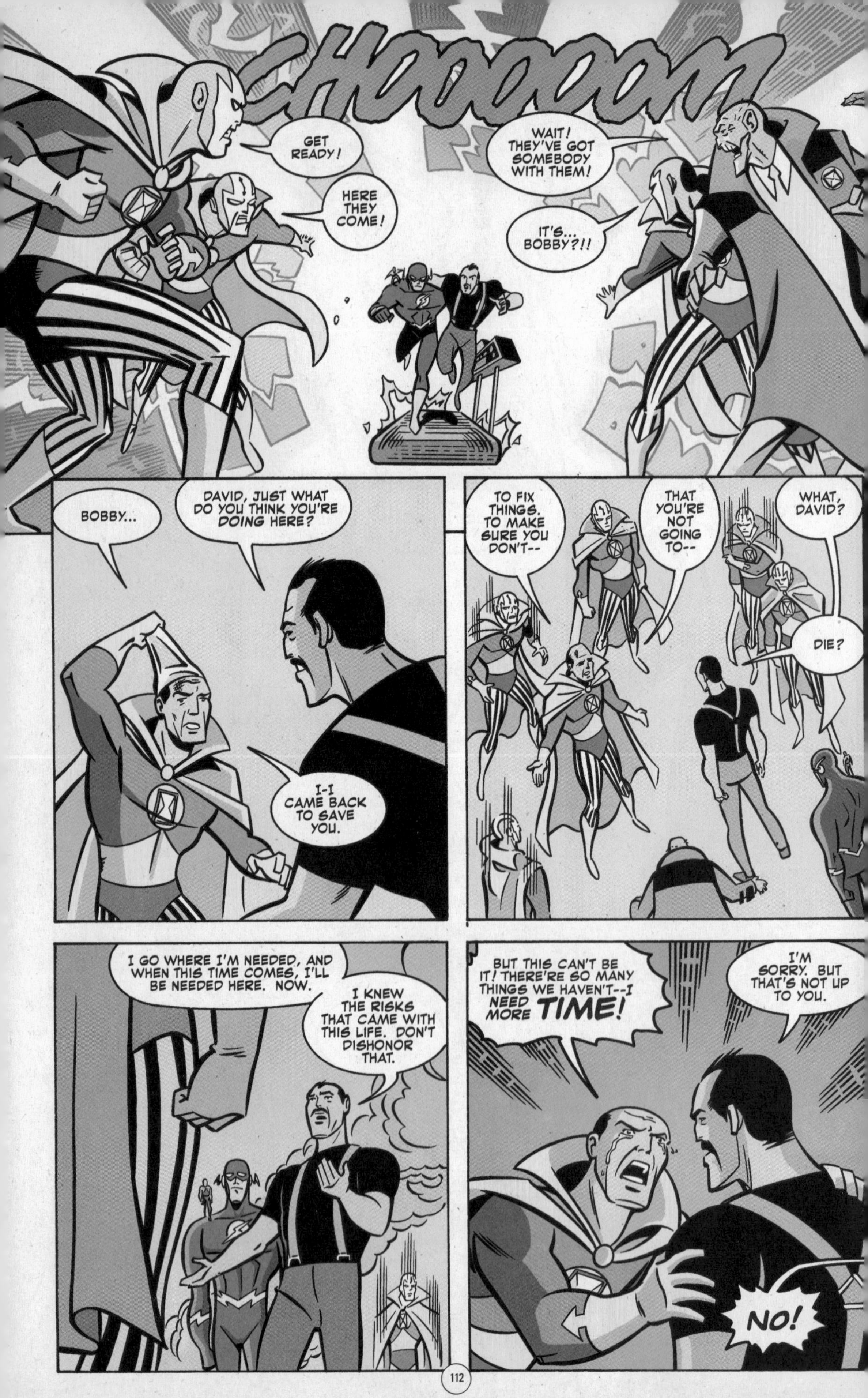
CHOOOOOM
GET READY!
HERE THEY COME!
WAIT! THEY'VE GOT SOMEBODY WITH THEM!
IT'S... BOBBY?!!
BOBBY...
DAVID, JUST WHAT DO YOU THINK YOU'RE DOING HERE?
I-I CAME BACK TO SAVE YOU.
TO FIX THINGS. TO MAKE SURE YOU DON'T--
THAT YOU'RE NOT GOING TO--
WHAT, DAVID?
DIE?
I GO WHERE I'M NEEDED, AND WHEN THIS TIME COMES, I'LL BE NEEDED HERE. NOW.
I KNEW THE RISKS THAT CAME WITH THIS LIFE. DON'T DISHONOR THAT.
BUT THIS CAN'T BE IT! THERE'RE SO MANY THINGS WE HAVEN'T--I NEED MORE TIME!
I'M SORRY. BUT THAT'S NOT UP TO YOU.
NO!

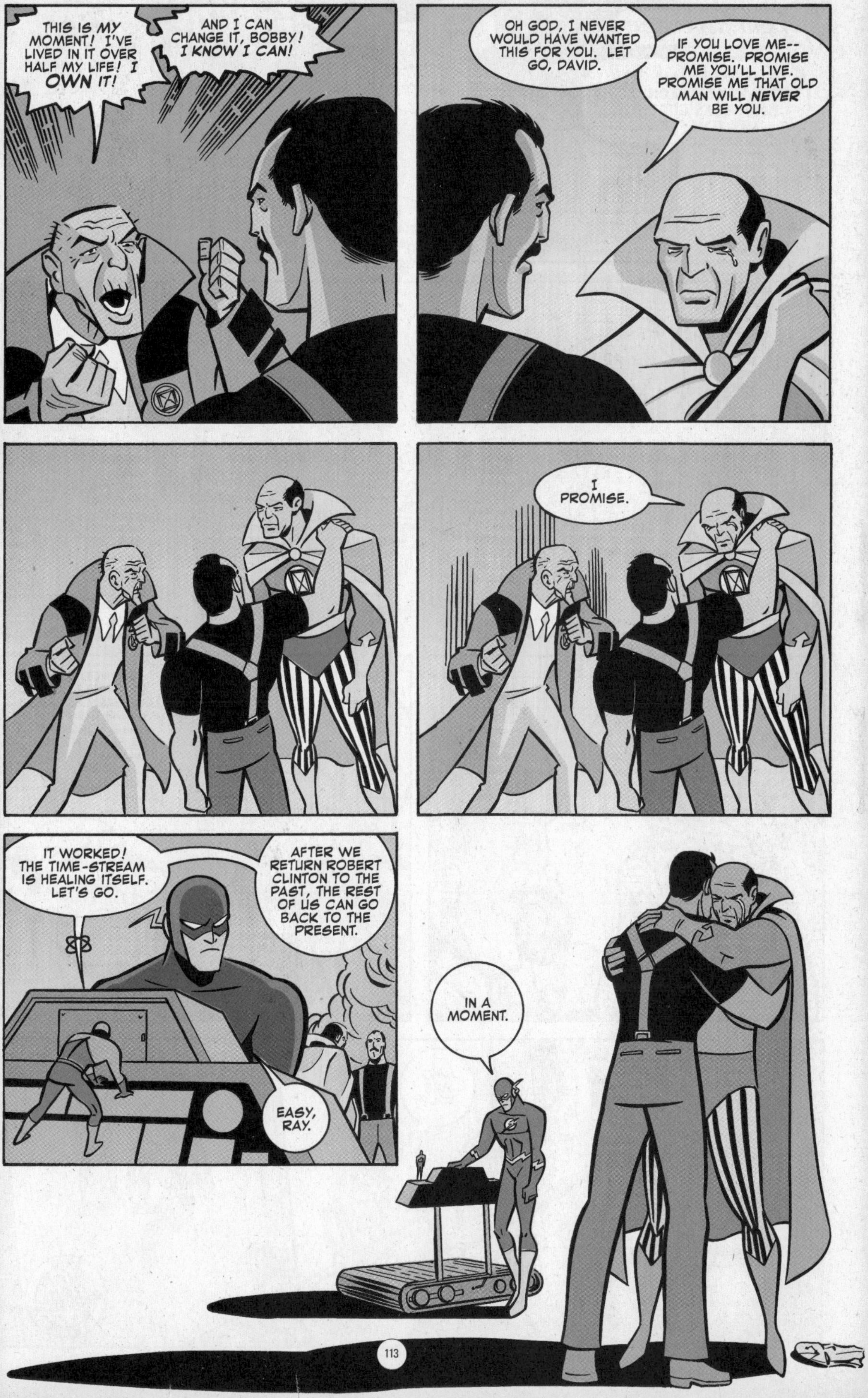
THIS IS MY MOMENT! I'VE LIVED IN IT OVER HALF MY LIFE! I OWN IT!
AND I CAN CHANGE IT, BOBBY! I KNOW I CAN!
OH GOD, I NEVER WOULD HAVE WANTED THIS FOR YOU. LET GO, DAVID.
IF YOU LOVE ME-- PROMISE. PROMISE ME YOU'LL LIVE. PROMISE ME THAT OLD MAN WILL NEVER BE YOU.
I PROMISE.
IT WORKED! THE TIME-STREAM IS HEALING ITSELF. LET'S GO.
AFTER WE RETURN ROBERT CLINTON TO THE PAST, THE REST OF US CAN GO BACK TO THE PRESENT.
EASY, RAY.
IN A MOMENT.

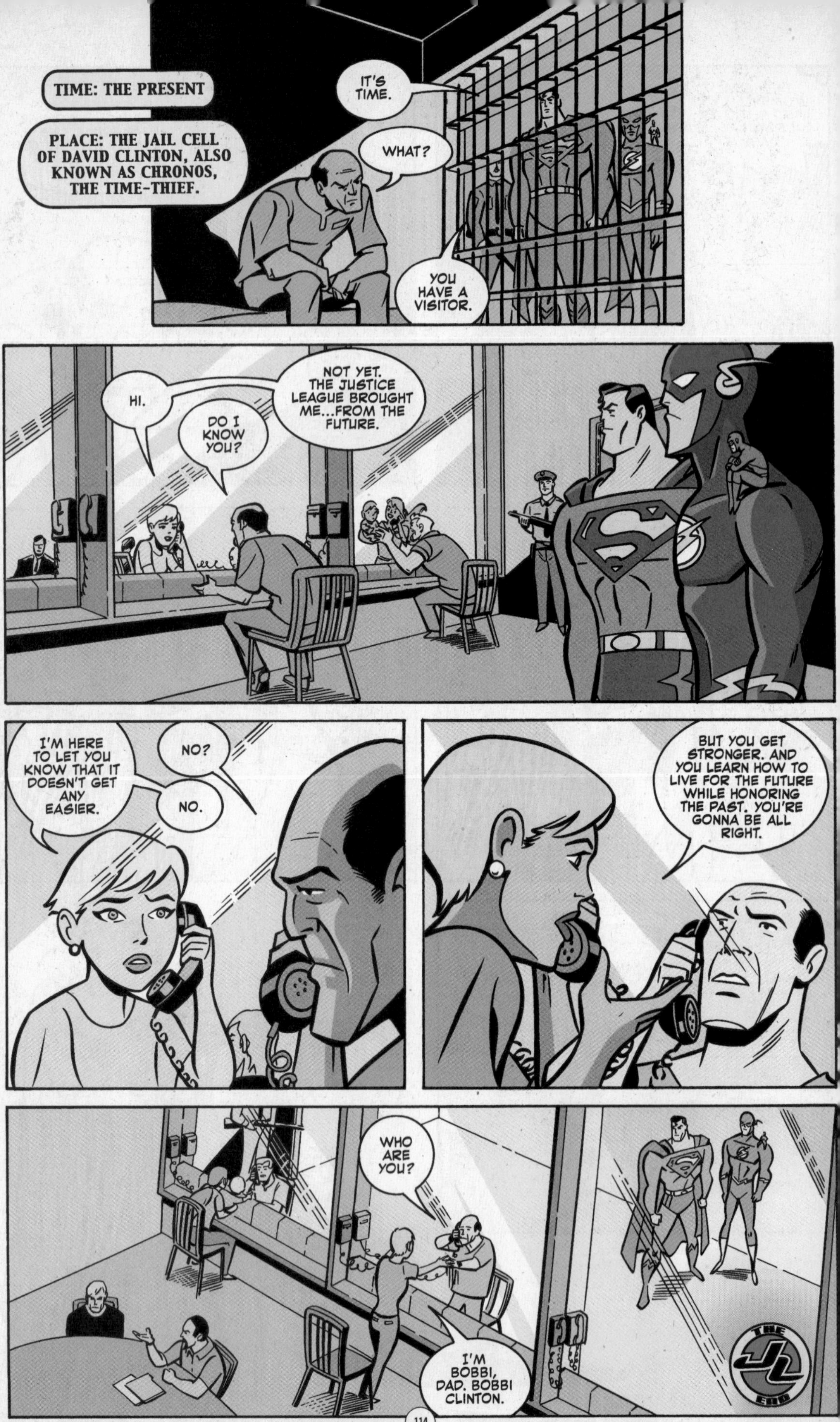
TIME: THE PRESENT
PLACE: THE JAIL CELL OF DAVID CLINTON, ALSO KNOWN AS CHRONOS, THE TIME-THIEF.
IT'S TIME.
WHAT?
YOU HAVE A VISITOR.
HI.
DO I KNOW YOU?
NOT YET. THE JUSTICE LEAGUE BROUGHT ME...FROM THE FUTURE.
I'M HERE TO LET YOU KNOW THAT IT DOESN'T GET ANY EASIER.
NO?
NO.
BUT YOU GET STRONGER. AND YOU LEARN HOW TO LIVE FOR THE FUTURE WHILE HONORING THE PAST. YOU'RE GONNA BE ALL RIGHT.
WHO ARE YOU?
I'M BOBBI, DAD. BOBBI CLINTON.
THE END

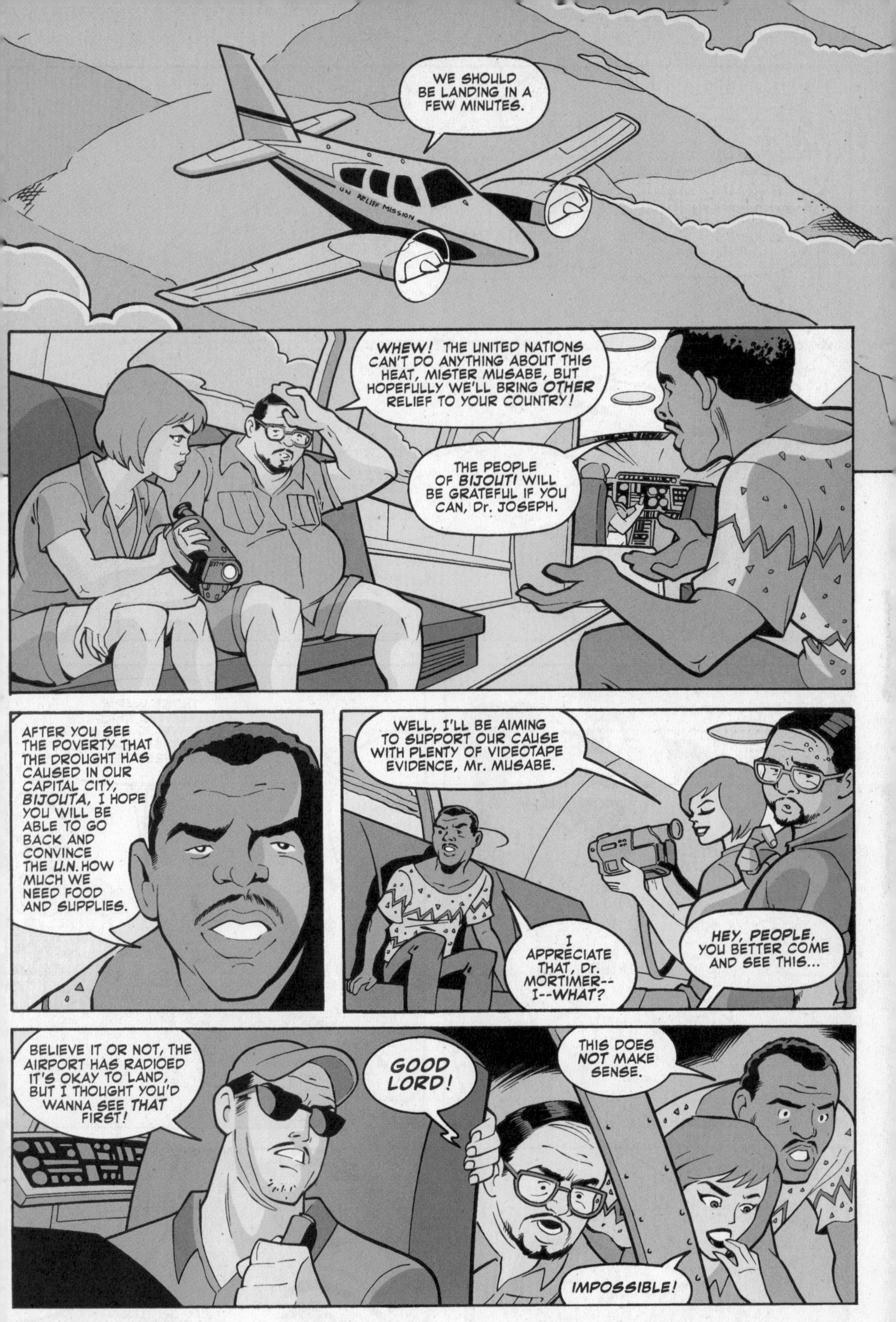
WE SHOULD BE LANDING IN A FEW MINUTES.
U.N. RELIEF MISSION
WHEW! THE UNITED NATIONS CAN'T DO ANYTHING ABOUT THIS HEAT, MISTER MUSABE, BUT HOPEFULLY WE'LL BRING OTHER RELIEF TO YOUR COUNTRY!
THE PEOPLE OF BIJOUTI WILL BE GRATEFUL IF YOU CAN, Dr. JOSEPH.
AFTER YOU SEE THE POVERTY THAT THE DROUGHT HAS CAUSED IN OUR CAPITAL CITY, BIJOUTA, I HOPE YOU WILL BE ABLE TO GO BACK AND CONVINCE THE U.N. HOW MUCH WE NEED FOOD AND SUPPLIES.
WELL, I'LL BE AIMING TO SUPPORT OUR CAUSE WITH PLENTY OF VIDEOTAPE EVIDENCE, Mr. MUSABE.
I APPRECIATE THAT, Dr. MORTIMER-- I--WHAT?
HEY, PEOPLE, YOU BETTER COME AND SEE THIS...
BELIEVE IT OR NOT, THE AIRPORT HAS RADIOED IT'S OKAY TO LAND, BUT I THOUGHT YOU'D WANNA SEE THAT FIRST!
GOOD LORD!
THIS DOES NOT MAKE SENSE.
IMPOSSIBLE!

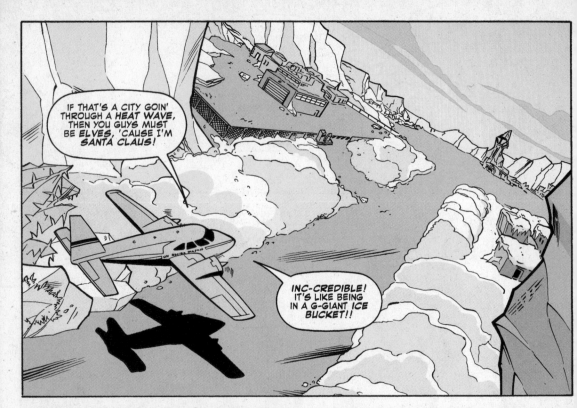

IF THAT'S A CITY GOIN' THROUGH A *HEAT WAVE*, THEN YOU GUYS MUST BE *ELVES*, 'CAUSE I'M *SANTA CLAUS*!

INC-CREDIBLE! IT'S LIKE BEING IN A G-GIANT *ICE BUCKET!!*

BUT I WAS HERE J-JUST FOUR DAYS AGO! MY CITY WAS NOT LIKE THIS!

WHERE DID THIS COME FROM? A FREAK WEATHER EFFECT?

THOSE WARM CLOTHES THE CHILDREN WEAR, WE DO NOT HAVE SUCH THINGS HERE--WE NEVER *NEED* THEM...

BIJOUTI'S NEEDS ARE THE CONCERN OF ITS *NEW GOVERNMENT*...

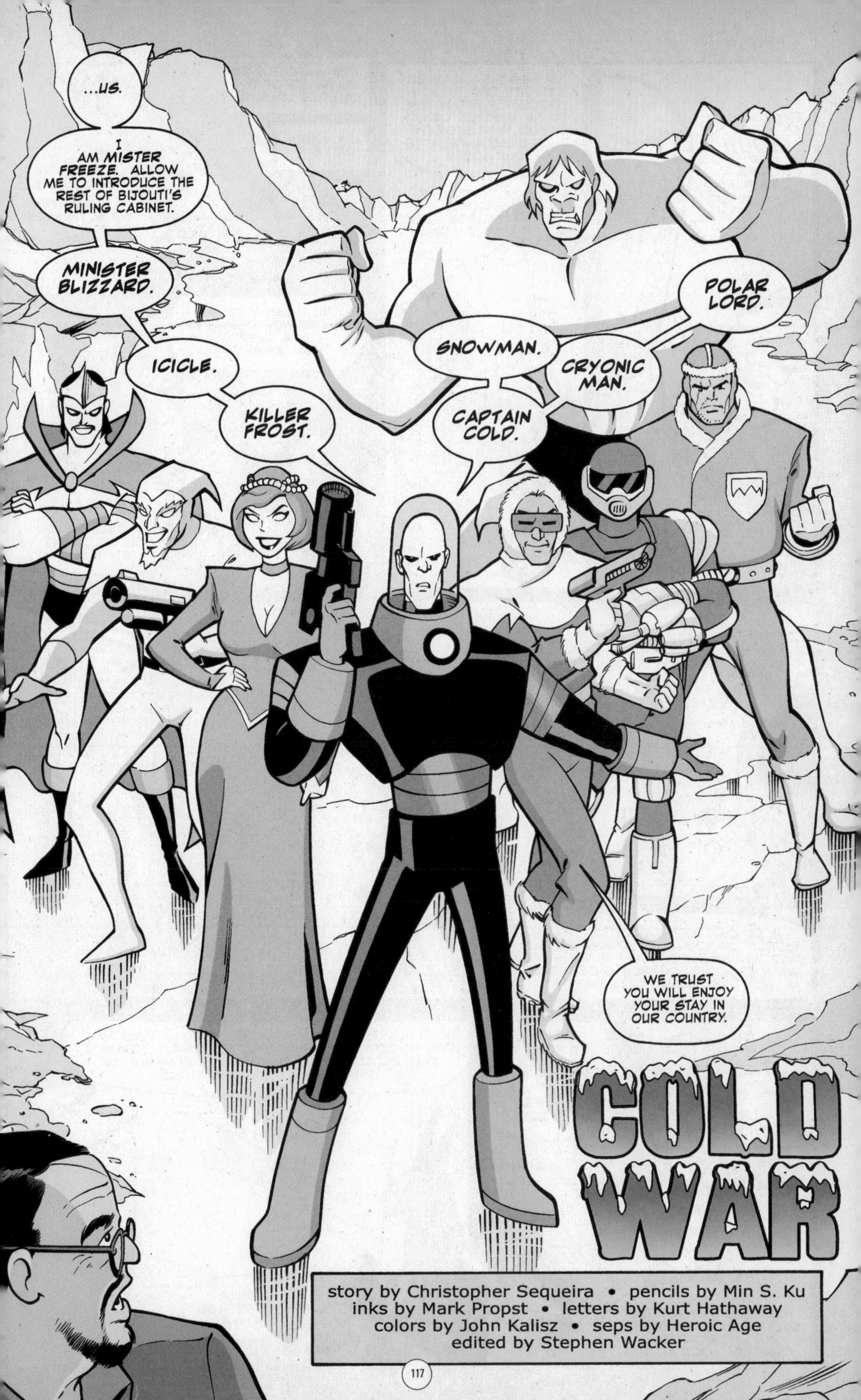
...US.
I AM MISTER FREEZE. ALLOW ME TO INTRODUCE THE REST OF BIJOUTI'S RULING CABINET.
MINISTER BLIZZARD.
ICICLE.
KILLER FROST.
SNOWMAN.
CAPTAIN COLD.
CRYONIC MAN.
POLAR LORD.
WE TRUST YOU WILL ENJOY YOUR STAY IN OUR COUNTRY.
COLD WAR
story by Christopher Sequeira • pencils by Min S. Ku
inks by Mark Propst • letters by Kurt Hathaway
colors by John Kalisz • seps by Heroic Age
edited by Stephen Wacker

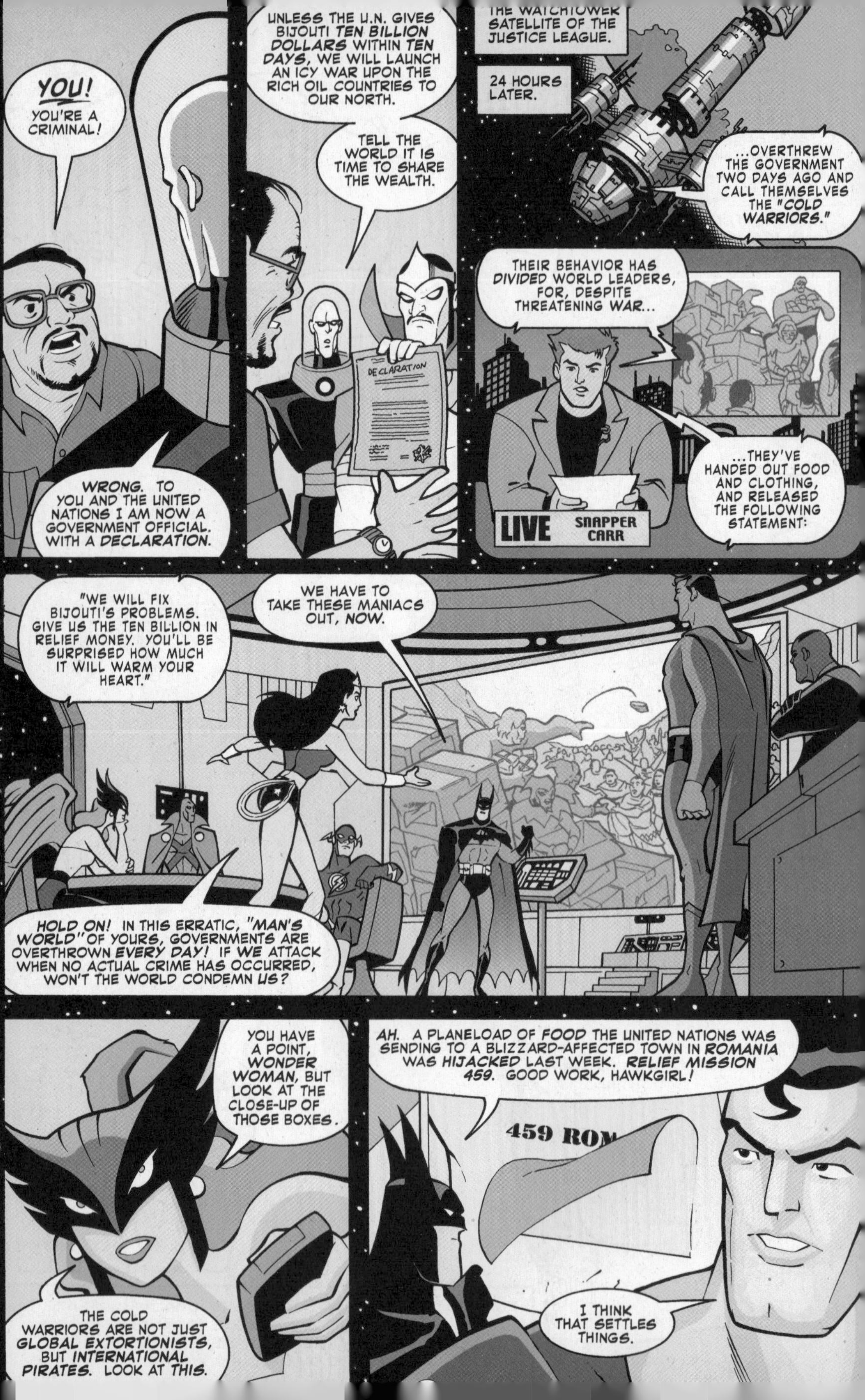
YOU! YOU'RE A CRIMINAL!
WRONG. TO YOU AND THE UNITED NATIONS I AM NOW A GOVERNMENT OFFICIAL. WITH A DECLARATION.
UNLESS THE U.N. GIVES BIJOUTI TEN BILLION DOLLARS WITHIN TEN DAYS, WE WILL LAUNCH AN ICY WAR UPON THE RICH OIL COUNTRIES TO OUR NORTH.
TELL THE WORLD IT IS TIME TO SHARE THE WEALTH.
DECLARATION
THE WATCHTOWER SATELLITE OF THE JUSTICE LEAGUE.
24 HOURS LATER.
...OVERTHREW THE GOVERNMENT TWO DAYS AGO AND CALL THEMSELVES THE "COLD WARRIORS."
THEIR BEHAVIOR HAS DIVIDED WORLD LEADERS, FOR, DESPITE THREATENING WAR...
LIVE
SNAPPER CARR
...THEY'VE HANDED OUT FOOD AND CLOTHING, AND RELEASED THE FOLLOWING STATEMENT:
"WE WILL FIX BIJOUTI'S PROBLEMS. GIVE US THE TEN BILLION IN RELIEF MONEY. YOU'LL BE SURPRISED HOW MUCH IT WILL WARM YOUR HEART."
WE HAVE TO TAKE THESE MANIACS OUT, NOW.
HOLD ON! IN THIS ERRATIC, "MAN'S WORLD" OF YOURS, GOVERNMENTS ARE OVERTHROWN EVERY DAY! IF WE ATTACK WHEN NO ACTUAL CRIME HAS OCCURRED, WON'T THE WORLD CONDEMN US?
YOU HAVE A POINT, WONDER WOMAN, BUT LOOK AT THE CLOSE-UP OF THOSE BOXES.
THE COLD WARRIORS ARE NOT JUST GLOBAL EXTORTIONISTS, BUT INTERNATIONAL PIRATES. LOOK AT THIS.
AH. A PLANELOAD OF FOOD THE UNITED NATIONS WAS SENDING TO A BLIZZARD-AFFECTED TOWN IN ROMANIA WAS HIJACKED LAST WEEK. RELIEF MISSION 459. GOOD WORK, HAWKGIRL!
459 ROM
I THINK THAT SETTLES THINGS.

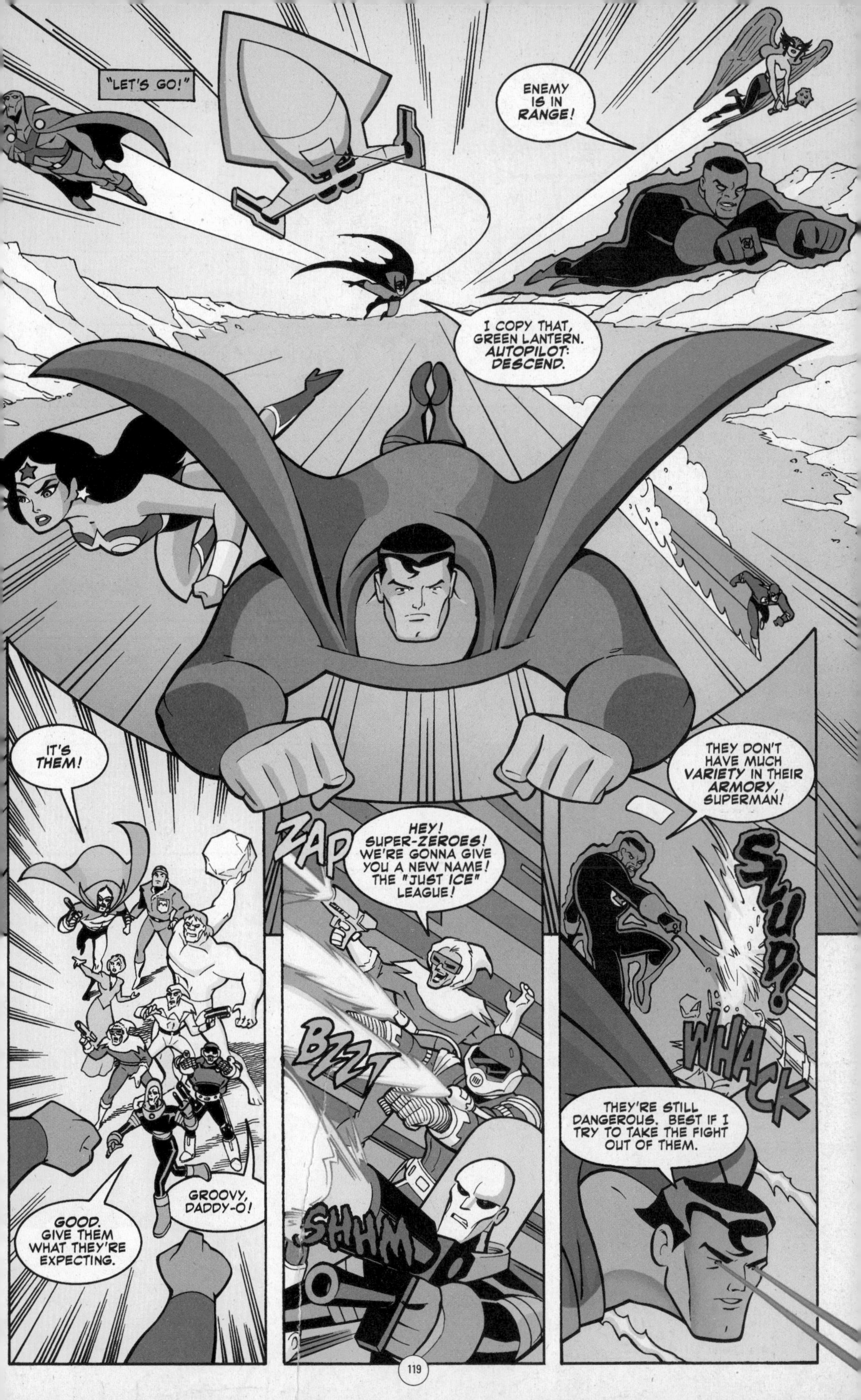

"LET'S GO!"
ENEMY IS IN RANGE!
I COPY THAT, GREEN LANTERN. AUTOPILOT: DESCEND.
IT'S THEM!
GOOD. GIVE THEM WHAT THEY'RE EXPECTING.
GROOVY, DADDY-O!
ZAP
HEY! SUPER-ZEROES! WE'RE GONNA GIVE YOU A NEW NAME! THE "JUST ICE" LEAGUE!
BZZT
SHHM
THEY DON'T HAVE MUCH VARIETY IN THEIR ARMORY, SUPERMAN!
SNUD!
WHACK
THEY'RE STILL DANGEROUS. BEST IF I TRY TO TAKE THE FIGHT OUT OF THEM.

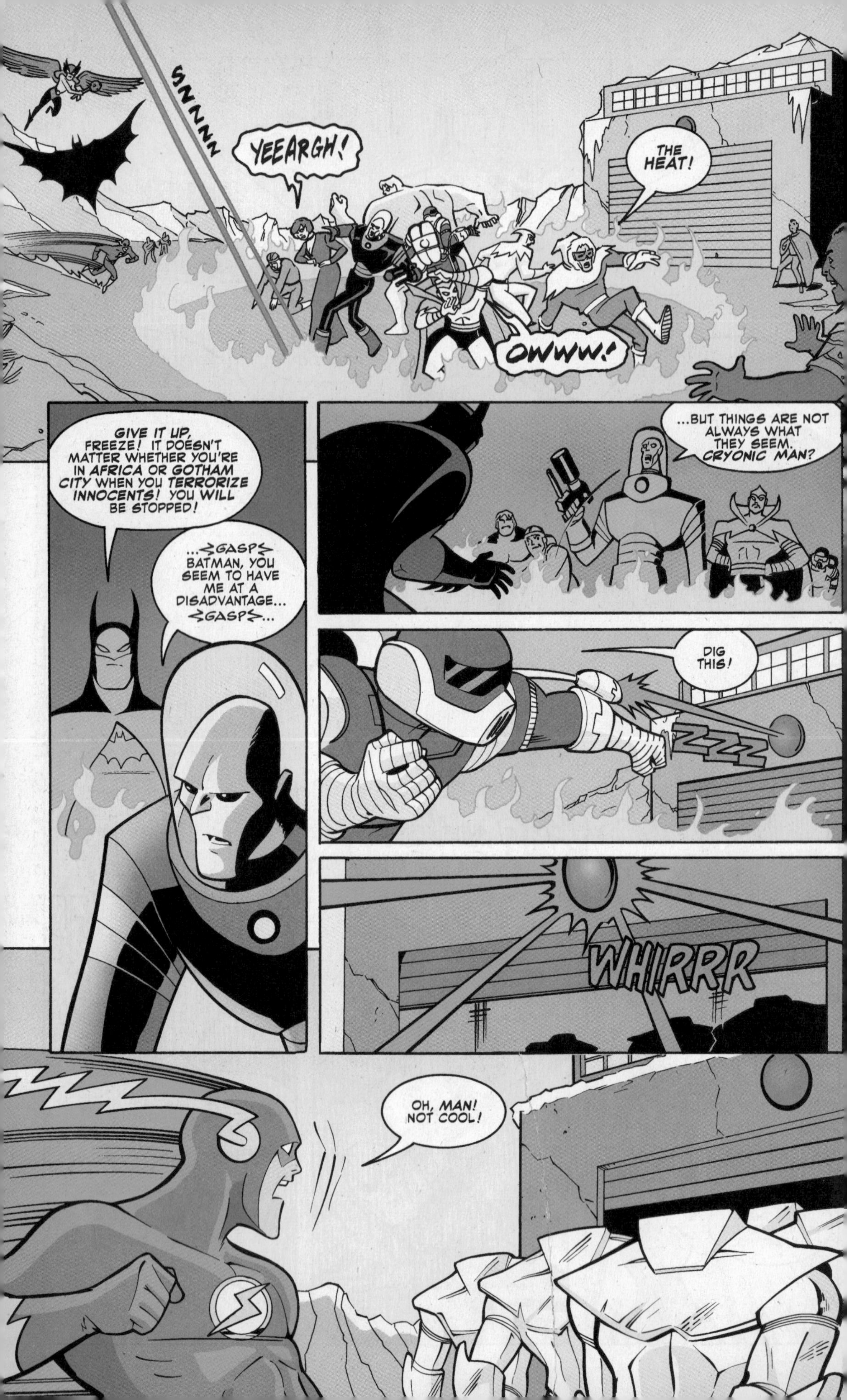
SNNNNN
YEEARGH!
THE HEAT!
OWWW!
GIVE IT UP, FREEZE! IT DOESN'T MATTER WHETHER YOU'RE IN AFRICA OR GOTHAM CITY WHEN YOU TERRORIZE INNOCENTS! YOU WILL BE STOPPED!
...GASP BATMAN, YOU SEEM TO HAVE ME AT A DISADVANTAGE... GASP...
...BUT THINGS ARE NOT ALWAYS WHAT THEY SEEM. CRYONIC MAN?
DIG THIS!
WHIRRR
OH, MAN! NOT COOL!

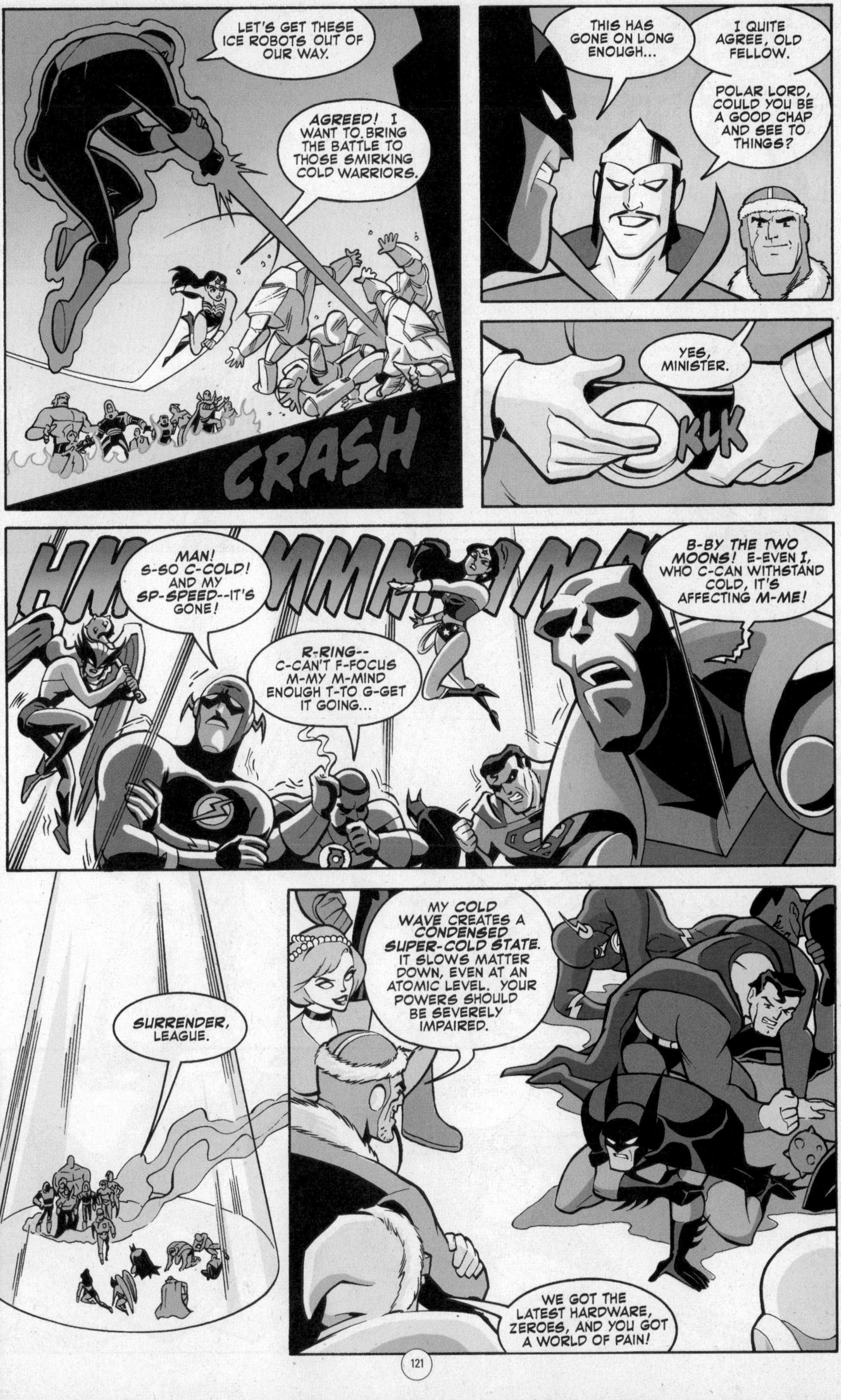
LET'S GET THESE ICE ROBOTS OUT OF OUR WAY.
AGREED! I WANT TO BRING THE BATTLE TO THOSE SMIRKING COLD WARRIORS.
CRASH
THIS HAS GONE ON LONG ENOUGH...
I QUITE AGREE, OLD FELLOW.
POLAR LORD, COULD YOU BE A GOOD CHAP AND SEE TO THINGS?
YES, MINISTER.
KLK
MAN! S-SO C-COLD! AND MY SP-SPEED--IT'S GONE!
R-RING-- C-CAN'T F-FOCUS M-MY M-MIND ENOUGH T-TO G-GET IT GOING...
B-BY THE TWO MOONS! E-EVEN I, WHO C-CAN WITHSTAND COLD, IT'S AFFECTING M-ME!
SURRENDER, LEAGUE.
MY COLD WAVE CREATES A CONDENSED SUPER-COLD STATE. IT SLOWS MATTER DOWN, EVEN AT AN ATOMIC LEVEL. YOUR POWERS SHOULD BE SEVERELY IMPAIRED.
WE GOT THE LATEST HARDWARE, ZEROES, AND YOU GOT A WORLD OF PAIN!

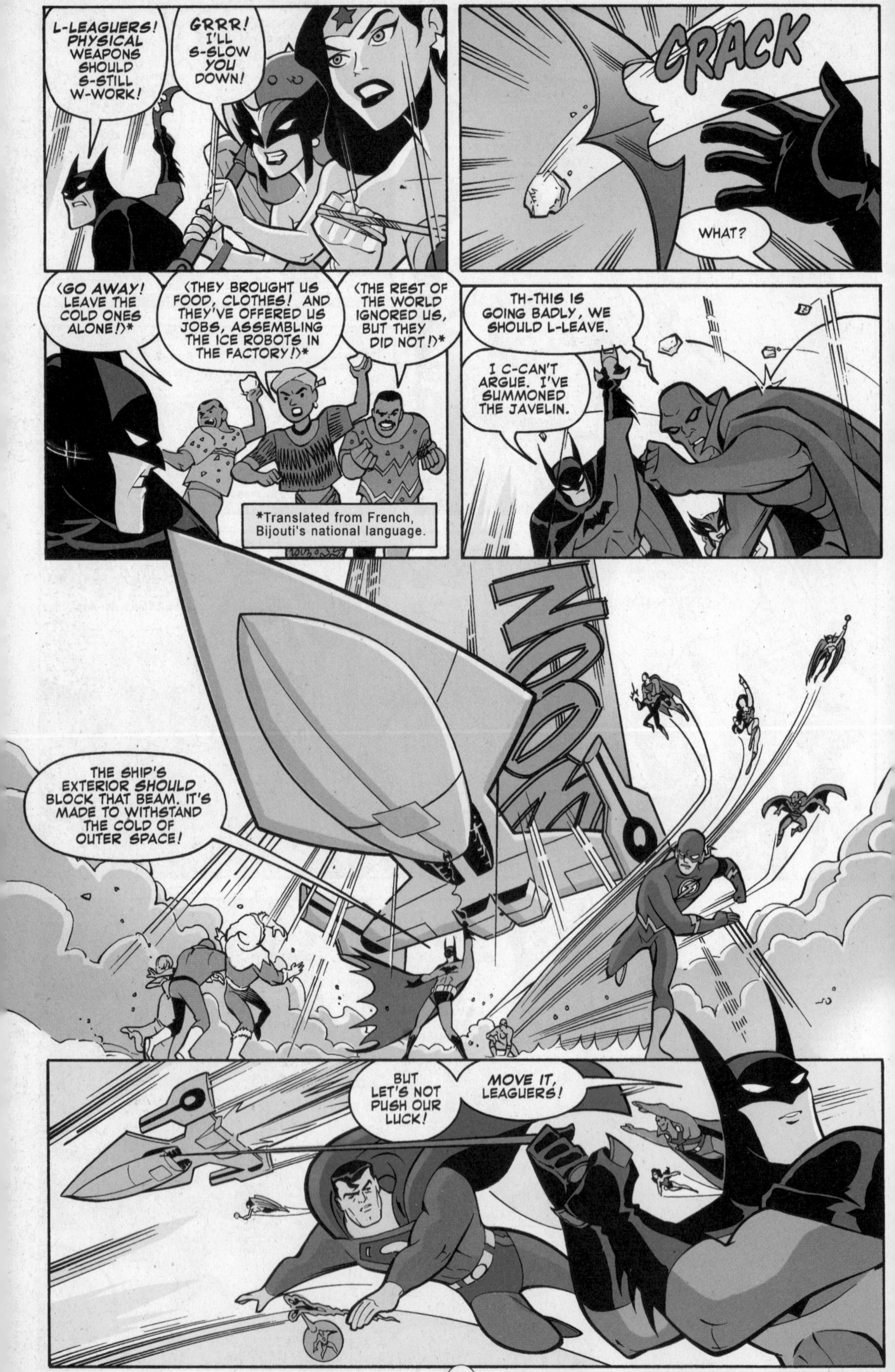
L-LEAGUERS! PHYSICAL WEAPONS SHOULD S-STILL W-WORK!
GRRR! I'LL S-SLOW YOU DOWN!
CRACK
WHAT?
‹GO AWAY! LEAVE THE COLD ONES ALONE!›*
‹THEY BROUGHT US FOOD, CLOTHES! AND THEY'VE OFFERED US JOBS, ASSEMBLING THE ICE ROBOTS IN THE FACTORY!›*
‹THE REST OF THE WORLD IGNORED US, BUT THEY DID NOT!›*
*Translated from French, Bijouti's national language.
TH-THIS IS GOING BADLY, WE SHOULD L-LEAVE.
I C-CAN'T ARGUE. I'VE SUMMONED THE JAVELIN.
WOOOM
THE SHIP'S EXTERIOR SHOULD BLOCK THAT BEAM. IT'S MADE TO WITHSTAND THE COLD OF OUTER SPACE!
BUT LET'S NOT PUSH OUR LUCK!
MOVE IT, LEAGUERS!

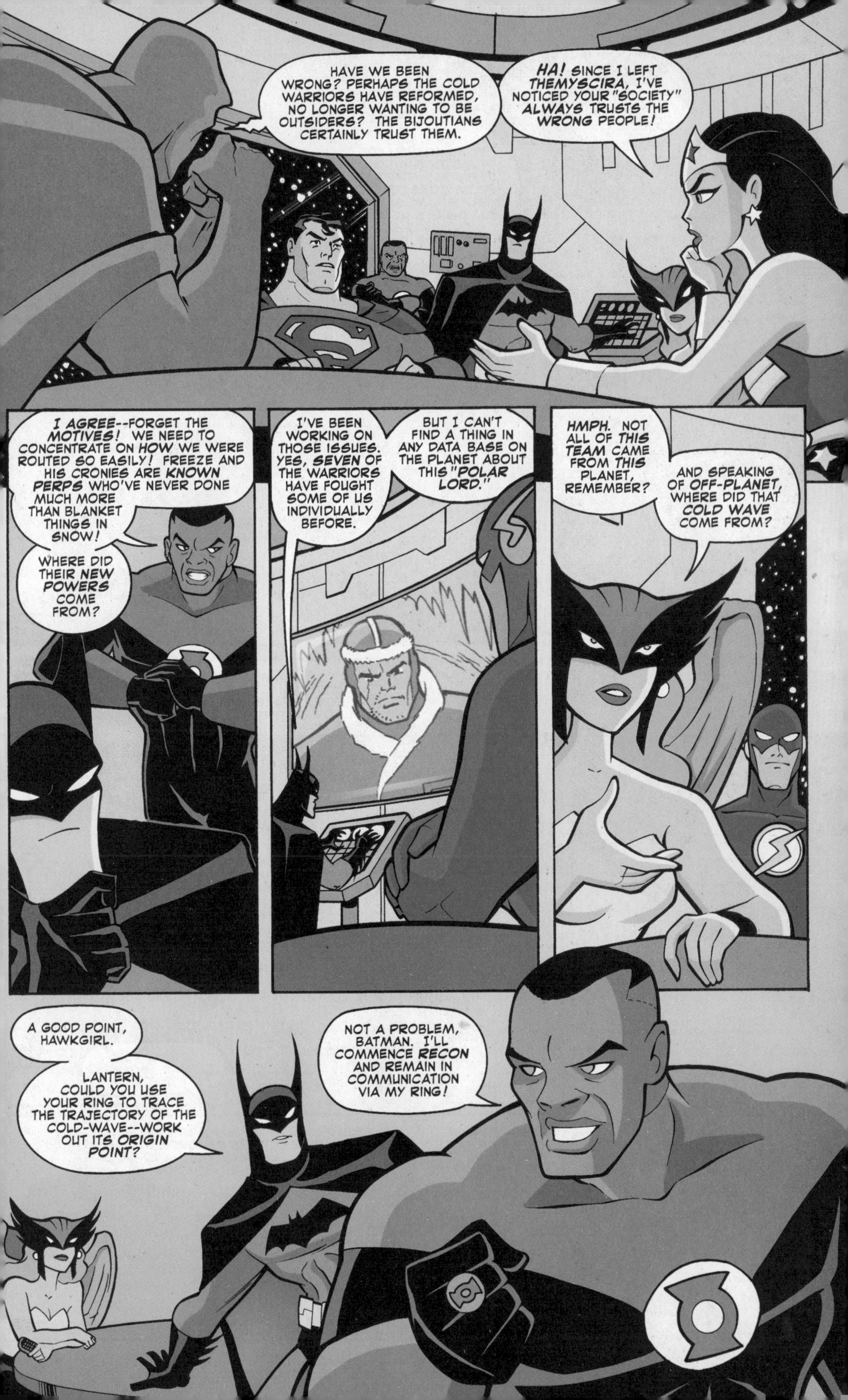
HAVE WE BEEN WRONG? PERHAPS THE COLD WARRIORS HAVE REFORMED, NO LONGER WANTING TO BE OUTSIDERS? THE BIJOUTIANS CERTAINLY TRUST THEM.
HA! SINCE I LEFT THEMYSCIRA, I'VE NOTICED YOUR "SOCIETY" ALWAYS TRUSTS THE WRONG PEOPLE!
I AGREE--FORGET THE MOTIVES! WE NEED TO CONCENTRATE ON HOW WE WERE ROUTED SO EASILY! FREEZE AND HIS CRONIES ARE KNOWN PERPS WHO'VE NEVER DONE MUCH MORE THAN BLANKET THINGS IN SNOW!
WHERE DID THEIR NEW POWERS COME FROM?
I'VE BEEN WORKING ON THOSE ISSUES. YES, SEVEN OF THE WARRIORS HAVE FOUGHT SOME OF US INDIVIDUALLY BEFORE.
BUT I CAN'T FIND A THING IN ANY DATA BASE ON THE PLANET ABOUT THIS "POLAR LORD."
HMPH. NOT ALL OF THIS TEAM CAME FROM THIS PLANET, REMEMBER?
AND SPEAKING OF OFF-PLANET, WHERE DID THAT COLD WAVE COME FROM?
A GOOD POINT, HAWKGIRL.
LANTERN, COULD YOU USE YOUR RING TO TRACE THE TRAJECTORY OF THE COLD-WAVE--WORK OUT ITS ORIGIN POINT?
NOT A PROBLEM, BATMAN. I'LL COMMENCE RECON AND REMAIN IN COMMUNICATION VIA MY RING!

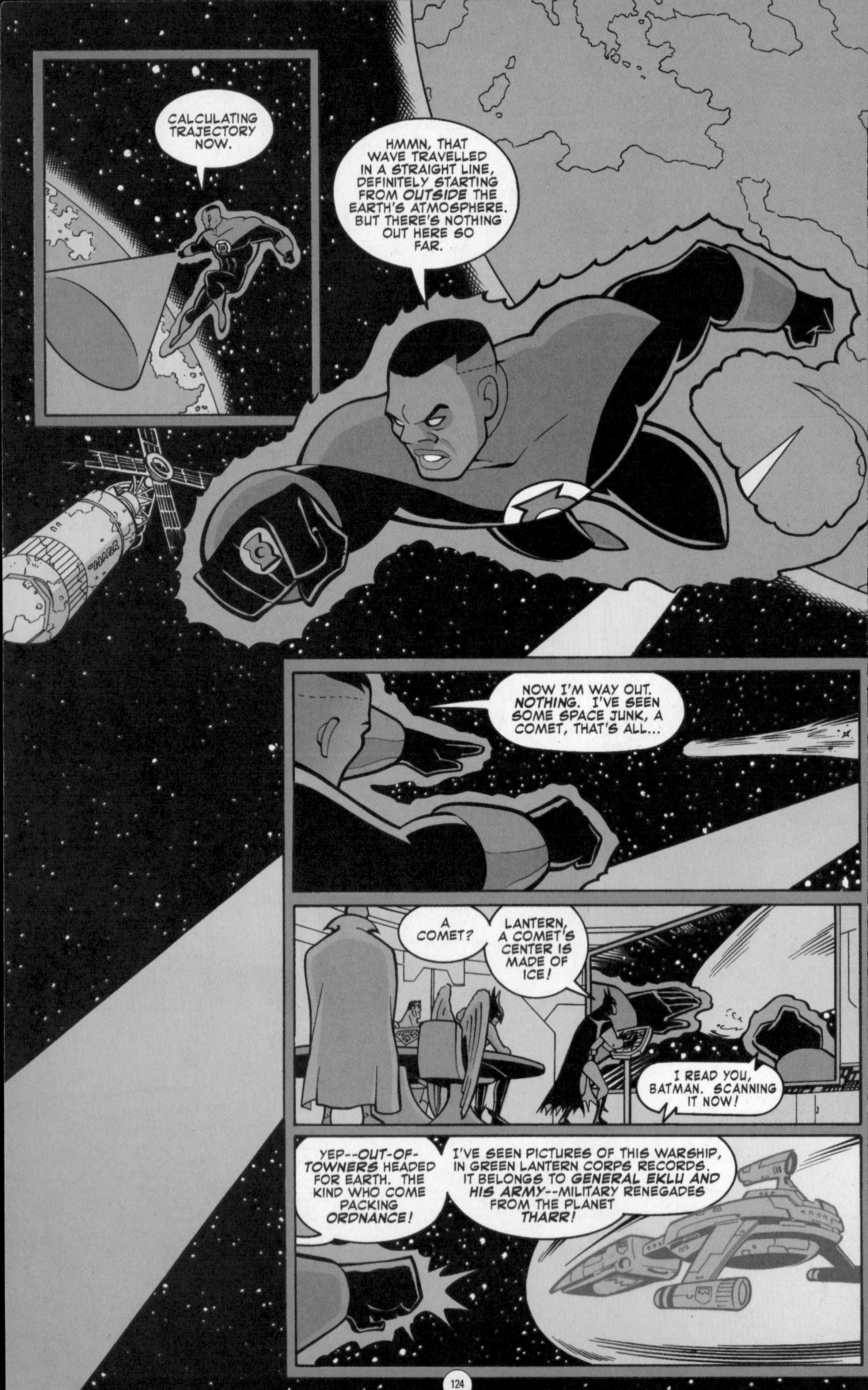
CALCULATING TRAJECTORY NOW.
HMMN, THAT WAVE TRAVELLED IN A STRAIGHT LINE, DEFINITELY STARTING FROM OUTSIDE THE EARTH'S ATMOSPHERE. BUT THERE'S NOTHING OUT HERE SO FAR.
NOW I'M WAY OUT. NOTHING. I'VE SEEN SOME SPACE JUNK, A COMET, THAT'S ALL...
A COMET?
LANTERN, A COMET'S CENTER IS MADE OF ICE!
I READ YOU, BATMAN. SCANNING IT NOW!
YEP--OUT-OF-TOWNERS HEADED FOR EARTH. THE KIND WHO COME PACKING ORDNANCE!
I'VE SEEN PICTURES OF THIS WARSHIP, IN GREEN LANTERN CORPS RECORDS. IT BELONGS TO GENERAL EKLU AND HIS ARMY--MILITARY RENEGADES FROM THE PLANET THARR!

AND ALL THARRIANS HAVE COLD POWERS AND COLD-BASED TECHNOLOGY TO COMPENSATE FOR THEIR HOT PLANET! POLAR LORD MUST BE GENERAL EKLU!

LANTERN! I CAN BE THERE IN *MINUTES* IF YOU WANT TO INTERCEPT THEM!

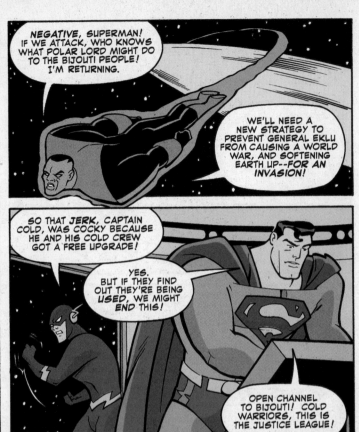

NEGATIVE, SUPERMAN! IF WE ATTACK, WHO KNOWS WHAT POLAR LORD MIGHT DO TO THE BIJOUTI PEOPLE! I'M RETURNING.

WE'LL NEED A NEW STRATEGY TO PREVENT GENERAL EKLU FROM CAUSING A WORLD WAR, AND SOFTENING EARTH UP--FOR AN INVASION!

SO THAT *JERK*, CAPTAIN COLD, WAS COCKY BECAUSE HE AND HIS COLD CREW GOT A *FREE* UPGRADE!

YES. BUT IF THEY FIND OUT THEY'RE BEING *USED*, WE MIGHT END THIS!

OPEN CHANNEL TO BIJOUTI! COLD WARRIORS, THIS IS THE JUSTICE LEAGUE!

SUPERMAN, NICE OF YOU TO CALL.

FREEZE, WE HAVE PROOF THAT POLAR LORD IS AN ALIEN TYRANT FROM A PLANET CALLED *THARR*. YOU AND YOUR FRIENDS ARE BEING *MANIPULATED* IN A PLOT TO INVADE EARTH!

ARE YOU CLAIMING WE'RE BEING SET UP?

I SAY, YOU MEAN POLAR LORD'S GOT HIS OWN AGENDA?

THAT WE'RE WORKING FOR AN ALIEN?

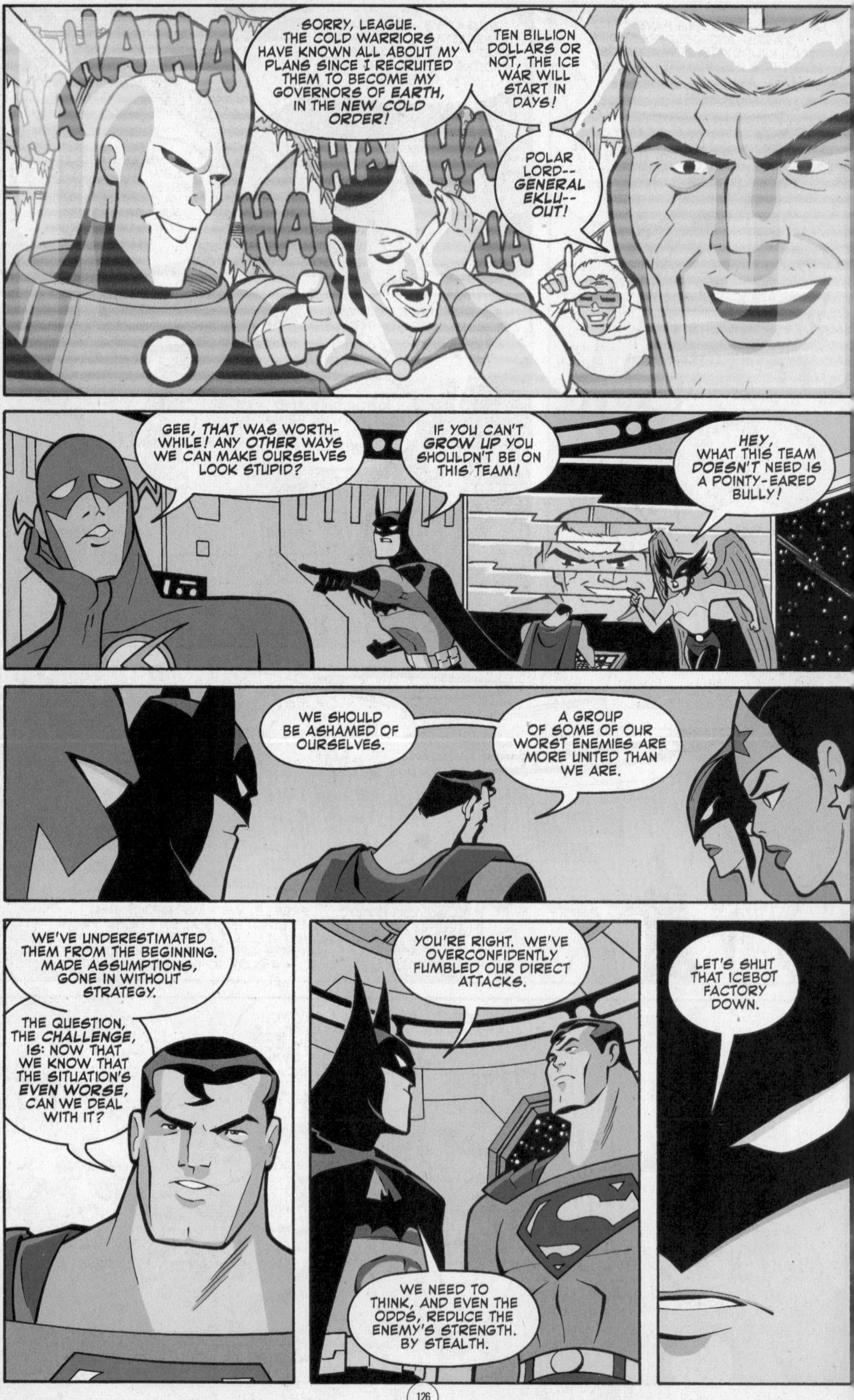
HA HA HA HA
SORRY, LEAGUE. THE COLD WARRIORS HAVE KNOWN ALL ABOUT MY PLANS SINCE I RECRUITED THEM TO BECOME MY GOVERNORS OF EARTH, IN THE NEW COLD ORDER!
TEN BILLION DOLLARS OR NOT, THE ICE WAR WILL START IN DAYS!
POLAR LORD-- GENERAL EKLU-- OUT!
HA HA HA HA
GEE, THAT WAS WORTH-WHILE! ANY OTHER WAYS WE CAN MAKE OURSELVES LOOK STUPID?
IF YOU CAN'T GROW UP YOU SHOULDN'T BE ON THIS TEAM!
HEY, WHAT THIS TEAM DOESN'T NEED IS A POINTY-EARED BULLY!
WE SHOULD BE ASHAMED OF OURSELVES.
A GROUP OF SOME OF OUR WORST ENEMIES ARE MORE UNITED THAN WE ARE.
WE'VE UNDERESTIMATED THEM FROM THE BEGINNING. MADE ASSUMPTIONS, GONE IN WITHOUT STRATEGY.
THE QUESTION, THE CHALLENGE, IS: NOW THAT WE KNOW THAT THE SITUATION'S EVEN WORSE, CAN WE DEAL WITH IT?
YOU'RE RIGHT. WE'VE OVERCONFIDENTLY FUMBLED OUR DIRECT ATTACKS.
WE NEED TO THINK, AND EVEN THE ODDS, REDUCE THE ENEMY'S STRENGTH. BY STEALTH.
LET'S SHUT THAT ICEBOT FACTORY DOWN.

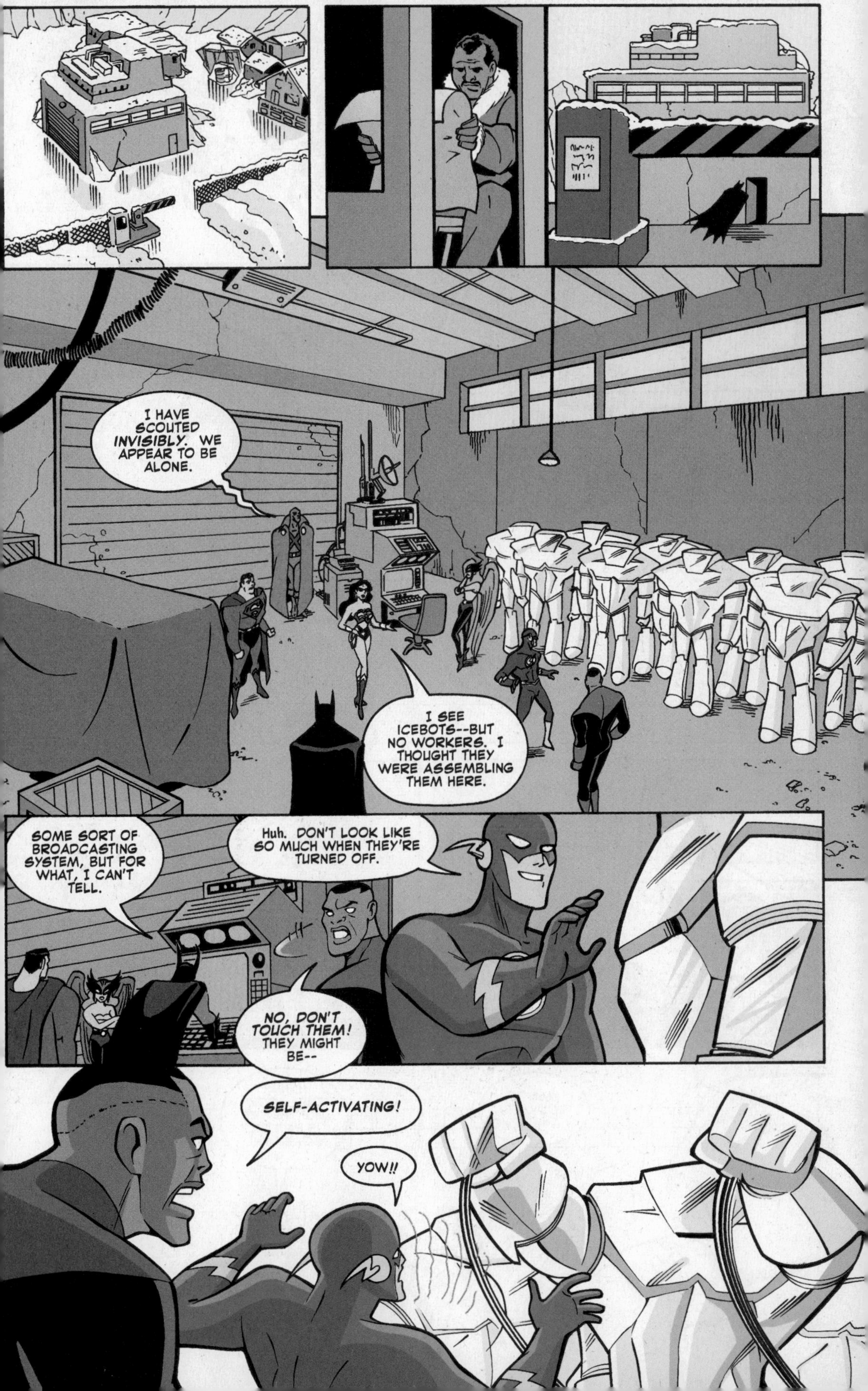

I HAVE SCOUTED INVISIBLY. WE APPEAR TO BE ALONE.
I SEE ICEBOTS--BUT NO WORKERS. I THOUGHT THEY WERE ASSEMBLING THEM HERE.
SOME SORT OF BROADCASTING SYSTEM, BUT FOR WHAT, I CAN'T TELL.
Huh. DON'T LOOK LIKE SO MUCH WHEN THEY'RE TURNED OFF.
NO, DON'T TOUCH THEM! THEY MIGHT BE--
SELF-ACTIVATING!
YOW!!

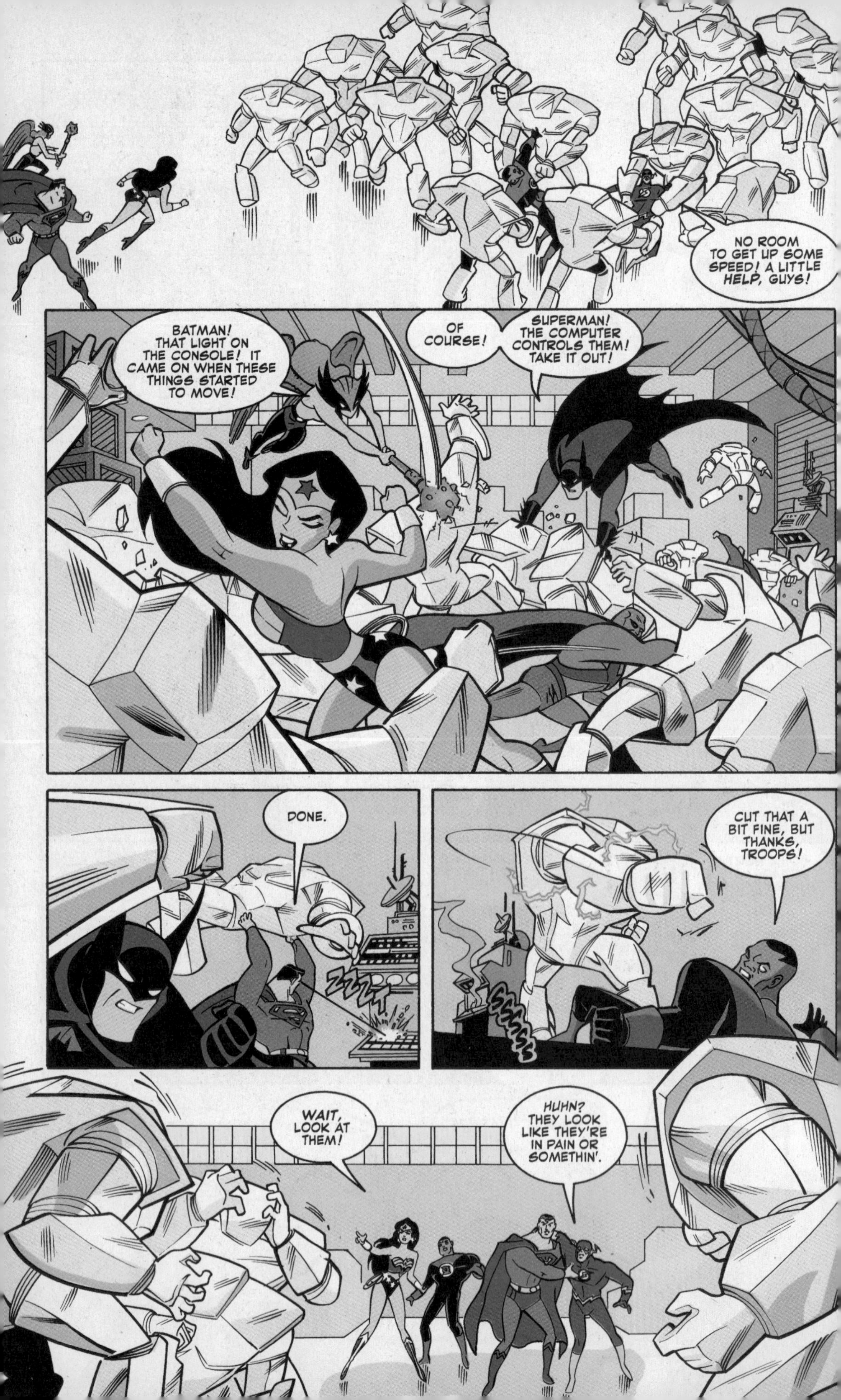
NO ROOM TO GET UP SOME SPEED! A LITTLE HELP, GUYS!
BATMAN! THAT LIGHT ON THE CONSOLE! IT CAME ON WHEN THESE THINGS STARTED TO MOVE!
OF COURSE!
SUPERMAN! THE COMPUTER CONTROLS THEM! TAKE IT OUT!
DONE.
ZZZT
CUT THAT A BIT FINE, BUT THANKS, TROOPS!
SSSSS
WAIT, LOOK AT THEM!
HUHN? THEY LOOK LIKE THEY'RE IN PAIN OR SOMETHIN'.

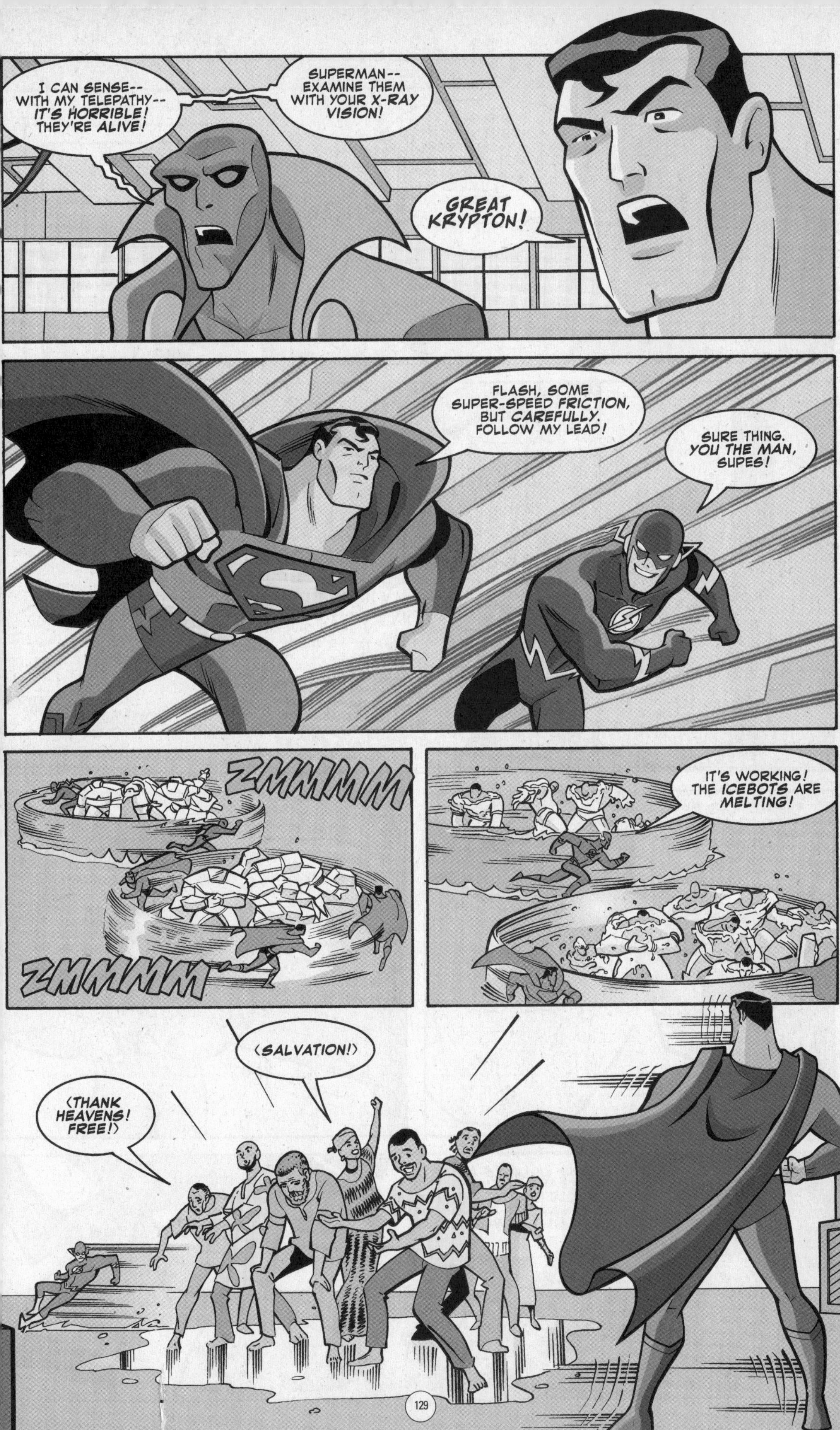
I CAN SENSE-- WITH MY TELEPATHY-- IT'S HORRIBLE! THEY'RE ALIVE!
SUPERMAN-- EXAMINE THEM WITH YOUR X-RAY VISION!
GREAT KRYPTON!
FLASH, SOME SUPER-SPEED FRICTION, BUT CAREFULLY. FOLLOW MY LEAD!
SURE THING. YOU THE MAN, SUPES!
ZMMMMM
ZMMMMM
IT'S WORKING! THE ICEBOTS ARE MELTING!
(SALVATION!)
(THANK HEAVENS! FREE!)

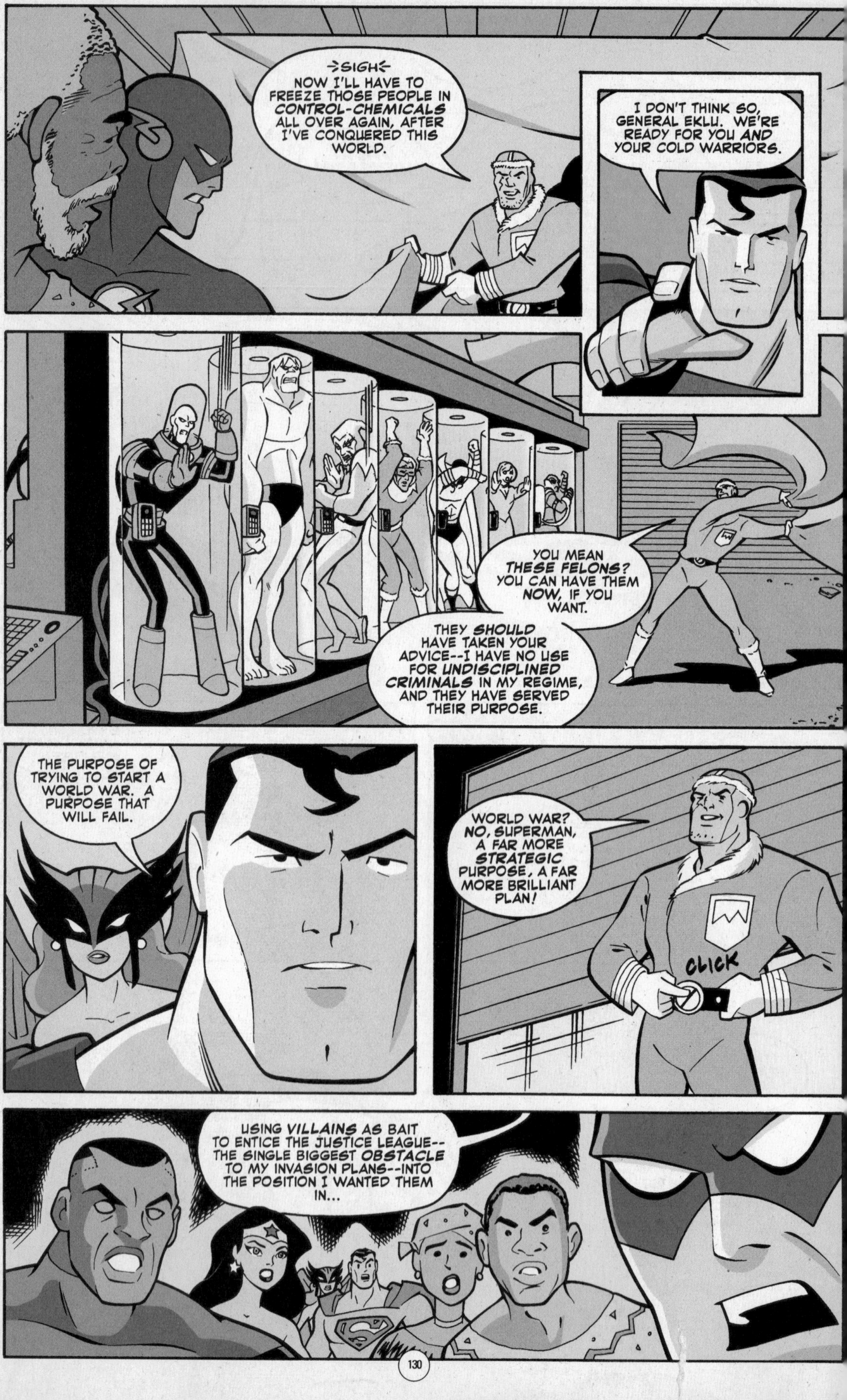

SIGH
NOW I'LL HAVE TO FREEZE THOSE PEOPLE IN CONTROL-CHEMICALS ALL OVER AGAIN, AFTER I'VE CONQUERED THIS WORLD.
I DON'T THINK SO, GENERAL EKLU. WE'RE READY FOR YOU AND YOUR COLD WARRIORS.
YOU MEAN THESE FELONS? YOU CAN HAVE THEM NOW, IF YOU WANT.
THEY SHOULD HAVE TAKEN YOUR ADVICE--I HAVE NO USE FOR UNDISCIPLINED CRIMINALS IN MY REGIME, AND THEY HAVE SERVED THEIR PURPOSE.
THE PURPOSE OF TRYING TO START A WORLD WAR. A PURPOSE THAT WILL FAIL.
WORLD WAR? NO, SUPERMAN, A FAR MORE STRATEGIC PURPOSE, A FAR MORE BRILLIANT PLAN!
CLICK
USING VILLAINS AS BAIT TO ENTICE THE JUSTICE LEAGUE--THE SINGLE BIGGEST OBSTACLE TO MY INVASION PLANS--INTO THE POSITION I WANTED THEM IN...

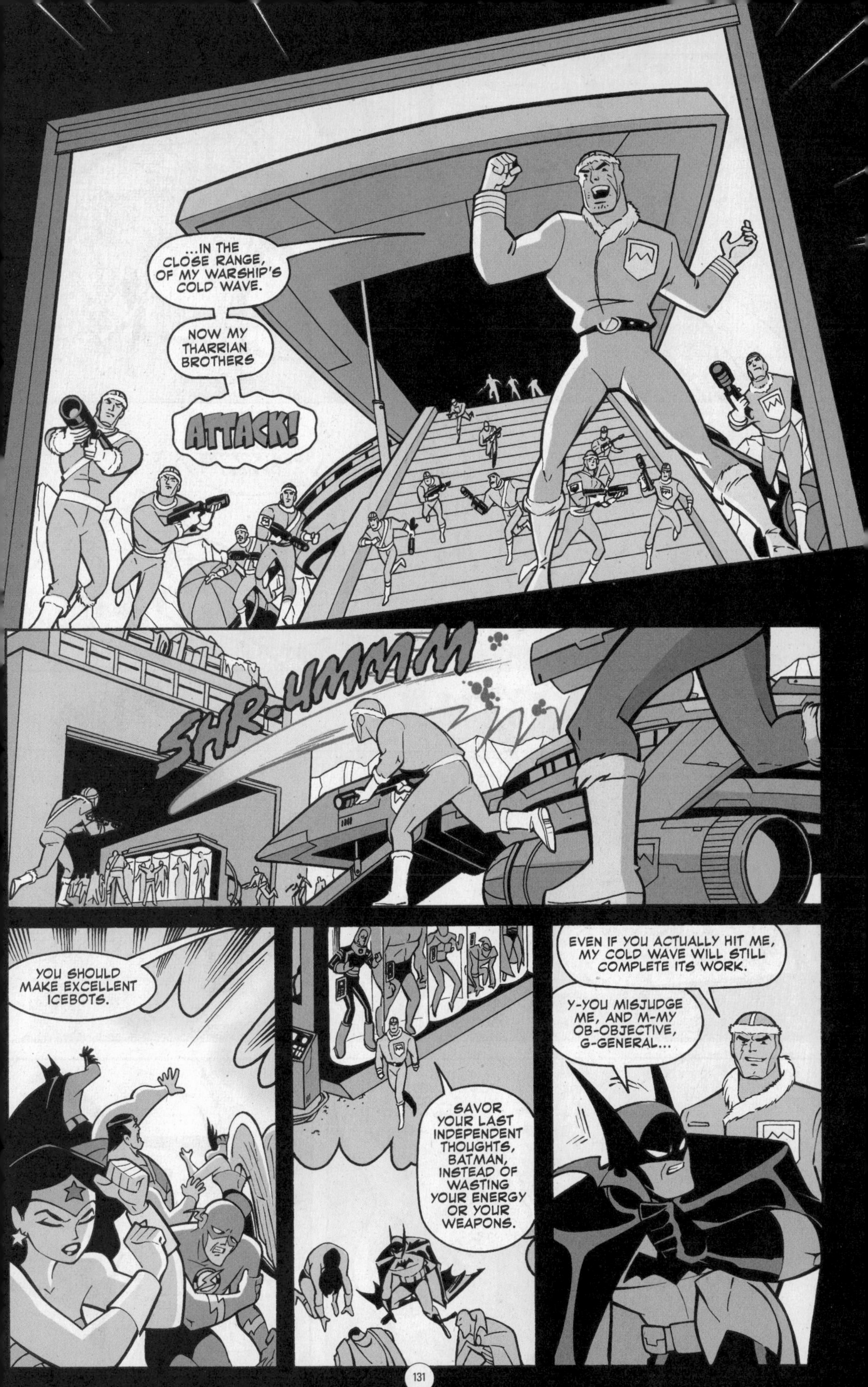

...IN THE CLOSE RANGE, OF MY WARSHIP'S COLD WAVE.
NOW MY THARRIAN BROTHERS
ATTACK!
SHR-UMMMM
YOU SHOULD MAKE EXCELLENT ICEBOTS.
SAVOR YOUR LAST INDEPENDENT THOUGHTS, BATMAN, INSTEAD OF WASTING YOUR ENERGY OR YOUR WEAPONS.
EVEN IF YOU ACTUALLY HIT ME, MY COLD WAVE WILL STILL COMPLETE ITS WORK.
Y-YOU MISJUDGE ME, AND M-MY OB-OBJECTIVE, G-GENERAL...

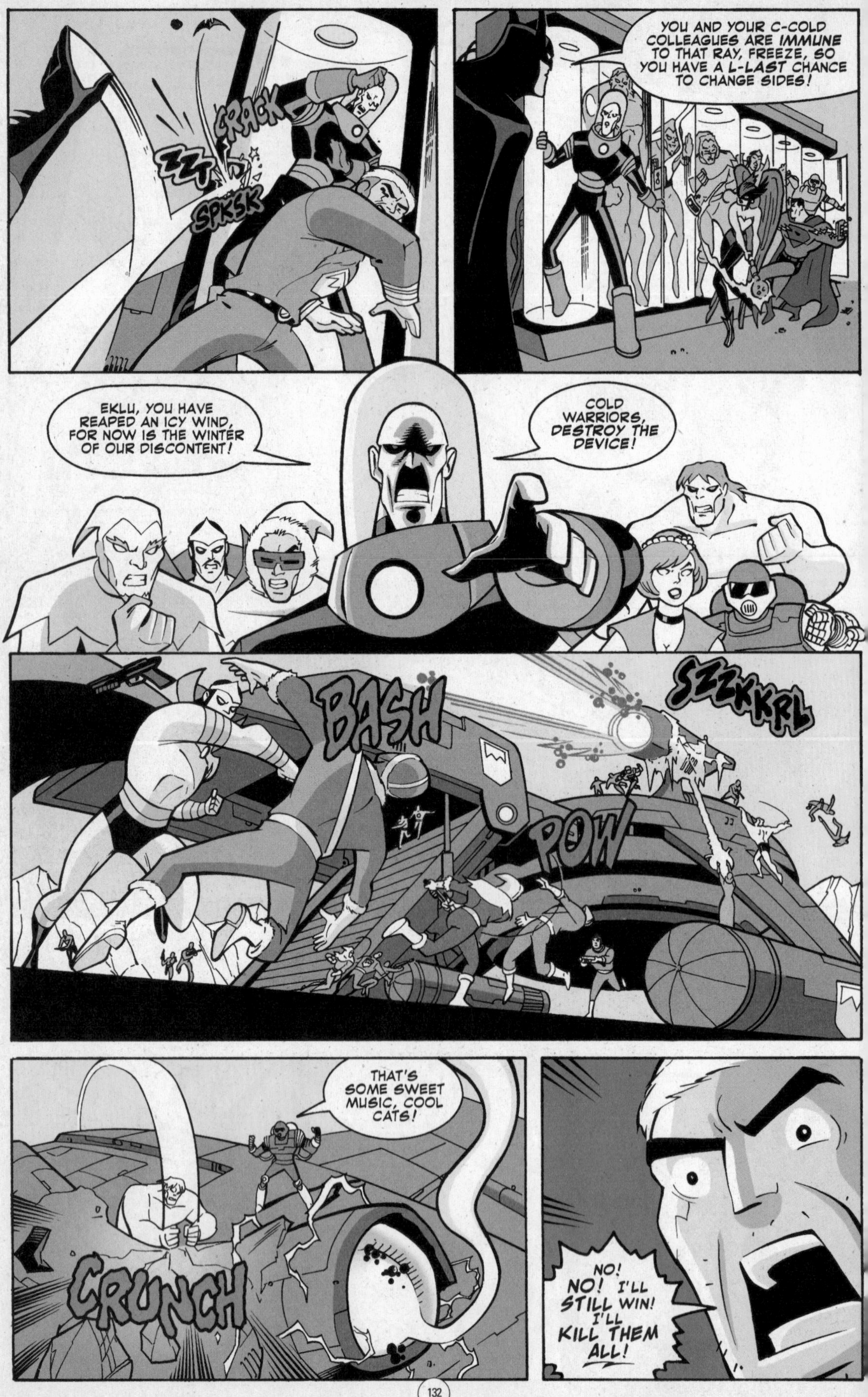
CRACK
ZZT
SPKSK
YOU AND YOUR C-COLD COLLEAGUES ARE IMMUNE TO THAT RAY, FREEZE, SO YOU HAVE A L-LAST CHANCE TO CHANGE SIDES!
EKLU, YOU HAVE REAPED AN ICY WIND, FOR NOW IS THE WINTER OF OUR DISCONTENT!
COLD WARRIORS, DESTROY THE DEVICE!
BASH
SZZKKRL
POW
THAT'S SOME SWEET MUSIC, COOL CATS!
CRUNCH
NO! NO! I'LL STILL WIN! I'LL KILL THEM ALL!

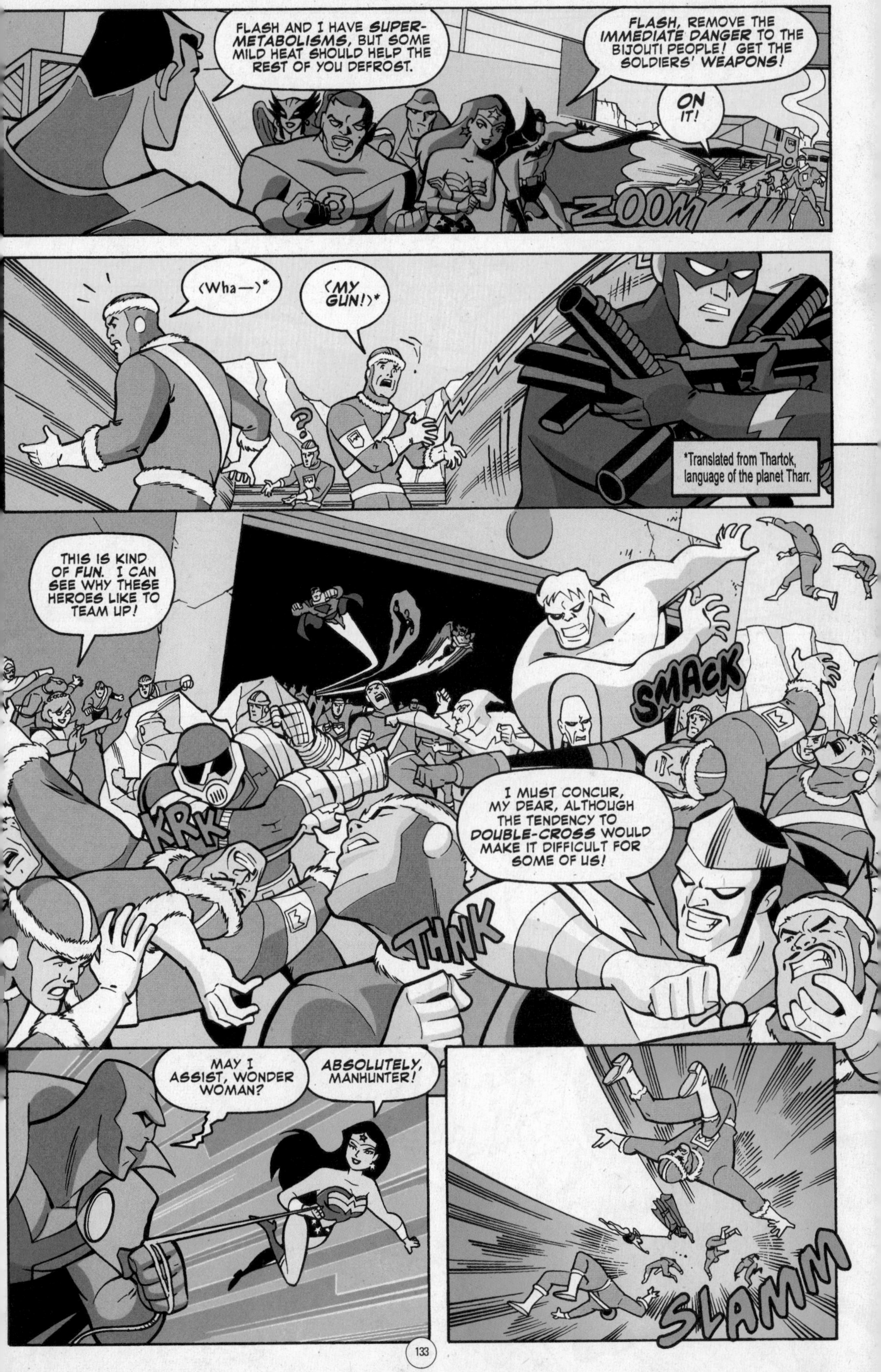
FLASH AND I HAVE SUPER-METABOLISMS, BUT SOME MILD HEAT SHOULD HELP THE REST OF YOU DEFROST.
FLASH, REMOVE THE IMMEDIATE DANGER TO THE BIJOUTI PEOPLE! GET THE SOLDIERS' WEAPONS!
ON IT!
ZOOM
‹Wha—›*
‹MY GUN!›*
*Translated from Thartok, language of the planet Tharr.
THIS IS KIND OF FUN. I CAN SEE WHY THESE HEROES LIKE TO TEAM UP!
SMACK
KRK
I MUST CONCUR, MY DEAR, ALTHOUGH THE TENDENCY TO DOUBLE-CROSS WOULD MAKE IT DIFFICULT FOR SOME OF US!
THNK
MAY I ASSIST, WONDER WOMAN?
ABSOLUTELY, MANHUNTER!
SLAMM

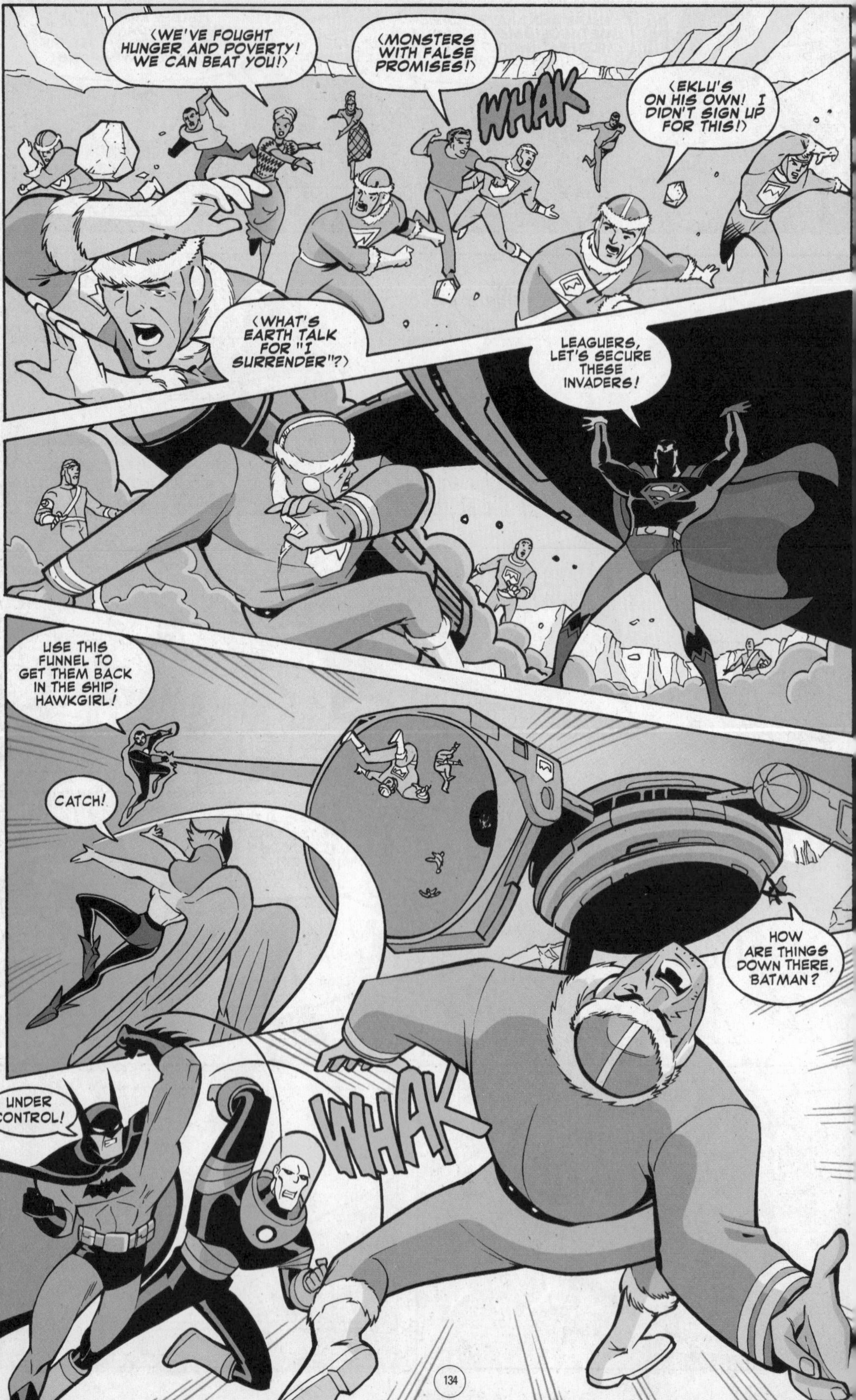
‹WE'VE FOUGHT HUNGER AND POVERTY! WE CAN BEAT YOU!›
‹MONSTERS WITH FALSE PROMISES!›
WHAK
‹EKLU'S ON HIS OWN! I DIDN'T SIGN UP FOR THIS!›
‹WHAT'S EARTH TALK FOR "I SURRENDER"?›
LEAGUERS, LET'S SECURE THESE INVADERS!
USE THIS FUNNEL TO GET THEM BACK IN THE SHIP, HAWKGIRL!
CATCH!
HOW ARE THINGS DOWN THERE, BATMAN?
UNDER CONTROL!
WHAK

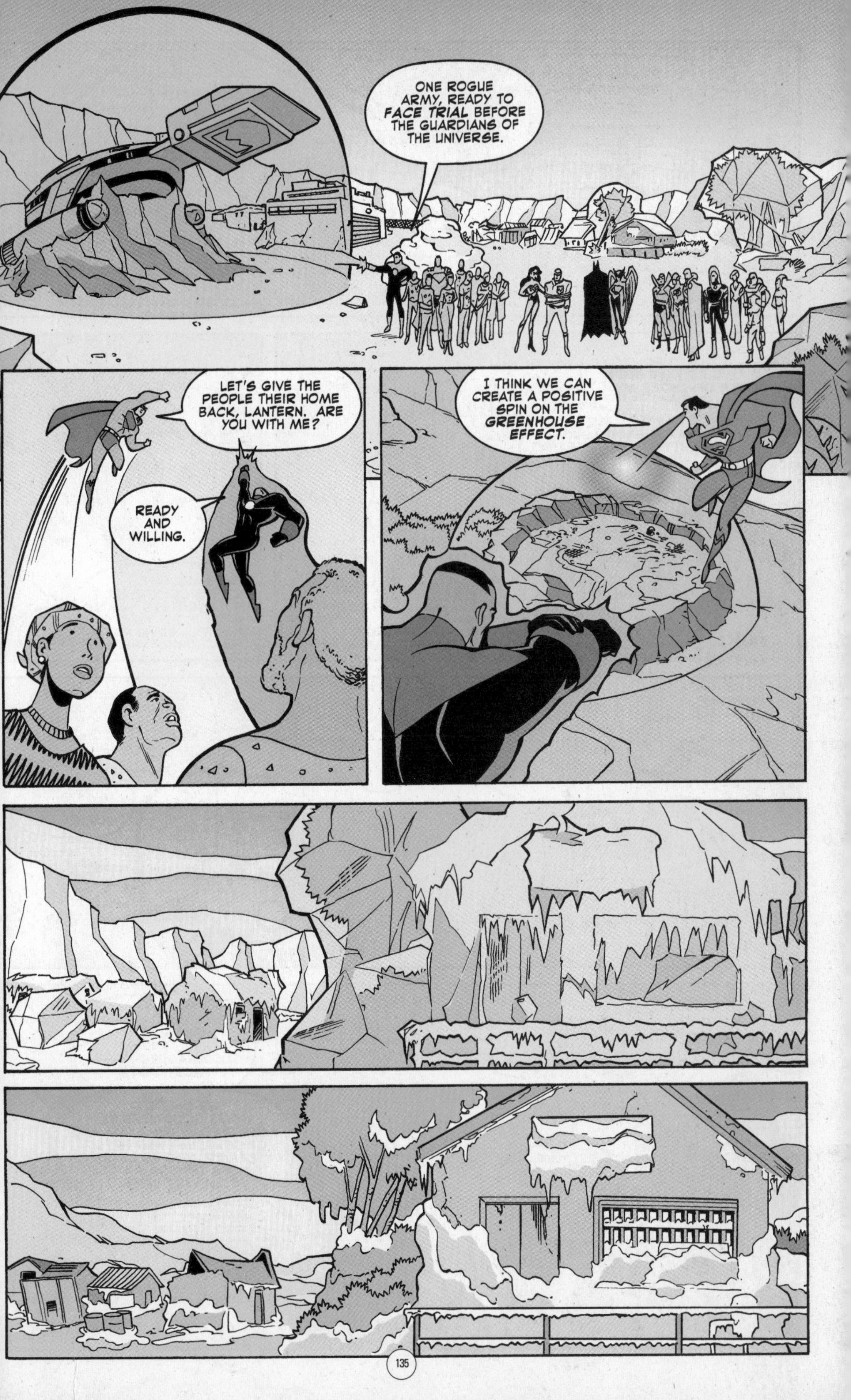
ONE ROGUE ARMY, READY TO FACE TRIAL BEFORE THE GUARDIANS OF THE UNIVERSE.
LET'S GIVE THE PEOPLE THEIR HOME BACK, LANTERN. ARE YOU WITH ME?
READY AND WILLING.
I THINK WE CAN CREATE A POSITIVE SPIN ON THE GREENHOUSE EFFECT.

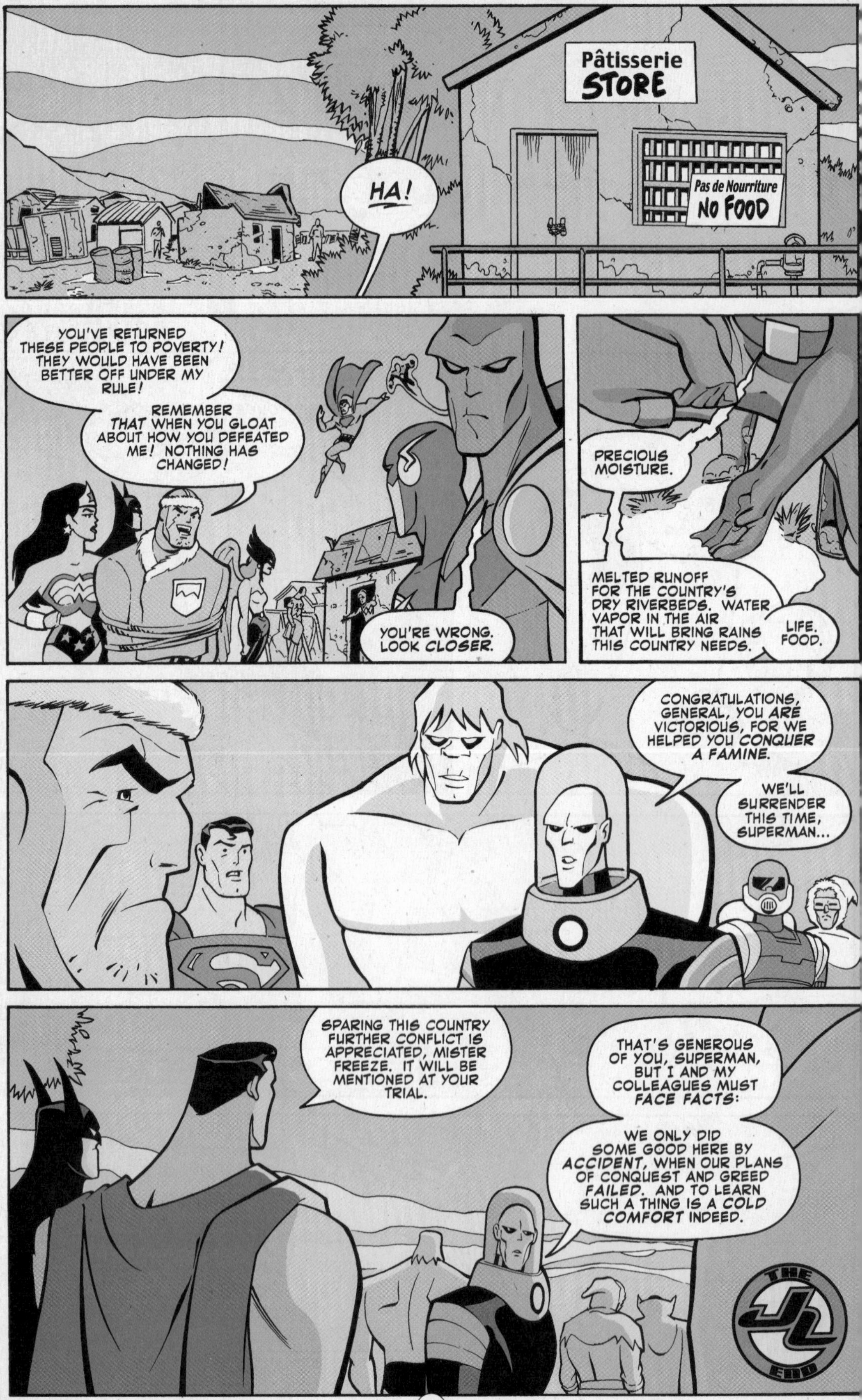
Pâtisserie STORE
Pas de Nourriture NO FOOD
HA!
YOU'VE RETURNED THESE PEOPLE TO POVERTY! THEY WOULD HAVE BEEN BETTER OFF UNDER MY RULE!
REMEMBER THAT WHEN YOU GLOAT ABOUT HOW YOU DEFEATED ME! NOTHING HAS CHANGED!
YOU'RE WRONG. LOOK CLOSER.
PRECIOUS MOISTURE.
MELTED RUNOFF FOR THE COUNTRY'S DRY RIVERBEDS. WATER VAPOR IN THE AIR THAT WILL BRING RAINS THIS COUNTRY NEEDS.
LIFE. FOOD.
CONGRATULATIONS, GENERAL, YOU ARE VICTORIOUS, FOR WE HELPED YOU CONQUER A FAMINE.
WE'LL SURRENDER THIS TIME, SUPERMAN...
SPARING THIS COUNTRY FURTHER CONFLICT IS APPRECIATED, MISTER FREEZE. IT WILL BE MENTIONED AT YOUR TRIAL.
THAT'S GENEROUS OF YOU, SUPERMAN, BUT I AND MY COLLEAGUES MUST FACE FACTS:
WE ONLY DID SOME GOOD HERE BY ACCIDENT, WHEN OUR PLANS OF CONQUEST AND GREED FAILED. AND TO LEARN SUCH A THING IS A COLD COMFORT INDEED.
THE END

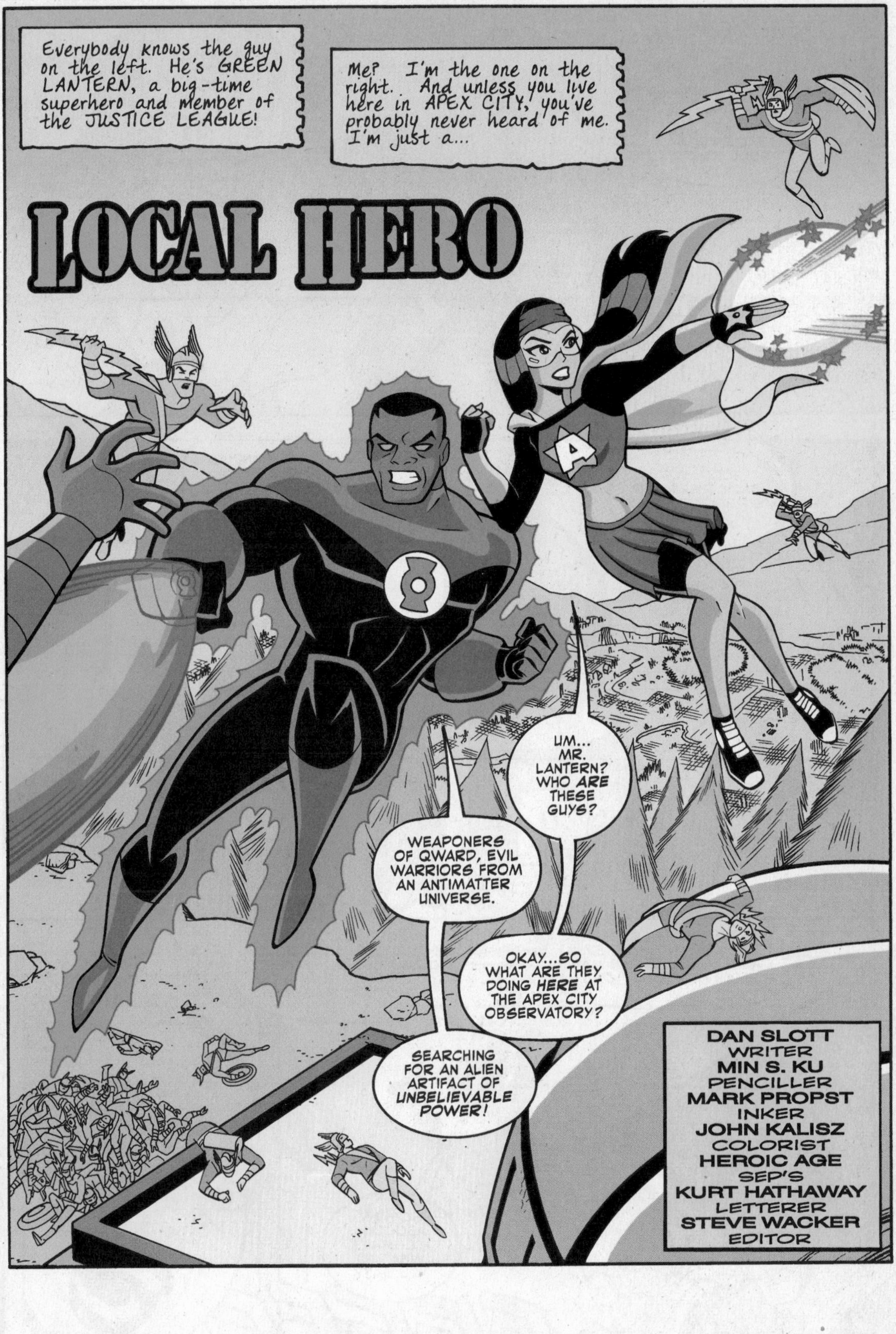

Everybody knows the guy on the left. He's GREEN LANTERN, a big-time superhero and member of the JUSTICE LEAGUE!
Me? I'm the one on the right. And unless you live here in APEX CITY, you've probably never heard of me. I'm just a...
LOCAL HERO
UM... MR. LANTERN? WHO ARE THESE GUYS?
WEAPONERS OF QWARD, EVIL WARRIORS FROM AN ANTIMATTER UNIVERSE.
OKAY...SO WHAT ARE THEY DOING HERE AT THE APEX CITY OBSERVATORY?
SEARCHING FOR AN ALIEN ARTIFACT OF UNBELIEVABLE POWER!
DAN SLOTT WRITER
MIN S. KU PENCILLER
MARK PROPST INKER
JOHN KALISZ COLORIST
HEROIC AGE SEP'S
KURT HATHAWAY LETTERER
STEVE WACKER EDITOR

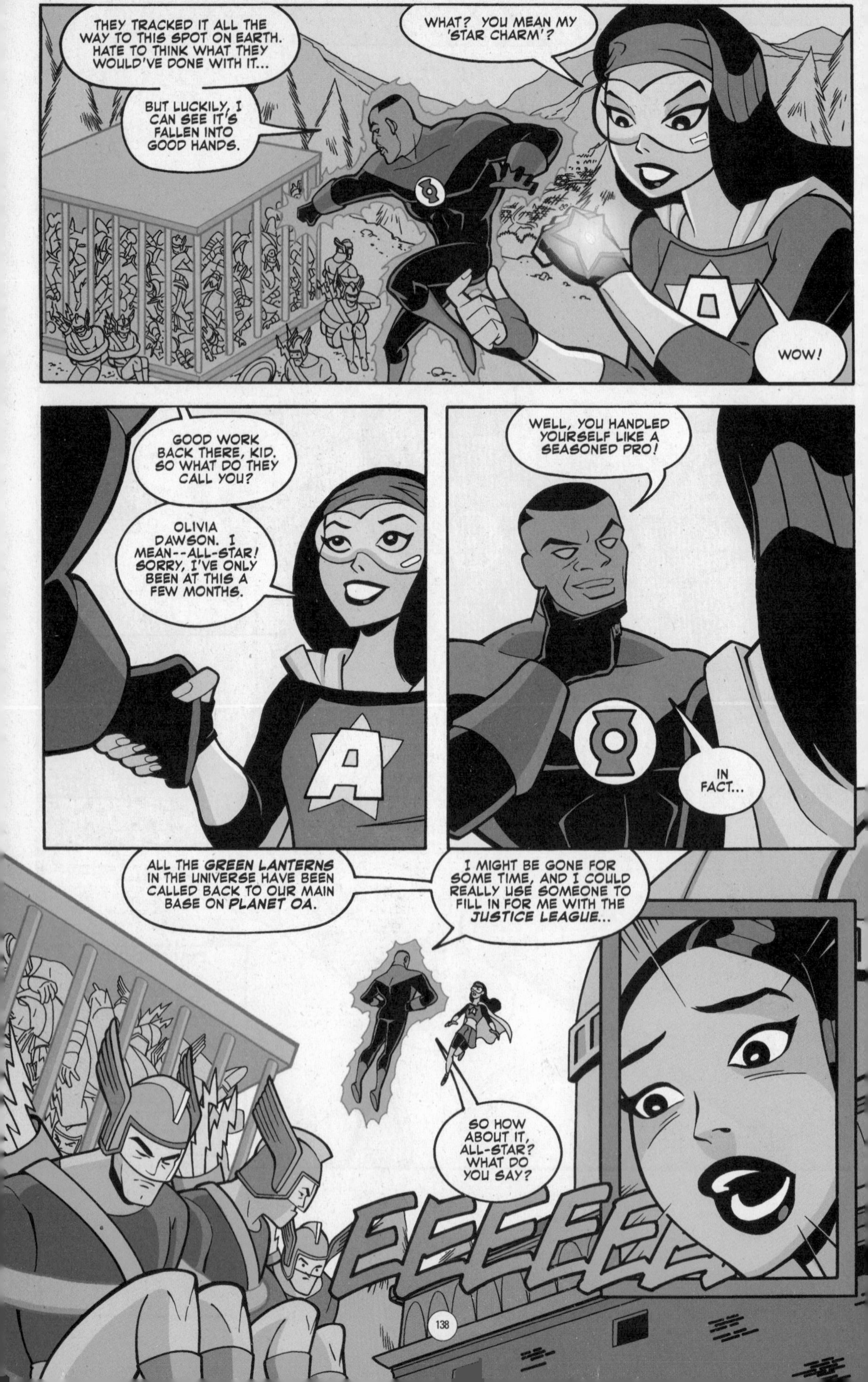
THEY TRACKED IT ALL THE WAY TO THIS SPOT ON EARTH. HATE TO THINK WHAT THEY WOULD'VE DONE WITH IT...
BUT LUCKILY, I CAN SEE IT'S FALLEN INTO GOOD HANDS.
WHAT? YOU MEAN MY 'STAR CHARM'?
WOW!
GOOD WORK BACK THERE, KID. SO WHAT DO THEY CALL YOU?
OLIVIA DAWSON. I MEAN--ALL-STAR! SORRY, I'VE ONLY BEEN AT THIS A FEW MONTHS.
WELL, YOU HANDLED YOURSELF LIKE A SEASONED PRO!
IN FACT...
ALL THE GREEN LANTERNS IN THE UNIVERSE HAVE BEEN CALLED BACK TO OUR MAIN BASE ON PLANET OA.
I MIGHT BE GONE FOR SOME TIME, AND I COULD REALLY USE SOMEONE TO FILL IN FOR ME WITH THE JUSTICE LEAGUE...
SO HOW ABOUT IT, ALL-STAR? WHAT DO YOU SAY?
EEEEEE

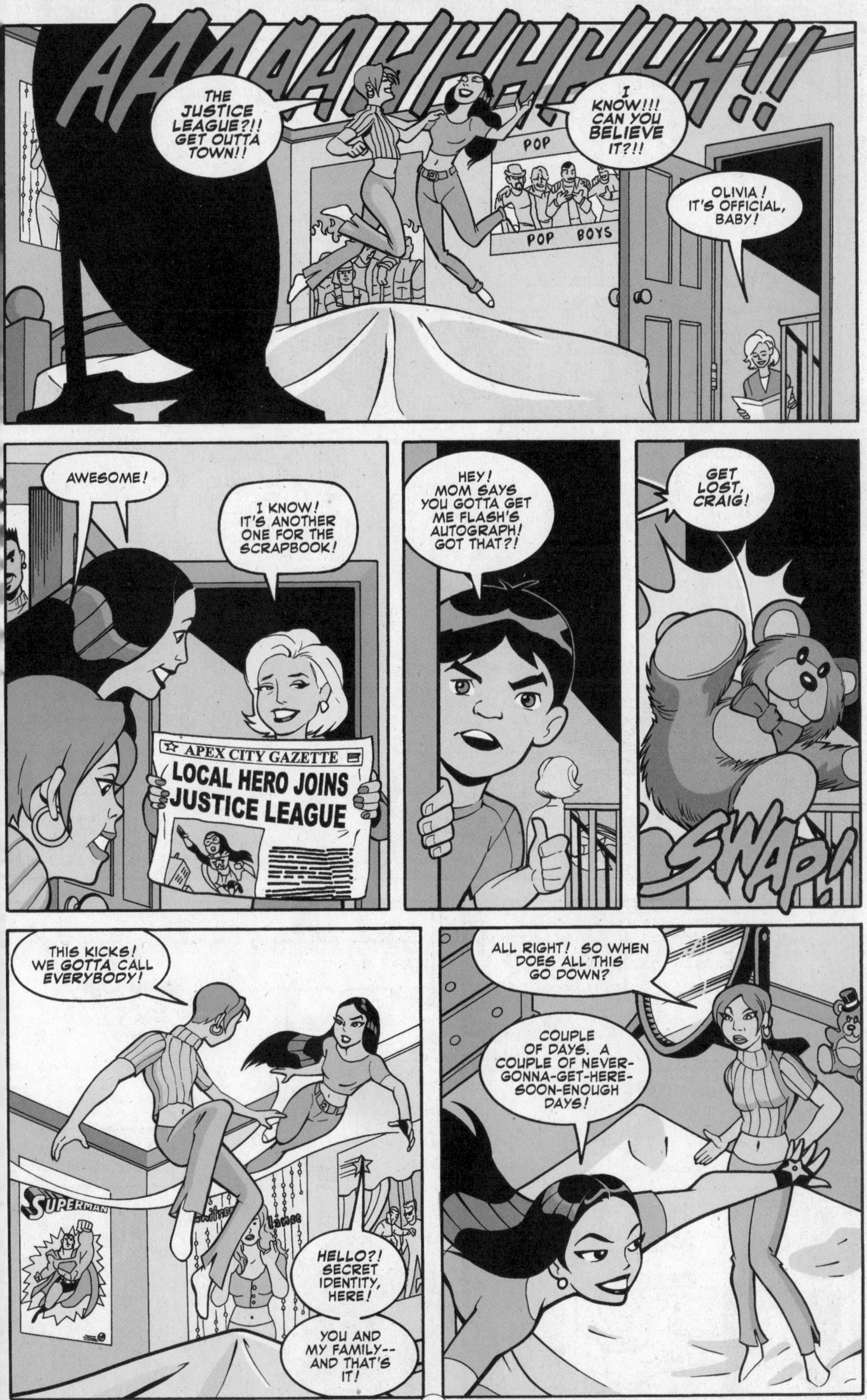
AAAAAAHHHHHHH!!
THE JUSTICE LEAGUE?!! GET OUTTA TOWN!!
I KNOW!!! CAN YOU BELIEVE IT?!!
POP
POP BOYS
OLIVIA! IT'S OFFICIAL, BABY!
AWESOME!
I KNOW! IT'S ANOTHER ONE FOR THE SCRAPBOOK!
APEX CITY GAZETTE
LOCAL HERO JOINS JUSTICE LEAGUE
HEY! MOM SAYS YOU GOTTA GET ME FLASH'S AUTOGRAPH! GOT THAT?!
GET LOST, CRAIG!
SWAP!
THIS KICKS! WE GOTTA CALL EVERYBODY!
SUPERMAN
HELLO?! SECRET IDENTITY, HERE!
YOU AND MY FAMILY-- AND THAT'S IT!
ALL RIGHT! SO WHEN DOES ALL THIS GO DOWN?
COUPLE OF DAYS. A COUPLE OF NEVER-GONNA-GET-HERE-SOON-ENOUGH DAYS!

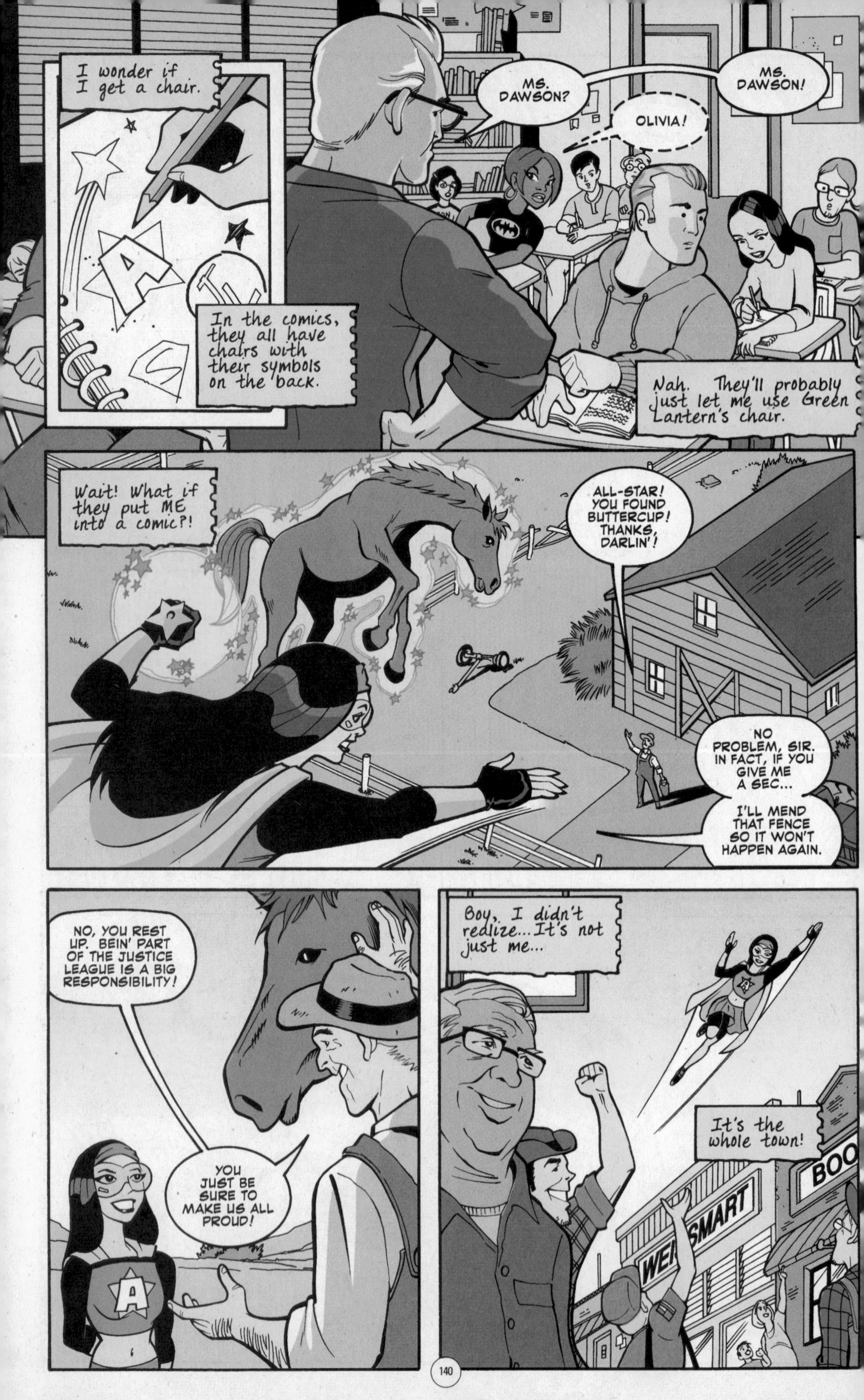
I wonder if I get a chair.
MS. DAWSON?
MS. DAWSON!
OLIVIA!
In the comics, they all have chairs with their symbols on the back.
Nah. They'll probably just let me use Green Lantern's chair.
Wait! What if they put ME into a comic?!
ALL-STAR! YOU FOUND BUTTERCUP! THANKS, DARLIN'!
NO PROBLEM, SIR. IN FACT, IF YOU GIVE ME A SEC...
I'LL MEND THAT FENCE SO IT WON'T HAPPEN AGAIN.
NO, YOU REST UP. BEIN' PART OF THE JUSTICE LEAGUE IS A BIG RESPONSIBILITY!
YOU JUST BE SURE TO MAKE US ALL PROUD!
Boy, I didn't realize... It's not just me...
It's the whole town!
SMART
BOO

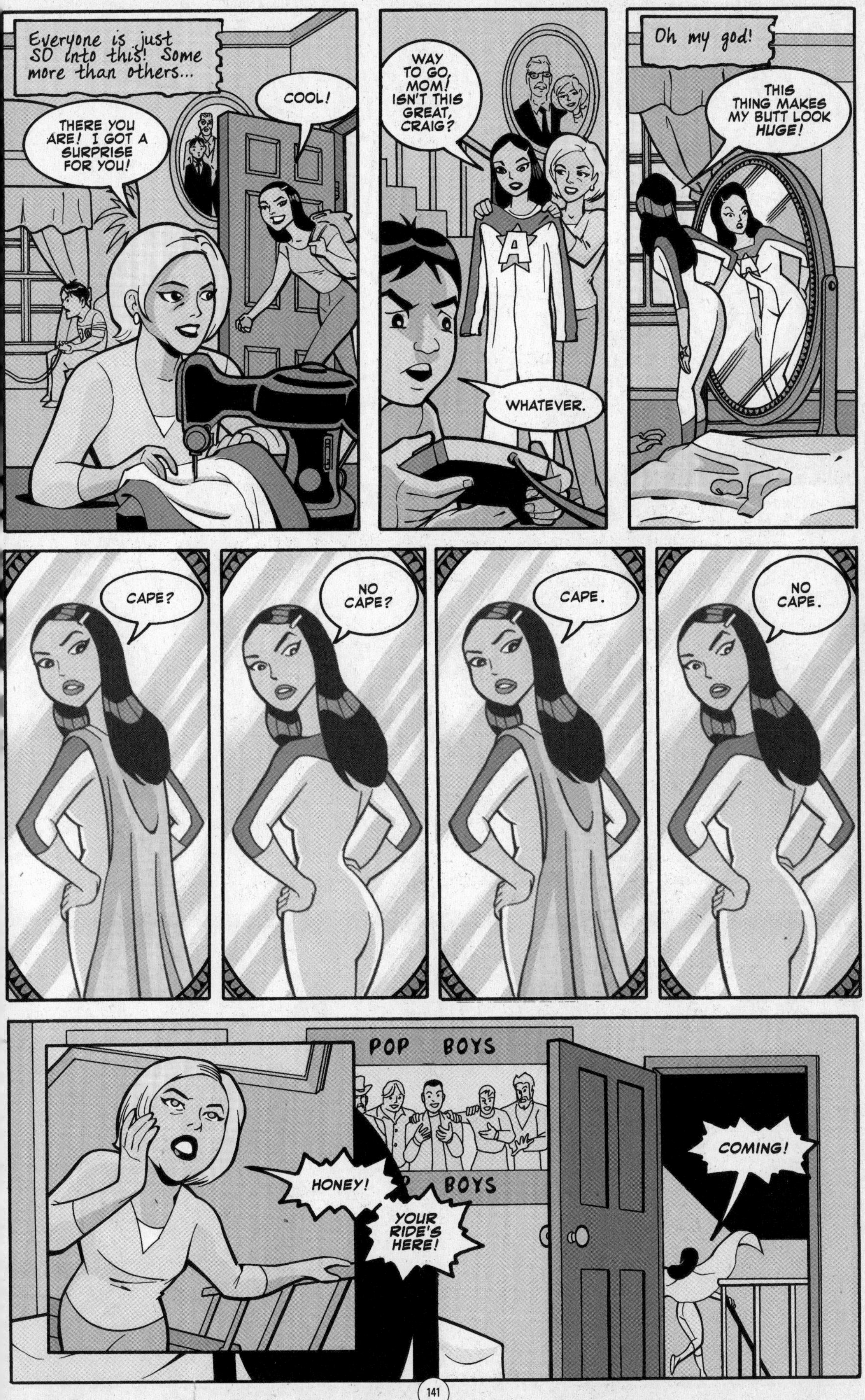
Everyone is just SO into this! Some more than others...
THERE YOU ARE! I GOT A SURPRISE FOR YOU!
COOL!
WAY TO GO, MOM! ISN'T THIS GREAT, CRAIG?
WHATEVER.
Oh my god!
THIS THING MAKES MY BUTT LOOK HUGE!
CAPE?
NO CAPE?
CAPE.
NO CAPE.
POP BOYS
HONEY!
YOUR RIDE'S HERE!
COMING!

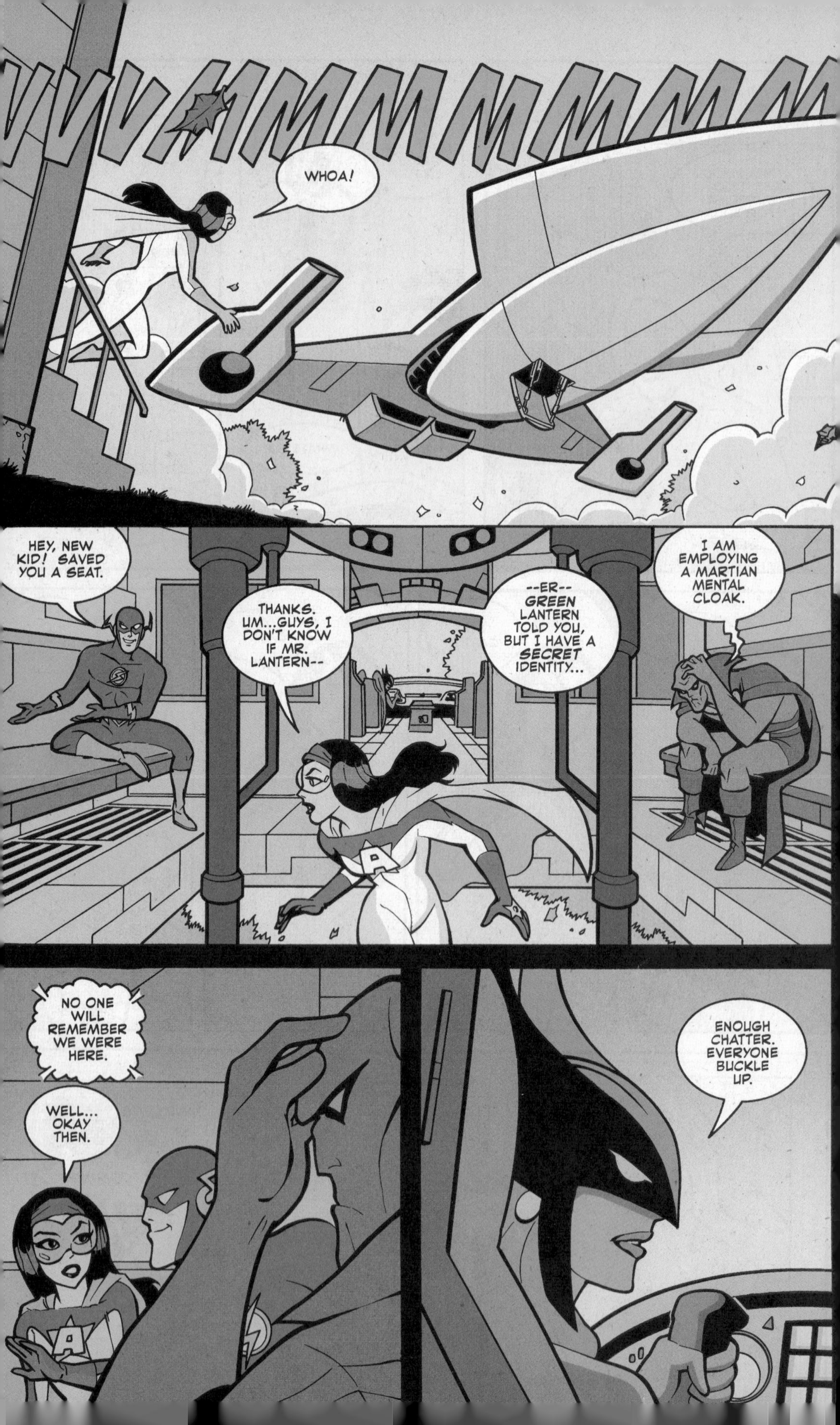
VVVVMMMMMMMMM
WHOA!
HEY, NEW KID! SAVED YOU A SEAT.
THANKS. UM...GUYS, I DON'T KNOW IF MR. LANTERN--
--ER-- GREEN LANTERN TOLD YOU, BUT I HAVE A SECRET IDENTITY...
I AM EMPLOYING A MARTIAN MENTAL CLOAK.
NO ONE WILL REMEMBER WE WERE HERE.
WELL... OKAY THEN.
ENOUGH CHATTER. EVERYONE BUCKLE UP.

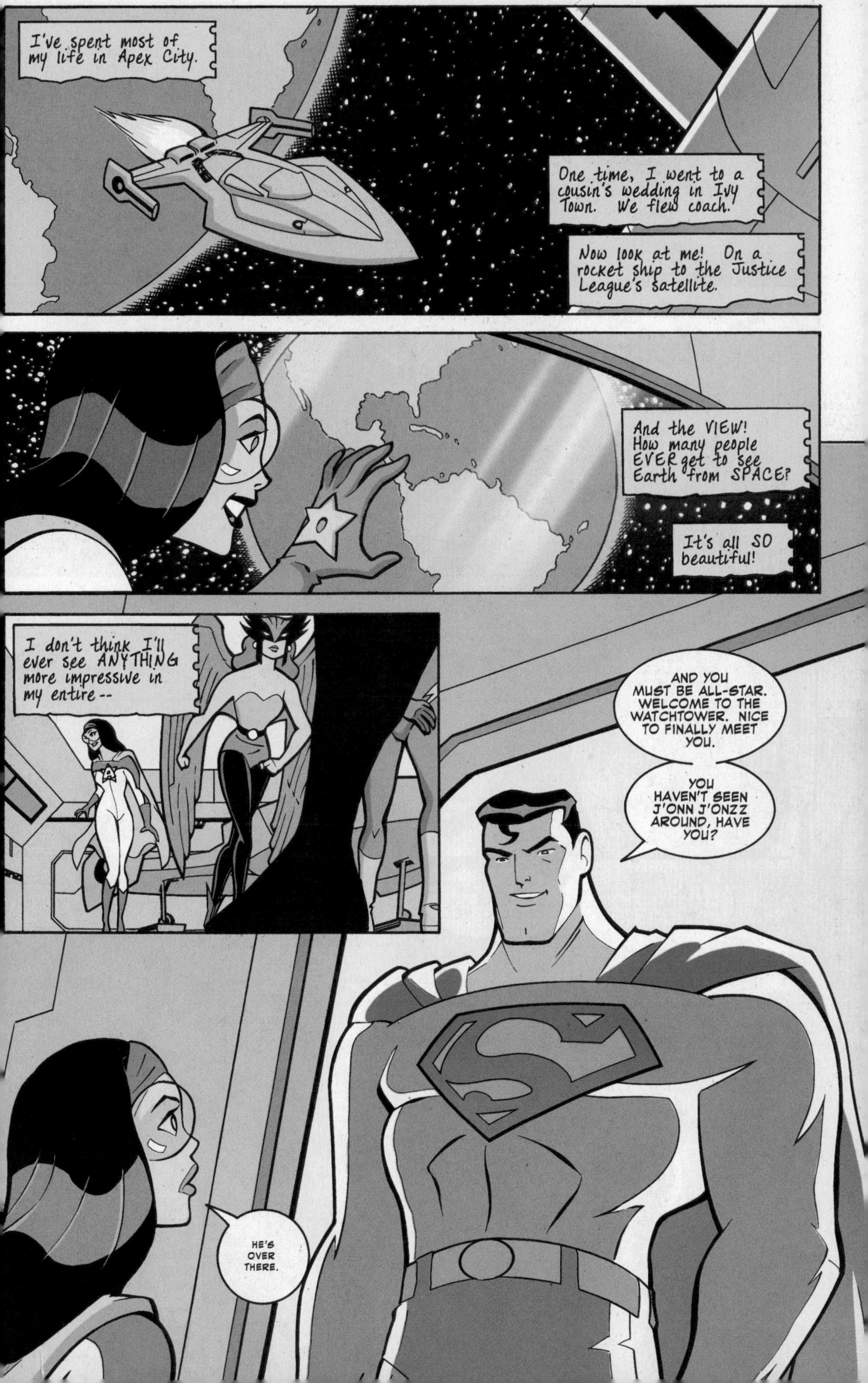

I've spent most of my life in Apex City.
One time, I went to a cousin's wedding in Ivy Town. We flew coach.
Now look at me! On a rocket ship to the Justice League's satellite.
And the VIEW! How many people EVER get to see Earth from SPACE?
It's all SO beautiful!
I don't think I'll ever see ANYTHING more impressive in my entire --
AND YOU MUST BE ALL-STAR. WELCOME TO THE WATCHTOWER. NICE TO FINALLY MEET YOU.
YOU HAVEN'T SEEN J'ONN J'ONZZ AROUND, HAVE YOU?
HE'S OVER THERE.

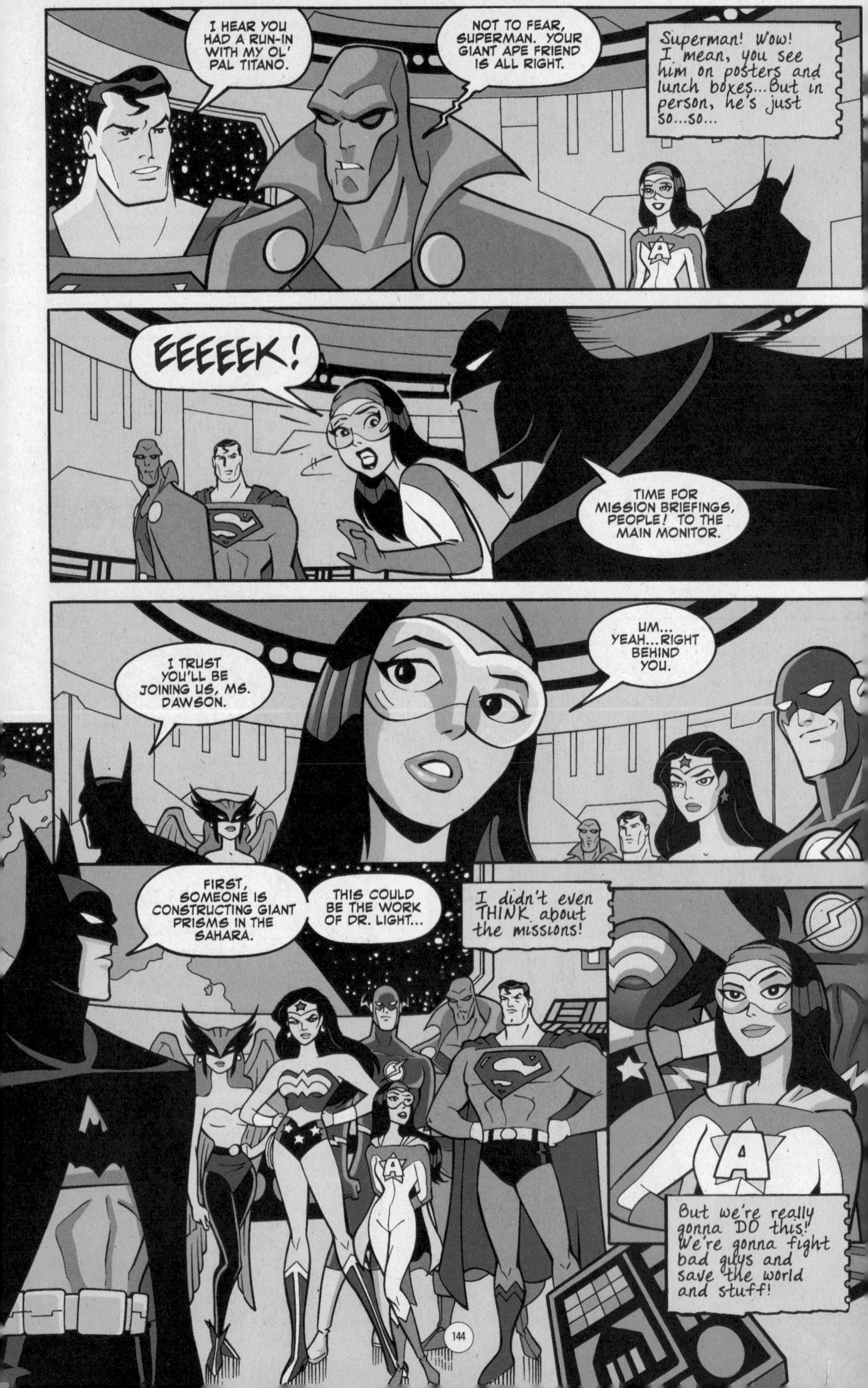
I HEAR YOU HAD A RUN-IN WITH MY OL' PAL TITANO.
NOT TO FEAR, SUPERMAN. YOUR GIANT APE FRIEND IS ALL RIGHT.
Superman! Wow! I mean, you see him on posters and lunch boxes...But in person, he's just so...so...
EEEEEK!
TIME FOR MISSION BRIEFINGS, PEOPLE! TO THE MAIN MONITOR.
I TRUST YOU'LL BE JOINING US, MS. DAWSON.
UM... YEAH...RIGHT BEHIND YOU.
FIRST, SOMEONE IS CONSTRUCTING GIANT PRISMS IN THE SAHARA.
THIS COULD BE THE WORK OF DR. LIGHT...
I didn't even THINK about the missions!
But we're really gonna DO this! We're gonna fight bad guys and save the world and stuff!

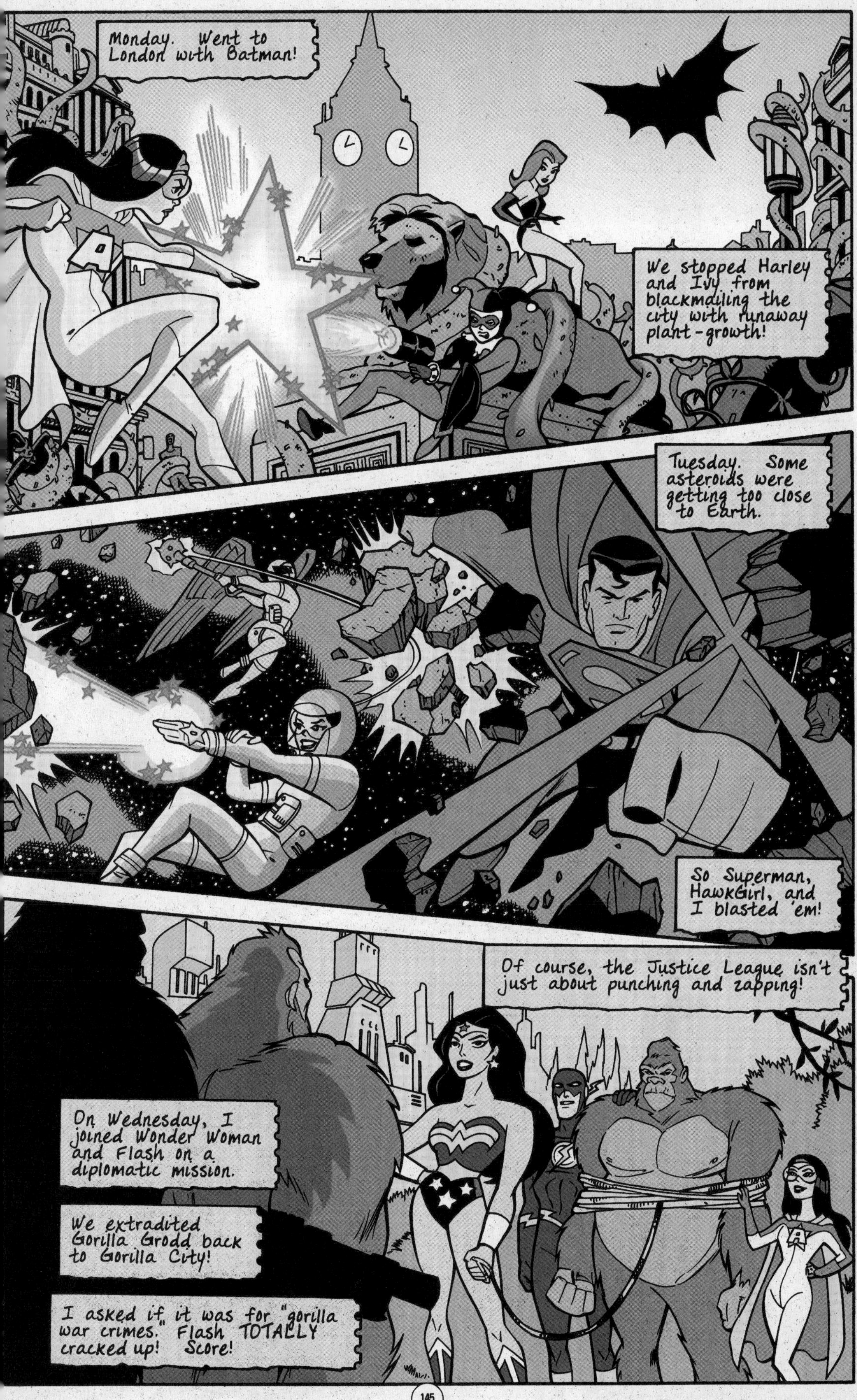
Monday. Went to London with Batman!
We stopped Harley and Ivy from blackmailing the city with runaway plant-growth!
Tuesday. Some asteroids were getting too close to Earth.
So Superman, HawkGirl, and I blasted 'em!
Of course, the Justice League isn't just about punching and zapping!
On Wednesday, I joined Wonder Woman and Flash on a diplomatic mission.
We extradited Gorilla Grodd back to Gorilla City!
I asked if it was for "gorilla war crimes." Flash TOTALLY cracked up! Score!

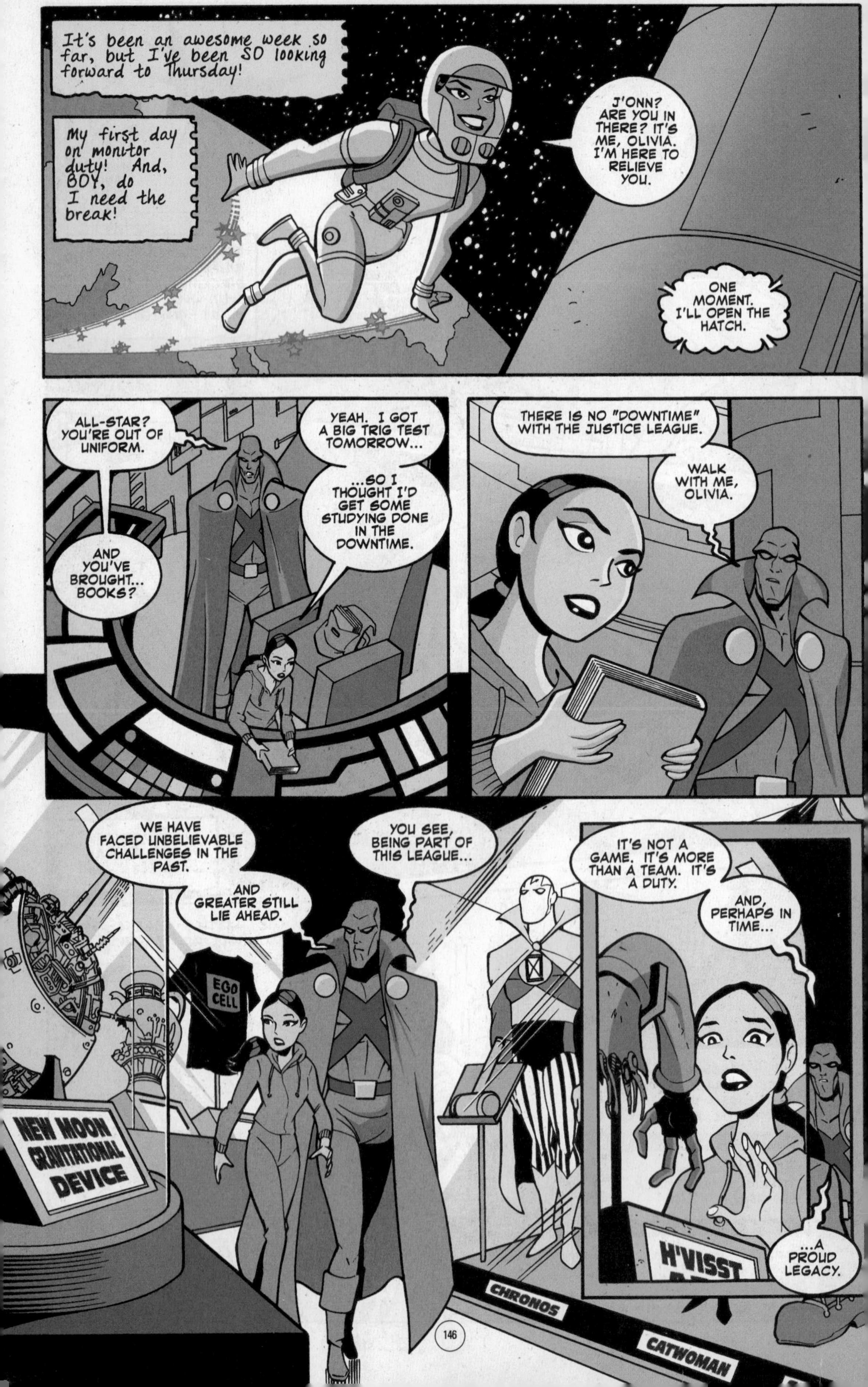
It's been an awesome week so far, but I've been SO looking forward to Thursday!
My first day on monitor duty! And, BOY, do I need the break!
J'ONN? ARE YOU IN THERE? IT'S ME, OLIVIA. I'M HERE TO RELIEVE YOU.
ONE MOMENT. I'LL OPEN THE HATCH.
ALL-STAR? YOU'RE OUT OF UNIFORM.
AND YOU'VE BROUGHT... BOOKS?
YEAH. I GOT A BIG TRIG TEST TOMORROW...
...SO I THOUGHT I'D GET SOME STUDYING DONE IN THE DOWNTIME.
THERE IS NO "DOWNTIME" WITH THE JUSTICE LEAGUE.
WALK WITH ME, OLIVIA.
WE HAVE FACED UNBELIEVABLE CHALLENGES IN THE PAST.
AND GREATER STILL LIE AHEAD.
YOU SEE, BEING PART OF THIS LEAGUE...
IT'S NOT A GAME. IT'S MORE THAN A TEAM. IT'S A DUTY.
AND, PERHAPS IN TIME...
...A PROUD LEGACY.
EGO CELL
NEW MOON GRAVITATIONAL DEVICE
H'VISST
CHRONOS
CATWOMAN

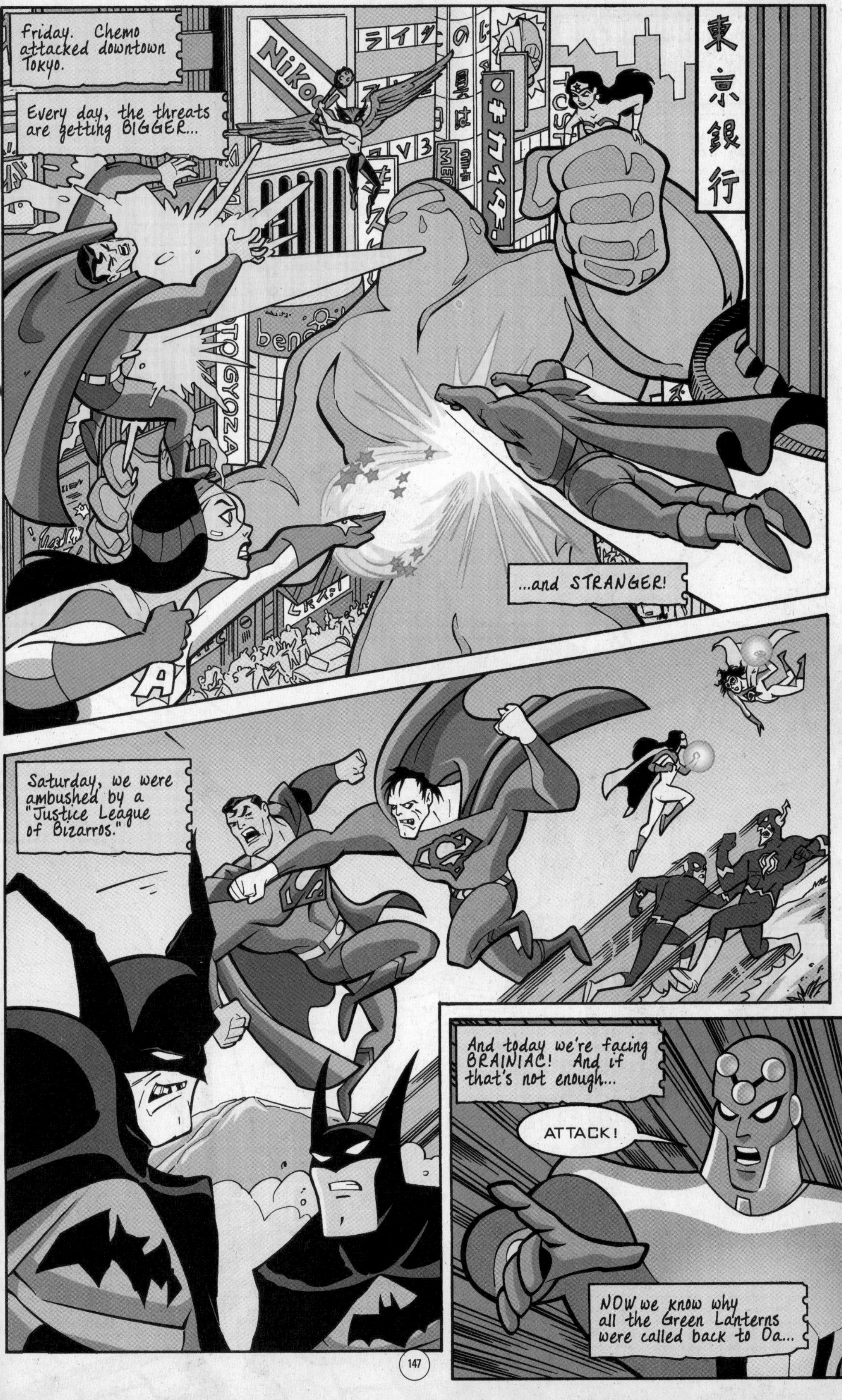

friday. Chemo attacked downtown Tokyo.
Every day, the threats are getting BIGGER...
...and STRANGER!
Saturday, we were ambushed by a "Justice League of Bizarros."
And today we're facing BRAINIAC! And if that's not enough...
ATTACK!
NOW we know why all the Green Lanterns were called back to Oa...

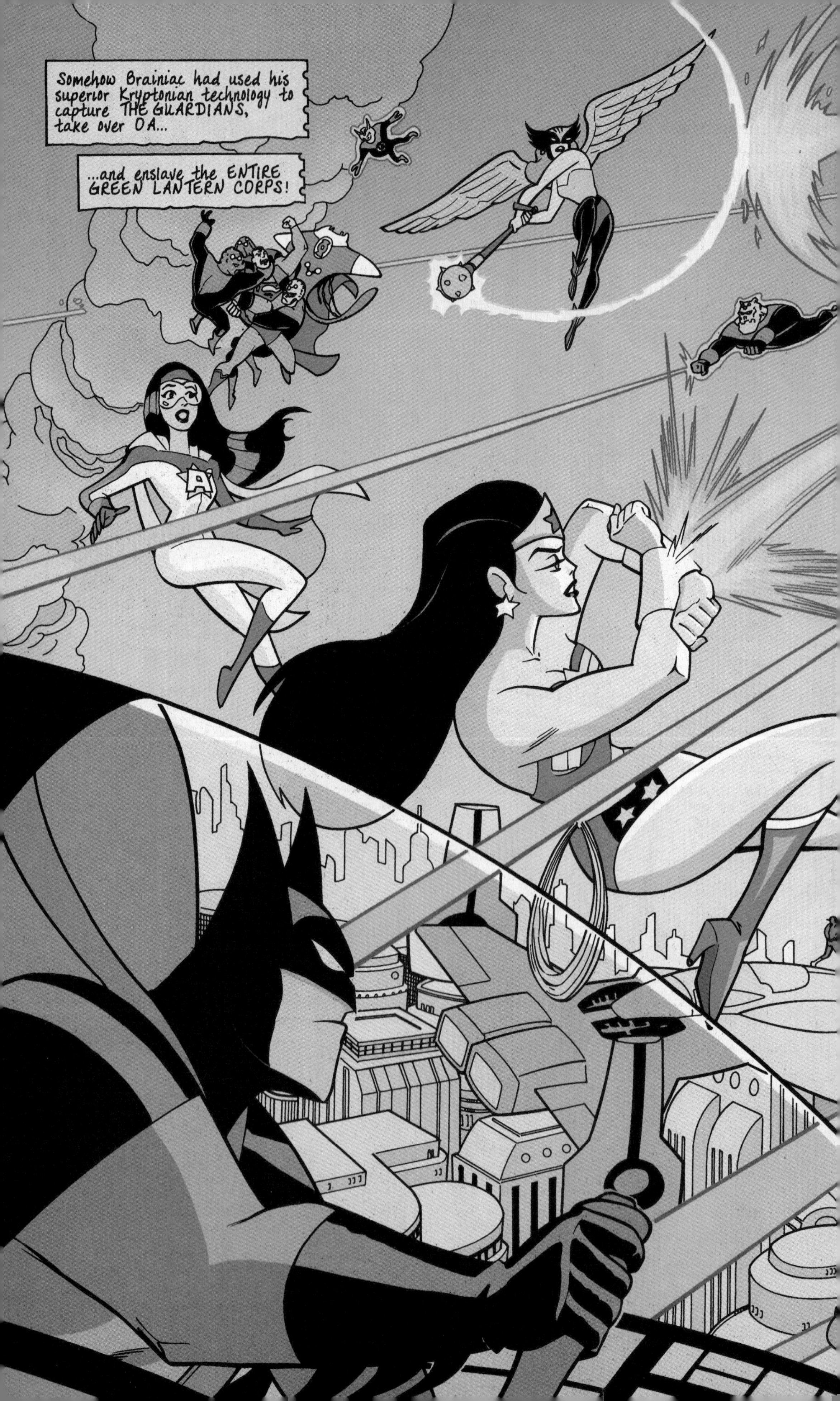
Somehow Brainiac had used his superior Kryptonian technology to capture THE GUARDIANS, take over OA...
...and enslave the ENTIRE GREEN LANTERN CORPS!

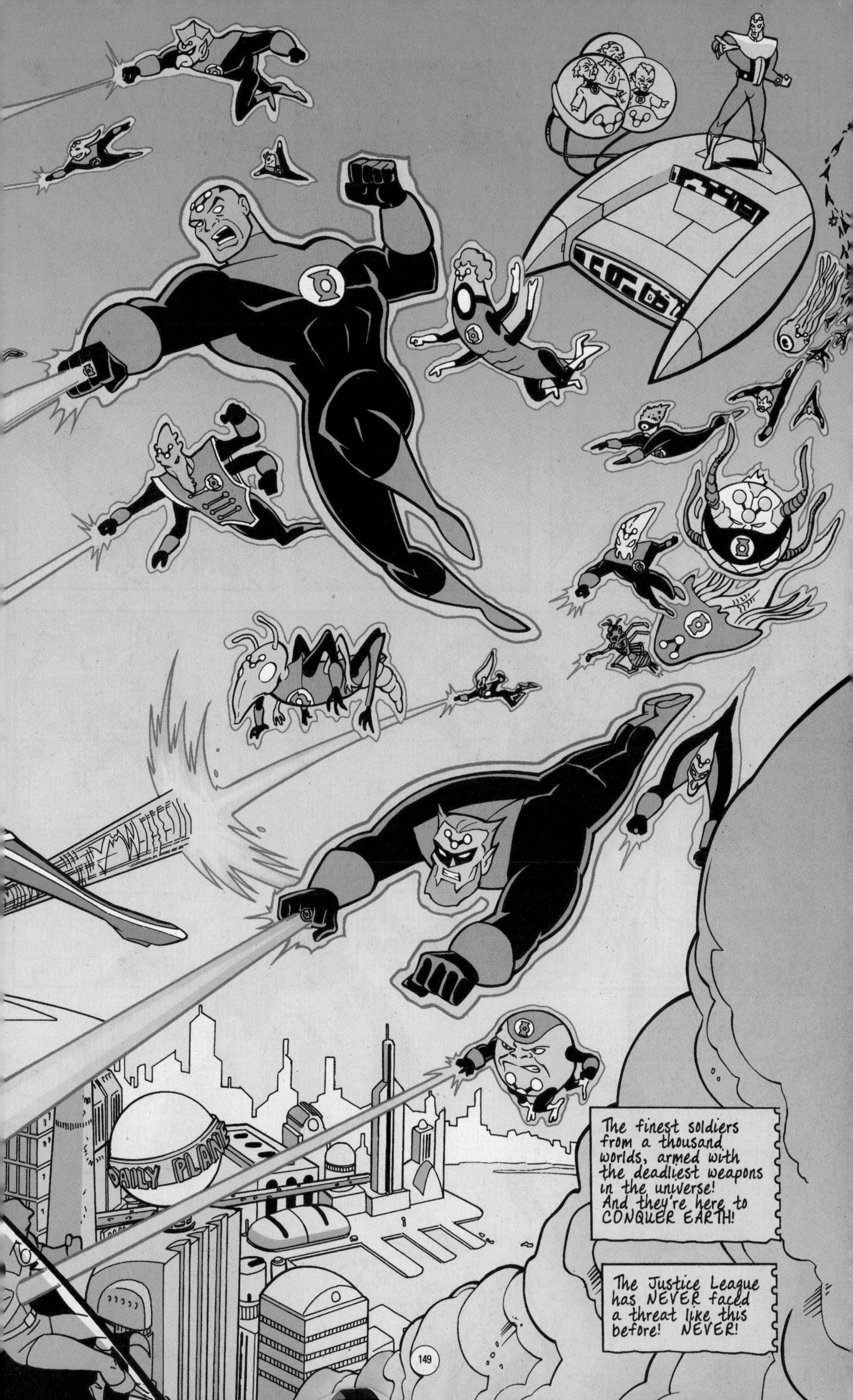
DAILY PLANET
The finest soldiers from a thousand worlds, armed with the deadliest weapons in the universe! And they're here to CONQUER EARTH!
The Justice League has NEVER faced a threat like this before! NEVER!

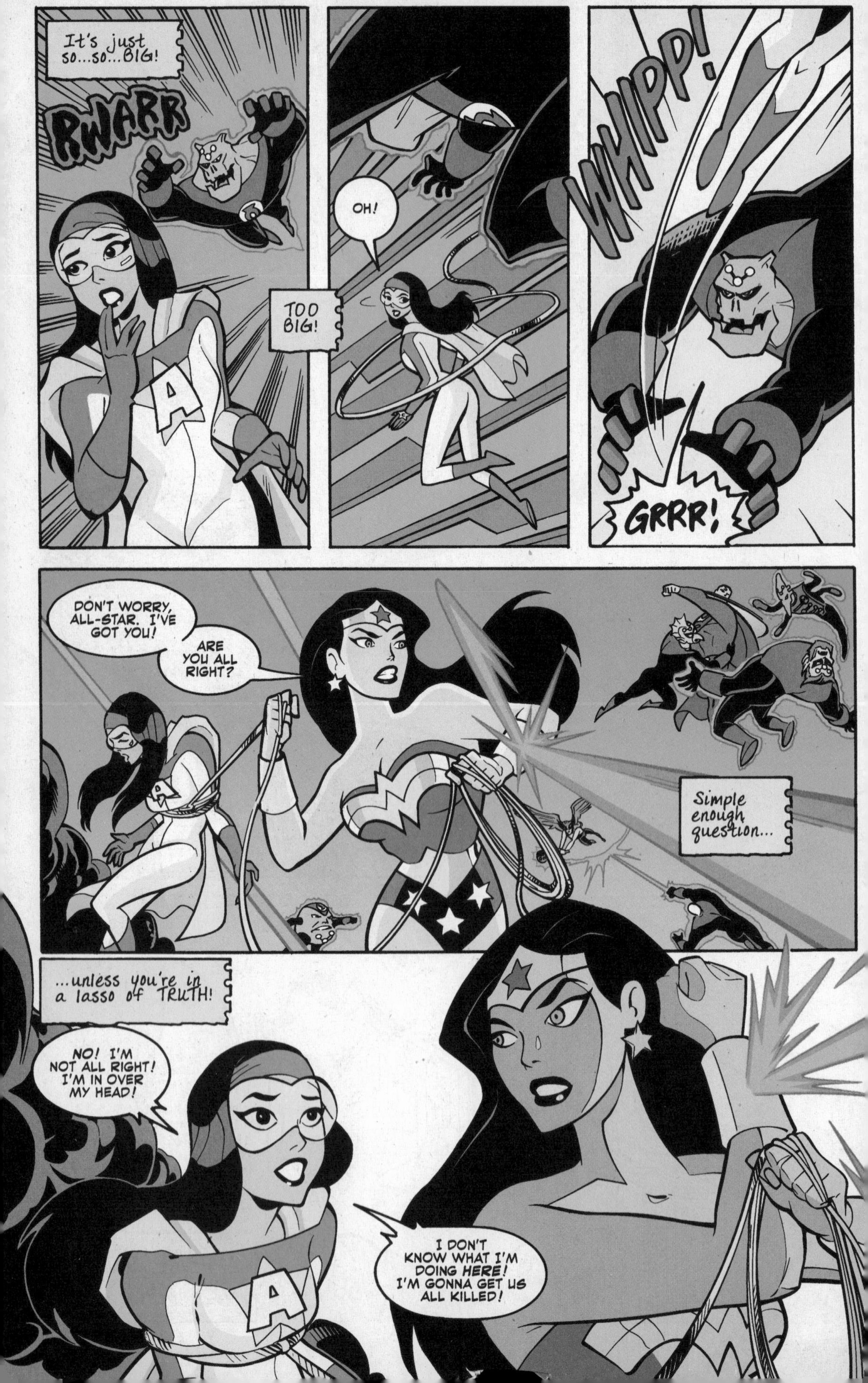

It's just so...so...BIG!
RWARR
OH!
TOO BIG!
WHIPP!
GRRR!
DON'T WORRY, ALL-STAR. I'VE GOT YOU!
ARE YOU ALL RIGHT?
Simple enough question...
...unless you're in a lasso of TRUTH!
NO! I'M NOT ALL RIGHT! I'M IN OVER MY HEAD!
I DON'T KNOW WHAT I'M DOING HERE! I'M GONNA GET US ALL KILLED!

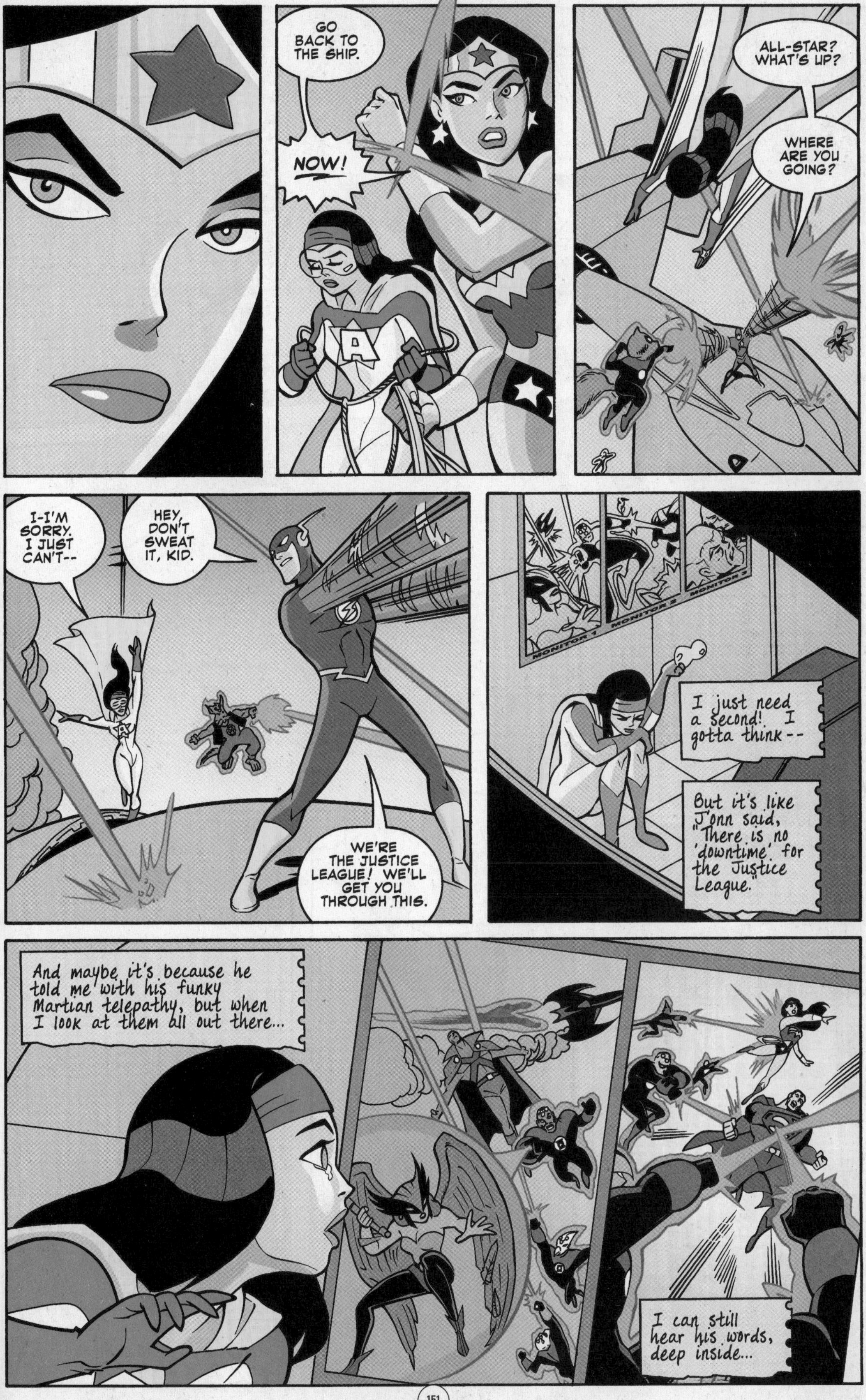
GO BACK TO THE SHIP.
NOW!
ALL-STAR? WHAT'S UP?
WHERE ARE YOU GOING?
I-I'M SORRY. I JUST CAN'T--
HEY, DON'T SWEAT IT, KID.
WE'RE THE JUSTICE LEAGUE! WE'LL GET YOU THROUGH THIS.
MONITOR 1
MONITOR 2
MONITOR 3
I just need a second! I gotta think--
But it's like J'onn said, "There is no 'downtime' for the Justice League."
And maybe it's because he told me with his funky Martian telepathy, but when I look at them all out there...
I can still hear his words, deep inside...

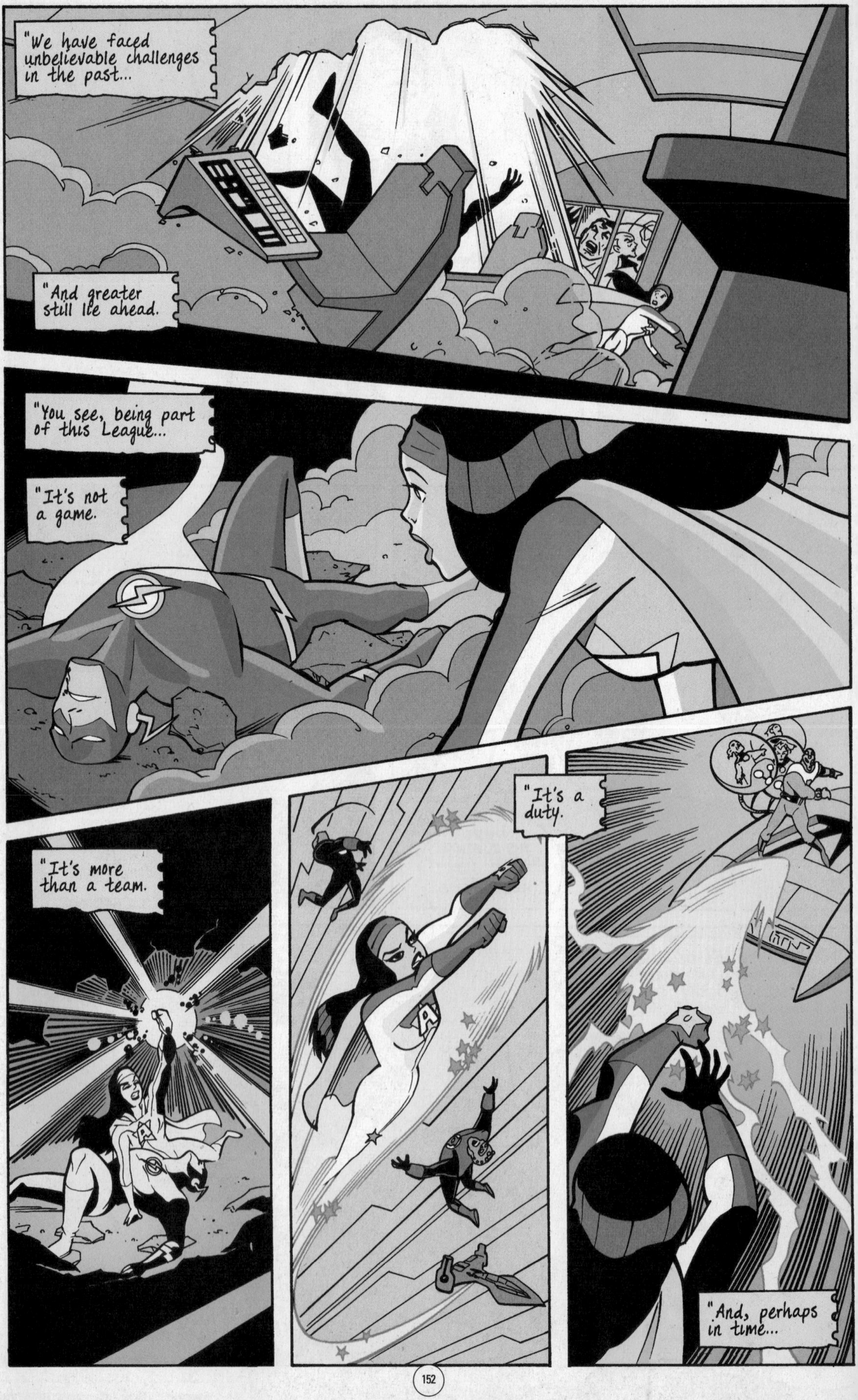
"We have faced unbelievable challenges in the past...
"And greater still lie ahead.
"You see, being part of this League...
"It's not a game.
"It's more than a team.
"It's a duty.
"And, perhaps in time...

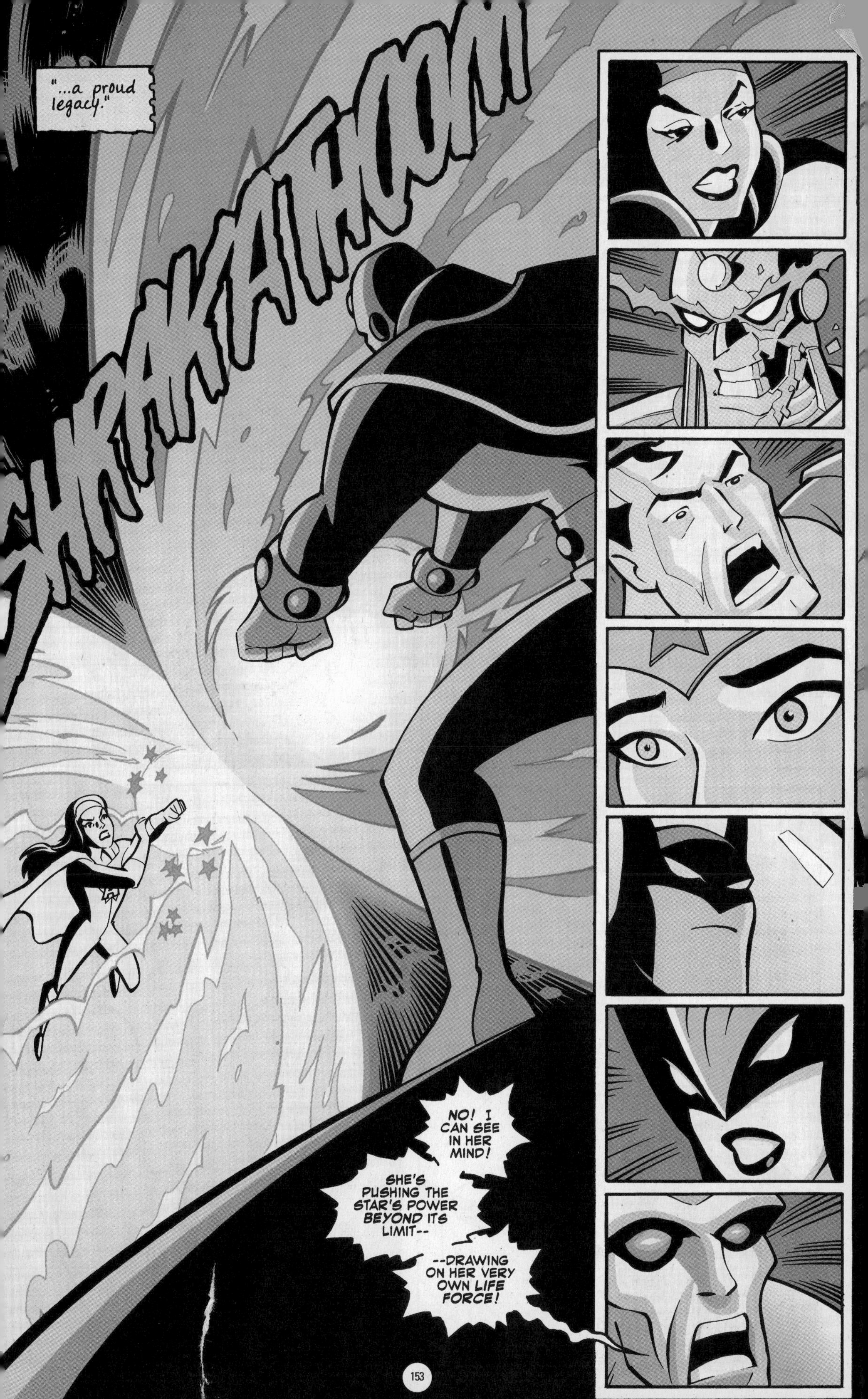
"...a proud legacy."
SHRAKATHOOM
NO! I CAN SEE IN HER MIND!
SHE'S PUSHING THE STAR'S POWER BEYOND ITS LIMIT--
--DRAWING ON HER VERY OWN LIFE FORCE!

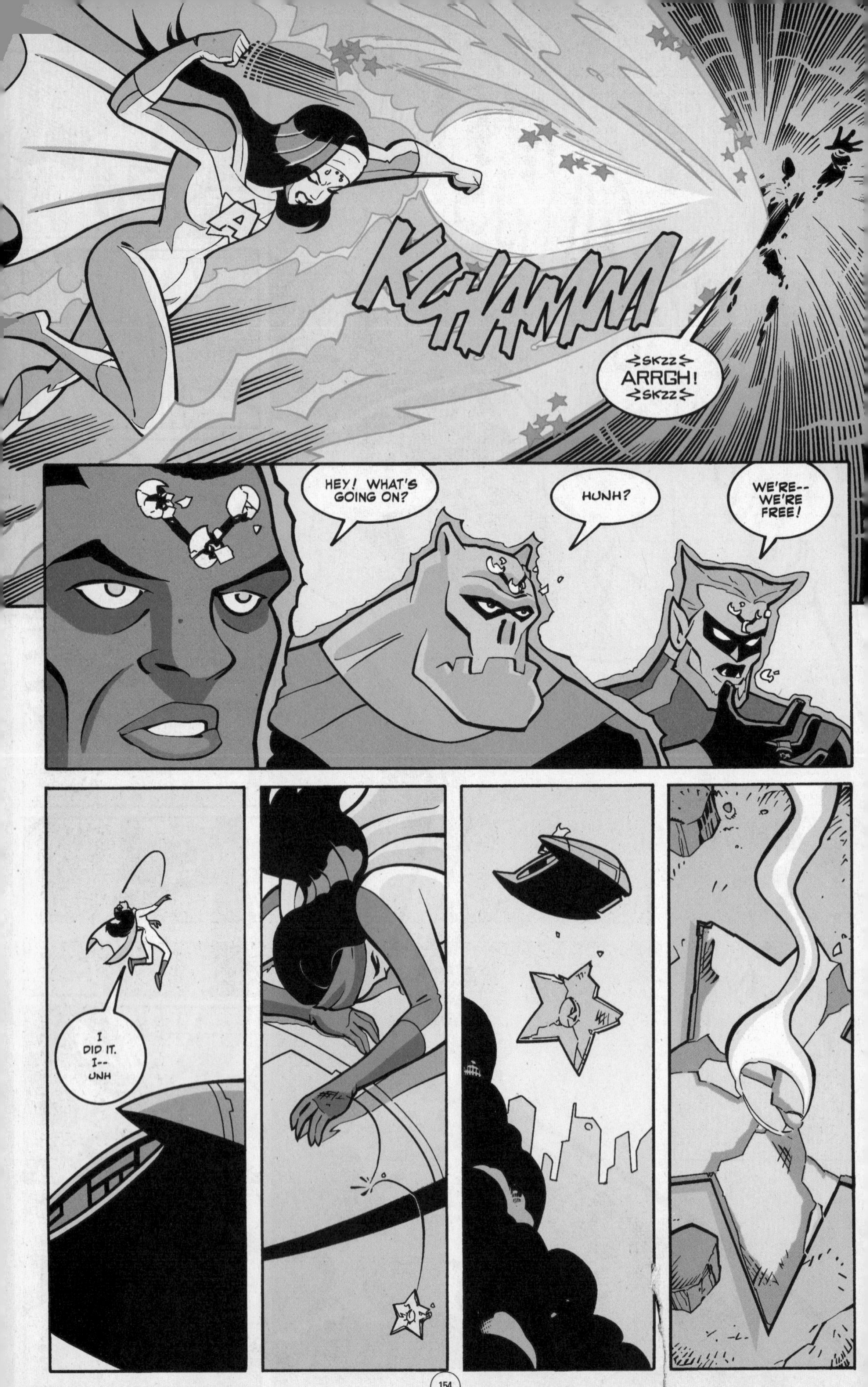
KCHAMMM
≶SKZZ≶ ARRGH! ≶SKZZ≶
HEY! WHAT'S GOING ON?
HUNH?
WE'RE-- WE'RE FREE!
I DID IT. I-- UNH

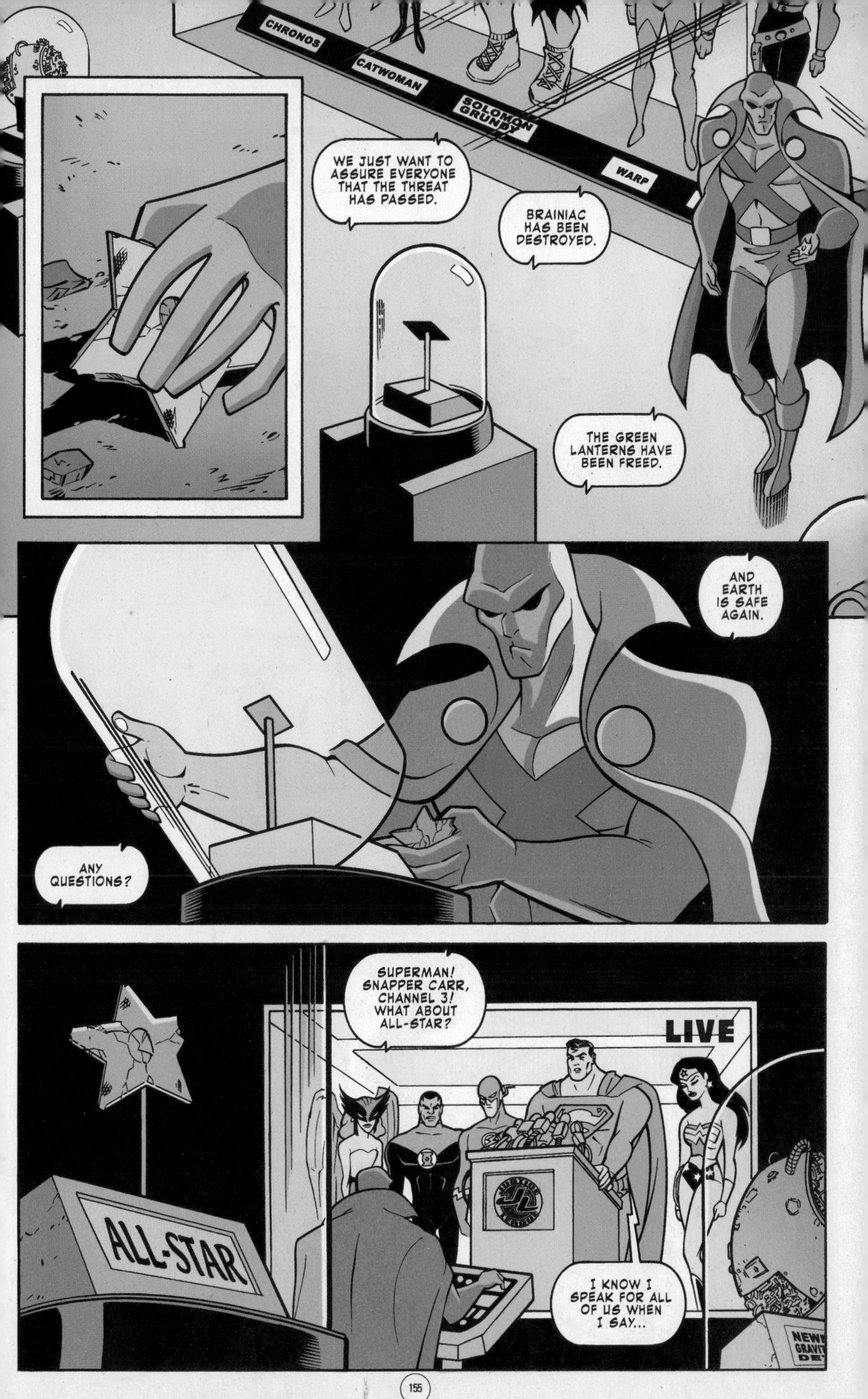
CHRONOS
CATWOMAN
SOLOMON GRUNDY
WARP
WE JUST WANT TO ASSURE EVERYONE THAT THE THREAT HAS PASSED.
BRAINIAC HAS BEEN DESTROYED.
THE GREEN LANTERNS HAVE BEEN FREED.
AND EARTH IS SAFE AGAIN.
ANY QUESTIONS?
SUPERMAN! SNAPPER CARR, CHANNEL 3! WHAT ABOUT ALL-STAR?
LIVE
ALL-STAR
I KNOW I SPEAK FOR ALL OF US WHEN I SAY...

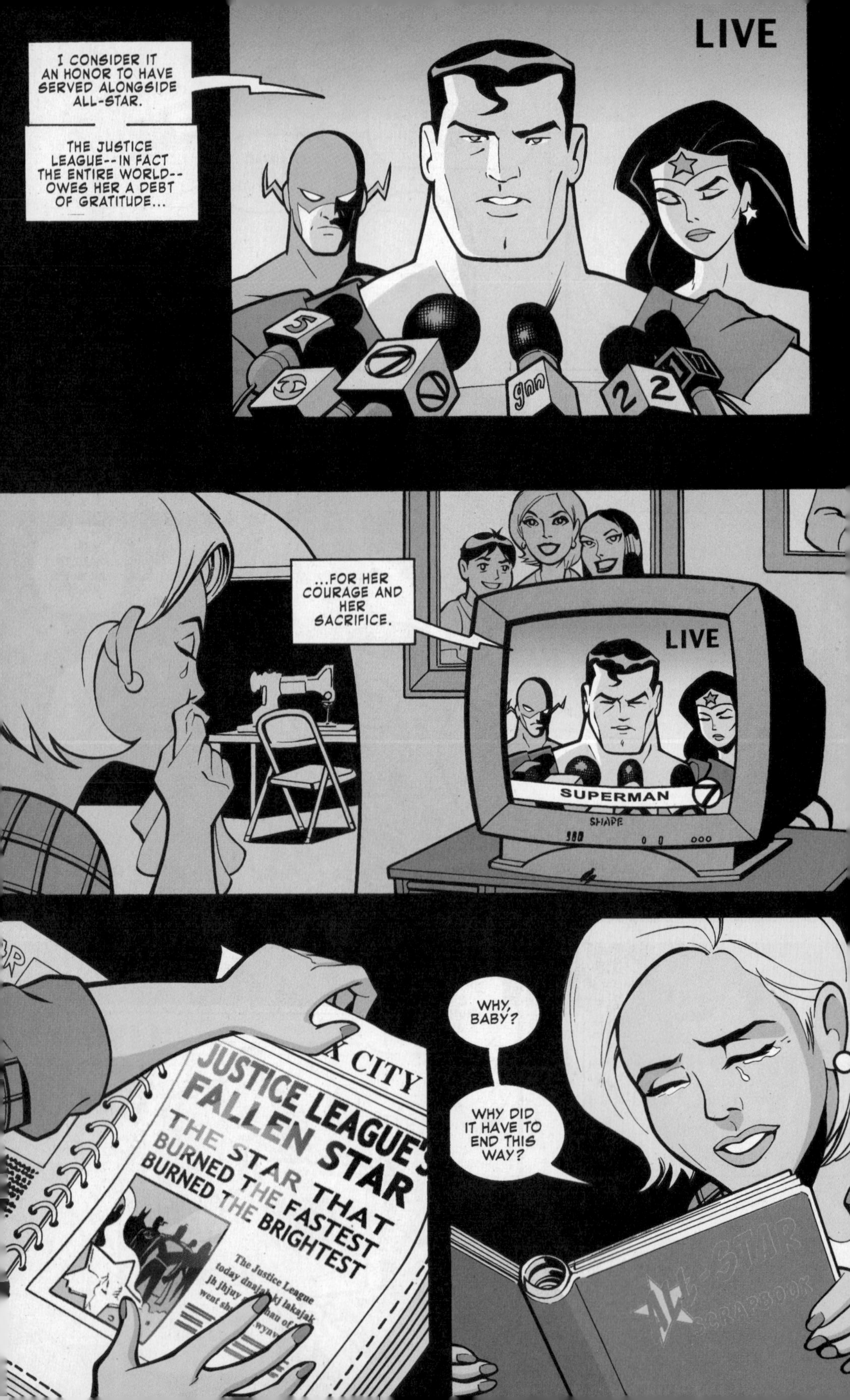
LIVE
I CONSIDER IT AN HONOR TO HAVE SERVED ALONGSIDE ALL-STAR.
THE JUSTICE LEAGUE--IN FACT THE ENTIRE WORLD--OWES HER A DEBT OF GRATITUDE...
...FOR HER COURAGE AND HER SACRIFICE.
LIVE
SUPERMAN
JUSTICE LEAGUE'S FALLEN STAR
THE STAR THAT BURNED THE FASTEST BURNED THE BRIGHTEST
The Justice League
WHY, BABY?
WHY DID IT HAVE TO END THIS WAY?

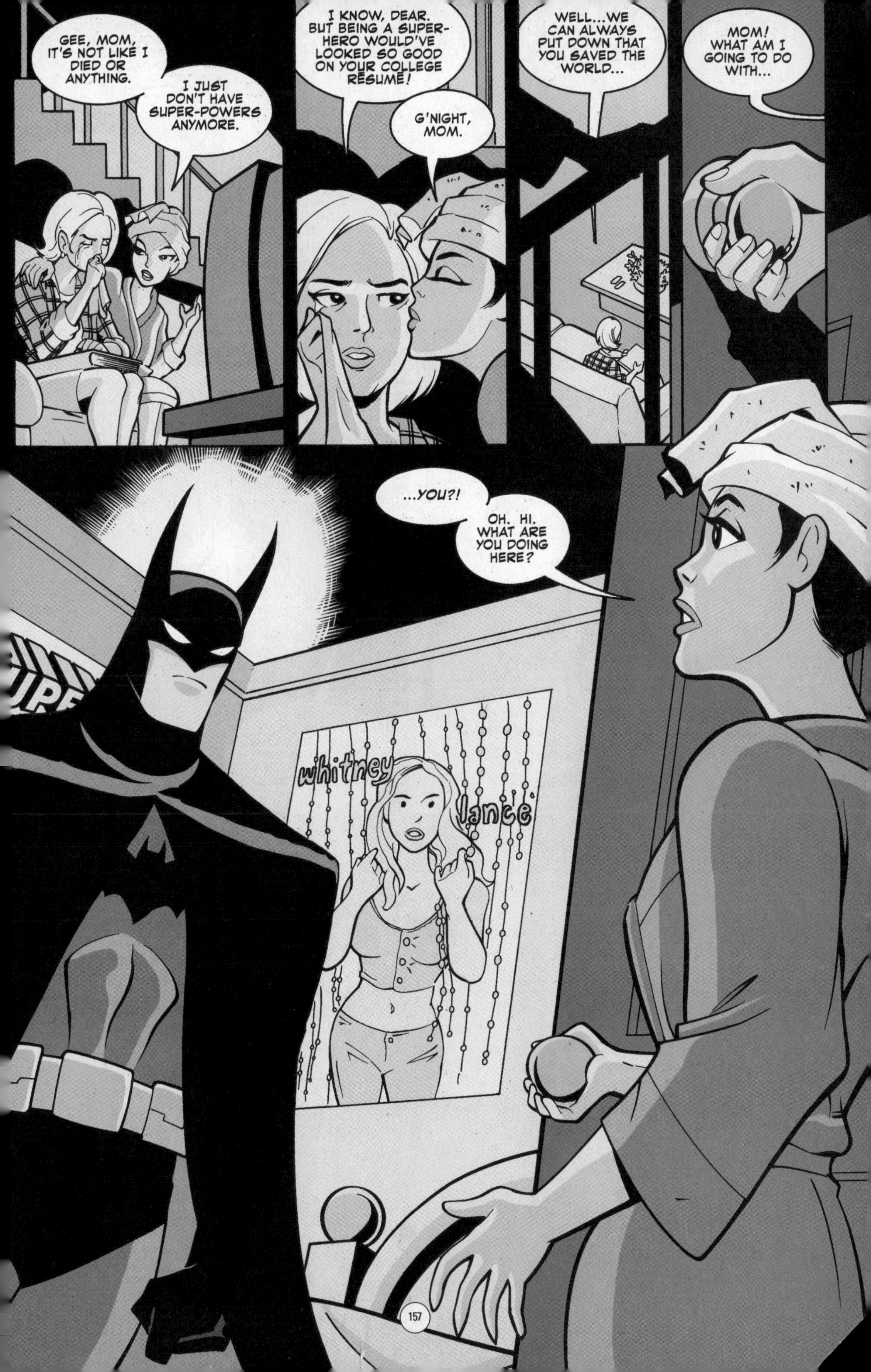
GEE, MOM, IT'S NOT LIKE I DIED OR ANYTHING.
I JUST DON'T HAVE SUPER-POWERS ANYMORE.
I KNOW, DEAR. BUT BEING A SUPER-HERO WOULD'VE LOOKED SO GOOD ON YOUR COLLEGE RESUMÉ!
G'NIGHT, MOM.
WELL...WE CAN ALWAYS PUT DOWN THAT YOU SAVED THE WORLD...
MOM! WHAT AM I GOING TO DO WITH...
...YOU?!
OH. HI. WHAT ARE YOU DOING HERE?
whitney
lance

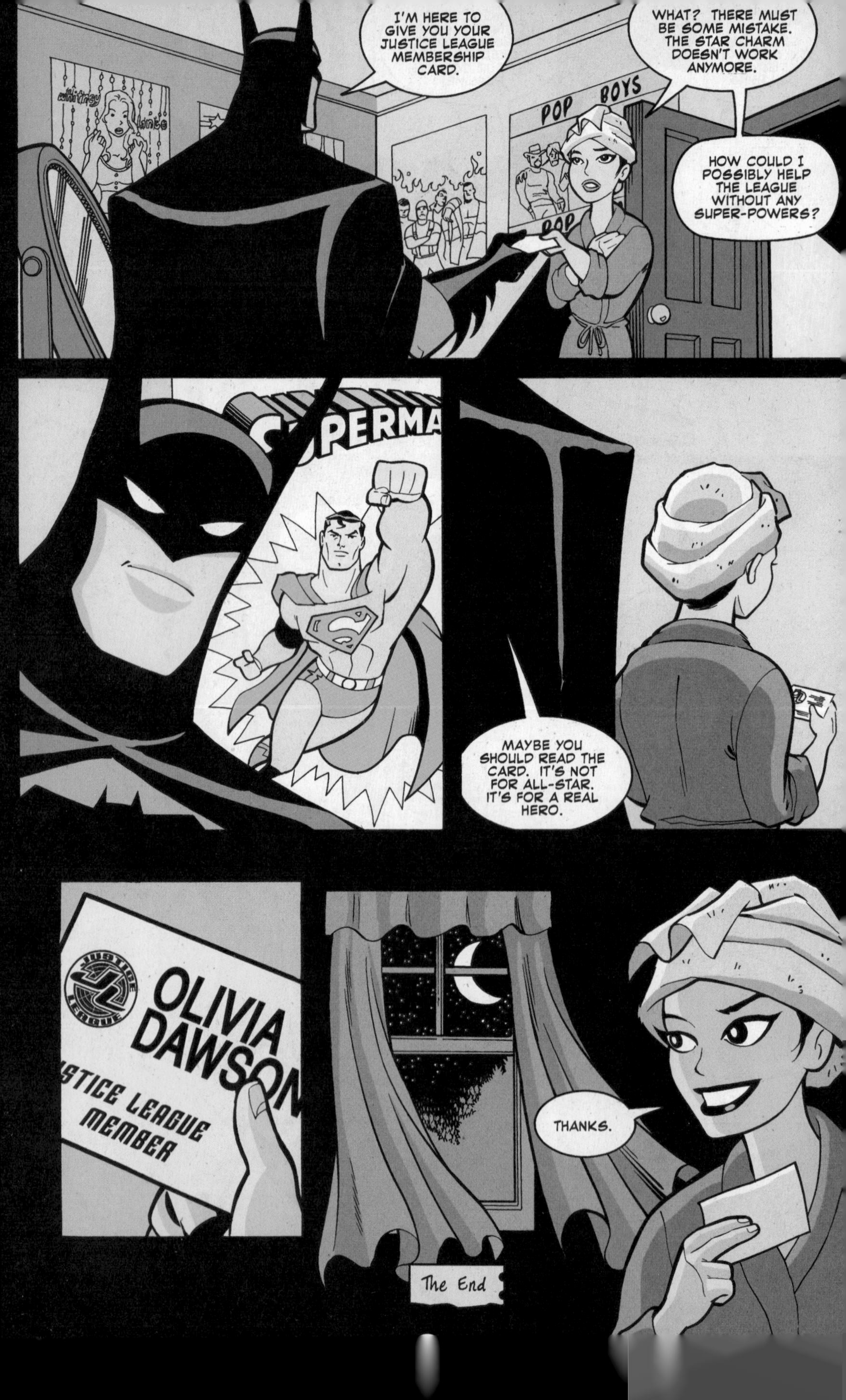

I'M HERE TO GIVE YOU YOUR JUSTICE LEAGUE MEMBERSHIP CARD.
WHAT? THERE MUST BE SOME MISTAKE. THE STAR CHARM DOESN'T WORK ANYMORE.
HOW COULD I POSSIBLY HELP THE LEAGUE WITHOUT ANY SUPER-POWERS?
POP BOYS
SUPERMA
MAYBE YOU SHOULD READ THE CARD. IT'S NOT FOR ALL-STAR. IT'S FOR A REAL HERO.
OLIVIA DAWSON
JUSTICE LEAGUE MEMBER
THANKS.
The End

C O V E R S

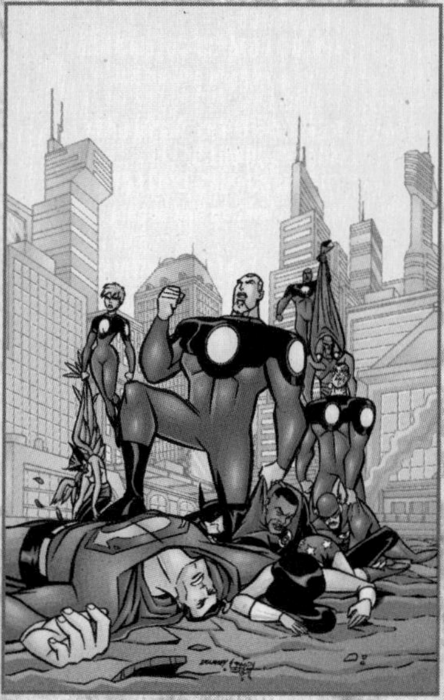
John Delaney & Randy Elliott

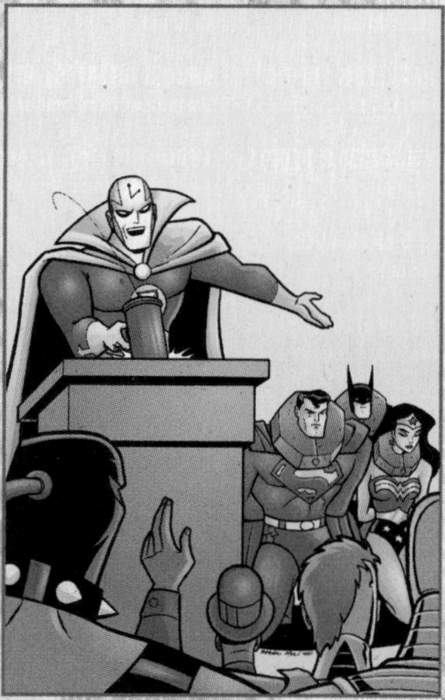
Min S. Ku

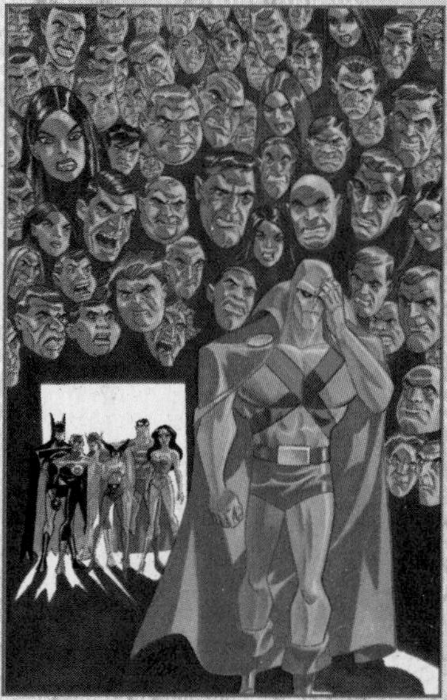
Butch Lukic

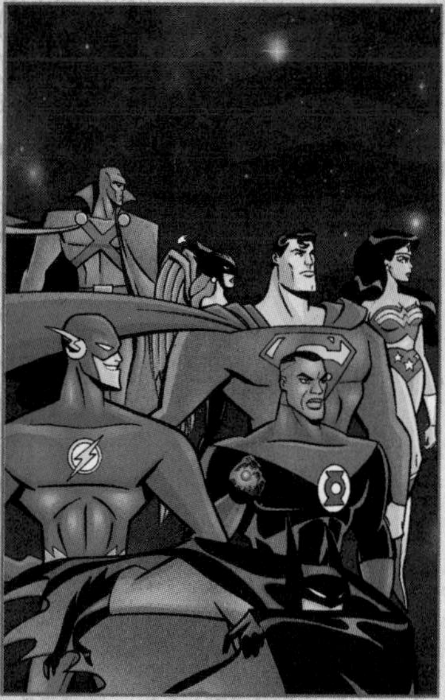
John Delaney & Rick Burchett

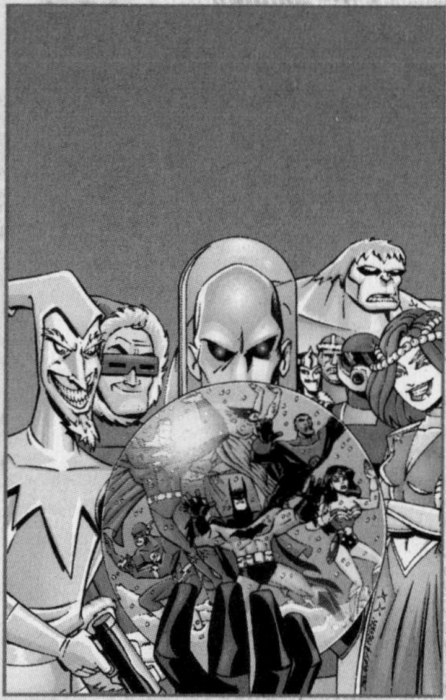
John Delaney & Paul Neary

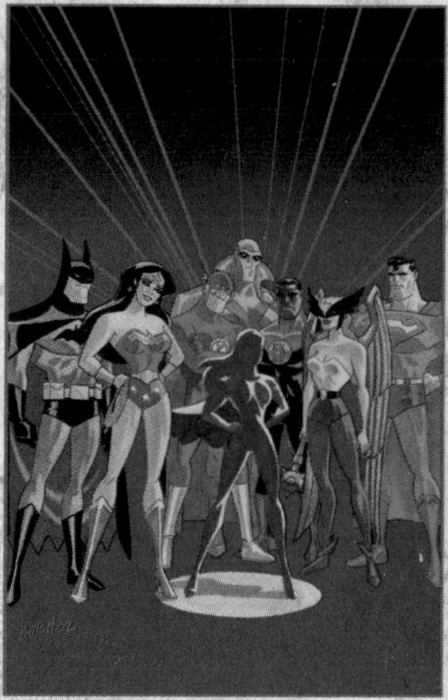
Butch Lukic

THE STARS OF THE
DC UNIVERSE
CAN ALSO BE FOUND IN THESE BOOKS: